ACCLAIM FOR ONE OF THE LEGENDARY GRAND MASTERS OF SPECULATIVE FICTION—INTERNATIONAL BESTSELLER ARTHUR C. CLARKE

❍ ❍ ❍

"Arthur Clarke is probably the most critically admired of all currently active writers of science fiction . . . awesomely informed about physics and astronomy, and blessed with one of the most astounding imaginations I ever encountered in print."

—*The New York Times*

"Our most important visionary writer."

—*Playboy*

"Intellectually provocative."

—*Newsday*

"Sets the standard for science fiction that is both high-tech and high-class."

—*Entertainment Weekly*

"Remarkable."

—*Los Angeles Times Book Review*

Books by Arthur C. Clarke

The Fountains of Paradise

The City and the Stars/The Sands of Mars
(omnibus)

The Ghost from the Grand Banks/The Deep Range
(omnibus)

Cradle
(written with Gentry Lee)

Available from Warner Aspect

ARTHUR C. CLARKE

THE CITY AND THE STARS

and

THE SANDS OF MARS

A Time Warner Company

Warner Books, Inc., 1271 Avenue of the Americas, New York, NY 10020

Visit our Web site at www.twbookmark.com.

For information on Time Warner Trade Publishing's online program, visit www.ipublish.com.

A Time Warner Company

Printed in the United States of America

First Warner Books Trade Printing: September 2001

10 9 8 7 6 5 4 3 2 1

Library of Congress Cataloging-in-Publication Data

Clarke, Arthur Charles
The city and the stars; and, The sands of mars / Arthur C. Clarke.
p. cm.
ISBN 0-446-67796-5
1. Science fiction 2. Mars (Planet)—Fiction. I. Clarke, Arthur Charles, 1917-
Sands of Mars. II. Title.

PR6005.L36 C58 2001
823'.914—dc21 2001017739

Book design by Bernadette Evangelist
Cover design by Jon Valk / Don Puckey
Cover illustration by Don Dixon

THE CITY AND THE STARS

To the memory of Val Cleaver
And Johnnie Maxwell,
Who listened patiently through
Many versions of this tale

Introduction

It is a matter of great satisfaction to me that *The City and the Stars* has been continuously in print ever since its first publication in 1956. Its precursor, *Against the Fall of Night,* is also still in print. Some years ago, this fact caused much confusion to a psychiatrist friend of mine.

She was examining a patient who also happened to be one of my readers. (This was not, she assured me, part of his problem.) They started discussing the plotline of the last novel they'd read and quickly found themselves in complete disagreement over details. In fact, the patient gave such a lucid and coherent account of the story *he* remembered that the doctor—who was convinced that everything happened quite differently—began to wonder which of them was in need of treatment.

It turned out, of course, that the psychiatrist had read *The City and the Stars,* the patient *Against the Fall of Night*—and neither knew that the other novel existed. As such a situation could lead to tragic results, I have now been careful to insert cross-references in both books.

Though this story is set more than a billion years in the future, computer technology has already almost caught up with me. Anyone who has played interactive video games will feel right at home in "The Cave of the White Worms." Not for the first time, I feel that I am involved in a self-fulfilling prophecy.

But there is another "prophecy," on the very last page of the story, whose truth or falsehood neither I nor any other man will ever know:

One day the energies of the Black Sun would fail and it would release its prisoner. And then, at the end of the Universe, as Time itself was faltering to a stop, Vanamonde and the Mad Mind must meet each other among the corpses of the stars.

I can still remember—half a lifetime later!—feeling that something outside of me was dictating those words, and even now they raise the hairs on the back of my neck.

For I appear to have anticipated, by about twenty years, one of the most unexpected results of modern cosmology. My "Black Sun" is obviously a Black Hole (the term did not come into use until the 1960s), and in 1974 Stephen Hawking made the stunning discovery that Black Holes are not permanent but can "die," just as I suggested. (To be technical, they "evaporate" by quantum tunneling.) And then they can become informational white noise sources, shooting out (if you wait long enough) anything you care to specify. Including Mad Minds. . . .

I cannot help wondering if I have also anticipated—and even explained—another creature in the cosmic zoo. The Universe of today's astronomers is a far more violent and exotic place than it was believed to be only a generation ago. Among its most surprising features are tightly focused beams of energy, jetting from the hearts of galaxies and extending out across thousands of light years.

"Star Wars"? Let us hope not. See Chapter 24 for an alternative.

For many years, and for many reasons, *The City and the Stars* was my best-loved book; now it has a new lease on life, both in text, and in music. To my delight and surprise, it is the basis of an oratorio by the British composer David Bedford, which should have had its premiere in London's Royal Festival Hall by the time this edition is published.

Colombo, Sri Lanka
September 2000

Preface

For the benefit of those who have read my first novel, *Against the Fall of Night,* and will recognize some of the material in the present work, a few words of explanation are in order.

Against the Fall of Night was begun in 1937 and, after four or five drafts, was completed in 1946, though for various reasons beyond the author's control book publication was delayed until some years later. Although this work was well received, it had most of the defects of a first novel, and my initial dissatisfaction with it increased steadily over the years. Moreover, the progress of science during the two decades since the story was first conceived made many of the original ideas naïve, and opened up vistas and possibilities quite unimagined when the book was originally planned. In particular, certain developments in information theory suggested revolutions in the human way of life even more profound than those which atomic energy is already introducing, and I wished to incorporate these into the book I had attempted, but so far failed, to write.

A sea voyage from England to Australia gave an opportunity of getting to grips with the uncompleted job, which was finished just before I set out to the Great Barrier Reef. The knowledge that I was to spend some months diving among sharks of doubtful docility was an additional spur to action. It may or may not be true, as Doctor Johnson stated, that nothing settles a man's mind so much as the knowledge that he will be hanged in the morning, but for my part I can testify that the thought of not returning from the Reef was the main reason why the book was completed at that particular time, and the ghost that had haunted me for almost twenty years was finally exorcised.

About a quarter of the present work appeared in *Against the Fall of Night*; it is my belief, however, that even those who read the earlier book will find that this is virtually a new novel. If not, at least I hope they will grant an author the right to have second thoughts. I promise them that this is my last word on the immortal city of Diaspar, in the long twilight of Earth.

Arthur C. Clarke

London, September, 1954—S.S. Himalaya—
Sydney, March, 1955

Like a glowing jewel, the city lay upon the breast of the desert. Once it had known change and alteration, but now Time passed it by. Night and day fled across the desert's face, but in the streets of Diaspar it was always afternoon, and darkness never came. The long winter nights might dust the desert with frost, as the last moisture left in the thin air of Earth congealed—but the city knew neither heat nor cold. It had no contact with the outer world; it was a universe itself.

Men had built cities before, but never a city such as this. Some had lasted for centuries, some for millenniums, before Time had swept away even their names. Diaspar alone had challenged Eternity, defending itself and all it sheltered against the slow attrition of the ages, the ravages of decay, and the corruption of rust.

Since the city was built, the oceans of Earth had passed away and the desert had encompassed all the globe. The last mountains had been ground to dust by the winds and the rain, and the world was too weary to bring forth more. The city did not care; Earth itself could crumble and Diaspar would still protect the children of its makers, bearing them and their treasures safely down the stream of time.

They had forgotten much, but they did not know it. They were as perfectly fitted to their environment as it was to them—for both had been designed together. What was beyond the walls of the city was no concern of theirs; it was something that had been shut out of their minds. Diaspar was all that existed, all that they needed, all that they could imagine. It mattered nothing to them that Man had once possessed the stars.

Yet sometimes the ancient myths rose up to haunt them, and they stirred uneasily as they remembered the legends of the Empire, when Diaspar was young and drew its lifeblood from the commerce of many suns. They did not wish to bring back the old days, for they were content in their eternal autumn. The glories of the Empire belonged to the past, and could remain there—for they remembered how the Empire had met its end, and at the thought of the Invaders the chill of space itself came seeping into their bones.

Then they would turn once more to the life and warmth of the city, to the long golden age whose beginning was already lost and whose end was yet more distant. Other men had dreamed of such an age, but they alone had achieved it.

They had lived in the same city, had walked the same miraculously unchanging streets, while more than a billion years had worn away.

CHAPTER

It had taken them many hours to fight their way out of the Cave of the White Worms. Even now, they could not be sure that some of the pallid monsters were not pursuing them—and the power of their weapons was almost exhausted. Ahead, the floating arrow of light that had been their mysterious guide through the labyrinths of the Crystal Mountain still beckoned them on. They had no choice but to follow it, though as it had done so many times before it might lead them into yet more frightful dangers.

Alvin glanced back to see if all his companions were still with him. Alystra was close behind, carrying the sphere of cold but ever-burning light that had revealed such horrors and such beauty since their adventure had begun. The pale white radiance flooded the narrow corridor and splashed from the glittering walls; while its power lasted, they could see where they were going and could detect the presence of any visible dangers. But the greatest dangers in these caves, Alvin knew too well, were not the visible ones at all.

Behind Alystra, struggling with the weight of their projectors, came Narillian and Floranus. Alvin wondered briefly why those projectors were so heavy, since it would have been such a simple matter to provide them with gravity neutralizers. He was always thinking of points like this, even in the midst of the most desperate adventures. When such thoughts crossed his mind, it seemed as if the structure of reality trembled for an instant, and that behind the world of the senses he caught a glimpse of another and totally different universe. . . .

The corridor ended in a blank wall. Had the arrow betrayed them again? No—even as they approached, the rock began to crumble into dust. Through the wall pierced a spinning metal spear, which broadened rapidly into a giant screw. Alvin and his friends moved back, waiting for the machine to force its way into the cave. With a deafening screech of metal upon rock—which surely must echo through all the recesses of the Mountain, and waken all its nightmare brood!—the subterrene smashed through the wall and came to rest beside them. A massive door opened, and Callistron appeared, shouting to them to hurry. ("Why Callistron?" wondered Alvin. "What's *he* doing here?") A moment later they were in safety, and the machine lurched forward as it began its journey through the depths of the earth.

The adventure was over. Soon, as always happened, they would be home, and all the wonder, the terror, and the excitement would be behind them. They were tired and content.

Alvin could tell from the tilt of the floor that the subterrene was heading down into the earth. Presumably Callistron knew what he was doing, and this was the way that led to home. Yet it seemed a pity. . . .

"Callistron," he said suddenly, "why don't we go upward? No one knows what the Crystal Mountain really looks like. How wonderful it would be to come out somewhere on its slopes, to see the sky and all the land around it. We've been underground long enough."

Even as he said these words, he somehow knew that they were wrong. Alystra gave a strangled scream, the interior of the subterrene wavered like an image seen through water, and behind and beyond the metal walls that surrounded him Alvin once more glimpsed that other universe. The two worlds seemed in conflict, first one and then the other predominating. Then, quite suddenly, it was all over. There was a snapping, rending sensation—and the dream had ended. Alvin was back in Diaspar, in his own familiar room, floating a foot or two above the floor as the gravity field protected him from the bruising contact of brute matter.

He was himself again. *This* was reality—and he knew exactly what would happen next.

Alystra was the first to appear. She was more upset than annoyed, for she was very much in love with Alvin.

"Oh, Alvin!" she lamented, as she looked down at him from the wall in which she had apparently materialized, "It was such an exciting adventure! Why did you have to spoil it?"

"I'm sorry. I didn't intend to—I just thought it would be a good idea . . ."

He was interrupted by the simultaneous arrival of Callistron and Floranus.

"Now listen, Alvin," began Callistron. "This is the *third* time you've interrupted a saga. You broke the sequence yesterday by wanting to climb out of the Valley of Rainbows. And the day before you upset everything by trying to get back to the Origin in that time track we were exploring. If you won't keep the rules, you'll have to go by yourself."

He vanished in high dudgeon, taking Floranus with him. Narillian never appeared at all; he was probably too fed up with the whole affair. Only the image of Alystra was left, looking sadly down at Alvin.

Alvin tilted the gravity field, rose to his feet, and walked toward the table he had materialized. A bowl of exotic fruit appeared upon it—not the food he had intended, for in his confusion his thoughts had wandered. Not wishing to reveal his error, he picked up the least dangerous-looking of the fruits and started to suck it cautiously.

"Well," said Alystra at last, "what are you going to do?"

"I can't help it," he said a little sulkily. "I think the rules are stupid. Besides, how can I remember them when I'm living a saga? I just behave in the way that seems natural. Didn't *you* want to look at the mountain?"

Alystra's eyes widened with horror.

"That would have meant going outside!" she gasped.

Alvin knew that it was useless to argue further. Here was the barrier that sundered him from all the people of his world, and which might doom him to a life of frustration.He was always wanting to go outside, both in reality and in dream. Yet to everyone in Diaspar, "outside" was a nightmare that they could not face. They would never talk about it if it could be avoided; it was something unclean and evil. Not even Jeserac, his tutor, would tell him why.

Alystra was still watching him with puzzled but tender eyes. "You're unhappy, Alvin," she said. "No one should be unhappy in Diaspar. Let me come over and talk to you."

Ungallantly, Alvin shook his head. He knew where *that* would lead, and at the moment he wanted to be alone. Doubly disappointed, Alystra faded from view.

In a city of ten million human beings, thought Alvin, there was no one to whom he could really talk. Eriston and Etania were fond of him in their way, but now that their term of guardianship was ending, they were happy enough to leave him to shape his own amusements and his own life. In the last few years, as his divergence from the standard pattern became more and more obvious, he had often felt his parents' resentment. Not with him—that, perhaps, was something he could have faced and fought—but with the sheer bad luck that had chosen them from all the city's millions, to meet him when he walked out of the Hall of Creation twenty years ago.

Twenty years. He could remember the first moment, and the first words he had ever heard: "Welcome, Alvin. I am Eriston, your appointed father. This is Etania, your mother." The words had meant nothing then, but his mind had recorded them with flawless accuracy. He remembered how he had looked down at his body; it was an inch or two taller now, but had scarcely altered since the moment of his birth. He had come almost fully grown into the world, and would leave it a thousand years hence.

Before that first memory, there was nothing. One day, perhaps, that nothingness would come again, but that was a thought too remote to touch his emotions in any way.

He turned his mind once more toward the mystery of his birth. It did not seem strange to Alvin that he might be created, in a single moment of time, by the powers and forces that materialized all the other objects of his everyday life. No; *that* was not the mystery. The enigma he had never been able to solve, and which no one would ever explain to him, was his uniqueness.

Unique. It was a strange, sad word—and a strange, sad thing to be. When it was applied to him—as he had often heard it done when no one thought he was listening—it seemed to possess ominous undertones that threatened more than his own happiness.

His parents, his tutor, everyone he knew, had tried to protect him from the truth, as if anxious to preserve the innocence of his long childhood. The pretense must soon be ended; in a few days he would be a full citizen of Diaspar, and nothing could be withheld from him that he wished to know.

Why, for example, did he not fit into the sagas? Of all the thousands of forms of recreation in the city, these were the most popular. When you entered a saga, you were not merely a passive observer, as in the crude entertainments or primitive times which Alvin had sometimes sampled. You were an active participant and possessed—or seemed to possess—free will. The events and scenes which were the raw material of your adventures might have been prepared beforehand by forgotten artists, but there was enough flexibility to allow for wide variation. You could go into these phantom worlds with your friends, seeking the excitement that did not exist in Diaspar—and as long as the dream lasted there was no way in which it could be distinguished from reality. Indeed, who could be certain that Diaspar itself was not the dream?

No one could ever exhaust all the sagas that had been conceived and recorded since the city began. They played upon all the emotions and were of infinitely varying subtlety. Some—those popular among the very young—were uncomplicated dramas of adventure and discovery. Others were purely explorations of psychological states, while others again were exercises in logic or mathematics which could provide the keenest of delights to more sophisticated minds.

Yet though the sagas seemed to satisfy his companions, they left Alvin with a feeling of incompleteness. For all their color and excitement, their varying locales and themes, there was something missing.

The sagas, he decided, never really got anywhere. They were always painted on such a narrow canvas. There were no great vistas, none of the rolling landscapes for which his soul craved. Above all, there was never a hint of the immensity in which the exploits of ancient man had really taken place—the luminous void between the stars and planets. The artists who had planned the sagas had been infected by the same strange phobia that ruled all the citizens of Diaspar. Even their vicarious adventures must take place cozily indoors, in subterranean caverns, or in neat little valleys surrounded by mountains that shut out all the rest of the world.

There was only one explanation. Far back in time, perhaps before Diaspar was founded, something had happened that had not only destroyed Man's curiosity and ambition, but had sent him homeward from the stars to cower for shelter in the tiny closed world of Earth's last city. He had renounced the Universe and returned to the artificial womb of Diaspar. The flaming, invincible urge that had once driven him over the

Galaxy, and to the islands of mist beyond, had altogether died. No ships had entered the Solar System for countless aeons; out there among the stars the descendants of Man might still be building empires and wrecking suns—Earth neither knew nor cared.

Earth did not. But Alvin did.

CHAPTER

The room was dark save for one glowing wall, upon which the tides of color ebbed and flowed as Alvin wrestled with his dreams. Part of the pattern satisfied him; he had fallen in love with the soaring lines of the mountains as they leaped out of the sea. There was a power and pride about those ascending curves; he had studied them for a long time, and then fed them into the memory unit of the visualizer, where they would be preserved while he experimented with the rest of the picture. Yet something was eluding him, though what it was he did not know. Again and again he had tried to fill in the blank spaces, while the instrument read the shifting patterns in his mind and materialized them upon the wall. It was no good. The lines were blurred and uncertain, the colors muddy and dull. If the artist did not know his goal, even the most miraculous of tools could not find it for him.

Alvin canceled his unsatisfactory scribblings and stared morosely at the three-quarters-empty rectangle he had been trying to fill with beauty. On a sudden impulse, he doubled the size of the existing design and shifted it to the center of the frame. No—that was a lazy way out, and the balance was all wrong. Worse still, the change of scale had revealed the defects in his construction, the lack of certainty in those at-first-sight confident lines. He would have to start all over again.

"Total erasure," he ordered the machine. The blue of the sea faded; the mountains dissolved like mist, until only the blank wall remained. They were as if they had never been—as if they were lost in the limbo that had taken all Earth's seas and mountains ages before Alvin was born.

The light came flooding back into the room and the luminous rectangle upon which Alvin had projected his dreams merged into its surroundings, to become one with the other walls. But were they walls? To anyone who had never seen such a place before, this was a very peculiar room indeed. It was utterly featureless and completely devoid of furniture, so that it seemed as if Alvin stood at the center of a sphere. No visible dividing lines separated walls from floor or ceiling. There was nothing on which the eye could focus; the space enclosing Alvin might have been ten feet or ten miles across, for all that the sense of vision could have told. It would have been hard to resist the temptation to walk forward, hands outstretched, to discover the physical limits of this extraordinary place.

Yet such rooms had been "home" to most of the human race for the greater part of its history. Alvin had only to frame the appropriate thought, and the walls would become windows opening upon any part of the city he chose. Another wish, and machines which he had never seen would fill the chamber with the projected images of any articles of furniture he might need. Whether they were "real" or not was a problem that had bothered few men for the last billion years. Certainly they were no less real than that other impostor, solid matter, and when they were no longer required they could be returned to the phantom world of the city's Memory Banks. Like everything else in Diaspar, they would never wear out—and they would never change, unless their stored patterns were canceled by a deliberate act of will.

Alvin had partly reconstructed his room when a persistent,

bell-like chime sounded in his ear. He mentally framed the admission signal, and the wall upon which he had just been painting dissolved once more. As he had expected, there stood his parents, with Jeserac a little behind them. The presence of his tutor meant that this was no ordinary family reunion—but he knew that already.

The illusion was perfect, and it was not lost when Eriston spoke. In reality, as Alvin was well aware, Eriston, Etania, and Jeserac were all miles apart, for the builders of the city had conquered space as completely as they had subjugated time. Alvin was not even certain where his parents lived among the multitudinous spires and intricate labyrinths of Diaspar, for they had both moved since he had last been physically in their presence.

"Alvin," began Eriston, "it is just twenty years since your mother and I first met you. You know what that means. Our guardianship is now ended, and you are free to do as you please."

There was a trace—but merely a trace—of sadness in Eriston's voice. There was considerably more relief, as if Eriston was glad that a state of affairs that had existed for some time in fact now had legal recognition. Alvin had anticipated his freedom by a good many years.

"I understand," he answered. "I thank you for watching over me, and I will remember you in all my lives." That was the formal response; he had heard it so often that all meaning had been leached away from it—it was merely a pattern of sounds with no particular significance. Yet "all my lives" was a strange expression, when one stopped to consider it. He knew vaguely what it meant; now the time had come for him to know exactly. There were many things in Diaspar which he did not understand, and which he would have to learn in the centuries that lay ahead of him.

For a moment it seemed as if Etania wished to speak. She raised one hand, disturbing the iridescent gossamer of her gown, then let it fall back to her side. Then she turned helplessly to Jeserac, and for the first time Alvin realized that his parents were worried. His memory swiftly scanned the events of the past few weeks. No, there was nothing in his recent life that could have caused this faint uncertainty, this air of mild alarm that seemed to surround both Eriston and Etania.

Jeserac, however, appeared to be in command of the situation. He gave an inquiring look at Eriston and Etania, satisfied himself that they had nothing more to say, and launched forth on the dissertation he had waited many years to make.

"Alvin," he began, "for twenty years you have been my pupil, and I have done my best to teach you the ways of the city, and to lead you to the heritage which is yours. You have asked me many questions, and not all of them have I been able to answer. Some things you were not ready to learn, and some I did not know myself. Now your infancy is over, though your childhood is scarcely begun. It is still my duty to guide you, if you need my help. In two hundred years, Alvin, you may begin to know something of this city and a little of its history. Even I, who am nearing the end of this life, have seen less than a quarter of Diaspar, and perhaps less than a thousandth of its treasures."

There was nothing so far that Alvin did not know, but there was no way of hurrying Jeserac. The old man looked steadfastly at him across the gulf of centuries, his words weighed down with the uncomputable wisdom acquired during a long lifetime's contact with men and machines.

"Tell me, Alvin," he said, "have you ever asked yourself *where* you were before you were born—before you found yourself facing Etania and Eriston at the Hall of Creation?"

"I assumed I was nowhere—that I was nothing but a pattern in the mind of the city, waiting to be created—like this."

A low couch glimmered and thickened into reality beside Alvin. He sat down upon it and waited for Jeserac to continue.

"You are correct, of course," came the reply. "But that is

merely part of the answer—and a very small part indeed. Until now, you have met only children of your own age, and they have been ignorant of the truth. Soon they will remember, but you will not, so we must prepare you to face the facts.

"For over a billion years, Alvin, the human race has lived in this city. Since the Galactic Empire fell, and the Invaders went back to the stars, this has been our world. Outside the walls of Diaspar, there is nothing except the desert of which our legends speak.

"We know little about our primitive ancestors, except that they were very short-lived beings and that, strange though it seems, they could reproduce themselves without the aid of memory units or matter organizers. In a complex and apparently uncontrollable process, the key patterns of each human being were preserved in microscopic cell structures actually created inside the body. If you are interested, the biologists can tell you more about it, but the method is of no great importance since it was abandoned at the dawn of history.

"A human being, like any other object, is defined by its structure—its pattern. The pattern of a man, and still more the pattern which specifies a man's mind, is incredibly complex. Yet Nature was able to pack that pattern into a tiny cell, too small for the eye to see.

"What Nature can do, Man can do also, in his own way. We do not know how long the task took. A million years, perhaps—but what is that? In the end our ancestors learned how to analyze and store the information that would define any specific human being—and to use that information to re-create the original, as you have just created that couch.

"I know that such things interest you, Alvin, but I cannot tell you exactly how it is done. The way in which information is stored is of no importance; all that matters is the information itself. It may be in the form of written words on paper, of varying magnetic fields, or patterns of electric charge. Men have used all these methods of storage, and many others. Suffice to say that long ago they were able to store themselves—or, to be more precise, the disembodied patterns from which they could be called back into existence.

"So much, you already know. This is the way our ancestors gave us virtual immortality, yet avoided the problems raised by the abolition of death. A thousand years in one body is long enough for any man; at the end of that time, his mind is clogged with memories, and he asks only for rest—or a new beginning.

"In a little while, Alvin, I shall prepare to leave this life. I shall go back through my memories, editing them and canceling those I do not wish to keep. Then I shall walk into the Hall of Creation, but through a door which you have never seen. This old body will cease to exist, and so will consciousness itself. Nothing will be left of Jeserac but a galaxy of electrons frozen in the heart of a crystal.

"I shall sleep, Alvin, and without dreams. Then one day, perhaps a hundred thousand years from now, I shall find myself in a new body, meeting those who have been chosen to be my guardians. They will look after me as Eriston and Etania have guided you, for at first I will know nothing of Diaspar and will have no memories of what I was before. Those memories will slowly return, at the end of my infancy, and I will build upon them as I move forward into my new cycle of existence.

"That is the pattern of our lives, Alvin. We have all been here many, many times before, though as the intervals of nonexistence vary according to apparently random laws this present population will never repeat itself again. The new Jeserac will have new and different friends and interests, but the old Jeserac—as much of him as I wish to save—will still exist.

"That is not all. At any moment, Alvin, only a hundredth of the citizens of Diaspar live and walk its streets. The vast majority slumber in the Memory Banks, waiting for the signal that will call them forth onto the stage of existence once again.

So we have continuity, yet change—immortality, but not stagnation.

"I know what you are wondering, Alvin. You want to know when you will recall the memories of your earlier lives, as your companions are already doing.

"There are no such memories, for you are unique. We have tried to keep this knowledge from you as long as we could, so that no shadow should lie across your childhood—though I think you must have guessed part of the truth already. We did not suspect it ourselves until five years ago, but now there is no doubt.

"You, Alvin, are something that has happened in Diaspar only a handful of times since the founding of the city. Perhaps you have been lying dormant in the Memory Banks through all the ages—or perhaps you were created only twenty years ago by some random permutation. You may have been planned in the beginning by the designers of the city, or you may be a purposeless accident of our own time.

"We do not know. All that we do know is this: You, Alvin, alone of the human race, have never lived before. In literal truth, you are the first child to be born on earth for at least ten million years."

Chapter

When Jeserac and his parents had faded from view, Alvin lay for a long time trying to hold his mind empty of thought. He closed his room around him, so that no one could interrupt his trance.

He was not sleeping; sleep was something he had never experienced, for that belonged to a world of night and day, and here there was only day. This was the nearest he could come to that forgotten state, and though it was not really essential to him he knew that it would help compose his mind.

He had learned little new; almost everything that Jeserac had told him he had already guessed. But it was one thing to have guessed it, another to have had that guess confirmed beyond possibility of refutation.

How would it affect his life, if at all? He could not be sure, and uncertainty was a novel sensation to Alvin. Perhaps it would make no difference whatsoever; if he did not adjust completely to Diaspar in this life, he would do so in the next—or the next.

Even as he framed the thought, Alvin's mind rejected it. Diaspar might be sufficient for the rest of humanity, but it was not enough for him. He did not doubt that one could spend a thousand lifetimes without exhausting all its wonders, or sampling all the permutations of experience it could provide. These things he could do—but if he could not do more, he would never be content.

There was only one problem to be faced. What more *was* there to do?

The unanswered question jolted him out of his reverie. He could not stay here while he was in this restless mood, and there was only one place in the city where he could find some peace of mind.

The wall flickered partially out of existence as he stepped through to the corridor, and its polarized molecules resisted his passage like a feeble wind blowing against his face. There were many ways in which he could be carried effortlessly to his goal, but he preferred to walk. His room was almost at the main city level, and a short passage brought him out onto a spiral ramp which led down to the street. He ignored the moving way, and kept to the narrow sidewalk—an eccentric thing to do, since he had several miles to travel. But Alvin liked the exercise, for it soothed his mind. Besides, there was so much to see that it seemed a pity to race past the latest marvels of Diaspar when you had eternity ahead of you.

It was the custom of the city's artists—and everyone in Diaspar was an artist at some time or another—to display their current productions along the side of the moving ways, so that the passers-by could admire their work. In this manner, it was usually only a few days before the entire population had critically examined any noteworthy creation, and also expressed its views upon it. The resulting verdict, recorded automatically by opinion-sampling devices which no one had ever been able to suborn or deceive—and there had been enough attempts—decided the fate of the masterpiece. If there was a sufficiently affirmative vote, its matrix would go into the memory of the city so that anyone who wished, at any future date, could possess a reproduction utterly indistinguishable from the original.

The less successful pieces went the way of all such works. They were either dissolved back into their original elements or ended in the homes of the artists' friends.

Alvin saw only one *objet d'art* on his journey that had any appeal to him. It was a creation of pure light, vaguely reminiscent of an unfolding flower. Slowly growing from a minute core of color, it would expand into complex spirals and curtains, then suddenly collapse and begin the cycle over again. Yet not precisely, for no two cycles were identical. Though Alvin watched through a score of pulsations, each time there were subtle and indefinable differences, even though the basic pattern remained the same.

He knew why he liked this piece of intangible sculpture. Its expanding rhythm gave an impression of space—even of escape. For that reason, it would probably not appeal to many of Alvin's compatriots. He made a note of the artist's name and decided to call him at the earliest opportunity.

All the roads, both moving and stationary, came to an end when they reached the park that was the green heart of the city. Here, in a circular space over three miles across, was a memory of what Earth had been in the days before the desert swallowed all but Diaspar. First there was a wide belt of grass, then low trees which grew thicker and thicker as one walked forward beneath their shade. At the same time the ground sloped gently downward, so that when at last one emerged from the narrow forest all sign of the city had vanished, hidden by the screen of trees.

The wide stream that lay ahead of Alvin was called, simply, the River. It possessed, and it needed, no other name. At intervals it was spanned by narrow bridges, and it flowed around the park in a complete, closed circle, broken by occasional lagoons. That a swiftly moving river could return upon itself after a course of less than six miles had never struck Alvin as at all unusual; indeed, he would not have thought twice about the matter if at some point in its circuit the River had flowed uphill. There were far stranger things than this in Diaspar.

A dozen young people were swimming in one of the little lagoons, and Alvin paused to watch them. He knew most of them by sight, if not by name, and for a moment was tempted to join in their play. Then the secret he was bearing decided him against it, and he contented himself with the role of spectator.

Physically, there was no way of telling which of these young citizens had walked out of the Hall of Creation this year and which had lived in Diaspar as long as Alvin. Though there were considerable variations in height and weight, they had no correlation with age. People were simply born that way, and although on the average the taller the person, the greater the age, this was not a reliable rule to apply unless one was dealing in centuries.

The face was a safer guide. Some of the newborn were taller than Alvin, but they had a look of immaturity, an expression of wondering surprise at the world in which they now found themselves that revealed them at once. It was strange to think that, slumbering untapped in their minds, were infinite vistas of lives that they would soon remember. Alvin envied them, yet he was not sure if he should. One's first existence was a precious gift which would never be repeated. It was wonderful to view life for the very first time, as in the freshness of the dawn. If only there were others like him, with whom he could share his thoughts and feelings!

Yet physically he was cast in precisely the same mold as those children playing in the water. The human body had changed not at all in the billion years since the building of Diaspar, since the basic design had been eternally frozen in the Memory Banks of the city. It had changed, however, a good deal from its original primitive form, though most of the alterations were internal and not visible to the eye. Man had rebuilt himself many times in his long history, in the effort to abolish those ills to which the flesh was once heir.

Such unnecessary appurtenances as nails and teeth had vanished. Hair was confined to the head; not a trace was left on the body. The feature that would most have surprised a man of the Dawn Ages was, perhaps, the disappearance of the navel. Its inexplicable absence would have given him much food for thought, and at first sight he would also have been baffled by the problem of distinguishing male from female. He might even have been tempted to assume that there was no longer any difference, which would have been a grave error. In the appropriate circumstances, there was no doubt about the masculinity of any male in Diaspar. It was merely that his equipment was now more neatly packaged when not required; internal stowage had vastly improved upon Nature's original inelegant and indeed downright hazardous arrangements.

It was true that reproduction was no longer the concern of the body, being far too important a matter to be left to games of chance played with chromosomes as dice. Yet, though conception and birth were not even memories, sex remained. Even in ancient times, not one-hundredth part of sexual activity had been concerned with reproduction. The disappearance of that mere one per cent had changed the pattern of human society and the meaning of such words as "father" and "mother"—but desire remained, though now its satisfaction had no profounder aim than that of any of the other pleasures of the senses.

Alvin left his playful contemporaries and continued on toward the center of the park. There were faintly marked paths here, crossing and crisscrossing through low shrubbery and occasionally diving into narrow ravines between great lichen-covered boulders. Once he came across a small polyhedral machine, no larger than a man's head, floating among the branches of a tree. No one knew how many varieties of robot there were in Diaspar; they kept out of the way and minded their business so effectively that it was quite unusual to see one.

Presently the ground began to rise again; Alvin was approaching the little hill that was at the exact center of the park, and therefore of the city itself. There were fewer obstacles and detours, and he had a clear view to the summit of the hill and the simple building that surmounted it. He was a little out of breath by the time he had reached his goal, and was glad to rest against one of the rose-pink columns and to look back over the way he had come.

There are some forms of architecture that can never change because they have reached perfection. The Tomb of Yarlan Zey might have been designed by the temple builders of the first civilizations man had ever known, though they would have found it impossible to imagine of what material it was made. The roof was open to the sky, and the single chamber was paved with great slabs which only at first sight resembled natural stone. For geological ages human feet had crossed and recrossed that floor and left no trace upon its inconceivably stubborn material.

The creator of the great park—the builder, some said, of Diaspar itself—sat with slightly downcast eyes, as if examining the plans spread across his knees. His face wore that curiously elusive expression that had baffled the world for so many generations. Some had dismissed it as no more than an idle whim of the artist's, but to others it seemed that Yarlan Zey was smiling at some secret jest.

The whole building was an enigma, for nothing concerning it could be traced in the historical records of the city. Alvin was not even sure what the word "Tomb" meant; Jeserac could probably tell him, because he was fond of collecting obsolete words and sprinkling his conversation with them, to the confusion of his listeners.

From this central vantage point, Alvin could look clear across the park, above the screening trees, and out to the city itself. The nearest buildings were almost two miles away, and formed a low belt completely surrounding the park. Beyond them, rank after rank in ascending height, were the towers and terraces that made up the main bulk of the city. They stretched for mile upon mile, slowly climbing up the sky, becoming ever more complex and monumentally impressive. Diaspar had been planned as an entity; it was a single mighty machine. Yet though its outward appearance was almost overwhelming in its complexity, it merely hinted at the hidden marvels of technology without which all these great buildings would be lifeless sepulchers.

Alvin stared out toward the limits of his world. Ten—twenty miles away, their details lost in distance, were the outer ramparts of the city, upon which seemed to rest the roof of the sky. There was nothing beyond them—nothing at all except the aching emptiness of the desert in which a man would soon go mad.

Then why did that emptiness call to him, as it called to no one else whom he had ever met? Alvin did not know. He stared out across the colored spires and battlements that now enclosed the whole dominion of mankind, as if seeking an answer to his question.

He did not find it. But at that moment, as his heart yearned for the unattainable, he made his decision.

He knew now what he was going to do with life.

Chapter

Jeserac was not very helpful, though he was not as uncooperative as Alvin had half expected. He had been asked such questions before in his long career as mentor, and did not believe that even a Unique like Alvin could produce many surprises or set him problems which he could not solve.

It was true that Alvin was beginning to show certain minor eccentricities of behavior, which might eventually need correction. He did not join as fully as he should in the incredibly elaborate social life of the city or in the fantasy worlds of his companions. He showed no great interest in the higher realms of thought, though at his age that was hardly surprising. More remarkable was his erratic love life; he could not be expected to form any relatively stable partnerships for at least a century, yet the brevity of his affairs was already famous. They were intense while they lasted—but not one of them had lasted for more than a few weeks. Alvin, it seemed, could interest himself thoroughly only in one thing at a time. There were times when he would join wholeheartedly in the erotic games of his companions, or disappear with the partner of his choice for several days. But once the mood had passed, there would be long spells when he seemed totally uninterested in what should have been a major occupation at his age. This was probably bad for him, and it was certainly bad for his discarded lovers, who wandered despondently around the city and took an unusually long time to find consolation elsewhere. Alystra, Jeserac had noticed, had now arrived at this unhappy stage.

It was not that Alvin was heartless or inconsiderate. In love, as in everything else, it seemed that he was searching for a goal that Diaspar could not provide.

None of these characteristics worried Jeserac. A Unique might be expected to behave in such a manner, and in due course Alvin would conform to the general pattern of the city. No single individual, however eccentric or brilliant, could affect the enormous inertia of a society that had remained virtually unchanged for over a billion years. Jeserac did not merely believe in stability; he could conceive of nothing else.

"The problem that worries you is a very old one," he told Alvin, "but you will be surprised how many people take the world so much for granted that it never bothers them or even crosses their mind. It is true that the human race once occupied an infinitely greater space than this city. You have seen something of what Earth was like before the deserts came and the oceans vanished. Those records you are so fond of projecting are the earliest we possess; they are the only ones that show Earth as it was before the Invaders came. I do not imagine that many people have ever seen them; those limitless, open spaces are something we cannot bear to contemplate.

"And even Earth, of course, was only a grain of sand in the Galactic Empire. What the gulfs between the stars must have been like is a nightmare no sane man would try to imagine. Our ancestors crossed them at the dawn of history when they went out to build the Empire. They crossed them again for the last time when the Invaders drove them back to Earth.

"The legend is—and it is only a legend—that we made a pact with the Invaders. They could have the Universe if they needed it so badly, we would be content with the world on which we were born.

"We have kept that pact and forgotten the vain dreams of our childhood, as you too will forget them, Alvin. The men who built this city, and designed the society that went with it, were lords of mind as well as matter. They put everything that the human race would ever need inside these walls—and then made sure that we would never leave them.

"Oh, the physical barriers are the least important ones. Perhaps there are routes that lead out of the city, but I do not think you would go along them for very far, even if you found them. And if you succeeded in the attempt, what good would it do? Your body would not last long in the desert, when the city could no longer protect or nourish it."

"If there is a route out of the city," said Alvin slowly, "then what is there to stop me from leaving?"

"That is a foolish question," answered Jeserac. "I think you already know the answer."

Jeserac was right, but not in the way he imagined. Alvin knew—or, rather, he had guessed. His companions had given him the answer, both in their waking life and in the dream adventures he had shared with them. They would never be able to leave Diaspar; what Jeserac did not know was that the compulsion which ruled their lives had no power over Alvin. Whether his uniqueness was due to accident or to an ancient design, he did not know, but this was one of its results. He wondered how many others he had yet to discover.

No one ever hurried in Diaspar, and this was a rule which even Alvin seldom broke. He considered the problem carefully for several weeks, and spent much time searching the earliest of the city's historical memories. For hours on end he would lie, supported by the impalpable arms of an antigravity field, while the hypnone projector opened his mind to the past. When the record was finished, the machine would blur and vanish—but still Alvin would lie staring into nothingness before he came back through the ages to meet reality again. He would see again the endless leagues of blue water, vaster than the land itself, rolling their waves against golden shores. His ears would ring with the boom of breakers stilled these billion years. He would remember the forests and the prairies, and the strange beasts that had once shared the world with Man.

Very few of these ancient records existed; it was generally accepted, though none knew the reason why, that somewhere between the coming of the Invaders and the building of Diaspar all memories of primitive times had been lost. So complete had been the obliteration that it was hard to believe it could have happened by accident alone. Mankind had lost its past, save for a few chronicles that might be wholly legendary. Before Diaspar there was simply the Dawn Ages. In that limbo were merged inextricably together the first men to tame fire and the first to release atomic energy—the first men to build a log canoe and the first to reach the stars. On the far side of this desert of time, they were all neighbors.

Alvin had intended to make this trip alone once more, but solitude was not always something that could be arranged in Diaspar. He had barely left his room when he encountered Alystra, who made no attempt to pretend that her presence was accidental.

It had never occurred to Alvin that Alystra was beautiful, for he had never seen human ugliness. When beauty is universal, it loses its power to move the heart, and only its absence can produce any emotional effect.

For a moment Alvin was annoyed by the meeting, with its reminder of passions that no longer moved him. He was still too young and self-reliant to feel the need for any lasting relationships, and when the time came he might find it hard to make them. Even in his most intimate moments, the barrier of his uniqueness came between him and his lovers. For all his fully formed body, he was still a child and would remain so for decades yet, while his companions one by one recalled the memories of their past lives and left him far behind. He had seen it happen before, and it made him wary of giving himself unreservedly to any other person. Even Alystra, who seemed so naïve and artless now, would soon become a complex of memories and talents beyond his imagination.

His mild annoyance vanished almost at once. There was no reason why Alystra should not come with him if she desired. He was not selfish and did not wish to clutch this new experience to his bosom like a miser. Indeed, he might be able to learn much from her reactions.

She asked no questions, which was unusual, as the express channel swept them out of the crowded heart of the city. Together they worked their way to the central high-speed section, never bothering to glance at the miracle beneath their feet. An engineer of the ancient world would have gone slowly mad trying to understand how an apparently solid roadway could be fixed at the sides while toward the center it moved at a steadily increasing velocity. But to Alvin and Alystra, it seemed perfectly natural that types of matter should exist that had the properties of solids in one direction and of liquids in another.

Around them the buildings rose higher and higher as if the city was strengthening its bulwarks against the outer world. How strange it would be, thought Alvin, if these towering walls became as transparent as glass, and one could watch the life within. Scattered throughout the space around him were friends he knew, friends he would one day know, and strangers he would never meet—though there could be very few of these, since in the course of his lifetime he would meet almost all the people in Diaspar. Most of them would be sitting in their separate rooms, but they would not be alone. They had only to form the wish and they could be, in all but physical fact, in the presence of any other person they chose. They were not bored, for they had access to everything that had happened in the realms of imagination or reality since the days when the city was built. To men whose minds were thus constituted, it was a completely satisfying existence. That it was also a wholly futile one, even Alvin did not yet comprehend.

As Alvin and Alystra moved outward from the city's heart, the number of people they saw in the streets slowly decreased, and there was no one in sight when they were brought to a smooth halt against a long platform of brightly colored marble. They stepped across the frozen whirlpool of matter where the substance of the moving way flowed back to its origin, and faced a wall pierced with brightly lighted tunnels. Alvin selected one without hesitation and stepped into it, with Alystra close behind. The peristaltic field seized them at once and propelled them forward as they lay back luxuriously, watching their surroundings.

It no longer seemed possible that they were in a tunnel far underground. The art that had used all of Diaspar for its canvas had been busy here, and above them the skies seemed open to the winds of heaven. All around were the spires of the city, gleaming in the sunlight. It was not the city that Alvin knew, but the Diaspar of a much earlier age. Although most of the great buildings were familiar, there were subtle differences that added to the interest of the scene. Alvin wished he could linger, but he had never found any way of retarding his progress through the tunnel.

All too soon they were set gently down in a large elliptical chamber, completely surrounded by windows. Through these they could catch tantalizing glimpses of gardens ablaze with brilliant flowers. There were gardens still in Diaspar, but these had existed only in the mind of the artist who conceived them. Certainly there were no such flowers as these in the world today.

Alystra was enchanted by their beauty, and was obviously under the impression that this was what Alvin had brought her to see. He watched her for a while as she ran gaily from scene to scene, enjoying her delight in each new discovery. There were hundreds of such places in the half-deserted buildings around the periphery of Diaspar, kept in perfect order by the hidden powers which watched over them. One day the tide of life might flow this way once more, but until then this ancient garden was a secret which they alone shared.

"We've further to go," said Alvin at last. "This is only the beginning." He stepped through one of the windows and the illusion was shattered. There was no garden behind the glass, but a circular passageway curving steeply upward. He could still see Alystra, a few feet away, though he knew that she could not see him. But she did not hesitate, and a moment later was standing beside him in the passage.

Beneath their feet the floor began to creep slowly forward, as if eager to lead them to their goal. They walked along it for a few paces, until their speed was so great that further effort would be wasted.

The corridor still inclined upward, and in a hundred feet had curved through a complete right angle. But only logic knew this; to all the senses it was as if one was now being hurried along an absolutely level corridor. The fact that they were in reality moving straight up a vertical shaft thousands of feet deep gave them no sense of insecurity, for a failure of the polarizing field was unthinkable.

Presently the corridor began to slope "downward" again until once more it had turned through a right angle. The movement of the floor slowed imperceptibly until it came to rest at the end of a long hall lined with mirrors, and Alvin knew that there was no hope of hurrying Alystra here. It was not merely that some feminine characteristics had survived unchanged since Eve; no one could have resisted the fascination of this place. There was nothing like it, as far as Alvin knew, in the rest of Diaspar. Through some whim of the artist, only a few of the mirrors reflected the scene as it really was—and even those, Alvin was convinced, were constantly changing their position. The rest certainly reflected *something,* but it was faintly disconcerting to see oneself walking amid ever-changing and quite imaginary surroundings.

Sometimes there were people going to and fro in the world behind the mirror, and more than once Alvin had seen faces that he recognized. He realized well enough that he had not been looking at any friends he knew in this existence. Through the mind of the unknown artist he had been seeing into the past, watching the previous incarnations of people who walked the world today. It saddened him, by reminding him of his own uniqueness, to think that however long he waited before these changing scenes he would never meet any ancient echo of himself.

"Do you know where we are?" Alvin asked Alystra when they had completed the tour of the mirrors. Alystra shook her head. "Somewhere near the edge of the city, I suppose," she answered carelessly. "We seem to have gone a long way, but I've no idea how far."

"We're in the Tower of Loranne," replied Alvin. "This is one of the highest points in Diaspar. Come—I'll show you." He caught Alystra's hand and led her out of the hall. There were no exits visible to the eye, but at various points the pattern on the floor indicated side corridors. As one approached the mirrors at these points, the reflections seemed to fuse into an archway of light and one could step through into another passage. Alystra lost all conscious track of their twistings and turnings, and at last they emerged into a long, perfectly straight tunnel through which blew a cold and steady wind. It stretched horizontally for hundreds of feet in either direction, and its far ends were tiny circles of light.

"I don't like this place," Alystra complained. "It's cold." She had probably never before experienced real coldness in her life, and Alvin felt somewhat guilty. He should have warned her to bring a cloak—and a good one, for all clothes in Diaspar were purely ornamental and quite useless as a protection.

Since her discomfort was entirely his fault, he handed over

his cloak without a word. There was no trace of gallantry in this; the equality of the sexes had been complete for far too long for such conventions to survive. Had matters been the other way around, Alystra would have given Alvin her cloak and he would have as automatically accepted.

It was not unpleasant walking with the wind behind them, and they soon reached the end of the tunnel. A wide-meshed filigree of stone prevented them from going farther, which was just as well, for they stood on the brink of nothingness. The great air duct opened on the sheer face of the tower, and below them was a vertical drop of at least a thousand feet. They were high upon the outer ramparts of the city, and Diaspar lay spread beneath them as few in their world could ever have seen it.

The view was the obverse of the one that Alvin had obtained from the center of the park. He could look down upon the concentric waves of stone and metal as they descended in mile-long sweeps toward the heart of the city. Far away, partly hidden by the intervening towers, he could glimpse the distant fields and trees and the eternally circling river. Further still, the remoter bastions of Diaspar climbed once more toward the sky.

Beside him, Alystra was sharing the view with pleasure but with no surprise. She had seen the city countless times before from other, almost equally well-placed vantage points—and in considerably more comfort.

"That's our world—all of it," said Alvin. "Now I want to show you something else." He turned away from the grating and began to walk toward the distant circle of light at the far end of the tunnel. The wind was cold against his lightly clad body, but he scarcely noticed the discomfort as he walked forward into the air stream.

He had gone only a little way when he realized that Alystra was making no attempt to follow. She stood watching, her borrowed cloak streaming down the wind, one hand half raised to her face. Alvin saw her lips move, but the words did not reach him. He looked back at her first with astonishment, then with an impatience that was not totally devoid of pity. What Jeserac had said was true. She could not follow him. She had realized the meaning of that remote circle of light from which the wind blew forever into Diaspar. Behind Alystra was the known world, full of wonder yet empty of surprise, drifting like a brilliant but tightly closed bubble down the river of time. Ahead, separated from her by no more than the span of a few footsteps, was the empty wilderness—the world of the desert—the world of the Invaders.

Alvin walked back to join her and was surprised to find that she was trembling. "Why are you frightened?" he asked. "We're still safely here in Diaspar. You've looked out of that window behind us—surely you can look out of this one as well!"

Alystra was staring at him as if he was some strange monster. By her standards, indeed, he was.

"I couldn't do it," she said at last. "Even thinking about it makes me feel colder than this wind. Don't go any farther, Alvin!"

"But there's no logic in it!" Alvin persisted remorselessly. "What possible harm would it do you to walk to the end of this corridor and look out? It's strange and lonely out there, but it isn't horrible. In fact, the longer I look the more beautiful I think—"

Alystra did not stay to hear him finish. She turned on her heels and fled back down the long ramp that had brought them up through the floor of this tunnel. Alvin made no attempt to stop her, since that would have involved the bad manners of imposing one's will upon another. Persuasion, he could see, would have been utterly useless. He knew that Alystra would not pause until she had returned to her companions. There was no danger that she would lose herself in the labyrinths of the city, for she would have no difficulty in retracing her footsteps. An instinctive ability to extricate himself from even the most complex of mazes had been merely one of the many accomplishments Man had learned since he started to live in cities. The long-extinct rat had been forced to acquire similar skills when he left the fields and threw in his lot with humanity.

Alvin waited for a moment, as if half-expecting Alystra to return. He was not surprised at her reaction—only at its violence and irrationality. Though he was sincerely sorry that she had gone, he could not help wishing that she had remembered to leave the cloak.

It was not only cold, but it was also hard work moving against the wind which sighed through the lungs of the city. Alvin was fighting both the air current and whatever force it was that kept it moving. Not until he had reached the stone grille, and could lock his arms around its bars, could he afford to relax. There was just sufficient room for him to force his head through the opening, and even so his view was slightly restricted, as the entrance to the duct was partly recessed into the city's wall.

Yet he could see enough. Thousands of feet below, the sunlight was taking leave of the desert. The almost horizontal rays struck through the grating and threw a weird pattern of gold and shadow far down the tunnel. Alvin shaded his eyes against the glare and peered down at the land upon which no man had walked for unknown ages.

He might have been looking at an eternally frozen sea. For mile after mile, the sand dunes undulated into the west, their contours grossly exaggerated by the slanting light. Here and there some caprice of the wind had carved curious whirlpools and gullies in the sand, so that it was sometimes hard to realize that none of this sculpture was the work of intelligence. At a very great distance, so far away indeed that he had no way of judging their remoteness, was a range of softly rounded hills. They had been a disappointment to Alvin; he would have given much to have seen in reality the soaring mountains of the ancient records and of his own dreams.

The sun lay upon the rim of the hills, its light tamed and reddened by the hundreds of miles of atmosphere it was traversing. There were two great black spots upon its disc; Alvin had learned from his studies that such things existed, but he was surprised that he could see them so easily. They seemed almost like a pair of eyes peering back at him as he crouched in his lonely spy hole with the wind whistling ceaselessly past his ears.

There was no twilight. With the going of the sun, the pools of shadow lying among the sand dunes flowed swiftly together in one vast lake of darkness. Color ebbed from the sky; the warm reds and golds drained away leaving an antarctic blue that deepened and deepened into night. Alvin waited for that breathless moment that he alone of all mankind had known—the moment when the first star shivers into life.

It had been many weeks since he had last come to this place, and he knew that the pattern of the night sky must have changed meanwhile. Even so, he was not prepared for his first glimpse of the Seven Suns.

They could have no other name; the phrase leaped unbidden to his lips. They formed a tiny, very compact and astonishingly symmetrical group against the afterglow of sunset. Six of them were arranged in a slightly flattened ellipse, which, Alvin was sure, was in reality a perfect circle, slightly tilted toward the line of vision. Each star was a different color; he could pick out red, blue, gold, and green, but the other tints eluded his eye. At the precise center of the formation was a single white giant—the brightest star in all the visible sky. The whole group looked exactly like a piece of jewelry; it seemed incredible, and beyond all stretching of the laws of chance, that Nature could ever have contrived so perfect a pattern.

As his eyes grew slowly accustomed to the darkness, Alvin could make out the great misty veil that had once been called the Milky Way. It stretched from the zenith down to the horizon, and the Seven Suns were entangled in its folds. The other stars had now emerged to challenge them, and their random groupings only emphasized the enigma of that perfect symmetry. It was almost as if some power had deliberately opposed the disorder of the natural Universe by setting its sign upon the stars.

Ten times, no more, the Galaxy had turned upon its axis since Man first walked on Earth. By its own standards, that was but a moment. Yet in that short period it had changed completely—changed far more than it had any right to do in the natural course of events. The great suns that had once burned so fiercely in the pride of youth were now guttering to their doom. But Alvin had never seen the heavens in their ancient glory, and so was unaware of all that had been lost.

The cold, seeping through into his bones, drove him back to the city. He extricated himself from the grating and rubbed the circulation back into his limbs. Ahead of him, down the tunnel, the light streaming out from Diaspar was so brilliant that for a moment he had to avert his eyes. Outside the city there were such things as day and night, but within it there was only eternal day. As the sun descended the sky above Diaspar would fill with light and no one would notice when the natural illumination vanished. Even before men had lost the need for sleep, they had driven darkness from their cities. The only night that ever came to Diaspar was a rare and unpredictable obscuration that sometimes visited the park and transformed it into a place of mystery.

Alvin came slowly back through the hall of mirrors, his mind still filled with night and stars. He felt inspired and yet depressed. There seemed no way in which he could ever escape out into that enormous emptiness—and no rational purpose in doing so. Jeserac had said that a man would soon die out in the desert, and Alvin could well believe him. Perhaps he might one day discover some way of leaving Diaspar, but if he did, he knew that he must soon return. To reach the desert would be an amusing game, no more. It was a game he could share with no one, and it would lead him nowhere. But at least it would be worth doing if it helped to quench the longing in his soul.

As if unwilling to return to the familiar world, Alvin lingered among the reflections from the past. He stood before one of the great mirrors and watched the scenes that came and went within its depths. Whatever mechanism produced these images was controlled by his presence, and to some extent by his thoughts. The mirrors were always blank when he first came into the room, but filled with action as soon as he moved among them.

He seemed to be standing in a large open courtyard which he had never seen in reality, but which probably still existed somewhere in Diaspar. It was unusually crowded, and some kind of public meeting seemed to be in progress. Two men were arguing politely on a raised platform while their supporters stood around and made interjections from time to time. The complete silence added to the charm of the scene, for imagination immediately went to work supplying the missing sounds. What were they debating? Alvin wondered. Perhaps it was not a real scene from the past, but a purely created episode. The careful balance of figures, the slightly formal movements, all made it seem a little too neat for life.

He studied the faces in the crowd, seeking for anyone he could recognize. There was no one here that he knew, but he might be looking at friends he would not meet for centuries to come. How many possible patterns of human physiognomy were there? The number was enormous, but it was still finite, especially when all the unesthetic variations had been eliminated.

The people in the mirror world continued their long-forgotten argument, ignoring the image of Alvin which stood motionless among them. Sometimes it was very hard to believe that he was not part of the scene himself, for the illusion was so flawless. When one of the phantoms in the mirror appeared to move behind Alvin, it vanished just as a real object would have done; and when one moved in front of him, he was the one who was eclipsed.

He was preparing to leave when he noticed an oddly dressed man standing a little apart from the main group. His movements, his clothes, everything about him, seemed slightly out of place in this assembly. He spoiled the pattern; like Alvin, he was an anachronism.

He was a good deal more than that. He was real, and he was looking at Alvin with a slightly quizzical smile.

CHAPTER

In his short lifetime, Alvin had met less than one-thousandth of the inhabitants of Diaspar. He was not surprised, therefore, that the man confronting him was a stranger. What did surprise him was to meet anyone at all here in this deserted tower, so near the frontier of the unknown.

He turned his back on the mirror world and faced the intruder. Before he could speak, the other had addressed him.

"You are Alvin, I believe. When I discovered that someone was coming here, I should have guessed it was you."

The remark was obviously not intended to give offense; it was a simple statement of fact, and Alvin accepted it as such. He was not surprised to be recognized; whether he liked it or not, the fact of his uniqueness, and its unrevealed potentialities, had made him known to everyone in the city.

"I am Khedron," continued the stranger, as if that explained everything. "They call me the Jester."

Alvin looked blank, and Khedron shrugged his shoulders in mock resignation.

"Ah, such is fame! Still, you are young and there have been no jests in your lifetime. Your ignorance is excused."

There was something refreshingly unusual about Khedron.

Alvin searched his mind for the meaning of the strange word "Jester"; it evoked the faintest of memories, but he could not identify it. There were many such titles in the complex social structure of the city, and it took a lifetime to learn them all.

"Do you often come here?" Alvin asked, a little jealously. He had grown to regard the Tower of Loranne as his personal property and felt slightly annoyed that its marvels were known to anyone else. But had Khedron, he wondered, ever looked out across the desert or seen the stars sinking down into the west?

"No," said Khedron, almost as if answering his unspoken thoughts. "I have never been here before. But it is my pleasure to learn of unusual happenings in the city and it is a very long time since anyone went to the Tower of Loranne."

Alvin wondered fleetingly how Khedron knew of his earlier visits, but quickly dismissed the matter from his mind. Diaspar was full of eyes and ears and other more subtle sense organs which kept the city aware of all that was happening within it. Anyone who was sufficiently interested could no doubt find a way of tapping these channels.

"Even if it is unusual for anyone to come here," said Alvin, still fencing verbally, "why should you be interested?"

"Because in Diaspar," replied Khedron, "the unusual is my prerogative. I had marked you down a long time ago; I knew we should meet some day. After my fashion, I too am unique. Oh, not in the way that you are; this is not my first life. I have walked a thousand times out of the Hall of Creation. But somewhere back at the beginning I was chosen to be Jester, and there is only one Jester at a time in Diaspar. Most people think that is one too many."

There was an irony about Khedron's speech that left Alvin still floundering. It was not the best of manners to ask direct personal questions, but after all Khedron had raised the subject.

"I'm sorry about my ignorance," said Alvin. "But what is a Jester, and what does he do?"

"You ask 'what,'" replied Khedron, "so I'll start by telling you 'why.' It's a long story, but I think you will be interested."

"I am interested in everything," said Alvin, truthfully enough.

"Very well. The men—if they were men, which I sometimes doubt—who designed Diaspar had to solve an incredibly complex problem. Diaspar is not merely a machine, you know—it is a living organism, and an immortal one. We are so accustomed to our society that we can't appreciate how strange it would have seemed to our first ancestors. Here we have a tiny, closed world which never changes except in its minor details, and yet which is perfectly stable, age after age. It has probably lasted longer than the rest of human history—yet in *that* history there were, so it is believed, countless thousands of separate cultures and civilizations which endured for a little while and then perished. How did Diaspar achieve its extraordinary stability?"

Alvin was surprised that anyone should ask so elementary a question, and his hopes of learning something new began to wane.

"Through the Memory Banks, of course," he replied. "Diaspar is always composed of the same people, though their actual groupings change as their bodies are created or destroyed."

Khedron shook his head.

"That is only a very small part of the answer. With exactly the same people, you could build many different patterns of society. I can't prove that, and I've no direct evidence of it, but I believe it's true. The designers of the city did not merely fix its population; they fixed the laws governing its behavior. We're scarcely aware that those laws exist, but we obey them. Diaspar is a frozen culture, which cannot change outside of narrow limits. The Memory Banks store many other things outside the patterns of our bodies and personalities. They store the image of the city itself, holding its every atom rigid against all the changes that time can bring. Look at this pavement—it was laid down millions of years ago, and countless feet have walked upon it. Can you see any sign of wear? Unprotected matter, however adamant, would have been ground to dust ages ago. But as long as there is power to operate the Memory Banks, and as long as the matrices they contain can still control the patterns of the city, the physical structure of Diaspar will never change."

"But there have been *some* changes," protested Alvin. "Many buildings have been torn down since the city was built, and new ones erected."

"Of course—but only by discharging the information stored in the Memory Banks and then setting up new patterns. In any case, I was merely mentioning that as an example of the way the city preserves itself physically. The point I want to make is that in the same way there are machines in Diaspar that preserve our social structure. They watch for any changes, and correct them before they become too great. How do they do it? I don't know—perhaps by selecting those who emerge from the Hall of Creation. Perhaps by tampering with our personality patterns; we may think we have free will, but can we be certain of that?

"In any event, the problem was solved. Diaspar has survived and come safely down the ages, like a great ship carrying as its cargo all that is left of the human race. It is a tremendous achievement in social engineering, though whether it is worth doing is quite another matter.

"Stability, however, is not enough. It leads too easily to stagnation, and thence to decadence. The designers of the city took elaborate steps to avoid this, though these deserted buildings suggest that they did not entirely succeed. I, Khedron the Jester, am part of that plan. A very small part, perhaps. I like to think otherwise, but I can never be sure."

"And just what is that part?" asked Alvin, still very much in the dark, and becoming a little exasperated.

"Let us say that I introduce calculated amounts of disorder into the city. To explain my operations would be to destroy their effectiveness. Judge me by my deeds, though they are few, rather than my words, though they are many."

Alvin had never before met anyone quite like Khedron. The Jester was a real personality—a character who stood head and shoulders above the general level of uniformity which was typical of Diaspar. Though there seemed no hope of discovering precisely what his duties were and how he carried them out, that was of minor importance. All that mattered, Alvin sensed, was that here was someone to whom he could talk—when there was a gap in the monologue—and who might give him answers to many of the problems that had puzzled him for so long.

They went back together down through the corridors of the Tower of Loranne, and emerged beside the deserted moving way. Not until they were once more in the streets did it occur to Alvin that Khedron had never asked him what he had been doing out here at the edge of the unknown. He suspected that Khedron knew, and was interested but not surprised. Something told him that it would be very difficult to surprise Khedron.

They exchanged index numbers, so that they could call each other whenever they wished. Alvin was anxious to see more of the Jester, though he fancied that his company might prove exhausting if it was too prolonged. Before they met again, however, he wanted to find what his friends, and particularly Jeserac, could tell him about Khedron.

"Until our next meeting," said Khedron, and promptly vanished. Alvin was somewhat annoyed. If you met anyone when you were merely projecting yourself, and were not present in the flesh, it was good manners to make that clear from the beginning. It could sometimes put the party who was ignorant of the facts at a considerable disadvantage. Probably Khedron had been quietly at home all the time—wherever his home might be. The number that he had given Alvin would insure that any messages would reach him, but did not reveal where he lived. That at lest was according to normal custom. You might be free enough with index numbers, but your actual address was something you disclosed only to your intimate friends.

As he made his way back into the city, Alvin pondered over all that Khedron had told him about Diaspar and its social organization. It was strange that he had met no one else who had ever seemed dissatisfied with their mode of life. Diaspar and its inhabitants had been designed as part of one master plan; they formed a perfect symbiosis. Throughout their long lives, the people of the city were never bored. Though their world might be a tiny one by the standard of earlier ages, its complexity was overwhelming, its wealth of wonder and treasure bcyond calculation. Here Man had gathered all the fruits of his genius, everything that had been saved from the ruin of the past. All the cities that had ever been, so it was said, had given something to Diaspar; before the coming of the Invaders, its name had been known on all the worlds that Man had lost. Into the building of Diaspar had gone all the skill, all the artistry of the Empire. When the great days were coming to an end, men of genius had remolded the city and given it the machines that made it immortal. Whatever might be forgotten, Diaspar would live and bear the descendants of Man safely down the stream of time.

They had achieved nothing except survival, and were content with that. There were a million things to occupy their lives between the hour when they came, almost full-grown, from the Hall of Creation and the hour when, their bodies scarcely older, they returned to the Memory Banks of the city. In a world where all men and women possess an intelligence that would once have been the mark of genius, there can be no danger of boredom. The delights of conversation and argument, the intricate formalities of social intercourse—these alone were enough to occupy a goodly portion of a lifetime. Beyond those were the great formal debates, when the whole city would listen entranced while its keenest minds met in combat or strove to scale those mountain peaks of philosophy which are never conquered yet whose challenge never palls.

No man or woman was without some absorbing intellectual interest. Eriston, for example, spent much of his time in prolonged soliloquies with the Central Computer, which virtually ran the city, yet which had leisure for scores of simultaneous discussions with anyone who cared to match his wits against it. For three hundred years, Eriston had been trying to construct logical paradoxes which the machine could not resolve. He did not expect to make serious progress before he had used up several lifetimes.

Etania's interests were of a more esthetic nature. She designed and constructed, with the aid of the matter organizers, three-dimensional interlacing patterns of such beautiful complexity that they were really extremely advanced problems in topology. Her work could be seen all over Diaspar, and some of her patterns had been incorporated in the floors of the great halls of choreography, where they were used as the basis for evolving new ballet creations and dance motifs.

Such occupations might have seemed arid to those who did not possess the intellect to appreciate their subtleties. Yet there was no one in Diaspar who could not understand something of what Eriston and Etania were trying to do and did not have some equally consuming interest of his own.

Athletics and various sports, including many only rendered possible by the control of gravity, made pleasant the first few centuries of youth. For adventure and the exercise of the imagination, the sagas provided all that anyone could desire. They were the inevitable end product of that striving for realism which began when men started to reproduce moving images and to record sounds, and then to use these techniques to enact scenes from real or imaginary life. In the sagas, the illusion was perfect because all the sense impressions involved were fed directly into the mind and any conflicting sensations were diverted. The entranced spectator was cut off from reality as long as the adventure lasted; it was as if he lived a dream yet believed he was awake.

In a world of order and stability, which in its broad outlines had not changed for a billion years, it was perhaps not surprising to find an absorbing interest in games of chance. Humanity had always been fascinated by the mystery of the falling dice, the turn of a card, the spin of the pointer. At its lowest level, this interest was based on mere cupidity—and that was an emotion that could have no place in a world where everyone possessed all that they could reasonably need. Even when this motive was ruled out, however, the purely intellectual fascination of chance remained to seduce the most sophisticated minds. Machines that behaved in a purely random way—events whose outcome could never be predicted, no matter how much information one had—from these philosopher and gambler could derive equal enjoyment.

And there still remained, for all men to share, the linked worlds of love and art. Linked, because love without art is merely the slaking of desire, and art cannot be enjoyed unless it is approached with love.

Men had sought beauty in many forms—in sequences of sound, in lines upon paper, in surfaces of stone, in the movements of the human body, in colors ranged through space. All these media still survived in Diaspar, and down the ages others had been added to them. No one was yet certain if all the possibilities of art had been discovered; or if it had any meaning outside the mind of man.

And the same was true of love.

Chapter

Jeserac sat motionless within a whirlpool of numbers. The first thousand primes, expressed in the binary scale that had been used for all arithmetical operations since electronic computers were invented, marched in order before him. Endless ranks of 1's and 0's paraded past, bringing before Jeserac's eyes the complete sequence of all those numbers that possessed no factors except themselves and unity. There was a mystery about the primes that had always fascinated Man, and they held his imagination still.

Jeserac was no mathematician, though sometimes he liked to believe he was. All he could do was to search among the infinite array of primes for special relationships and rules which more talented men might incorporate in general laws. He could find how numbers behaved, but he could not explain why. It was his pleasure to hack his way through the arithmetical jungle, and sometimes he discovered wonders that more skillful explorers had missed.

He set up the matrix of all possible integers, and started his computer stringing the primes across its surface as beads might be arranged at the intersections of a mesh. Jeserac had done this a hundred times before, and it had never taught him anything. But he was fascinated by the way in which the numbers he was studying were scattered, apparently according to no laws, across the spectrum of the integers. He knew the laws of distribution that had already been discovered, but always hoped to discover more.

He could scarcely complain about the interruption. If he had wished to remain undisturbed, he should have set his annunciator accordingly. As the gentle chime sounded in his ear, the wall of numbers shivered, the digits blurred together, and Jeserac returned to the world of mere reality.

He recognized Khedron at once, and was none too pleased. Jeserac did not care to be disturbed from his ordered way of life, and Khedron represented the unpredictable. However, he greeted his visitor politely enough and concealed all trace of his mild concern.

When two people met for the first time in Diaspar—or even for the hundredth—it was customary to spend an hour or so in an exchange of courtesies before getting down to business, if any. Khedron somewhat offended Jeserac by racing through these formalities in a mere fifteen minutes and then saying abruptly: “I’d like to talk to you about Alvin. You’re his tutor, I believe.”

“That is true,” replied Jeserac. “I still see him several times a week—as often as he wishes.”

“And would you say that he was an apt pupil?”

Jeserac thought that over; it was a difficult question to answer. The pupil-tutor relationship was extremely important and was, indeed, one of the foundations of life in Diaspar. On the average, ten thousand new minds came into the city every year. Their previous memories were still latent, and for the first twenty years of their existence everything around them was fresh and strange. They had to be taught to use the myriad machines and devices that were the background of everyday life, and they had to learn their way through the most complex society Man had ever built.

Part of this instruction came from the couples chosen to be the parents of the new citizens. The selection was by lot, and the duties were not onerous. Eriston and Etania had devoted no more than a third of their time to Alvin's upbringing, and they had done all that was expected of them.

Jeserac's duties were confined to the more formal aspects of Alvin's education; it was assumed that his parents would teach him how to behave in society and introduce him to an ever-widening circle of friends. They were responsible for Alvin's character, Jeserac for his mind.

"I find it rather hard to answer your question," Jeserac replied. "Certainly there is nothing wrong with Alvin's intelligence, but many of the things that should concern him seem to be a matter of complete indifference. On the other hand, he shows a morbid curiosity regarding subjects which we do not generally discuss."

"The world outside Diaspar, for example?"

"Yes—but how did you know?"

Khedron hesitated for a moment, wondering how far he should take Jeserac into his confidence. He knew that Jeserac was kindly and well-intentioned, but he knew also that he must be bound by the same taboos that controlled everyone in Diaspar—everyone except Alvin.

"I guessed it," he said at last.

Jeserac settled down more comfortably in the depths of the chair he had just materialized. This was an interesting situation, and he wanted to analyze it as fully as possible. There was not much he could learn, however, unless Khedron was willing to co-operate.

He should have anticipated that Alvin would one day meet the Jester, with unpredictable consequences. Khedron was the only other person in the city who could be called eccentric—and even his eccentricity had been planned by the designers of Diaspar. Long ago it had been discovered that without some crime or disorder, Utopia soon became unbearably dull.

Crime, however, from the nature of things, could not be guaranteed to remain at the optimum level which the social equation demanded. If it was licensed and regulated, it ceased to be crime.

The office of Jester was the solution—as first sight naïve, yet actually profoundly subtle—which the city's designers had evolved. In all the history of Diaspar there were less than two hundred persons whose mental inheritance fitted them for this peculiar role. They had certain privileges that protected them from the consequences of their actions, though there had been Jesters who had overstepped the mark and paid the only penalty that Diaspar could impose—that of being banished into the future before their current incarnation had ended.

On rare and unforeseeable occasions, the Jester would turn the city upside-down by some prank which might be no more than an elaborate practical joke, or which might be a calculated assault on some currently cherished belief or way of life. All things considered, the name "Jester" was a highly appropriate one. There had once been men with very similar duties, operating with the same license, in the days when there were courts and kings.

"It will help," said Jeserac, "if we are frank with one another. We both know that Alvin is a Unique—that he has never experienced any earlier life in Diaspar. Perhaps you can guess, better than I can, the implications of that. I doubt if anything that happens in the city is totally unplanned, so there must be a purpose in his creation. Whether he will achieve that purpose—whatever it is—I do not know. Nor do I know whether it is good or bad. I cannot guess what it is."

"Suppose it concerns something external to the city?"

Jeserac smiled patiently; the Jester was having his little joke, as was only to be expected.

"I have told him what lies there; he knows that there is nothing outside Diaspar except the desert. Take him there if you can; perhaps *you* know a way. When he sees the reality, it may cure the strangeness in his mind."

"I think he has already seen it," said Khedron softly. But he said it to himself, and not to Jeserac.

"I do not believe that Alvin is happy," Jeserac continued. "He has formed no real attachments, and it is hard to see how he can while he still suffers from this obsession. But after all, he is very young. He may grow out of this phase, and become part of the pattern of the city."

Jeserac was talking to reassure himself; Khedron wondered if he really believed what he was saying.

"Tell me, Jeserac," asked Khedron abruptly, "does Alvin know that he is not the first Unique?"

Jeserac looked startled, then a little defiant.

"I might have guessed," he said ruefully, "that *you* would know that. How many Uniques have there been in the whole history of Diaspar? As many as ten?"

"Fourteen," answered Khedron without hesitation. "Not counting Alvin.

"You have better information than I can command," said Jeserac wryly. "Perhaps you can tell me what happened to those Uniques?"

"They disappeared."

"Thank you: I knew that already. That is why I have told Alvin as little as possible about his predecessors: it would hardly help him in his present mood. Can I rely on your co-operation?"

"For the moment—yes. I want to study him myself; mysteries have always intrigued me, and there are too few in Diaspar. Besides, I think that Fate may be arranging a jest beside which all my efforts will look very modest indeed. In that case, I want to make sure that I am present at its climax."

"You are rather too fond of talking in riddles," complained Jeserac. "Exactly what are you anticipating?"

"I doubt if my guesses will be any better than yours. But I

believe this—neither you nor I nor anyone in Diaspar will be able to stop Alvin when he has decided what he wants to do. We have a very interesting few centuries ahead of us."

Jeserac sat motionless for a long time, his mathematics forgotten, after the image of Khedron had faded from sight. A sense of foreboding, the like of which he had never known before, hung heavily upon him. For a fleeting moment he wondered if he should request an audience with the Council—but would that not be making a ridiculous fuss about nothing? Perhaps the whole affair was some complicated and obscure jest of Khedron's, though he could not imagine why he had been chosen to be its butt.

He thought the matter over carefully, examining the problem from every angle. After little more than an hour, he made a characteristic decision.

He would wait and see.

Alvin wasted no time learning all that he could about Khedron. Jeserac, as usual, was his main source of information. The old tutor gave a carefully factual account of his meeting with the Jester, and added what little he knew about the other's mode of life. Insofar as such a thing was possible in Diaspar, Khedron was a recluse: no one knew where he lived or anything about his way of life. The last jest he had contrived had been a rather childish prank involving a general paralysis of the moving ways. That had been fifty years ago; a century earlier he had let loose a particularly revolting dragon which had wandered around the city eating every existing specimen of the works of the currently most popular sculptor. The artist himself, justifiably alarmed when the beast's single-minded diet became obvious, had gone into hiding and not emerged until the monster had vanished as mysteriously as it had appeared.

One thing was obvious from these accounts. Khedron must have a profound understanding of the machines and powers that ruled the city, and could make them obey his will in ways which no one else could do. Presumably there must be some overriding control which prevented any too-ambitious Jester from causing permanent and irreparable damage to the complex structure of Diaspar.

Alvin filed all this information away, but made no move to contact Khedron. Though he had many questions to ask the Jester, his stubborn streak of independence—perhaps the most truly unique of all his qualities—made him determined to discover all he could by his own unaided efforts. He had embarked on a project that might keep him busy for years, but as long as he felt that he was moving toward his goal he was happy.

Like some traveler of old mapping out an unknown land, he had begun the systematic exploration of Diaspar. He spent his weeks and days prowling through the lonely towers at the margin of the city, in the hope that somewhere he might discover a way out into the world beyond. During the course of his search he found a dozen of the great air vents opening high above the desert, but they were all barred—and even if the bars had not been there, the sheer drop of almost a mile was sufficient obstacle.

He found no other exits, though he explored a thousand corridors and ten thousand empty chambers. All these buildings were in that perfect and spotless condition which the people of Diaspar took for granted as part of the normal order of things. Sometimes Alvin would meet a wandering robot, obviously on a tour of inspection, and he never failed to question the machine. He learned nothing, because the machines he encountered were not keyed to respond to human speech or thoughts. Though they were aware of his presence, for they floated politely aside to let him pass, they refused to engage in conversation.

There were times when Alvin did not see another human being for days. When he felt hungry, he would go into one of the living apartments and order a meal. Miraculous machines to whose existence he seldom gave a thought would wake to life after aeons of slumber. The patterns they had stored in their memories would flicker on the edge of reality, organizing and directing the matter they controlled. And so a meal prepared by a master chef a hundred million years before would be called again into existence to delight the palate or merely to satisfy the appetite.

The loneliness of this deserted world—the empty shell surrounding the living heart of the city—did not depress Alvin. He was used to loneliness, even when he was among those he called his friends. This ardent exploration, absorbing all his energy and interest, made him forget for the moment the mystery of his heritage and the anomaly that cut him off from all his fellows.

He had explored less than one-hundredth of the city's rim when he decided that he was wasting his time. His decision was not the result of impatience, but of sheer common sense. If needs be, he was prepared to come back and finish the task, even if it took him the remainder of his life. He had seen enough, however, to convince him that if a way out of Diaspar did exist, it would not be found as easily as this. He might waste centuries in fruitless search unless he called upon the assistance of wiser men.

Jeserac had told him flatly that he knew no road out of Diaspar, and doubted if one existed. The information machines, when Alvin had questioned them, had searched their almost infinite memories in vain. They could tell him every detail of the city's history back to the beginning of recorded times—back to the barrier beyond which the Dawn Ages lay forever hidden. But they could not answer Alvin's simple question, or else some higher power had forbidden them to do so.

He would have to see Khedron again.

Chapter

"You took your time," said Khedron, "but I knew you would call sooner or later."

This confidence annoyed Alvin; he did not like to think that his behavior could be predicted so accurately. He wondered if the Jester had watched all his fruitless searching and knew exactly what he had been doing.

"I am trying to find a way out of the city," he said bluntly. "There *must* be one, and I think you could help me find it."

Khedron was silent for a moment. There was still time, if he wished, to turn back from the road that stretched before him, and which led into a future beyond all his powers of prophecy. No one else would have hesitated; no other man in the city, even if he had the power, would have dared to disturb the ghosts of an age that had been dead for millions of centuries. Perhaps there was no danger, perhaps nothing could alter the perpetual changelessness of Diaspar. But if there was any risk of something strange and new coming into the world, this might be the last chance to ward it off.

Khedron was content with the order of things as it was. True, he might upset that order from time to time—but only by a little. He was a critic, not a revolutionary. On the placidly flowing river of time, he wished only to make a few ripples: he shrank from diverting its course. The desire for adventure, other than that of the mind, had been eliminated from him as carefully and thoroughly as from all the other citizens of Diaspar.

Yet he still possessed, though it was almost extinguished, that spark of curiosity that was once Man's greatest gift. He was still prepared to take a risk.

He looked at Alvin and tried to remember his own youth, his own dreams of half a thousand years before. Any moment of his past that he cared to choose was still clear and sharp when he turned his memory upon it. Like beads upon a string, this life and all the ones before it stretched back through the ages; he could seize and re-examine any one he wished. Most of those older Khedrons were strangers to him now; the basic patterns might be the same, but the weight of experience separated him from them forever. If he wished, he could wash his mind clear of all his earlier incarnations, when next he walked back into the Hall of Creation to sleep until the city called him forth again. But that would be a kind of death, and he was not ready for that yet. He was still prepared to go on collecting all that life could offer, like a chambered nautilus patiently adding new cells to its slowly expanding spiral.

In his youth, he had been no different from his companions. It was not until he came of age and the latent memories of his earlier lives came flooding back that he had taken up the role for which he had been destined long ago. Sometimes he felt resentment that the intelligences which had contrived Diaspar with such infinite skill could even now, after all these ages, make him move like a puppet across their stage. Here, perhaps, was a chance of obtaining a long-delayed revenge. A new actor had appeared who might ring down the curtain for the last time on a play that already had seen far too many acts.

Sympathy, for one whose loneliness must be even greater than his own; an ennui produced by ages of repetition; and an impish sense of fun—these were the discordant factors that prompted Khedron to act.

"I may be able to help you," he told Alvin, "or I may not. I don't wish to raise any false hopes. Meet me in half an hour at the intersection of Radius 3 and Ring 2. If I cannot do anything else, at least I can promise you an interesting journey."

Alvin was at the rendezvous ten minutes ahead of time, though it was on the other side of the city. He waited impatiently as the moving ways swept eternally past him, bearing the placid and contented people of the city about their unimportant business. At last he saw the tall figure of Khedron appear in the distance, and a moment later he was for the first time in the physical presence of the Jester. This was no projected image; when they touched palms in the ancient greeting, Khedron was real enough.

The Jester sat down on one of the marble balustrades and regarded Alvin with a curious intentness.

"I wonder," he said, "if you know what you are asking. And I wonder what you would do if you obtained it. Do you *really* imagine that you could leave the city, even if you found a way?"

"I am sure of it," replied Alvin, bravely enough, though Khedron could sense the uncertainty in his voice.

"Then let me tell you something which you may not know. You see those towers there?" Khedron pointed to the twin peaks of Power Central and Council Hall, staring at each other across a canyon a mile deep. "Suppose I were to lay a perfectly firm plank between those two towers—a plank only six inches wide. Could you walk across it?"

Alvin hesitated.

"I don't know," he answered. "I wouldn't like to try."

"I'm quite sure you could never do it. You'd get giddy and fall off before you'd gone a dozen paces. Yet if that same plank was supported just clear of the ground, you'd be able to walk along it without difficulty."

"And what does that prove?"

"A simple point I'm trying to make. In the two experiments I've described, the plank would be exactly the same in both cases. One of those wheeled robots you sometimes meet could cross it just as easily if it was bridging those towers as if it was laid along the ground. *We* couldn't, because we have a fear of heights. It may be irrational, but it's too powerful to be ignored. It is built into us; we are born with it.

"In the same way, we have a fear of space. Show any man in Diaspar a road out of the city—a road that might be just like this road in front of us now—and he could not go far along it. He would have to turn back, as you would turn back if you started to cross a plank between those towers."

"But why?" asked Alvin. "There must have been a time—"

"I know, I know," said Khedron. "Men once went out over the whole world, and to the stars themselves. Something changed them and gave them this fear with which they are now born. You alone imagine that you do not possess it. Well, we shall see. I'm taking you to Council Hall."

The Hall was one of the largest buildings in the city, and was almost entirely given over to the machines that were the real administrators of Diaspar. Not far from its summit was the chamber where the Council met on those infrequent occasions when it had any business to discuss.

The wide entrance swallowed them up, and Khedron strode forward into the golden gloom. Alvin had never entered Council Hall before; there was no rule against it—there were few rules against anything in Diaspar—but like everyone else he had a certain half-religious awe of the place. In a world that had no gods, Council Hall was the nearest thing to a temple.

Khedron never hesitated as he led Alvin along corridors and down ramps that were obviously made for wheeled machines, not human traffic. Some of these ramps zigzagged down into the depths at such steep angles that it would have been impossible to keep a footing on them had not gravity been twisted to compensate for the slope.

They came at last to a closed door, which slid silently open as they approached, then barred their retreat. Ahead was another door, which did not open as they came up to it. Khedron made no move to touch the door, but stood motionless in front of it. After a short pause, a quiet voice said: "Please state your names."

"I am Khedron the Jester. My companion is Alvin."

"And your business?"

"Sheer curiosity."

Rather to Alvin's surprise, the door opened at once. In his experience, if one gave facetious replies to machines it always led to confusion and one had to go back to the beginning. The machine that had interrogated Khedron must have been a very sophisticated one—far up in the hierarchy of the Central Computer.

They met no more barriers, but Alvin suspected that they had passed many tests of which he had no knowledge. A short corridor brought them out abruptly into a huge circular chamber with a sunken floor, and set in that floor was something so astonishing that for a moment Alvin was overwhelmed with wonder. He was looking down upon the entire city of Diaspar, spread out before him with its tallest buildings barely reaching to his shoulder.

He spent so long picking out familiar places and observing unexpected vistas that it was some time before he paid any notice to the rest of the chamber. Its walls were covered with a microscopically detailed pattern of black and white squares; the pattern itself was completely irregular, and when he moved his eyes quickly he got the impression that it was flickering swiftly, though it never changed. At frequent intervals around the chamber were manually controlled machines of some type, each complete with a vision screen and a seat for the operator.

Khedron let Alvin look his fill. Then he pointed to the diminutive city and said: "Do you know what that is?"

Alvin was tempted to answer, "A model, I suppose," but that answer was so obvious that he was sure it must be wrong. So he shook his head and waited for Khedron to answer his own question.

"You remember," said the Jester, "that I once told you how the city was maintained—how the Memory Banks hold its pattern frozen forever. Those Banks are all around us, with all their immeasurable store of information, completely defining the city as it is today. Every atom of Diaspar is somehow keyed, by forces we have forgotten, to the matrices buried in these walls."

He waved toward the perfect, infinitely detailed simulacrum of Diaspar that lay below them.

"That is no model; it does not really exist. It is merely the projected image of the pattern held in the Memory Banks, and therefore it is absolutely identical with the city itself. These viewing machines here enable one to magnify any desired portion, to look at it life size or larger. They are used when it is necessary to make alterations in the design, though it is a very long time since that was done. If you want to know what Diaspar is like, this is the place to come. You can learn more here in a few days than you would in a lifetime of actual exploring."

"It's wonderful," said Alvin. "How many people know that it exists?"

"Oh, a good many, but it seldom concerns them. The Council comes down here from time to time; no alterations to the city can be made unless they are all here. And not even then, if the Central Computer doesn't approve of the proposed change. I doubt if this room is visited more than two or three times a year."

Alvin wanted to know how Khedron had access to it, and then remembered that many of his more elaborate jests must have involved a knowledge of the city's inner mechanisms that could have come only from very profound study. It must be one of the Jester's privileges to go anywhere and learn anything; he could have no better guide to the secrets of Diaspar.

"What you are looking for may not exist," said Khedron, "but if it does, this is where you will find it. Let me show you how to operate the monitors."

For the next hour Alvin sat before one of the vision screens, learning to use the controls. He could select at will any point in the city, and examine it with any degree of magnification. Streets and towers and walls and moving ways flashed across the screen as he changed the co-ordinates; it was as though he was an all-seeing, disembodied spirit that could move effortlessly over the whole of Diaspar, unhindered by any physical obstructions.

Yet it was not, in reality, Diaspar that he was examining. He was moving through the memory cells, looking at the dream image of the city—the dream that had had the power to hold the real Diaspar untouched by time for a billion years. He could see only that part of the city which was permanent; the people who walked its streets were no part of this frozen image. For his purpose, that did not matter. His concern now was purely with the creation of stone and metal in which he was imprisoned, and not those who shared—however willingly—his confinement.

He searched for and presently found the Tower of Loranne, and moved swiftly through the corridors and passageways which he had already explored in reality. As the image of the stone grille expanded before his eyes, he could almost feel the cold wind that had blown ceaselessly through it for perhaps half the entire history of mankind, and that was blowing now. He came up to the grille, looked out—and saw nothing. For a moment the shock was so great that he almost doubted his own memory; had his vision of the desert been nothing more than a dream?

Then he remembered the truth. The desert was no part of Diaspar, and therefore no image of it existed in the phantom world he was exploring. Anything might lie beyond that grille in reality; this monitor screen could never show it.

Yet it could show him something that no living man had ever seen. Alvin advanced his viewpoint through the grille, out into the nothingness beyond the city. He turned the control which altered the direction of vision, so that he looked backward along the way that he had come. And there behind him lay Diaspar—seen from the outside.

To the computers, the memory circuits, and all the multitudinous mechanisms that created the image at which Alvin was looking, it was merely a simple problem of perspective. They "knew" the form of the city; therefore they could show it as it would appear from the outside. Yet even though he could appreciate how the trick was done, the effect on Alvin was overwhelming. In spirit, if not reality, he had escaped from the city. He appeared to be hanging in space, a few feet away from the sheer wall of the Tower of Loranne. For a moment he stared at the smooth gray surface before his eyes; then he touched the control and let his viewpoint drop toward the ground.

Now that he knew the possibilities of this wonderful instrument, his plan of action was clear. There was no need to spend months and years exploring Diaspar from the inside, room by room and corridor by corridor. From this new vantage point he could wing his way along the outside of the city, and could see at once any openings that might lead to the desert and the world beyond.

The sense of victory, of achievement, made him feel lightheaded and anxious to share his joy. He turned to Khedron, wishing to thank the Jester for having made this possible. But Khedron was gone, and it took only a moment's thought to realize why.

Alvin was perhaps the only man in Diaspar who could look

unaffected upon the images that were now drifting across the screen. Khedron could help him in his search, but even the Jester shared the strange terror of the Universe which had pinned mankind for so long inside its little world. He had left Alvin to continue his quest alone.

The sense of loneliness, which for a little while had lifted from Alvin's soul, pressed down upon him once more. But this was no time for melancholy; there was too much to do. He turned back to the monitor screen, set the image of the city wall drifting slowly across it, and began his search.

Diaspar saw little of Alvin for the next few weeks, though only a few people noticed his absence. Jeserac, when he discovered that his erstwhile pupil was spending all his time at Council Hall instead of prowling around the frontier of the city, felt slightly relieved, imagining that Alvin could come to no trouble there. Eriston and Etania called his room once or twice, found that he was out and thought nothing of it. Alystra was a little more persistent.

For her own peace of mind, it was a pity that she had become infatuated with Alvin, when there were so many more suitable choices. Alystra had never had any difficulty in finding partners, but by comparison with Alvin all the other men she knew were nonentities, cast from the same featureless mold. She would not lose him without a struggle; his aloofness and indifference set a challenge which she could not resist.

Yet perhaps her motives were not entirely selfish, and were maternal rather than sexual. Though birth had been forgotten, the feminine instincts of protection and sympathy still remained. Alvin might appear to be stubborn and self-reliant and determined to have his own way, yet Alystra could sense his inner loneliness.

When she found that Alvin had disappeared, she promptly asked Jeserac what had happened to him. Jeserac, with only a momentary hesitation, told her. If Alvin did not want company, the answer was in his own hands. His tutor neither approved nor disapproved of this relationship. On the whole, he rather liked Alystra and hoped that her influence would help Alvin to adjust himself to life in Diaspar.

The fact that Alvin was spending his time at Council Hall could only mean that he was engaged on some research project, and this knowledge at least served to quell any suspicions Alystra might have concerning possible rivals. But though her jealousy was not aroused, her curiosity was. She sometimes reproached herself for abandoning Alvin in the Tower of Loranne, though she knew that if the circumstances were repeated she would do exactly the same thing again. There was no way of understanding Alvin's mind, she told herself, unless she could discover what he was trying to do.

She walked purposefully into the main hall, impressed but not overawed by the hush that fell as soon as she passed through the entrance. The information machines were ranged side by side against the far wall, and she chose one at random.

As soon as the recognition signal lighted up, she said, "I am looking for Alvin; he is somewhere in this building. Where can I find him?"

Even after a lifetime, one never grew wholly accustomed to the complete absence of time lag when an information machine replied to an ordinary question. There were people who knew—or claimed to know—how it was done, and talked learnedly of "access time" and "storage space" but that made the final result none the less marvelous. Any question of a purely factual nature, within the city's truly enormous range of available information, could be answered immediately. Only if complex calculations were involved before a reply could be given would there be any appreciable delay.

"He is with the monitors," came the reply. It was not very helpful, since the name conveyed nothing to Alystra. No machine ever volunteered more information than it was asked for, and learning to frame questions properly was an art which often took a long time to acquire.

"How do I reach him?" asked Alystra. She would find what the monitors were when she got to them.

"I cannot tell you unless you have the permission of the Council."

This was a most unexpected, even a disconcerting, development. There were very few places in Diaspar that could not be visited by anyone who pleased. Alystra was quite certain that Alvin had *not* obtained Council permission, and this could only mean that a higher authority was helping him.

The Council ruled Diaspar, but the Council itself could be overridden by a superior power—the all-but-infinite intellect of the Central Computer. It was difficult not to think of the Central Computer as a living entity, localized in a single spot, though actually it was the sum total of all the machines in Diaspar. Even if it was not alive in the biological sense, it certainly possessed at least as much awareness and self-consciousness as a human being. It must know what Alvin was doing, and, therefore, it must approve, otherwise it would have stopped him or referred him to the Council, as the information machine had done to Alystra.

There was no point in staying here. Alystra knew that any attempt to find Alvin—even if she knew exactly where he was in this enormous building—would be doomed to failure. Doors would fail to open; slideways would reverse when she stood on them, carrying her backward instead of forward; elevator fields would be mysteriously inert, refusing to lift her from one floor to another. If she persisted, she would be gently conveyed out into the street by a polite but firm robot, or else shuttled round and round Council Hall until she grew fed up and left under her own volition.

She was in a bad temper as she walked out into the street. She was also more than a little puzzled, and for the first time felt that there was some mystery here which made her personal desires and interests seem very trivial indeed. That did not mean that they would be any the less important to her. She had no idea what she was going to do next, but she was sure of one thing. Alvin was not the only person in Diaspar who could be stubborn and persistent.

Chapter

The image on the monitor screen faded as Alvin raised his hands from the control panel and cleared the circuits. For a moment he sat quite motionless, looking into the blank rectangle that had occupied all his conscious mind for so many weeks. He had circumnavigated his world; across that screen had passed every square foot of the outer wall of Diaspar. He knew the city better than any living man save perhaps Khedron; and he knew now that there was no way through the walls.

The feeling that possessed him was not mere despondency; he had never really expected that it would be as easy as this, that he would find what he sought at the first attempt. What was important was that he had eliminated one possibility. Now he must deal with the others.

He rose to his feet and walked over to the image of the city which almost filled the chamber. It was hard not to think of it as an actual model, though he knew that in reality it was no more than an optical projection of the pattern in the memory cells he had been exploring. When he altered the monitor controls and set his viewpoint moving through Diaspar, a spot of light would travel over the surface of this replica, so that he could see exactly where he was going. It had been a useful guide in the early days, but he soon had grown so skillful at setting the co-ordinates that he had not needed this aid.

The city lay spread out beneath him; he looked down upon it like a god. Yet he scarcely saw it as he considered, one by one, the steps he should now take.

If all else failed, there was one solution to the problem. Diaspar might be held in a perpetual stasis by its eternity circuits, frozen forever according to the pattern in the memory cells, but that pattern could itself be altered, and the city would then change with it. It would be possible to redesign a section of the outer wall so that it contained a doorway, feed this pattern into the monitors, and let the city reshape itself to the new conception.

Alvin suspected that the large areas of the monitor control board whose purpose Khedron had not explained to him were concerned with such alterations. It would be useless to experiment with them; controls that could alter the very structure of the city were firmly locked and could be operated only with the authority of the Council and the approval of the Central Computer. There was very little chance that the Council would grant him what he asked, even if he was prepared for decades or even centuries of patient pleading. That was not a prospect that appealed to him in the least.

He turned his thoughts toward the sky. Sometimes he had imagined, in fantasies which he was half-ashamed to recall, that he had regained the freedom of the air which man had renounced so long ago. Once, he knew, the skies of Earth had been filled with strange shapes. Out of space the great ships had come, bearing unknown treasures, to berth at the legendary Port of Diaspar. But the Port had been beyond the limits of the city; aeons ago it had been buried by the drifting sand. He could dream that somewhere in the mazes of Diaspar a flying machine might still be hidden, but he did not really believe it. Even in the days when small, personal flyers had been in common use, it was most unlikely that they had ever been allowed to operate inside the limits of the city.

For a moment he lost himself in the old, familiar dream. He imagined that he was master of the sky, that the world lay spread out beneath him, inviting him to travel where he willed. It was not the world of his own time that he saw, but the lost world of the dawn—a rich and living panorama of hills and lakes and forests. He felt a bitter envy of his unknown ancestors, who had flown with such freedom over all the earth and who had let its beauty die.

This mind-drugging reverie was useless; he tore himself back to the present and to the problem at hand. If the sky was unattainable and the way by land was barred, what remained?

Once again he had come to the point when he needed help, when he could make no further progress by his own efforts. He disliked admitting the fact, but was honest enough not to deny it. Inevitably, his thoughts turned to Khedron.

Alvin had never been able to decide whether he liked the Jester. He was very glad that they had met, and was grateful to Khedron for the assistance and implicit sympathy he had given him on his quest. There was no one else in Diaspar with whom he had so much in common, yet there was some element in the other's personality that jarred upon him. Perhaps it was Khedron's air of ironic detachment, which sometimes gave Alvin the impression that he was laughing secretly at all his efforts, even while he seemed to be doing his best to help. Because of this, as well as his own natural stubbornness and independence, Alvin hesitated to approach the Jester except as a last resort.

They arranged to meet in a small, circular court not far from Council Hall. There were many such secluded spots in the city, perhaps only a few yards from some busy thoroughfare, yet completely cut off from it. Usually they could be reached only on foot after a rather roundabout walk; sometimes, indeed, they were at the center of skillfully contrived mazes which enhanced their isolation. It was rather typical of Khedron that he should have chosen such a place for a rendezvous.

The court was little more than fifty paces across, and was in reality located deep within the interior of some great building. Yet it appeared to have no definite physical limits, being bounded by a translucent blue-green material which glowed with a faint internal light. However, though there were no visible limits, the court had been so laid out that there was no danger of feeling lost in infinite space. Low walls, less than waist high and broken at intervals so that one could pass through them, managed to give the impression of safe confinement without which no one in Diaspar could ever feel entirely happy.

Khedron was examining one of these walls when Alvin arrived. It was covered with an intricate mosaic of colored tiles, so fantastically involved that Alvin did not even attempt to unravel it.

"Look at this mosaic, Alvin," said the Jester. "Do you notice anything strange about it?"

"No," confessed Alvin after a brief examination. "I don't care for it—but there's nothing strange about *that.*"

Khedron ran his fingers over the colored tiles. "You are not very observant," he said. "Look at these edges here—see how they become rounded and softened. This is something that one very seldom sees in Diaspar, Alvin. It is wear—the crumbling away of matter under the assault of time. I can remember when this pattern was new, only eighty thousand years ago, in my last lifetime. If I come back to this spot a dozen lives from now, these tiles will have been worn completely away."

"I don't see anything very surprising about that," answered Alvin. "There are other works of art in the city not good enough to be preserved in the memory circuits, but not bad enough to be destroyed outright. One day, I suppose, some other artist will come along and do a better job. And his work won't be allowed to wear out."

"I knew the man who designed this wall," said Khedron, his fingers still exploring the cracks in the mosaic. "Strange that I can remember that fact, when I don't recall the man himself. I could not have liked him, so I must have erased him from my mind." He gave a short laugh. "Perhaps I designed it myself, during one of my artistic phases, and was so annoyed when the city refused to make it eternal that I decided to forget the whole affair. There—I knew that piece was coming loose!"

He had managed to pull out a single flake of golden tile, and looked very pleased at this minor sabotage. He threw the fragment on the ground, adding, "Now the maintenance robots will have to do something about it!"

There was a lesson for him here, Alvin knew. That strange instinct known as intuition, which seemed to follow short cuts not accessible to mere logic, told him that. He looked at the golden shard lying at his feet, trying to link it somehow to the problem that now dominated his mind.

It was not hard to find the answer, once he realized that it existed.

"I see what you are trying to tell me," he said to Khedron. "There are objects in Diaspar that aren't preserved in the memory circuits, so I could never find them through the monitors at Council Hall. If I was to go there and focus on this court, there would be no sign of the wall we're sitting on."

"I think you might find the wall. But there would be no mosaic on it."

"Yes, I can see that," said Alvin, too impatient now to bother about such hairsplitting. "And in the same way, parts of the city might exist that had never been preserved in the eternity circuits, but which hadn't yet worn away. Still, I don't really see how that helps me. I *know* that the outer wall exists—and that it has no openings in it."

"Perhaps there is no way out," answered Khedron. "I can

promise you nothing. But I think there is still a great deal that the monitors can teach us—if the Central Computer will let them. And it seems to have taken rather a liking to you."

Alvin pondered over this remark on their way to Council Hall. Until now, he had assumed that it was entirely through Khedron's influence that he had been able to gain access to the monitors. It had not occurred to him that it might be through some intrinsic quality of his own. Being a Unique had many disadvantages; it was only right that it should have some compensations.

The unchanging image of the city still dominated the chamber in which Alvin had spent so many hours. He looked at it now with a new understanding; all that he saw here existed—but all of Diaspar might not be mirrored. Yet, surely, any discordancies must be trivial, and, as far as he could see, undetectable.

"I attempted to do this many years ago," said Khedron, as he sat down at the monitor desk, "but the controls were locked against me. Perhaps they will obey me now."

Slowly, and then with mounting confidence as he regained access to long-forgotten skills, Khedron's fingertips moved over the control desk, resting for a moment at the nodal points in the sensitive grid buried in the panel before him.

"I think that's correct," he said at last. "Anyway we'll soon see."

The screen glowed into life, but instead of the picture that Alvin had expected, there appeared a somewhat baffling message:

REGRESSION WILL COMMENCE AS SOON AS YOU HAVE SET RATE CONTROL

"Foolish of me," muttered Khedron. "I got everything else right and forgot the most important thing of all." His fingers now moved with a confident assurance over the board, and as the message faded from the screen he swung around in his seat so that he could look at the replica of the city.

"Watch this, Alvin," he said. "I think we are both going to learn something new about Diaspar."

Alvin waited patiently, but nothing happened. The image of the city floated there before his eyes in all its familiar wonder and beauty—though he was conscious of neither now. He was about to ask Khedron what he should look for when a sudden movement caught his attention, and he turned his head quickly to follow it. It had been no more than a half-glimpsed flash or flicker, and he was too late to see what had made it. Nothing had altered; Diaspar was just as he had always known it. Then he saw that Khedron was watching him with a sardonic smile, so he looked again at the city. This time, the thing happened before his eyes.

One of the buildings at the edge of the park suddenly vanished, and was replaced instantly by another of quite different design. The transformation was so abrupt that had Alvin been blinking he would have missed it. He stared in amazement at the subtly altered city, but even during the first shock of astonishment his mind was seeking for the answer. He remembered the words that had appeared on the monitor screen—REGRESSION WILL COMMENCE—and he knew at once what was happening.

"That's the city as it was thousands of years ago," he said to Khedron. "We're going back in time."

"A picturesque but hardly accurate way of putting it," replied the Jester. "What is actually happening is that the monitor is remembering the earlier versions of the city. When any modifications were made, the memory circuits were not simply emptied; the information in them was taken to subsidiary storage units, so that it could be recalled whenever needed. I have set the monitor to regress through those units at the rate of a thousand years a second. Already, we're looking at the Diaspar of half a million years ago. We'll have to go much farther back than that to see any real changes—I'll increase the rate."

He turned back to the control board, and even as he did so, not one building but a whole block whipped out of existence and was replaced by a large oval amphitheater.

"Ah, the Arena!" said Khedron. "I can remember the fuss when we decided to get rid of that. It was hardly ever used, but a great many people felt sentimental about it."

The monitor was now recalling its memories at a far higher rate; the image of Diaspar was receding into the past at millions of years a minute, and changes were occurring so rapidly that the eye could not keep up with them. Alvin noticed that the alterations to the city appeared to come in cycles; there would be a long period of stasis, then a whole rash of rebuilding would break out, followed by another pause. It was almost as if Diaspar were a living organism, which had to regain its strength after each explosion of growth.

Through all these changes, the basic design of the city had not altered. Buildings came and went, but the pattern of streets seemed eternal, and the park remained as the green heart of Diaspar. Alvin wondered how far back the monitor could go. Could it return to the founding of the city, and pass through the veil that sundered known history from the myths and legends of the Dawn?

Already they had gone five hundred million years into the past. Outside the walls of Diaspar, beyond the knowledge of the monitors, it would be a different Earth. Perhaps there might be oceans and forests, even other cities which Man had not yet deserted in the long retreat to his final home.

The minutes drifted past, each minute an aeon in the little universe of the monitors. Soon, thought Alvin, the earliest of all these stored memories must be reached and the regression would end. But fascinating though this lesson was, he did not see how it could help him to escape from the city as it was here and now.

With a sudden, soundless implosion, Diaspar contracted to a fraction of its former size. The park vanished; the boundary wall of linked, titanic towers instantly evaporated. This city was open to the world, for the radial roads stretched out to the limits of the monitor image without obstruction. Here was Diaspar as it had been before the great change came upon mankind.

"We can go no farther," said Khedron, pointing to the monitor screen. On it had appeared the words: REGRESSION CONCLUDED. "This must be the earliest version of the city that has been preserved in the memory cells. Before that, I doubt if the eternity circuits were used, and the buildings were allowed to wear out naturally."

For a long time, Alvin stared at this model of the ancient city. He thought of the traffic those roads had borne, as men came and went freely to all the corners of the world—and to other worlds as well. Those men were his ancestors; he felt a closer kinship to them than to the people who now shared his life. He wished that he could see them and share their thoughts, as they moved through the streets of that billion-year-remote Diaspar. Yet those thoughts could not have been happy ones, for they must have been living then beneath the shadow of the Invaders. In a few more centuries, they were to turn their faces from the glory they had won and build a wall against the Universe.

Khedron ran the monitor backward and forward a dozen times through the brief period of history that had wrought the transformation. The change from a small open city to a much larger closed one had taken little more than a thousand years. In that time, the machines that had served Diaspar so faithfully must have been designed and built, and the knowledge that would enable them to carry out their tasks had been fed into their memory circuits. Into the memory circuits, also, must have gone the essential patterns of all the men who were now alive, so that when the right impulse called them forth again they could be clothed in matter and would emerge reborn from the Hall of Creation. In some sense, Alvin realized, he must have existed in that ancient world. It was possible, of course, that he was completely synthetic—that his entire personality had been designed by artist-technicians who had worked with tools of inconceivable complexity toward some clearly envisaged goal. Yet he thought it more likely that he was a composite of men who had once lived and walked on Earth.

Very little of the old Diaspar had remained when the new city was created; the park had obliterated it almost completely. Even before the transformation, there had been a small, grass-covered clearing at the center of Diaspar, surrounding the junction of all the radial streets. Afterward it had expanded tenfold, wiping out streets and buildings alike. The Tomb of Yarlan Zey had been brought into existence at this time, replacing a very large circular structure which had previously stood at the meeting point of all the streets. Alvin had never really believed the legends of the Tomb's antiquity, but now it seemed that they were true.

"I suppose," said Alvin, struck by a sudden thought, "that we can explore this image, just as we explored the image of today's Diaspar?"

Khedron's fingers flickered over the monitor control board, and the screen answered Alvin's question. The long-vanished city began to expand before his eyes as his viewpoint moved along the curiously narrow streets. This memory of the Diaspar that once had been was still as sharp and clear as the image of the city he lived in today. For a billion years, the information circuits had held it in ghostly pseudo-existence, waiting for the moment when someone should call it forth again. And it was not, thought Alvin, merely a memory he was seeing now. It was something more complex than that—it was the memory of a memory.

He did not know what he could learn from it, and whether it could help him in his quest. No matter; it was fascinating to look into the past and to see a world that had existed in the days when men still roamed among the stars. He pointed to the low, circular building that stood at the city's heart.

"Let's start there," he told Khedron. "That seems as good a place as any to begin."

Perhaps it was sheer luck; perhaps it was some ancient memory; perhaps it was elementary logic. It made no difference, since he would have arrived at this spot sooner or later—this spot upon which all the radial streets of the city converged.

It took him ten minutes to discover that they did not meet here for reasons of symmetry alone—ten minutes to know that his long search had met its reward.

CHAPTER

Alystra had found it very easy to follow Alvin and Khedron without their knowledge. They seemed in a great hurry—something which in itself was most unusual—and never looked back. It had been an amusing game to pursue them along the moving ways, hiding in the crowds yet always keeping them in sight. Toward the end their goal had been obvious; when they left the pattern of streets and went into the park, they could only be heading for the Tomb of Yarlan Zey. The park contained no other buildings, and people in such eager haste as Alvin and Khedron would not be interested merely in enjoying the scenery.

Because there was no way of concealing herself on the last few hundred yards to the Tomb, Alystra waited until Khedron and Alvin had disappeared into the marbled gloom. Then, as soon as they were out of sight, she hurried up the grass-covered slope. She felt fairly sure that she could hide behind one of the great pillars long enough to discover what Alvin and Khedron were doing; it did not matter if they detected her after that.

The Tomb consisted of two concentric rings of columns, enclosing a circular courtyard. Except in one sector, the columns screened off the interior completely, and Alystra avoided approaching through this opening, but entered the Tomb from the side. She cautiously negotiated the first ring of columns, saw that there was no one in sight, and tiptoed across to the second. Through the gaps, she could see Yarlan Zey looking out through the entrance, across the park he had built, and beyond that to the city over which he had watched for so many ages.

And there was no one else in all this marble solitude. The Tomb was empty.

At that moment, Alvin and Khedron were a hundred feet underground, in a small, boxlike room whose walls seemed to be flowing steadily upward. That was the only indication of movement; there was no trace of vibration to show that they were sinking swiftly into the earth, descending toward a goal that even now neither of them fully understood.

It had been absurdly easy, for the way had been prepared for them. (By whom? wondered Alvin. By the Central Computer? Or by Yarlan Zey himself, when he transformed the city?) The monitor screen had shown them the long, vertical shaft plunging into the depths, but they had followed its course only a little way when the image had blanked out. That meant, Alvin knew, that they were asking for information that the monitor did not possess, and perhaps never had possessed.

He had scarcely framed this thought when the screen came to life once more. On it appeared a brief message, printed in the simplified script that machines had used to communicate with men ever since they had achieved intellectual equality:

STAND WHERE THE STATUE GAZES—AND REMEMBER:
DIASPAR WAS NOT ALWAYS THUS

The last five words were in larger type, and the meaning of the entire message was obvious to Alvin at once. Mentally framed code messages had been used for ages to unlock doors or set machines in action. As for "Stand where the statue gazes"—that was really *too* simple.

"I wonder how many people have read this message?" said Alvin thoughtfully.

"Fourteen, to my knowledge," replied Khedron. "And there may have been others." He did not amplify this rather cryptic remark, and Alvin was in too great a hurry to reach the park to question him further.

They could not be certain that the mechanisms would still respond to the triggering impulse. When they reached the Tomb, it had taken them only a moment to locate the single slab, among all those paving the floor, upon which the gaze of Yarlan Zey was fixed. It was only at first sight that the statue seemed to be looking out across the city; if one stood directly in front of it, one could see that the eyes were downcast and that the elusive smile was directed toward a spot just inside the entrance to the Tomb. Once the secret was realized, there could be no doubt about it. Alvin moved to the next slab, and found that Yarlan Zey was no longer looking toward him.

He rejoined Khedron, and mentally echoed the words that the Jester spoke aloud: "Diaspar was not always thus." Instantly, as if the millions of years that had lapsed since their last operation had never existed, the waiting machines responded. The great slab of stone on which they were standing began to carry them smoothly into the depths.

Overhead, the patch of blue suddenly flickered out of existence. The shaft was no longer open; there was no danger that anyone should accidentally stumble into it. Alvin wondered fleetingly if another slab of stone had somehow been materialized to replace the one now supporting him and Khedron, then decided against it. The original slab probably still paved the Tomb; the one upon which they were standing might only exist for infinitesimal fractions of a second, being continuously re-created at greater and greater depths in the earth to give the illusion of steady downward movement.

Neither Alvin nor Khedron spoke as the walls flowed silently past them. Khedron was once again wrestling with his conscience, wondering if this time he had gone too far. He could not imagine where this route might lead, if indeed it led anywhere. For the first time in his life, he began to understand the real meaning of fear.

Alvin was not afraid; he was too excited. This was the sensation he had known in the Tower of Loranne, when he had looked out across the untrodden desert and seen the stars conquering the night sky. He had merely gazed at the unknown then; he was being carried toward it now.

The walls ceased to flow past them. A patch of light appeared at one side of their mysteriously moving room, grew brighter and brighter, and was suddenly a door. They stepped through it, took a few paces along the short corridor beyond—and then were standing in a great, circular cavern whose walls came together in a sweeping curve three hundred feet above their heads.

The column down whose interior they had descended seemed far too slim to support the millions of tons of rock above it; indeed, it did not seem to be an integral part of thc chamber at all, but gave the impression of being an afterthought. Khedron, following Alvin's gaze, arrived at the same conclusion.

"This column," he said, speaking rather jerkily, as if anxious to find something to say, "was built simply to house the shaft down which we came. It could never have carried the traffic that must have passed through here when Diaspar was still open to the world. *That* came through those tunnels over there; I suppose you recognize what they are?"

Alvin looked toward the walls of the chamber, more than a hundred yards away. Piercing them at regular intervals were large tunnels, twelve of them, radiating in all directions exactly as the moving ways still did today. He could see that they sloped gently upward, and now he recognized the familiar gray surface of the moving ways. These were only the severed stumps of the great roads; the strange material that gave them life was now frozen into immobility. When the park had been built, the hub of the moving way system had been buried. But it had never been destroyed.

Alvin began to walk toward the nearest of the tunnels. He had gone only a few paces when he realized that something was happening to the ground beneath his feet. *It was becoming transparent.* A few more yards, and he seemed to be standing in midair without visible support. He stopped and stared down into the void beneath him.

"Khedron!" he called. "Come and look at this!"

The other joined him, and together they gazed at the marvel beneath their feet. Faintly visible, at an indefinite depth, lay an enormous map—a great network of lines converging toward a spot beneath the central shaft. They stared at it in silence for a moment; then Khedron said quietly: "You realize what this is?"

"I think so," replied Alvin. "It's a map of the entire transport system, and those little circles must be the other cities of Earth. I can just see names beside them, but they're too faint to read."

"There must have been some form of internal illumination once," said Khedron absently. He was tracing the lines beneath his feet, following them with his eyes out toward the walls of the chamber.

"I thought so!" he exclaimed suddenly. "Do you see how all these radiating lines lead toward the small tunnels?"

Alvin had noticed that besides the great arches of the moving ways there were innumerable smaller tunnels leading out of the chamber—tunnels that sloped *downward* instead of up.

Khedron continued without waiting for a reply.

"It would be hard to think of a simpler system. People

would come down the moving ways, select the place they wished to visit, and then follow the appropriate line on the map."

"And what happened to them after that?" asked Alvin. Khedron was silent, his eyes searching out the mystery of those descending tunnels. There were thirty or forty of them, all looking exactly the same. Only the names on the map would have enabled one to distinguish between them, and those names were indecipherable now.

Alvin had wandered away and was circumnavigating the central pillar. Presently his voice came to Khedron, slightly muffled and overlaid with echoes from the walls of the chamber.

"What is it?" called Khedron, not wishing to move, because he had nearly succeeded in reading one of the dimly visible groups of characters. But Alvin's voice was insistent, so he went to join him.

Far beneath was the other half of the great map, its faint webwork radiating to the points of the compass. This time, however, not all of it was too dim to be clearly seen, for one of the lines—and only one—was brilliantly illuminated. It seemed to have no connection with the rest of the system, and pointed like a gleaming arrow to one of the downward-sloping tunnels. Near its end the line transfixed a circle of golden light, and against that circle was the single word LYS. That was all.

For a long time Alvin and Khedron stood gazing down at that silent symbol. To Khedron it was a challenge he knew he could never accept—and which, indeed, he would rather did not exist. But to Alvin it hinted at the fulfillment of all his dreams; though the word Lys meant nothing to him, he let it roll around his mouth, tasting its sibilance like some exotic flavor. The blood was pounding in his veins, and his cheeks were flushed as by a fever. He stared around this great concourse, trying to imagine it as it had been in the ancient days, when air transport had come to an end but the cities of Earth still had contact with one another. He thought of the countless millions of years that had passed with the traffic steadily dwindling and the lights on the great map dying one by one, until at last only this single line remained. How long, he wondered, had it gleamed there among its darkened companions, waiting to guide the steps that never came, until Yarlan Zey had sealed the moving ways and closed Diaspar against the world?

And that had been a billion years ago. Even then, Lys must have lost touch with Diaspar. It seemed impossible that it could have survived; perhaps, after all, the map meant nothing now.

Khedron broke into his reverie at last. He seemed nervous and ill at ease, not at all like the confident and self-assured person that he had always been in the city above.

"I do not think that we should go any farther now," he said. "It may not be safe until—until we are more prepared."

There was wisdom in this, but Alvin recognized the underlying note of fear in Khedron's voice. Had it not been for that, he might have been sensible, but a too-acute awareness of his own valor, combined with a contempt for Khedron's timidity, drove Alvin onward. It seemed foolish to have come so far, only to turn back when the goal might be in sight.

"I'm going down that tunnel," he said stubbornly, as if challenging Khedron to stop him. "I want to see where it leads." He set off resolutely, and after a moment's hesitation the Jester followed him along the arrow of light that burned beneath their feet.

As they stepped into the tunnel, they felt the familiar tug of the peristaltic field, and in a moment were being swept effortlessly into the depths. The journey lasted scarcely a minute; when the field released them they were standing at one end of a long narrow chamber in the form of a half-cylinder. At its distant end, two dimly lit tunnels stretched away toward infinity.

Men of almost every civilization that had existed since the

Dawn would have found their surroundings completely familiar, yet to Alvin and Khedron this was a glimpse of another world. The purpose of the long, streamlined machine that lay aimed like a projectile at the far tunnel was obvious, but that made it none the less novel. Its upper portion was transparent, and looking through the walls Alvin could see rows of luxuriously appointed seats. There was no sign of any entrance, and the entire machine was floating about a foot above a single metal rod that stretched away into the distance, disappearing in one of the tunnels. A few yards away another rod led to the second tunnel, but no machine floated above it. Alvin knew, as surely as if he had been told, that somewhere beneath unknown, far-off Lys, that second machine was waiting in another such chamber as this.

Khedron began to talk, a little too swiftly.

"What a peculiar transport system! It could only handle a hundred people at a time, so they could not have expected much traffic. And why did they go to all this trouble to bury themselves in the Earth if the skies were still open? Perhaps the Invaders would not even permit them to fly, though I find that hard to believe. Or was this built during the transition period, while men still traveled but did not wish to be reminded of space? They could go from city to city, and never see the sky and the stars." He gave a nervous laugh. "I feel sure of one thing, Alvin. When Lys existed, it was much like Diaspar. All cities must be essentially the same. No wonder that they were all abandoned in the end, and merged into Diaspar. What was the point of having more than one?"

Alvin scarcely heard him. He was busy examining the long projectile, trying to find the entrance. If the machine was controlled by some central or verbal code order, he might never be able to make it obey him, and it would remain a maddening enigma for the rest of his life.

The silently opening door took him completely unawares. There was no sound, no warning when a section of the wall simply faded from sight and the beautifully designed interior lay open before his eyes.

This was the moment of choice. Until this instant, he had always been able to turn back if he wished. But if he stepped inside that welcoming door, he knew what would happen, though not where it would lead. He would no longer be in control of his own destiny, but would have placed himself in the keeping of unknown forces.

He scarcely hesitated. He was afraid to hold back, being fearful that if he waited too long this moment might never come again—or that if it did, his courage might not match his desire for knowledge. Khedron opened his mouth in anxious protest, but before he could speak, Alvin had stepped through the entrance. He turned to face Khedron, who was standing framed in the barely visible rectangle of the doorway, and for a moment there was a strained silence while each waited for the other to speak.

The decision was made for them. There was a faint flicker of translucence, and the wall of the machine had closed again. Even as Alvin raised his hand in farewell, the long cylinder started to ease itself forward. Before it had entered the tunnel, it was already moving faster than a man could run.

There had been a time when, every day, millions of men made such journeys, in machines basically the same as this, as they shuttled between their homes and their humdrum jobs. Since that far-off day, Man had explored the Universe and returned again to Earth—had won an empire, and had it wrestled from his grasp. Now such a journey was being made again, in a machine wherein legions of forgotten and unadventurous men would have felt completely at home.

And it was to be the most momentous journey any human being had undertaken for a billion years.

Alystra had searched the Tomb a dozen times, though once was quite sufficient, for there was nowhere anyone could hide.

After the first shock of surprise, she had wondered if what she had followed across the park had not been Alvin and Khedron at all, but only their projections. But that made no sense; projections were materialized at any spot one wished to visit, without the trouble of going there in person. No sane person would "walk" his projected image a couple of miles, taking half an hour to reach his destination, when he could be there instantly. No; it was the real Alvin and the real Khedron that she had followed into the Tomb.

Somewhere, then, there must be a secret entrance. She might as well look for it while she was waiting for them to come back.

As luck would have it, she missed Khedron's reappearance, for she was examining a column behind the statue when he emerged on the other side of it. She heard his footsteps, turned toward him, and saw at once that he was alone.

"Where is Alvin?" she cried.

It was some time before the Jester answered. He looked distraught and irresolute, and Alystra had to repeat her question before he took any notice of her. He did not seem in the least surprised to find her there.

"I do not know where he is," he answered at last. "I can only tell you that he is on his way to Lys. Now you know as much as I do."

It was never wise to take Khedron's words at their face value. But Alystra needed no further assurance that the Jester was not playing his role today. He was telling her the truth—whatever it might mean.

CHAPTER

When the door closed behind him, Alvin slumped into the nearest seat. All strength seemed suddenly to have been drained from his legs: at last he knew, as he had never known before, that fear of the unknown that haunted all his fellow men. He felt himself trembling in every limb, and his sight became misty and uncertain. Could he have escaped from this speeding machine he would willingly have done so, even at the price of abandoning all his dreams.

It was not fear alone that overwhelmed him, but a sense of unutterable loneliness. All that he knew and loved was in Diaspar; even if he was going into no danger, he might never see his world again. He knew, as no man had known for ages, what it meant to leave one's home forever. In this moment of desolation, it seemed to him of no importance whether the path he was following led to peril or to safety; all that mattered to him now was that it led away from home.

The mood slowly passed; the dark shadows lifted from his mind. He began to pay attention to his surroundings, and to see what he could learn from the unbelievably ancient vehicle in which he was traveling. It did not strike Alvin as particularly strange or marvelous that this buried transport system should still function perfectly after such aeons of time. It was not preserved in the eternity circuits of the city's own monitors, but there must be similar circuits elsewhere guarding it from change or decay.

For the first time he noticed the indicator board that formed part of the forward wall. It carried a brief but reassuring message:

LYS
35 MINUTES

Even as he watched, the number changed to "34." That at least was useful information, though since he had no idea of the machine's speed it told him nothing about the length of the journey. The walls of the tunnel were one continual blur of gray, and the only sensation of movement was a very slight vibration he would never have noticed had he not looked for it.

Diaspar must be many miles away by now, and above him would be the desert with its shifting sand dunes. Perhaps at this very moment he was racing below the broken hills he had watched so often from the Tower of Loranne.

His imagination sped onward to Lys, as if impatient to arrive ahead of his body. What sort of a city would it be? No matter how hard he tried, he could only picture another and smaller version of Diaspar. He wondered if it still existed, then assured himself that not otherwise would this machine be carrying him swiftly through the Earth.

Suddenly there was a distinct change in the vibration underfoot. The vehicle was slowing down—there was no question of that. The time must have passed more swiftly than he had thought; somewhat surprised, Alvin glanced at the indicator.

LYS
23 MINUTES

Feeling puzzled, and a little worried, he pressed his face against the side of the machine. His speed was still blurring the walls of the tunnel into a featureless gray, yet now from time to time he could catch a glimpse of markings that disappeared almost as quickly as they came. And at each disappearance, they seemed to remain in his field of vision for a little longer.

Then, without any warning, the walls of the tunnel were snatched away on either side. The machine was passing, still at a very great speed, through an enormous empty space, far larger even than the chamber of the moving ways.

Peering in wonder through the transparent walls, Alvin could glimpse beneath him an intricate network of guiding rods, rods that crossed and crisscrossed to disappear into a maze of tunnels on either side. A flood of bluish light poured down from the arched dome of the ceiling, and silhouetted against the glare he could just make out the frameworks of great machines. The light was so brilliant that it pained the eyes, and Alvin knew that this place had not been intended for man. A moment later, his vehicle flashed past row after row of cylinders, lying motionless above their guide rails. They were much larger than the one in which he was traveling, and Alvin guessed that they must have been used for transporting freight. Around them were grouped incomprehensible, many-jointed mechanisms, all silent and stilled.

Almost as quickly as it had appeared, the vast and lonely chamber vanished behind him. Its passing left a feeling of awe in Alvin's mind; for the first time he really understood the meaning of that great, darkened map below Diaspar. The world was more full of wonder than he had ever dreamed.

Alvin glanced again at the indicator. It had not changed; he had taken less than a minute to flash through the great cavern. The machine was accelerating again; though there was little sense of motion, the tunnel walls were flowing past on either side at a speed he could not even guess.

It seemed an age before that indefinable change of vibration occurred again. Now the indicator was reading:

LYS
1 MINUTE

That minute was the longest that Alvin had ever known. More and more slowly moved the machine; this was no mere slackening of its speed. It was coming at last to rest.

Smoothly and silently the long cylinder slid out of the tunnel into a cavern that might have been the twin of the one below Diaspar. For a moment Alvin was too excited to see anything clearly; the door had been open for a considerable time before he realized that he could leave the vehicle. As he hurried out of the machine, he caught a last glimpse of the indicator. Its wording had now changed and its message was infinitely reassuring:

DIASPAR
35 MINUTES

As he began to search for a way out of the chamber, Alvin found the first hint that he might be in a civilization different from his own. The way to the surface clearly lay through a low, wide tunnel at one end of the cavern—and leading up through the tunnel was a flight of steps. Such a thing was extremely rare in Diaspar; the architects of the city had built ramps or sloping corridors whenever there was a change of level. This was a survival from the days when most robots had moved on wheels, and so found steps an impassable barrier.

The stairway was very short, and ended against doors that opened automatically at Alvin's approach. He walked into a small room like that which had carried him down the shaft under the Tomb of Yarlan Zey, and was not surprised when a few minutes later the doors opened again to reveal a vaulted corridor rising slowly to an archway that framed a semicircle of sky. There had been no sensation of movement, but Alvin knew that he must have risen many hundreds of feet. He hurried forward up the slope to the sunlit opening, all fear forgotten in his eagerness to see what lay before him.

He was standing at the brow of a low hill, and for an instant it seemed as if he were once again in the central park of Diaspar. Yet if this were indeed a park, it was too enormous for his mind to grasp. The city he had expected to see was nowhere visible. As far as the eye could reach there was nothing but forest and grass-covered plains.

Then Alvin lifted his eyes to the horizon, and there above the trees, sweeping from right to left in a great arc that encircled the world, was a line of stone which would have dwarfed the mightiest giants of Diaspar. It was so far away that its details were blurred by sheer distance, but there was something about its outlines that Alvin found puzzling. Then his eyes became at last accustomed to the scale of that colossal landscape, and he knew that those far-off walls had not been built by man.

Time had not conquered everything; Earth still possessed mountains of which she could be proud.

For a long time Alvin stood at the mouth of the tunnel, slowly growing accustomed to the strange world in which he had found himself. He was half stunned by the impact of sheer size and space; that ring of misty mountains could have enclosed a dozen cities as large as Diaspar. Search as he might, however, Alvin could see no trace of human life. Yet the road that led down the hillside seemed well-kept; he could do no better than accept its guidance.

At the foot of the hill, the road disappeared between great trees that almost hid the sun. As Alvin walked into their shadow, a strange medley of scents and sounds greeted him. The rustle of the wind among the leaves he had known before, but underlying that were a thousand vague noises that conveyed nothing to his mind. Unknown odors assailed him, smells that had been lost even to the memory of his race. The warmth, the profusion of scent and color, and the unseen presences of a million living things, smote him with almost physical violence.

He came upon the lake without any warning. The trees to the right suddenly ended, and before him was a great expanse of water, dotted with tiny islands. Never in his life had Alvin seen so much water; by comparison, the largest pools in Diaspar were scarcely more than puddles. He walked slowly down to the edge of the lake and cupped the warm water in his hands, letting it trickle through his fingers.

The great silver fish that suddenly forced its way through the underwater reeds was the first nonhuman creature that Alvin had ever seen. It should have been utterly strange to him, yet its shape teased his mind with a haunting familiarity. As it hung there in the pale green void, its fins a faint blur of motion, it seemed the very embodiment of power and speed. Here, incorporated in living flesh, were the graceful lines of the great ships that had once ruled the skies of Earth. Evolution and science had come to the same answers; and the work of Nature had lasted longer.

At last Alvin broke the lake's enchantment, and continued along the winding road. The forest closed around him once more, but only for a little while. Presently the road ended, in a great clearing half a mile wide and twice as long—and Alvin understood why he had seen no trace of man before.

The clearing was full of low, two-storied buildings, colored in soft shades that rested the eye even in the full glare of the sun. Most were of clean, straightforward design, but several were built in a complex architectural style involving the use of fluted columns and gracefully fretted stone. In these buildings, which seemed of great age, the immeasurably ancient device of the pointed arch was used.

As he walked slowly toward the village, Alvin was still struggling to grasp his new surroundings. Nothing was familiar; even the air had changed, with its hint of throbbing, unknown life. And the tall, golden-haired people going among the buildings with such unconscious grace were obviously of a different stock from the men of Diaspar.

They took no notice of Alvin, and that was strange, for his clothing was totally different from theirs. Since the temperature never changed in Diaspar, dress there was purely ornamental and often extremely elaborate. Here it seemed mainly functional, designed for use rather than display, and frequently consisted of a single sheet draped around the body.

It was not until Alvin was well inside the village that the people of Lys reacted to his presence, and then their response took a somewhat unexpected form. A group of five men emerged from one of the houses and began to walk purposefully toward him—almost as if, indeed, they had been expecting his arrival. Alvin felt a sudden, heady excitement, and the blood pounded in his veins. He thought of all the fateful meetings men must have had with other races on far-off worlds. Those he was meeting now were of his own species—but how had they diverged in the aeons that had sundered them from Diaspar?

The delegation came to a halt a few feet away from Alvin. Its leader smiled, holding out his hand in the ancient gesture of friendship.

"We thought it best to meet you here," he said. "Our home is very different from Diaspar, and the walk from the terminus gives visitors a chance to become—acclimatized."

Alvin accepted the outstretched hand, but for a moment was too surprised to reply. Now he understood why all the other villagers had ignored him so completely.

"You knew I was coming?" he said at length.

"Of course. We always know when the carriers start to move. Tell me—how did you discover the way? It has been such a long time since the last visit that we feared the secret had been lost."

The speaker was interrupted by one of his companions.

"I think we'd better restrain our curiosity, Gerane. Seranis is waiting."

The name "Seranis" was preceded by a word unfamiliar to Alvin, and he assumed that it was a title of some kind. He had no difficulty in understanding the others, and it never occurred to him that there was anything surprising about this. Diaspar and Lys shared the same linguistic heritage, and the ancient invention of sound recording had long ago frozen speech in an unbreakable mold.

Gerane gave a shrug of mock resignation. "Very well," he smiled. "Seranis has few privileges—I should not rob her of this one."

As they walked deeper into the village, Alvin studied the men around him. They appeared kindly and intelligent, but he was looking for ways in which they differed from a similar group in Diaspar. There were differences, but it was hard to define them. They were all somewhat taller than Alvin, and two of them showed the unmistakable marks of physical age. Their skins were very brown, and in all their movements they seemed to radiate a vigor and zest which Alvin found refreshing, though at the same time a little bewildering. He smiled as he remembered Khedron's prophecy that, if he ever reached Lys, he would find it exactly the same as Diaspar.

The people of the village now watched with frank curiosity as Alvin followed his guides; there was no longer any pretense that they took him for granted. Suddenly there were shrill, high-pitched shouts from the trees on the right, and a group of small, excited creatures burst out of the woods and crowded around Alvin. He stopped in utter amazement, unable to believe his eyes. Here was something that his world had lost so long ago that it lay in the realms of mythology. This was the way that life had once begun; these noisy, fascinating creatures were human children.

Alvin watched them with wondering disbelief—and with another sensation which tugged at his heart but which he could not yet identify. No other sight could have brought home to him so vividly his remoteness from the world he knew. Diaspar had paid, and paid in full, the price of immortality.

The party halted before the largest building Alvin had yet seen. It stood in the center of the village and from a flagpole on its small circular tower a green pennant floated along the breeze.

All but Gerane dropped behind as he entered the building. Inside it was quiet and cool; sunlight filtering through the translucent walls lit up everything with a soft, restful glow. The floor was smooth and resilient, inlaid with fine mosaics. On the walls, an artist of great ability and power had depicted a set of forest scenes. Mingled with these paintings were other murals which conveyed nothing to Alvin's mind, yet which were attractive and pleasant to look upon. Let into one wall was a rectangular screen filled with a shifting maze of colors—presumably a visophone receiver, though a rather small one.

They walked together up a short circular stairway that led them out onto the flat roof of the building. From this point, the entire village was visible, and Alvin could see that it consisted of about a hundred buildings. In the distance the trees opened out to enclose wide meadows, where animals of several different types were grazing. Alvin could not imagine what these were, most of them were quadrupeds, but some seemed to have six or even eight legs.

Seranis was waiting for him in the shadow of the tower. Alvin wondered how old she was; her long, golden hair was touched with gray, which he guessed must be some indication of age. The presence of children, with all the consequences that implied, had left him very confused. Where there was birth, then surely there must also be death, and the life span here in Lys might be very different from that in Diaspar. He could not tell whether Seranis was fifty, five hundred, or five thousand years old, but looking into her eyes he could sense that wisdom and depth of experience he sometimes felt when he was with Jeserac.

She pointed to a small seat, but though her eyes smiled a welcome she said nothing until Alvin had made himself comfortable—or as comfortable as he could be under that intense though friendly scrutiny. Then she sighed, and addressed Alvin in a low gentle voice.

"This is an occasion which does not often arise, so you will excuse me if I do not know the correct behavior. But there are certain rights due to a guest, even if an unexpected one. Before we talk, there is something about which I should warn you. I can read your mind."

She smiled at Alvin's obvious consternation, and added quickly: "There is no need to let that worry you. No right is respected more strongly than that of mental privacy. I will enter your mind only if you invite me to. But it would not be fair to hide this fact from you, and it will explain why we find speech somewhat slow and difficult. It is not often used here."

This revelation, though slightly alarming, did not surprise Alvin. Once both men and machines had possessed this power and the unchanging machines could still read their masters' orders. But in Diaspar, man himself had lost the gift he had once shared with his slaves.

"I do not know what brought you from your world to ours," continued Seranis, "but if you are looking for life, your search has ended. Apart from Diaspar, there is only desert beyond our mountains."

It was strange that Alvin, who had questioned accepted beliefs so often before, did not doubt the words of Seranis. His only reaction was one of sadness that all his teaching had been so nearly true.

"Tell me about Lys," he begged. "Why have you been cut off from Diaspar for so long, when you seem to know so much about us?"

Seranis smiled at his eagerness.

"Presently," she said. "But first I would like to know something about you. Tell me how you found the way here, and why you came."

Haltingly at first, and then with growing confidence. Alvin told his story. He had never spoken with such freedom before; here at last was someone who would not laugh at his dreams because they knew those dreams were true. Once or twice Seranis interrupted him with swift questions, when he mentioned some aspect of Diaspar that was unfamiliar to her. It was hard for Alvin to realize that things which were part of his everyday life would be meaningless to someone who had never lived in the city and knew nothing of its complex culture and social organization. Seranis listened with such understanding that he took her comprehension for granted; not until much later did he realize that many other minds besides hers were listening to his words.

When he had finished, there was silence for a while. Then Seranis looked at him and said quietly: "Why did you come to Lys?"

Alvin glanced at her in surprise.

"I've told you," he said. "I wanted to explore the world. Everyone told me that there was only desert beyond the city, but I had to see for myself."

"And was that the only reason?"

Alvin hesitated. When at last he answered, it was not the indomitable explorer who spoke, but the lost child who had been born into an alien world.

"No," he said softly, "that wasn't the only reason—though I did not know it until now. I was lonely."

"Lonely? In Diaspar?" There was a smile on the lips of Seranis, but sympathy in her eyes, and Alvin knew that she expected no further answer.

Now that he had told his story, he waited for her to keep her share of the bargain. Presently Seranis rose to her feet and began to pace to and fro on the roof.

"I know the questions you wish to ask," she said. "Some of them I can answer, but it would be wearisome to do it in words. If you will open your mind to me, I will tell you what you need to know. You can trust me: I will take nothing from you without your permission."

"What do you want me to do?" said Alvin cautiously.

"Will yourself to accept my help—look at my eyes—and forget everything," commanded Seranis.

Alvin was never sure what happened then. There was a total eclipse of all his senses, and though he could never remember acquiring it, when he looked into his mind the knowledge was there.

He saw back into the past, not clearly, but as a man on some high mountain might look out across a misty plain. He understood that Man had not always been a city dweller, and that since the machines gave him freedom from toil there had always been a rivalry between two different types of civilization. In the Dawn of Ages there had been thousands of cities, but a large part of mankind had preferred to live in relatively small communities. Universal transport and instantaneous communication had given them all the contact they required with the rest of the world, and they felt no need to live huddled together with millions of their fellows.

Lys had been little different, in the early days, from hundreds of other communities. But gradually, over the ages, it developed an independent culture which was one of the highest that mankind had ever known. It was a culture based largely upon the direct use of mental power, and this set it apart from the rest of human society, which came to rely more and more upon machines.

Through the aeons, as they advanced along their different roads, the gulf between Lys and the cities widened. It was bridged only in times of great crisis; when the Moon was falling, its destruction was carried out by the scientists of Lys. So also was the defense of Earth against the Invaders, who were held at bay in the final Battle of Shalmirane.

That great ordeal exhausted mankind; one by one the cities died and the desert rolled over them. As the population fell, humanity began the migration that was to make Diaspar the last and greatest of all cities.

Most of these changes did not affect Lys, but it had its own battle to fight—the battle against the desert. The natural barrier of the mountains was not enough, and many ages passed before the great oasis was made secure. The picture was blurred here, perhaps deliberately. Alvin could not see what had been done to give Lys the virtual eternity that Diaspar had achieved.

The voice of Seranis seemed to come to him from a great distance—yet it was not her voice alone, for it was merged into a symphony of words, as though many other tongues were chanting in unison with hers.

"That, very briefly, is our history. You will see that even in the Dawn Ages we had little to do with the cities, though their people often came into our land. We never hindered them, for many of our greatest men came from outside, but when the cities were dying we did not wish to be involved in their downfall. With the ending of air transport there was only one way into Lys—the carrier system from Diaspar. It was closed at your end, when the park was built—and you forgot us, though we have never forgotten you.

"Diaspar has surprised us. We expected it to go the way of all other cities, but instead it has achieved a stable culture that may last as long as Earth. It is not a culture that we admire, yet we are glad that those who wish to escape have been able to do so. More than you might think have made the journey, and they have almost always been outstanding men who brought something of value with them when they came to Lys."

The voice faded; the paralysis of Alvin's senses ebbed away and he was himself again. He saw with astonishment that the sun had fallen far below the trees and that the eastern sky already held a hint of night. Somewhere a great bell vibrated with a throbbing boom that pulsed slowly into silence, leaving the air tense with mystery and premonition. Alvin found himself trembling slightly, not with the first touch of the evening's chill, but through sheer awe and wonder at all that he had learned. It was very late, and he was far from home. He had a sudden need to see his friends again, and to be among the familiar sights and scenes of Diaspar.

"I must return," he said. "Khedron—my parents—they will be expecting me."

That was not wholly true; Khedron would certainly be wondering what had happened to him, but as far as Alvin was aware no one else knew that he had left Diaspar. He could not have explained the reason for this mild deceit, and was slightly ashamed of himself as soon as he had uttered the words.

Seranis looked at him thoughtfully.

"I am afraid it is not as easy as that," she said.

"What do you mean?" asked Alvin. "Won't the carrier that brought me here take me back again?" He still refused to face the idea that he might be held in Lys against his will, though the idea had briefly crossed his mind.

For the first time, Seranis seemed slightly ill at ease.

"We have been talking about you," she said—not explaining who the "we" might be, nor exactly how they had consulted together. "If you return to Diaspar, the whole city will know about us. Even if you promise to say nothing, you would find it impossible to keep our secret."

"Why should you wish it kept?" asked Alvin. "Surely it would be a good thing for both our peoples if they could meet again."

Seranis looked displeased.

"We do not think so," she said. "If the gates were opened, our land would be flooded with the idly curious and the sensation seekers. As it is now, only the best of your people have ever reached us."

This reply radiated so much unconscious superiority, yet was based on such false assumptions, that Alvin felt his annoyance quite eclipse his alarm.

"That isn't true," he said flatly. "I do not believe you would find another person in Diaspar who could leave the city, even if he wanted to—even if he knew that there was somewhere to go. If you let me return, it would make no difference to Lys."

"It is not my decision," explained Seranis, "and you underestimate the powers of the mind if you think that the barriers that keep your people inside their city can never be broken. However, we do not wish to hold you here against your will, but if you return to Diaspar we must erase all memories of Lys from your mind." She hesitated for a moment. "This has never risen before; all your predecessors came here to stay."

Here was a choice that Alvin refused to accept. He wanted to explore Lys, to learn all its secrets, to discover the ways in which they differed from his own home, but equally he was determined to return to Diaspar, so that he could prove to his friends that he had been no idle dreamer. He could not understand the reasons prompting this desire for secrecy; even if he had, it would not have made any difference in his behavior.

He realized that he must play for time or else convince Seranis that what she asked him was impossible.

"Khedron knows where I am," he said. "You cannot erase *his* memories."

Seranis smiled. It was a pleasant smile, and one that in any other circumstances would have been friendly enough. But behind it Alvin glimpsed, for the first time, the presence of overwhelming and implacable power.

"You underestimate us, Alvin," she replied. "That would be

very easy. I can reach Diaspar more quickly than I can cross Lys. Other men have come here before, and some of them told their friends where they were going. Yet those friends forget them, and they vanished from the history of Diaspar."

Alvin had been foolish to ignore this possibility, though it was obvious, now that Seranis had pointed it out. He wondered how many times, in the millions of years since the two cultures were separated, men from Lys had gone into Diaspar in order to preserve their jealously guarded secret. And he wondered just how extensive were the mental powers which these strange people possessed and did not hesitate to use.

Was it safe to make any plans at all? Seranis had promised that she would not read his mind without his consent, but he wondered if there might be circumstances in which that promise would not be kept.

"Surely," he said, "you don't expect me to make the decision at once. Cannot I see something of your country before I make my choice?"

"Of course," replied Seranis. "You can stay here as long as you wish, and still return to Diaspar eventually if you change your mind. But if you can decide within the next few days, it will be very much easier. You do not want your friends to be worried, and the longer you are missing the harder it will be for us to make the necessary adjustments."

Alvin could appreciate that; he would like to know just what those "adjustments" were. Presumably someone from Lys would contact Khedron—without the Jester ever being aware of it—and tamper with his mind. The fact of Alvin's disappearance could not be concealed, but the information that he and Khedron had discovered could be obliterated. As the ages passed, Alvin's name would join those of the other Uniques who had mysteriously vanished without trace and had then been forgotten.

There were many mysteries here, and he seemed no closer to solving any of them. Was there any purpose behind the curious, one-sided relationship between Lys and Diaspar, or was it merely a historical accident? Who and what were the Uniques, and if the people from Lys could enter Diaspar, why had they not canceled the memory circuits that held the clue to their existence? Perhaps that was the only question to which Alvin could give a plausible answer. The Central Computer might be too stubborn an opponent to tackle, and would hardly be affected by even the most advanced of mental techniques.

He put these problems aside; one day, when he had learned a great deal more, he might have some chance of answering them. It was idle to speculate, to build pyramids of surmise on a foundation of ignorance.

"Very well," he said, though not too graciously, for he was still annoyed that this unexpected obstacle had been placed in his path. "I'll give you my answer as soon as I can, if you will show me what your land is like."

"Good," said Seranis, and this time her smile held no hidden threat. "We are proud of Lys, and it will be a pleasure to show you how men can live without the aid of cities. Meanwhile, there is no need for you to worry—your friends will not be alarmed by your absence. We shall see to that, if only for our own protection."

It was the first time Seranis had ever made a promise that she could not keep.

CHAPTER

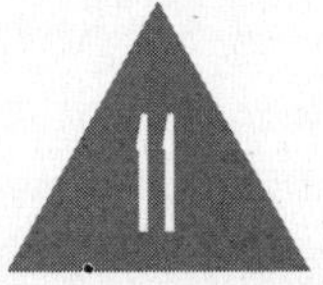

Try as she would, Alystra could extract no further information from Khedron. The Jester had recovered quickly from his initial shock, and from the panic that had sent him flying back to the surface when he found himself alone in the depths beneath the Tomb. He also felt ashamed of his cowardly behavior, and wondered if he would ever have the courage to return to the chamber of the moving ways and the network of world-ranging tunnels that radiated from it. Although he felt that Alvin had been impatient, if not indeed foolhardy, he did not really believe that he would run into any danger. He would return in his own good time. Khedron was certain of that. Well, almost certain; there was just enough doubt to make him feel the need for caution. It would be wise, he decided, to say as little as possible for the time being, and to pass the whole thing off as another joke.

Unfortunately for this plan, he had not been able to mask his emotions when Alystra encountered him on his return to the surface. She had seen the fear written so unmistakably in his eyes, and had at once interpreted it as meaning that Alvin was in danger. All Khedron's reassurances were in vain, and she became more and more angry with him as they walked together back through the park. At first Alystra had wanted to remain at the Tomb, waiting for Alvin to return in whatever mysterious manner he had vanished. Khedron had managed to convince her that this would be a waste of time, and was relieved when she followed him back to the city. There was a chance that Alvin might return almost at once, and he did not wish anyone else to discover the secret of Yarlan Zey.

By the time they had reached the city, it was obvious to Khedron that his evasive tactics had failed completely and that the situation was seriously out of hand. It was the first time in his life that he had ever been at a loss and had not felt himself capable of dealing with any problem that arose. His immediate and irrational fear was being slowly replaced by a profounder and more firmly based alarm. Until now, Khedron had given little thought to the consequences of his actions. His own interests, and a mild but genuine empathy toward Alvin, had been sufficient motive for all that he had done. Though he had given encouragement and assistance to Alvin, he had never believed that anything like this could ever really happen.

Despite the gulf of years and experience between them, Alvin's will had always been more powerful than his own. It was too late to do anything about it now; Khedron felt that events were sweeping him along toward a climax utterly beyond his control.

In view of this, it was a little unfair that Alystra obviously regarded him as Alvin's evil genius and showed an inclination to blame him for all that had happened. Alystra was not really vindictive, but she was annoyed, and part of her annoyance focused on Khedron. If any action of hers caused him trouble, she would be the last person to be sorry.

They parted in stony silence when they had reached the great circular way that surrounded the park. Khedron watched Alystra disappear into the distance and wondered wearily what plans were brewing in her mind.

There was only one thing of which he could be certain now.

Boredom would not be a serious problem for a considerable time to come.

Alystra acted swiftly and with intelligence. She did not bother to contact Eriston and Etania; Alvin's parents were pleasant nonentities for whom she felt some affection but no respect. They would only waste time in futile arguments and would then do exactly as Alystra was doing now.

Jeserac listened to her story without apparent emotion. If he was alarmed or surprised, he concealed it well—so well that Alystra was somewhat disappointed. It seemed to her that nothing so extraordinary and important as this had ever happened before, and Jeserac's matter-of-fact behavior made her feel deflated. When she had finished, he questioned her at some length, and hinted, without actually saying so, that she might have made a mistake. What reason was there for supposing that Alvin had really left the city? Perhaps it had been a trick at her expense; the fact that Khedron was involved made this seem highly probable. Alvin might be laughing at her, concealed somewhere in Diaspar, at this very moment.

The only positive reaction she got out of Jeserac was a promise to make inquiries and to contact her again within a day. In the meantime she was not to worry, and it would also be best if she said nothing to anyone else about the whole affair. There was no need to spread alarm over an incident that would probably be cleared up in a few hours.

Alystra left Jeserac in a mood of mild frustration. She would have been more satisfied could she have seen his behavior immediately after she had left.

Jeserac had friends on the Council; he had been a member himself in his long life, and might be again if he was unlucky. He called three of his most influential colleagues and cautiously aroused their interest. As Alvin's tutor, he was well aware of his own delicate position and was anxious to safeguard himself. For the present, the fewer who knew what had happened, the better.

It was immediately agreed that the first thing to do was to contact Khedron and ask him for an explanation. There was only one defect in the excellent plan. Khedron had anticipated it and was nowhere to be found.

If there was any ambiguity about Alvin's position, his hosts were very careful not to remind him of it. He was free to go anywhere he wished in Airlee, the little village over which Seranis ruled—though that was too strong a word to describe her position. Sometimes it seemed to Alvin that she was a benevolent dictator, but at others it appeared that she had no powers at all. So far he had failed completely to understand the social system of Lys, either because it was too simple or else so complex that its ramifications eluded him. All he had discovered for certain was that Lys was divided into innumerable villages, of which Airlee was a quite typical example. Yet in a sense there were no typical examples, for Alvin had been assured that every village tried to be as unlike its neighbors as possible. It was all extremely confusing.

Though it was very small, and contained less than a thousand people, Airlee was full of surprises. There was hardly a single aspect of life that did not differ from its counterpart in Diaspar. The differences extended even to such fundamentals as speech. Only the children used their voices for normal communication; the adults scarcely ever spoke, and after a while Alvin decided that they did so only out of politeness to him. It was a curiously frustrating experience to feel oneself enmeshed in a great net of soundless and undetectable words, but after a while Alvin grew accustomed to it. It seemed surprising that vocal speech had survived at all since there was no longer any use for it, but Alvin later discovered that the people of Lys were very fond of singing, and indeed of all forms of music. Without this incentive, it was very likely that they would long ago have become completely mute.

They were always busy, engaged in tasks or problems which

were usually incomprehensible to Alvin. When he could understand what they were doing, much of their work seemed quite unnecessary. A considerable part of their food, for example, was actually grown, and not synthesized in accordance with patterns worked out ages ago. When Alvin commented on this, it was patiently explained to him that the people of Lys liked to watch things grow, to carry out complicated genetic experiments and to evolve ever more subtle tastes and flavors. Airlee was famous for its fruits, but when Alvin ate some choice samples they seemed to him no better than those he could have conjured up in Diaspar by no more effort than raising a finger.

At first he wondered if the people of Lys had forgotten, or had never possessed, the powers and machines that he took for granted and upon which all life in Diaspar was based. He soon found that this was not the case. The tools and the knowledge were there, but they were used only when it was essential. The most striking example of this was provided by the transport system, if it could be dignified by such a name. For short distances, people walked, and seemed to enjoy it. If they were in a hurry, or had small loads to move, they used animals which had obviously been developed for the purpose. The freight-carrying species was a low, six-legged beast, very docile and strong but of poor intelligence. The racing animals were of a different breed altogether, normally walking on four legs but using only their heavily muscled hind limbs when they really got up speed. They could cross the entire width of Lys in a few hours, and the passenger rode in a pivoted seat strapped on the creature's back. Nothing in the world would have induced Alvin to risk such a ride, though it was a very popular sport among the younger men. Their finely bred steeds were the aristocrats of the animal world, and were well aware of it. They had fairly large vocabularies, and Alvin often overheard them talking boastfully among themselves about past and future victories. When he tried to be friendly and attempted to join in the conversation, they pretended that they could not understand him, and if he persisted would go bounding off in outraged dignity.

These two varieties of animal sufficed for all ordinary needs, and gave their owners a great deal of pleasure which no mechanical contrivances could have done. But when extreme speed was required or vast loads had to be moved, the machines were there, and were used without hesitation.

Though the animal life of Lys presented Alvin with a whole world of new interests and surprises, it was the two extremes of the human population range that fascinated him most of all. The very young and the very old—both were equally strange to him and equally amazing. Airlee's most senior inhabitant had barely attained his second century, and had only a few more years of life before him. When *he* had reached that age, Alvin reminded himself, his body would scarcely have altered, whereas this old man, who had no chain of future existences to look forward to as compensation, had almost exhausted his physical powers. His hair was completely white, and his face an unbelievably intricate mass of wrinkles. He seemed to spend most of his time sitting in the sun or walking slowly around the village exchanging soundless greetings with everyone he met. As far as Alvin could tell he was completely contented, asking no more of life, and was not distressed by its approaching end.

Here was a philosophy so much at variance with that of Diaspar as to be completely beyond Alvin's comprehension. Why should anyone accept death when it was so unnecessary, when you had the choice of living for a thousand years and then leaping forward through the millenniums to make a new start in a world that you had helped to shape? This was one mystery he was determined to solve as soon as he had the chance of discussing it frankly. It was very hard for him to believe that Lys had made this choice of its own free will, if it knew the alternative that existed.

He found part of his answer among the children, those little creatures who were as strange to him as any of the animals of Lys. He spent much of his time among them, watching them at their play and eventually being accepted by them as a friend. Sometimes it seemed to him that they were not human at all, their motives, their logic, and even their language were so alien. He would look unbelievingly at the adults and ask himself how it was possible that they could have evolved from these extraordinary creatures who seemed to spend most of their lives in a private world of their own.

And yet, even while they baffled him, they aroused within his heart a feeling he had never known before. When—which was not often, but sometimes happened—they burst into tears of utter frustration or despair, their tiny disappointments seemed to him more tragic than Man's long retreat after the loss of his Galactic Empire. That was something too huge and remote for comprehension, but the weeping of a child could pierce one to the heart.

Alvin had met love in Diaspar, but now he was learning something equally precious, and without which love itself could never reach its highest fulfillment but must remain forever incomplete. He was learning tenderness.

If Alvin was studying Lys, Lys was also studying him, and was not dissatisfied with what it had found. He had been in Airlee for three days when Seranis suggested that he might like to go further afield and see something more of her country. It was a proposal he accepted at once—on condition that he was not expected to ride one of the village's prize racing beasts.

"I can assure you," said Seranis, with a rare flash of humor, "that no one here would dream of risking one of their precious animals. Since this is an exceptional case, I will arrange transport in which you will feel more at home. Hilvar will act as your guide, but of course you can go wherever you please."

Alvin wondered if that was strictly true. He imagined that

there would be some objection if he tried to return to the little hill from whose summit he had first emerged into Lys. However, that did not worry him for the moment since he was in no hurry to go back to Diaspar, and indeed had given little thought to the problem after his initial meeting with Seranis. Life here was still so interesting and so novel that he was still quite content to live in the present.

He appreciated Seranis's gesture in offering her son as his guide, though doubtless Hilvar had been given careful instructions to see that he did not get into mischief. It had taken Alvin some time to get accustomed to Hilvar, for a reason which he could not very well explain to him without hurting his feelings. Physical perfection was so universal in Diaspar that personal beauty had been completely devalued; men noticed it no more than the air they breathed. This was not the case in Lys, and the most flattering adjective that could be applied to Hilvar was "homely." By Alvin's standards, he was downright ugly, and for a while he had deliberately avoided him. If Hilvar was aware of this, he showed no sign of it, and it was not long before his good-natured friendliness had broken through the barrier between them. The time was to come when Alvin would be so accustomed to Hilvar's broad, twisted smile, his strength, and his gentleness that he could scarcely believe he had ever found him unattractive, and would not have had him changed for any consideration in the world.

They left Airlee soon after dawn in a small vehicle which Hilvar called a ground-car, and which apparently worked on the same principle as the machine that had brought Alvin from Diaspar. It floated in the air a few inches above the turf, and although there was no sign of any guide rail, Hilvar told him that the cars could run only on predetermined routes. All the centers of population were linked together in this fashion, but during his entire stay in Lys Alvin never saw another ground-car in use.

Hilvar had put a great deal of effort into organizing this expedition, and was obviously looking forward to it quite as much as Alvin. He had planned the route with his own interests in mind, for natural history was his consuming passion and he hoped to find new types of insect life in the relatively uninhabited regions of Lys which they would be visiting. He intended to travel as far south as the machine could take them, and the rest of the way they would have to go on foot. Not realizing the full implications of this, Alvin made no objections.

They had a companion with them on the journey—Krif, the most spectacular of Hilvar's many pets. When Krif was resting, his six gauzy wings lay folded along his body, which glittered through them like a jeweled scepter. If something disturbed him, he would rise into the air with a flicker of iridescence and a faint whirring of invisible wings. Though the great insect would come when called and would—sometimes—obey simple orders, it was almost wholly mindless. Yet it had a definite personality of its own, and for some reason was suspicious of Alvin, whose sporadic attempts to gain its confidence always ended in failure.

To Alvin, the journey across Lys had a dreamlike unreality. Silent as a ghost, the machine slid across rolling plains and wound its way through forests, never deviating from its invisible track. It traveled perhaps ten times as fast as a man could comfortably walk; seldom indeed was any inhabitant of Lys in a greater hurry than that.

They passed through many villages, some larger than Airlee but most of them built along very similar lines. Alvin was interested to notice the subtle but significant differences in clothing and even physical appearance that occurred as they moved from one community to the next. The civilization of Lys was composed of hundreds of distinct cultures, each contributing some special talent toward the whole. The groundcar was well stocked with Airlee's most famous product, a small, yellow peach which was gratefully received whenever Hilvar gave away some samples. He often stopped to talk to friends and to introduce Alvin, who never ceased to be impressed by the simple courtesy with which everyone used vocal speech as soon as they knew who he was. It must often have been very tedious to them, but as far as he could judge they always resisted the temptation to lapse into telepathy and he never felt excluded from their conversation.

They made their longest pause at a tiny village almost hidden in a sea of tall golden grass, which soared high above their heads and which undulated in the gentle wind as if it was endowed with life. As they moved through it, they were continually overtaken by rolling waves as the countless blades bowed in unison above them. At first it was faintly disturbing, for Alvin had a foolish fancy that the grass was bending down to look at him, but after a while he found the continual motion quite restful.

Alvin soon discovered why they had made this stop. Among the little crowd that had already gathered before the car came gliding into the village was a shy, dark girl whom Hilvar introduced as Nyara. They were obviously very pleased to see one another again, and Alvin felt envious of their patent happiness at this brief reunion. Hilvar was clearly torn between his duties as a guide and his desire to have no other company but Nyara, and Alvin soon rescued him from his quandary by setting off on a tour of exploration by himself. There was not much to see in the little village, but he took his time.

When they started on their way again, there were many questions he was anxious to ask Hilvar. He could not imagine what love must be like in a telepathic society, and after a discreet interval he broached the subject. Hilvar was willing enough to explain, even though Alvin suspected that he had made his friend interrupt a prolonged and tender mental leave-taking.

In Lys, it seemed, all love began with mental contact, and it might be months or years before a couple actually met. In this way, Hilvar explained, there could be no false impressions, no deceptions on either side. Two people whose minds were open to one another could hide no secrets. If either attempted it, the other partner would know at once that something was being concealed.

Only very mature and well-balanced minds could afford such honesty; only love based upon absolute unselfishness could survive it. Alvin could well understand that such a love would be deeper and richer than anything his people could know; it could be so perfect, in fact, that he found it hard to believe that it could ever occur at all.

Yet Hilvar assured him that it did, and became starry-eyed and lost in his own reveries when Alvin pressed him to be more explicit. There were some things that could not be communicated; one either knew them or one did not. Alvin decided sadly that he could never attain the kind of mutual understanding which these fortunate people had made the very basis of their lives.

When the ground-car emerged from the savanna, which ended abruptly as though a frontier had been drawn beyond which the grass was not permitted to grow, there was a range of low, heavily wooded hills ahead of them. This was an outpost, Hilvar explained, of the main rampart guarding Lys. The real mountains lay beyond, but to Alvin even these small hills were an impressive and awe-inspiring sight.

The car came to a halt in a narrow, sheltered valley which was still flooded by the warmth and light of the descending sun. Hilvar looked at Alvin with a kind of wide-eyed candor which, one could have sworn, was totally innocent of any guile.

"This is where we start to walk," he said cheerfully, beginning to throw equipment out of the vehicle. "We can't ride any farther."

Alvin looked at the hills surrounding them, then at the comfortable seat in which he had been riding.

"Isn't there a way around?" he asked, not very hopefully.

"Of course," replied Hilvar. "But we're not going around. We're going to the top, which is much more interesting. I'll put the car on automatic so that it will be waiting for us when we get down the other side."

Determined not to give in without a struggle, Alvin made one last effort.

"It will soon be dark," he protested. "We'll never be able to go all that way before sunset."

"Exactly," said Hilvar, sorting packages and equipment with incredible speed. "We'll spend the night on the summit, and finish the journey in the morning."

For once, Alvin knew when he was beaten.

The gear that they were carrying looked very formidable, but though it was bulky it weighed practically nothing. It was all packed in gravity-polarizing containers that neutralized its weight, leaving only inertia to be contended with. As long as Alvin moved in a straight line, he was not conscious that he was carrying any load. Dealing with these containers required a little practice, for if he attempted to make a sudden change of direction his pack seemed to develop a stubborn personality and did its best to keep him on his original course, until he had overcome its momentum.

When Hilvar had adjusted all the straps and satisfied himself that everything was in order, they began to walk slowly up the valley. Alvin looked back wistfully as the ground-car retraced its track and disappeared from sight; he wondered how many hours would elapse before he could again relax in its comfort.

Nevertheless, it was very pleasant climbing upward with the mild sun beating on their backs, and seeing ever-new vistas unfold around them. There was a partly obliterated path which disappeared from time to time but which Hilvar seemed able to follow even when Alvin could see no trace of it. He asked Hilvar what had made the path, and was told that there were many small animals in these hills—some solitary, and some living in primitive communities which echoed many of the features of human civilization. A few had even discovered, or been taught, the use of tools and fire. It never occurred to Alvin that such creatures might be other than friendly; both he and Hilvar took this for granted, for it had been so many ages since anything on Earth had challenged the supremacy of Man.

They had been climbing for half an hour when Alvin first noticed the faint, reverberating murmur in the air around him. He could not detect its source, for it seemed to come from no particular direction. It never ceased, and it grew steadily louder as the landscape widened around them. He would have asked Hilvar what it was, but it had become necessary to save his breath for more essential purposes.

Alvin was in perfect health; indeed, he had never had an hour's illness in his life. But physical well-being, however important and necessary it might be, was not sufficient for the task he was facing now. He had the body, but he did not possess the skill. Hilvar's easy strides, the effortless surge of power which took him up every slope, filled Alvin with envy—and a determination not to give in while he could still place one foot in front of the other. He knew perfectly well that Hilvar was testing him, and did not resent the fact. It was a good-natured game, and he entered into the spirit of it even while the fatigue spread slowly through his legs.

Hilvar took pity on him when they had completed two-thirds of the ascent, and they rested for a while propped up against a westward-facing bank, letting the mellow sunlight drench their bodies. The throbbing thunder was very strong now, and although Alvin questioned him Hilvar refused to explain it. It would, he said, spoil the surprise if Alvin knew what to expect at the end of the climb.

They were now racing against the sun, but fortunately the final ascent was smooth and gentle. The trees that had covered the lower part of the hill had now thinned out, as if they too were tired of the fight against gravity, and for the last few hundred yards the ground was carpeted with short, wiry grass on which it was very pleasant to walk. As the summit came in sight, Hilvar put forth a sudden burst of energy and went racing up the slope. Alvin decided to ignore the challenge; indeed, he had no choice. He was quite content to plod steadily onward, and when he had caught up with Hilvar to collapse in contented exhaustion by his side.

Not until he had regained his breath was he able to appreciate the view spread out beneath him, and to see the origin of the endless thunder which now filled the air. The ground ahead fell away steeply from the crest of the hill—so steeply, indeed, that it soon became an almost vertical cliff. And leaping far out from the face of the cliff was a mighty ribbon of water, which curved out through space to crash into the rocks a thousand feet below. There it was lost in a shimmering mist of spray, while up from the depths rose that ceaseless, drumming thunder that reverberated in hollow echoes from the hills on either side.

Most of the waterfall was now in shadow, but the sunlight streaming past the mountain still illuminated the land beneath, adding the final touch of magic to the scene. For quivering in evanescent beauty above the base of the fall was the last rainbow left on Earth.

Hilvar waved his arm in a sweep which embraced the whole horizon.

"From here," he said, raising his voice so that it could be heard above the thunder of the waterfall, "you can see right across Lys."

Alvin could well believe him. To the north lay mile upon mile of forest, broken here and there by clearings and fields and the wandering threads of a hundred rivers. Hidden somewhere in that vast panorama was the village of Airlee, but it was hopeless to try to find it. Alvin fancied that he could catch a glimpse of the lake past which the path led to the entrance into Lys, but decided that his eyes had tricked him. Still farther north, trees and clearings alike were lost in a mottled carpet of green, rucked here and there by lines of hills. And beyond that, at the very edge of vision, the mountains that hemmed Lys from the desert lay like a bank of distant clouds.

East and west the view was little different, but to the south the mountains seemed only a few miles away. Alvin could see them very clearly, and he realized that they were far higher than the little peak on which he was standing. They were separated from him by country that was much wilder than the land through which he had just passed. In some indefinable way it seemed deserted and empty, as if Man had not lived here for many, many years.

Hilvar answered Alvin's unspoken question.

"Once that part of Lys was inhabited," he said. "I don't know why it was abandoned, and perhaps one day we shall move into it again. Only the animals live there now."

Indeed, there was nowhere any sign of human life—none of the clearings or well-disciplined rivers that spoke of Man's presence. Only in one spot was there any indication that he had ever lived here, for many miles away a solitary white ruin jutted above the forest roof like a broken fang. Elsewhere, the jungle had returned to its own.

The sun was sinking below the western walls of Lys. For a breathless moment, the distant mountains seemed to burn with golden flames; then the land they guarded was swiftly drowned with shadow and the night had come.

"We should have done this before," said Hilvar, practical as ever, as he started to unload their equipment. "It'll be pitch dark in five minutes—and cold, too."

Curious pieces of apparatus began to cover the grass. A slim tripod extended a vertical rod carrying a pear-shaped bulge at its upper end. Hilvar raised this until the pear was just clear of their heads, and gave some mental signal which Alvin could not intercept. At once their little encampment was flooded with light, and the darkness retreated. The pear gave not only light but also heat, for Alvin could feel a gentle, caressing glow that seemed to sink into his very bones.

Carrying the tripod in one hand and his pack in the other, Hilvar walked down the slope while Alvin hurried behind, doing his best to keep in the circle of light. He finally pitched camp in a small depression a few hundred yards below the crest of the hill, and started to put the rest of his equipment into operation.

First came a large hemisphere of some rigid and almost invisible material which englobed them completely and protected them from the cool breeze which had now begun to blow up the face of the hill. The dome appeared to be generated by a small rectangular box which Hilvar placed on the ground and then ignored completely, even to the extent of burying it beneath the rest of his paraphernalia. Perhaps this also projected the comfortable, semitransparent couches on which Alvin was so glad to relax. It was the first time he had seen furniture materialized in Lys, where it seemed to him that the houses were terribly cluttered up with permanent artifacts which would be much better kept safely out of the way in Memory Banks.

The meal which Hilvar produced from yet another of his receptacles was also the first purely synthetic one that Alvin had eaten since reaching Lys. There was a steady blast of air, sucked through some orifice in the dome overhead, as the matter-converter seized its raw material and performed its everyday miracle. On the whole, Alvin was much happier with purely synthetic food. The way in which the other kind was prepared struck him as being appallingly unhygienic, and at least with the matter-converters you knew exactly what you were eating.

They settled down for their evening meal as the night deepened around them and the stars came out. When they had finished, it was completely dark beyond their circle of light, and at the edge of that circle Alvin could see dim shapes moving as the creatures of the forest crept out of their hiding places. From time to time he caught the glint of reflected light as pale eyes stared back at him, but whatever beasts were watching out there would come no closer, so he could see nothing more of them.

It was very peaceful, and Alvin felt utterly content. For a while they lay on their couches and talked about the things that they had seen, the mystery that enmeshed them both, and the many ways in which their two cultures differed. Hilvar was fascinated by the miracle of the Eternity Circuits which had put Diaspar beyond the reach of time, and Alvin found some of his questions very hard to answer.

"What I don't understand," said Hilvar, "is how the designers of Diaspar made certain that nothing would ever go wrong with the memory circuits. You tell me that the information defining the city, and all the people who live in it, is stored as patterns of electric charge inside crystals. Well, crystals will last forever—but what about all the circuits associated with them? Aren't there ever any failures of *any* kind?"

"I asked Khedron that same question, and he told me that the Memory Banks are virtually triplicated. Any one of the three banks can maintain the city, and if anything goes wrong with one of them, the other two automatically correct it. Only if the same failure occurred simultaneously in two of the banks would any permanent damage be done—and the chances of that are infinitesimal."

"And how is the relation maintained between the pattern stored in the memory units and the actual structure of the city? Between the plan, as it were, and the thing it describes?"

Alvin was now completely out of his depth. He knew that the answer involved technologies that relied on the manipulation of space itself—but how one could lock an atom rigidly in the position defined by data stored elsewhere was something he could not begin to explain.

On a sudden inspiration, he pointed to the invisible dome protecting them from the night.

"Tell me how this roof above our heads is created by that box you're sitting on," he answered, "and then I'll explain how the Eternity Circuits work."

Hilvar laughed.

"I suppose it's a fair comparison. You'd have to ask one of our field theory experts if you wanted to know that. I certainly couldn't tell you."

The reply made Alvin very thoughtful. So there were still men in Lys who understood how their machines worked; that was more than could be said of Diaspar.

Thus they talked and argued, until presently Hilvar said: "I'm tired. What about you—are you going to sleep?"

Alvin rubbed his still-weary limbs.

"I'd likc to," he confessed, "but I'm not sure I can. It still seems a strange custom to me."

"It is a good deal more than a custom," smiled Hilvar. "I have been told that it was once a necessity to every human being. We still like to sleep at least once a day, even if only for a few hours. During that time the body refreshes itself, and the mind as well. Does no one in Diaspar *ever* sleep?"

"Only on very rare occasions," said Alvin. "Jeserac, my tutor, has done it once or twice, after he had made some exceptional mental effort. A well-designed body should have no need for such rest periods; we did away with them millions of years ago."

Even as he spoke these rather boastful words, his actions belied them. He felt a weariness such as he had never before known; it seemed to spread from his calves and thighs until it flowed through all his body. There was nothing unpleasant about the sensation—rather the reverse. Hilvar was watching him with an amused smile, and Alvin had enough faculties left to wonder if his companion was exercising any of his mental powers upon him. If so, he did not object in the least.

The light flooding down from the metal pear overhead sank to a faint glow, but the warmth it was radiating continued unabated. By the last flicker of light, Alvin's drowsy mind registered a curious fact which he would have to inquire about in the morning.

Hilvar had stripped off his clothes, and for the first time Alvin saw how much the two branches of the human race had diverged. Some of the changes were merely ones of emphasis or proportion, but others, such as the external genitals and the presence of teeth, nails, and definite body hair, were more fundamental. What puzzled him most of all, however, was the curious small hollow in the pit of Hilvar's stomach.

When, some days later, he suddenly remembered the subject, it took a good deal of explaining. By the time that Hilvar had made the functions of the navel quite clear, he had uttered many thousands of words and drawn half a dozen diagrams.

And both he and Alvin had made a great step forward in understanding the basis of each other's cultures.

Chapter

The night was at its deepest when Alvin woke. Something had disturbed him, some whisper of sound that had crept into his mind despite the endless thunder of the falls. He sat up in the darkness, straining his eyes across the hidden land, while with indrawn breath he listened to the drumming roar of the water and the softer, more fugitive sounds of the creatures of the night.

Nothing was visible. The starlight was too dim to reveal the miles of country that lay hundreds of feet below; only a jagged line of darker night eclipsing the stars told of the mountains on the southern horizon. In the darkness beside him Alvin heard his companion roll over and sit up.

"What is it?" came a whispered voice.

"I thought I heard a noise."

"What sort of noise?"

"I don't know: perhaps it was just imagination."

There was a silence while two pairs of eyes peered out into the mystery of the night. Then, suddenly, Hilvar caught Alvin's arm.

"Look!" he whispered.

Far to the south glowed a solitary point of light, too low in the heavens to be a star. It was a brilliant white, tinged with violet, and even as they watched it began to climb the spectrum of intensity, until the eye could no longer bear to look upon it. Then it exploded—and it seemed as if lightning had struck below the rim of the world. For a brief instant the mountains, and the land they encircled, were etched with fire against the darkness of the night. Ages later came the ghost of a far-off explosion, and in the woods below a sudden wind stirred among the trees. It died away swiftly, and one by one the routed stars crept back into the sky.

For the second time in his life, Alvin knew fear. It was not as personal and imminent as it had been in the chamber of the moving ways, when he had made the decision that took him to Lys. Perhaps it was awe rather than fear; he was looking into the face of the unknown, and it was as if he had already sensed that out there beyond the mountains was something he must go to meet.

"What was that?" he whispered at length.

There was a pause so long that he repeated the question.

"I am trying to find out," said Hilvar, and was silent again. Alvin guessed what he was doing and did not interrupt his friend's silent quest.

Presently Hilvar gave a little sigh of disappointment. "Everyone is asleep," he said. "There was no one who could tell me. We must wait until morning, unless I wake one of my friends. And I would not like to do that unless it is really important."

Alvin wondered what Hilvar would consider a matter of real importance. He was just going to suggest, a little sarcastically, that this might well merit interrupting someone's sleep. Before he could make the proposal, Hilvar spoke again.

"I've just remembered," he said, rather apologetically, "it's a long time since I came here, and I'm not quite certain about my bearings. But that must be Shalmirane."

"Shalmirane! Does it still exist?"

"Yes; I'd almost forgotten. Seranis once told me that the

fortress lies in those mountains. Of course, it's been in ruins for ages, but perhaps someone still lives there."

Shalmirane! To these children of two races, so widely differing in culture and history, this was indeed a name of magic. In all the long story of Earth, there had been no greater epic than the defense of Shalmirane against an invader who had conquered all the Universe. Though the true facts were utterly lost in the mists which had gathered so thickly around the Dawn Ages, the legends had never been forgotten and would last as long as man endured.

Presently Hilvar's voice came again out of the darkness.

"The people of the south could tell us more. I have some friends there; I will call them in the morning."

Alvin scarcely heard him; he was deep in his own thoughts, trying to remember all that he had ever heard of Shalmirane. It was little enough; after this immense lapse of time, no one could tell the truth from the legend. All that was certain was that the Battle of Shalmirane marked the end of Man's conquests and the beginning of his long decline.

Among those mountains, thought Alvin, might lie the answers to all the problems that had tormented him for so many years.

"How long," he said to Hilvar, "would it take us to reach the fortress?"

"I've never been there, but it's much farther than I intended to go. I doubt if we could do it in a day."

"Can't we use the ground-car?"

"No; the way lies through the mountains and no cars can go there."

Alvin thought it over. He was tired, his feet were sore, and the muscles of his thighs were still aching from the unaccustomed effort. It was very tempting to leave it for another time. Yet there might be no other time.

Beneath the dim light of the falling stars, not a few of which had died since Shalmirane was built, Alvin wrestled with his thoughts and presently made his decision. Nothing had changed; the mountains resumed their watch over the sleeping land. But a turning point in history had come and gone, and the human race was moving toward a strange new future.

Alvin and Hilvar slept no more that night, but broke camp with the first glow of dawn. The hill was drenched with dew, and Alvin marveled at the sparkling jewelry which weighed down each blade and leaf. The "swish" of the wet grass fascinated him as he plowed through it, and looking back up the hill he could see his path stretching behind him like a dark band across the shining ground.

The sun had just lifted above the eastern wall of Lys when they reached the outskirts of the forest. Here, Nature had returned to her own. Even Hilvar seemed somewhat lost among the gigantic trees that blocked the sunlight and cast pools of shadow on the jungle floor. Fortunately the river from the falls flowed south in a line too straight to be altogether natural and by keeping to its edge they could avoid the denser undergrowth. A good deal of Hilvar's time was spent in controlling Krif, who disappeared occasionally into the jungle or went skimming wildly across the water. Even Alvin, to whom everything was still so new, could feel that the forest had a fascination not possessed by the smaller, more cultivated woods of northern Lys. Few trees were alike; most of them were in various stages of devolution and some had reverted through the ages almost to their original, natural forms. Many were obviously not of Earth at all—probably not even of the Solar System. Watching like sentinels over the lesser trees were giant sequoias, three or four hundred feet high. Once they had been called the oldest things on Earth; they were still a little older than Man.

The river was widening now; ever and again it opened into small lakes, upon which tiny islands lay at anchor. There were insects here, brilliantly colored creatures swinging to and fro over the surface of the water. Once, despite Hilvar's commands,

Krif darted away to join his distant cousins. He disappeared instantly in a cloud of glittering wings, and the sound of angry buzzing floated toward them. A moment later the cloud erupted and Krif came back across the water, almost too quickly for the eye to follow. Thereafter he kept very close to Hilvar and did not stray again.

Toward evening they caught occasional glimpses of the mountains ahead. The river that had been so faithful a guide was flowing sluggishly now, as if it too were nearing the end of its journey. But it was clear that they could not reach the mountains by nightfall; well before sunset the forest had become so dark that further progress was impossible. The great trees lay in pools of shadow, and a cold wind was sweeping through the leaves. Alvin and Hilvar settled down for the night beside a giant redwood whose topmost branches were still ablaze with sunlight.

When at last the hidden sun went down, the light still lingered on the dancing waters. The two explorers—for such they now considered themselves, and such indeed they were—lay in the gathering gloom, watching the river and thinking of all that they had seen. Presently Alvin felt once again steal over him that sense of delicious drowsiness he had known for the first time on the previous night, and he gladly resigned himself to sleep. It might not be needed in the effortless life of Diaspar, but he welcomed it here. In the final moment before unconsciousness overcame him, he found himself wondering who last had come this way, and how long since.

The sun was high when they left the forest and stood at last before the mountain walks of Lys. Ahead of them the ground rose steeply to the sky in waves of barren rock. Here the river came to an end as spectacular as its beginning, for the ground opened in its path and it sank roaring from sight. Alvin wondered what happened to it, and through what subterranean caves it traveled before it emerged again into the light of day. Perhaps the lost oceans of Earth still existed, far down in the eternal darkness, and this ancient river still felt the call that drew it to the sea.

For a moment Hilvar stood looking at the whirlpool and the broken land beyond. Then he pointed to a gap in the hills.

"Shalmirane lies in that direction," he said confidently. Alvin did not ask how he knew; he assumed that Hilvar's mind had made brief contact with that of a friend many miles away, and the information he needed had been silently passed to him.

It did not take long to reach the gap, and when they had passed through it they found themselves facing a curious plateau with gently sloping sides. Alvin felt no tiredness now, and no fear—only a taut expectancy and a sense of approaching adventure. What he would discover, he had no conception. That he would discover something he did not doubt at all.

As they approached the summit, the nature of the ground altered abruptly. The lower slopes had consisted of porous, volcanic stone, piled here and there in great mounds of slag. Now the surface turned suddenly to hard, glassy sheets, smooth and treacherous, as if the rock had once run in molten rivers down the mountain.

The rim of the plateau was almost at their feet. Hilvar reached it first, and a few seconds later Alvin overtook him and stood speechless at his side. For they stood on the edge, not of the plateau they had expected, but of a giant bowl half a mile deep and three miles in diameter. Ahead of them the ground plunged steeply downward, slowly leveling out at the bottom of the valley and rising again, more and more steeply, to the opposite rim. The lowest part of the bowl was occupied by a circular lake, the surface of which trembled continually, as if agitated by incessant waves.

Although it lay in the full glare of the sun, the whole of that great depression was ebony black. What material formed the crater, Alvin and Hilvar could not even guess, but it was black as the rock of a world that had never known a sun. Nor was that all, for lying beneath their feet and ringing the entire crater was a seamless band of metal, some hundred feet wide, tarnished by immeasurable age but still showing no slightest sign of corrosion.

As their eyes grew accustomed to the unearthly scene, Alvin and Hilvar realized that the blackness of the bowl was not as absolute as they had thought. Here and there, so fugitive that they could only see them indirectly, tiny explosions of light were flickering in the ebony walls. They came at random, vanishing as soon as they were born, like the reflections of stars on a broken sea.

"It's wonderful!" gasped Alvin. "But what *is* it?"

"It looks like a reflector of some kind."

"But it's so black!"

"Only to our eyes, remember. We do not know what radiations they used."

"But surely there must be more than this! Where *is* the fortress?"

Hilvar pointed to the lake.

"Look carefully," he said.

Alvin stared through the quivering roof of the lake, trying to plumb the secrets it concealed within its depths. At first he could see nothing; then, in the shallows near its edge, he made out a faint reticulation of light and shade. He was able to trace the pattern out toward the center of the lake until the deepening water hid all further details.

The dark lake had engulfed the fortress. Down there lay the ruins of once mighty buildings, overthrown by time. Yet not all of them had been submerged, for on the far side of the crater Alvin now noticed piles of jumbled stones, and great blocks that must once have formed part of massive walls. The waters lapped around them, but had not yet risen far enough to complete their victory.

"We'll go around the lake," said Hilvar, speaking softly as if the majestic desolation had struck awe into his soul. "Perhaps we may find something in those ruins over there."

For the first few hundred yards the crater walls were so steep and smooth that it was difficult to stand upright, but after a while they reached the gentler slopes and could walk without difficulty. Near the border of the lake the smooth ebony of the surface was concealed by a thin layer of soil, which the winds of Lys must have brought here through the ages.

A quarter of a mile away, titanic blocks of stone were piled one upon the other, like the discarded toys of an infant giant. Here, a section of a massive wall was still recognizable; there, two carven obelisks marked what had once been a mighty entrance. Everywhere grew mosses and creeping plants, and tiny stunted trees. Even the wind was hushed.

So Alvin and Hilvar came to the ruins of Shalmirane. Against those walls, and against the energies they had housed, forces that could shatter a world to dust had flamed and thundered and been utterly defeated. Once these peaceful skies had blazed with fires torn from the hearts of suns, and the mountains of Lys must have quailed like living things beneath the fury of their masters.

No one had ever captured Shalmirane. But now the fortress, the impregnable fortress, had fallen at last—captured and destroyed by the patient tendrils of the ivy, the generations of blindly burrowing worms, and the slowly rising waters of the lake.

Overawed by its majesty, Alvin and Hilvar walked in silence toward the colossal wreck. They passed into the shadow of a broken wall, and entered a canyon where the mountains of stone had split asunder. Before them lay the lake, and presently they stood with the dark water lapping at their feet. Tiny waves, no more than a few inches high, broke endlessly upon the narrow shore.

Hilvar was the first to speak, and his voice held a hint of uncertainty which made Alvin glance at him in sudden surprise.

"There's something here I don't understand," he said slowly. "There's no wind, so what causes these ripples? The water should be perfectly still."

Before Alvin could think of any reply, Hilvar dropped to the ground, turned his head on one side, and immersed his right ear in the water. Alvin wondered what he hoped to discover in such a ludicrous position; then he realized that he was listening. With some repugnance—for the rayless waters looked singularly uninviting—he followed Hilvar's example.

The first shock of coldness lasted only for a second; when it passed he could hear, faint but distinct, a steady, rhythmic throbbing. It was as if he could hear, from far down in the depths of the lake, the beating of a giant heart.

They shook the water from their hair and stared at each other with silent surmise. Neither liked to say what he thought—that the lake was alive.

"It would be best," said Hilvar presently, "if we searched among these ruins and kept away from the lake."

"Do you think there's something down there?" asked Alvin, pointing to the enigmatic ripples that were still breaking against his feet. "Could it be dangerous?"

"Nothing that possesses a mind is dangerous," Hilvar replied. (Is that true? thought Alvin. What of the Invaders?) "I can detect no thoughts of any kind here, but I do not believe we are alone. It is very strange."

They walked slowly back toward the ruins of the fortress, each carrying in his mind the sound of that steady, muffled pulsing. It seemed to Alvin that mystery was piling upon mystery, and that for all his efforts he was getting further and further from any understanding of the truths he sought.

It did not seem that the ruins could teach them anything, but they searched carefully among the piles of rubble and the great mounds of stone. Here, perhaps, lay the graves of buried machines—the machines that had done their work so long ago. They would be useless now, thought Alvin, if the Invaders returned. Why had they never come back? But that was yet another mystery: he had enough enigmas to deal with—there was no need to seek for any more.

A few yards from the lake they found a small clearing among the rubble. It had been covered with weeds, but they were now blackened and charred by tremendous heat, so that they crumbled to ashes as Alvin and Hilvar approached, smearing their legs with streaks of charcoal. At the center of the clearing stood a metal tripod, firmly anchored to the ground, and supporting a circular ring which was tilted on its axis so that it pointed to a spot halfway up the sky. At first sight it seemed that the ring enclosed nothing; then, as Alvin looked more carefully, he saw that it was filled with a faint haze that tormented the eye by lurking at the edge of the visible spectrum. It was the glow of power, and from this mechanism, he did not doubt, had come the explosion of light that had lured them to Shalmirane.

They did not venture any closer, but stood looking at the machine from a safe distance. They were on the right track, thought Alvin; now it only remained to discover who, or what, had set this apparatus here, and what their purpose might be. That tilted ring—it was clearly aimed out into space. Had the flash they had observed been some kind of signal? That was a thought which had breath-taking implications.

"Alvin," said Hilvar suddenly, his voice quiet but urgent, "we have visitors."

Alvin spun on his heels and found himself staring at a triangle of lidless eyes. That, at least, was his first impression, then behind the staring eyes he saw the outlines of a small but complex machine. It was hanging in the air a few feet above the ground, and it was like no robot he had ever before seen.

Once the initial surprise had worn off, he felt himself the complete master of the situation. All his life he had given orders to machines, and the fact that this one was unfamiliar was of no importance. For that matter, he had never seen more than a few per cent of the robots that provided his daily needs in Diaspar.

"Can you speak?" he asked.

There was silence.

"Is anyone controlling you?"

Still silence.

"Go away. Come here. Rise. Fall."

None of the conventional control thoughts produced any effect. The machine remained contemptuously inactive. That suggested two possibilities. It was either too unintelligent to understand him or it was very intelligent indeed, with its own powers of choice and volition. In that case, he must treat it as an equal. Even then he might underestimate it, but it would bear him no resentment, for conceit was not a vice from which robots often suffered.

Hilvar could not help laughing at Alvin's obvious discomfiture. He was just about to suggest that he should take over the task of communicating, when the words died on his lips. The stillness of Shalmirane was shattered by an ominous and utterly unmistakable sound—the gurgling splash of a very large body emerging from water.

It was the second time since he had left Diaspar that Alvin wished he were at home. Then he remembered that this was not the spirit in which to meet adventure, and he began to walk slowly but deliberately toward the lake.

The creature now emerging from the dark water seemed a monstrous parody, in living matter, of the robot that was still subjecting them to its silent scrutiny. That same equilateral arrangement of eyes could be no coincidence; even the pattern of tentacles and little jointed limbs had been roughly reproduced. Beyond that, however, the resemblance ceased. The robot did not possess—it obviously did not require—the fringe of delicate, feathery palps which beat the water with a steady rhythm, the stubby multiple legs on which the beast was humping itself ashore, or the ventilating inlets, if that was what they were, which now wheezed fitfully in the thin air.

Most of the creature's body remained in the water; only the first ten feet reared itself into what was clearly an alien element. The entire beast was about fifty feet long, and even anyone with no knowledge of biology would have realized that there was something altogether wrong about it. It had an extraordinary air of improvisation and careless design, as if its components had been manufactured without much forethought and thrown roughly together when the need arose.

Despite its size and their initial doubts, neither Alvin nor Hilvar felt the slightest nervousness once they had had a clear look at the dweller in the lake. There was an engaging clumsiness about the creature which made it quite impossible to regard it as a serious menace, even if there was any reason to suppose it might be dangerous. The human race had long ago overcome its childhood terror of the merely alien in appearance. That was a fear which could no longer survive after the first contact with friendly extraterrestrial races.

"Let me deal with this," said Hilvar quietly. "I'm used to handling animals."

"But this isn't an animal," whispered Alvin in return. "I'm sure it's intelligent, and owns that robot."

"The robot may own *it*. In any case, its mentality must be very strange. I can still detect no sign of thought. Hello—what's happening?"

The monster had not moved from its half-raised position at the water's edge, which it seemed to be maintaining with considerable effort. But a semitransparent membrane had begun to form at the center of the triangle of eyes—a membrane that pulsed and quivered and presently started to emit audible sounds. They were low-pitched, resonant boomings which created no intelligible words, though it was obvious that the creature was trying to speak to them.

It was painful to watch this desperate attempt at communication. For several minutes the creature struggled in vain; then, quite suddenly, it seemed to realize that it had made a mistake. The throbbing membrane contracted in size, and the sounds it emitted rose several octaves in frequency until they entered the spectrum of normal speech. Recognizable words began to form, though they were still interspersed with gibberish. It was as if the creature was remembering a vocabulary it had known long ago but had had no occasion to use for many years.

Hilvar tried to give what assistance he could.

"We can understand you now," he said, speaking slowly and distinctly. "Can we help you? We saw the light you made. It brought us here from Lys."

At the word "Lys" the creature seemed to droop as if it had suffered some bitter disappointment.

"Lys," it repeated; it could not manage the "s" very well, so that the word sounded like "Lyd." "Always from Lys. No one else ever comes. We call the Great Ones, but they do not hear."

"Who are the Great Ones?" asked Alvin, leaning forward eagerly. The delicate, ever-moving palps waved briefly toward the sky.

"The Great Ones," it said. "From the planets of eternal day. They will come. The Master promised us."

This did not seem to make matters any clearer. Before Alvin could continue his cross-examination, Hilvar intervened again. His questioning was so patient, so sympathetic, and yet so penetrating that Alvin knew better than to interrupt, despite his eagerness. He did not like to admit that Hilvar was his superior in intelligence, but there was no doubt that his flair for handling animals extended even to this fantastic being. What was more, it seemed to respond to him. Its speech became more distinct as the conversation proceeded, and where at first it had been brusque to the point of rudeness, it presently elaborated its answers and volunteered information on its own.

Alvin lost all consciousness of the passage of time as Hilvar pieced together the incredible story. They could not discover the whole truth; there was endless room for conjecture and debate. As the creature answered Hilvar's questions ever more and more willingly, its appearance began to change. It slumped back into the lake, and the stubby legs that had been supporting it seemed to dissolve into the rest of its body. Presently a still more extraordinary change occurred; the three huge eyes slowly closed, shrank to pinpoints, and vanished completely. It was as if the creature had seen all that it wished to for the moment, and therefore had no further use for eyes.

Other and more subtle alterations were continually taking place, and eventually almost all that remained above the surface of the water was the vibrating diaphragm through which the creature spoke. Doubtless this too would be dissolved back into the original amorphous mass of protoplasm when it was no longer required.

Alvin found it hard to believe that intelligence could reside in so unstable a form—and his biggest surprise was yet to come. Though it seemed obvious that the creature was not of terrestrial origin, it was some time before even Hilvar, despite his greater knowledge of biology, realized the type of organism they were dealing with. It was not a single entity; in all their conversations with it, it always referred to itself as "we." In fact, it was nothing less than a colony of independent creatures, organized and controlled by unknown forces.

Animals of a remotely similar type—the medusae, for example—had once flourished in the ancient oceans of Earth. Some of them had been of great size, trailing their translucent bodies and forests of stinging tentacles over fifty or a hundred feet of water. But none of them had attained even the faintest flicker of intelligence, beyond the power to react to simple stimuli.

There was certainly intelligence here, though it was a failing, degenerating intelligence. Never was Alvin to forget this unearthly meeting, as Hilvar slowly pieced together the story of the Master, while the protean polyp groped for unfamiliar words, the dark lake lapped at the ruins of Shalmirane, and the trioptic robot watched them with unwavering eyes.

CHAPTER

The Master had come to earth amid the chaos of the Transition Centuries, when the Galactic Empire was crumbling but the lines of communication among the stars had not yet completely broken. He had been of human origin, though his home was a planet circling one of the Seven Suns. While still a young man, he had been forced to leave his native world, and its memory had haunted him all his life. His expulsion he blamed on vindictive enemies, but the fact was that he suffered from an incurable malady which, it seemed, attacked only Homo sapiens among all the intelligent races of the Universc. That disease was religious mania.

Throughout the earlier part of its history, the human race had brought forth an endless succession of prophets, seers, messiahs, and evangelists who convinced themselves and their followers that to them alone were the secrets of the Universe revealed. Some of them succeeded in establishing religions that survived for many generations and influenced billions of men; others were forgotten even before their deaths.

The rise of science, which with monotonous regularity refuted the cosmologies of the prophets and produced miracles which they could never match, eventually destroyed all these faiths. It did not destroy the awe, nor the reverence and humility, which all intelligent beings felt as they contemplated the stupendous Universe in which they found themselves. What it did weaken, and finally obliterate, were the countless religions, each of which claimed with unbelievable arrogance that it was the sole repository of the truth and that its millions of rivals and predecessors were all mistaken.

Yet, though they never possessed any real power once humanity had reached a very elementary level of civilization, all down the ages isolated cults had continued to appear, and however fantastic their creeds they had always managed to attract some disciples. They thrived with particular strength during periods of confusion and disorder, and it was not surprising that the Transition Centuries had seen a great outburst of irrationality. When reality was depressing, men tried to console themselves with myths.

The Master, even if he was expelled from his own world, did not leave it unprovided. The Seven Suns had been the center of galactic power and science, and he must have possessed influential friends. He had made his hegira in a small but speedy ship, reputed to be one of the fastest ever built. With him into exile he had taken another of the ultimate products of galactic science—the robot that was looking at Alvin and Hilvar even now.

No one had ever known the full talents and functions of this machine. To some extent, indeed, it had become the Master's alter ego; without it, the religion of the Great Ones would probably have collapsed after the Master's death. Together they had roved among the star clouds on a zigzag trail which led at last, certainly not by accident, back to the world from which the Master's ancestors had sprung.

Entire libraries had been written about that saga, each work therein inspiring a host of commentaries until, by a kind of chain reaction, the original volumes were lost beneath mountains of exegesis and annotation. The Master had stopped at many worlds, and made disciples among many races. His personality must have been an immensely powerful one for it to have inspired humans and nonhumans alike, and there was no doubt that a religion of such wide appeal must have contained much that was fine and noble. Probably the Master was the most successful—as he was also the last—of all mankind's messiahs. None of his predecessors could have won so many converts or had their teachings carried across such gulfs of time and space.

What those teachings were neither Alvin nor Hilvar could ever discover with any accuracy. The great polyp did its desperate best to convey them, but many of the words it used were meaningless and it had a habit of repeating sentences or whole speeches with a kind of swift mechanical delivery that made them very hard to follow. After a while Hilvar did his best to steer the conversation away from these meaningless morasses of theology in order to concentrate on ascertainable facts.

The Master and a band of his most faithful followers had arrived on Earth in the days before the cities had passed away, and while the Port of Diaspar was still open to the stars. They must have come in ships of many kinds; the polyps, for example, in one filled with the waters of the sea which was their natural home. Whether the movement was well received on Earth was not certain; but at least, it met no violent opposition, and after further wanderings it set up its final retreat among the forests and mountains of Lys.

At the close of his long life, the Master's thoughts had turned once more toward the home from which he had been exiled, and he had asked his friends to carry him out into the open so that he could watch the stars. He had waited, his strength waning, until the culmination of the Seven Suns, and toward the end he babbled many things which were to inspire yet more libraries of interpretation in future ages. Again and again he spoke of the "Great Ones" who had now left this universe of space and matter but who would surely one day return, and he charged his followers to remain to greet them when they came. Those were his last rational words. He was never again conscious of his surroundings, but just before the end he uttered one phrase that had come down the ages to haunt the minds of all who heard it: *"It is lovely to watch the colored shadows on the planets of eternal light."* Then he died.

At the Master's death, many of his followers broke away, but others remained faithful to his teachings, which they slowly elaborated through the ages. At first they believed that the Great Ones, whoever they were, would soon return, but that hope faded with the passing centuries. The story here grew very confused, and it seemed that truth and legend were inextricably intertwined. Alvin had only a vague picture of generations of fanatics, waiting for some great event which they did not understand to take place at some unknown future date.

The Great Ones never returned. Slowly the power of the movement failed as death and disillusion robbed it of its disciples. The short-lived human followers were the first to go, and there was something supremely ironic in the fact that the very last adherent of a human prophet was a creature utterly unlike Man.

The great polyp had become the Master's last disciple for a very simple reason. It was immortal. The billions of individual cells from which its body was built would die, but before that happened they would have reproduced themselves. At long intervals the monster would disintegrate into its myriad separate cells, which would go their own way and multiply by fission if their environment was suitable. During this phase the polyp did not exist as a self-conscious, intelligent entity—here Alvin was irresistibly reminded of the manner in which the inhabitants of Diaspar spent their quiescent millenniums in the city's Memory Banks.

In due time some mysterious biological force brought the scattered components together again, and the polyp began a new cycle of existence. It returned to awareness and recollected its earlier lives, though often imperfectly since accident sometimes damaged the cells that carried the delicate patterns of memory.

Perhaps no other form of life could have kept faith so long to a creed otherwise forgotten for a billion years. In a sense, the great polyp was a helpless victim of its biological nature. Because of its immortality, it could not change, but was forced to repeat eternally the same invariant pattern.

The religion of the Great Ones, in its later stages, had become identified with a veneration of the Seven Suns. When the Great Ones stubbornly refused to appear, attempts were made to signal their distant home. Long ago the signaling had become no more than a meaningless ritual, now maintained by an animal that had forgotten how to learn and a robot that had never known how to forget.

As the immeasurably ancient voice died away into the still air, Alvin found himself overwhelmed by a surge of pity. The misplaced devotion, the loyalty that had held to its futile course while suns and planets passed away—he could never have believed such a tale had he not seen the evidence before his eyes. More than ever before the extent of his ignorance saddened him. A tiny fragment of the past had been illuminated for a little while, but now the darkness had closed over it again.

The history of the Universe must be a mass of such disconnected threads, and no one could say which were important and which were trivial. This fantastic tale of the Master and the Great Ones seemed like another of the countless legends that had somehow survived from the civilizations of the Dawn. Yet the very existence of the huge polyp, and of the silently watching robot, made it impossible for Alvin to dismiss the whole story as a fable built of self-delusion upon a foundation of madness.

What was the relationship, he wondered, between these two entities, which though so different in every possible way had maintained their extraordinary partnership over such aeons of time? He was somehow certain that the robot was much the more important of the two. It had been the confidant of the Master and must still know all his secrets.

Alvin looked at the enigmatic machine that still regarded him so steadily. Why would it not speak? What thoughts were passing through its complicated and perhaps alien mind? Yet, surely, if it had been designed to serve the Master, its mind would not be altogether alien, and it should respond to human orders.

As he thought of all the secrets which that stubbornly mute machine must possess, Alvin felt a curiosity so great that it verged upon greed. It seemed unfair that such knowledge should be wasted and hidden from the world; here must lie wonders beyond even the ken of the Central Computer in Diaspar.

"Why won't your robot speak to us?" he asked the polyp, when Hilvar had momentarily run out of questions. The answer was one he had half expected.

"It was against the Master's wishes for it to speak with any voice but his, and his voice is silent now."

"But it will obey you?"

"Yes; the Master placed it in our charge. We can see through its eyes, wherever it goes. It watches over the machines that preserve this lake and keep its water pure. Yet it would be truer to call it our partner than our servant."

Alvin thought this over. An idea, still vague and half-formed, was beginning to take shape in his mind. Perhaps it was inspired by pure lust for knowledge and power; when he looked back on this moment he could never be certain just what his motives were. They might be largely selfish, but they also contained some element of compassion. If he could do so, he would like to break this futile sequence and release these creatures from their fantastic fate. He was not sure what could be done about the polyp, but it might be possible to cure the robot of its insanity and at the same time to release its priceless, pent-up memories.

"Are you certain," he said slowly, talking to the polyp but aiming his words at the robot, "that you are really carrying out the Master's wishes by remaining here? He desired the world to know of his teaching, but they have been lost while you hide here in Shalmirane. It was only by chance that we discovered you, and there may be many others who would like to hear the doctrine of the Great Ones."

Hilvar glanced at him sharply, obviously uncertain of his intentions. The polyp seemed agitated, and the steady beating of its respiratory equipment faltered for a few seconds. Then it replied, in a voice not altogether under control: "We have discussed this problem for many years. But we cannot leave Shalmirane, so the world must come to us, no matter how long it takes."

"I have a better idea," said Alvin eagerly. "it is true that *you* may have to stay here in the lake, but there is no reason why your companion should not come with us. He can return whenever he wishes or whenever you need him. Many things have changed since the Master died—things which you should know about, but which you can never understand if you stay here."

The robot never moved, but in its agony of indecision the polyp sank completely below the surface of the lake and remained there for several minutes. Perhaps it was having a soundless argument with its colleague; several times it began to re-emerge; thought better of it, and sank into the water again. Hilvar took this opportunity to exchange a few words with Alvin.

"I'd like to know what you are trying to do," he said softly, his voice half-bantering and half-serious. "Or don't you know yourself?"

"Surely," replied Alvin, "you feel sorry for these poor creatures? Don't you think it would be a kindness to rescue them?"

"I do, but I've learned enough about you to be fairly certain that altruism isn't one of your dominant emotions. You must have some other motive."

Alvin smiled ruefully. Even if Hilvar did not read his mind—and he had no reason to suppose that he did—he could undoubtedly read his character.

"Your people have remarkable mental powers," he replied, trying to divert the conversation from dangerous ground. "I think they might be able to do something for the robot, if not this animal." He spoke very softly, lest he be overheard. The precaution might have been a useless one, but if the robot did intercept his remarks it gave no sign of it.

Fortunately, before Hilvar could press the inquiry any further, the polyp emerged once more from the lake. In the last few minutes it had become a good deal smaller and its movements were more disorganized. Even as Alvin watched, a segment of its complex, translucent body broke away from the main bulk and then disintegrated into multitudes of smaller sections, which swiftly dispersed. The creature was beginning to break up before their eyes.

Its voice, when it spoke again, was very erratic and hard to understand.

"Next cycle starting," it jerked out in a kind of fluctuating whisper. "Did not expect it so soon—only few minutes left—stimulation too great—cannot hold together much longer."

Alvin and Hilvar stared at the creature in horrified fascination. Even though the process they were watching was a natural one, it was not pleasant to watch an intelligent creature apparently in its death throes. They also felt an obscure sense of guilt; it was irrational to have the feeling, since it was of no great importance when the polyp began another cycle, but they realized that the unusual effort and excitement caused by their presence was responsible for this premature metamorphosis.

Alvin realized that he would have to act quickly or his opportunity would be gone—perhaps only for a few years, perhaps for centuries.

"What have you decided?" he said eagerly. "Is the robot coming with us?"

There was an agonizing pause while the polyp tried to force its dissolving body to obey its will. The speech diaphragm fluttered, but no audible sound came from it. Then, as if in a despairing gesture of farewell, it waved its delicate palps feebly and let them fall back into the water, where they promptly broke adrift and went floating out into the lake. In a matter of minutes, the transformation was over. Nothing of the creature larger than an inch across remained. The water was full of tiny, greenish specks, which seemed to have a life and mobility of their own and which rapidly disappeared into the vastness of the lake.

The ripples on the surface had now altogether died away, and Alvin knew that the steady pulse beat that had sounded in the depths would now be stilled. The lake was dead again—or so it seemed. But that was an illusion; one day the unknown forces that had never failed to do their duty in the past would exert themselves again, and the polyp would be reborn. It was a strange and wonderful phenomenon, yet was it so much stranger than the organization of the human body, itself a vast colony of separate, living cells?

Alvin wasted little effort on such speculations. He was oppressed by his sense of failure, even though he had never clearly conceived the goal he was aiming for. A dazzling opportunity had been missed and might never again return. He stared sadly out across the lake, and it was some time before his mind registered the message which Hilvar was speaking quietly in his ear.

"Alvin," his friend said softly, "I think you have won your point."

He spun swiftly on his heels. The robot, which until now had been floating aloofly in the distance, never approaching within twenty feet of them, had moved up in silence and was now poised a yard above his head. Its unmoving eyes, with their wide angles of vision, gave no indication of its direction of interest. Probably it saw the entire hemisphere in front of it with equal clarity, but Alvin had little doubt that its attention was now focused upon him.

It was waiting for his next move. To some extent, at least, it was now under his control. It might follow him to Lys, perhaps even to Diaspar—unless it changed its mind. Until then, he was its probationary master.

Chapter

The journey back to Airlee lasted almost three days—partly because Alvin, for his own reasons, was in no hurry to return. The physical exploration of Lys had now taken second place to a more important and exciting project; he was slowly making contact with the strange, obsessed intelligence which had now become his companion.

He suspected that the robot was trying to use him for its own purposes, which would be no more than poetic justice. What its motives were he could never be quite certain, since it still stubbornly refused to speak to him. For some reason of his own—perhaps fear that it might reveal too many of his secrets—the Master must have placed very efficient blocks upon its speech circuits, and Alvin's attempts to clear them were completely unsuccessful. Even indirect questioning of the "If you say nothing I shall assume you mean 'Yes' " type failed; the robot was much too intelligent to be taken in by such simple tricks.

In other respects, however, it was more co-operative. It would obey any orders that did not require it to speak or reveal information. After a while Alvin found that he could control it, as he could direct the robots in Diaspar, by thought alone. This was a great step forward, and a little later the creature—it was hard to think of it as a mere machine—relaxed its guard still further and allowed him to see through its eyes. It did not object, it seemed, to such passive forms of communication, but it blocked all attempts at closer intimacy.

Hilvar's existence it ignored completely; it would obey none of his commands, and its mind was closed to all his probing. At first this was something of a disappointment to Alvin, who had hoped that Hilvar's greater mental powers would enable him to force open this treasure chest of hidden memories. It was not until later that he realized the advantage of possessing a servant who would obey no one else in all the world.

The member of the expedition who strongly objected to the robot was Krif. Perhaps he imagined that he now had a rival, or perhaps he disapproved, on general principles, of anything that flew without wings. When no one was looking, he had made several direct assaults on the robot, which had infuriated him still further by taking not the slightest notice of his attacks. Eventually Hilvar had been able to calm him down, and on the homeward journey in the ground-car he seemed to have resigned himself to the situation. Robot and insect escorted the vehicle as it glided silently through forest and field—each keeping to the side of its respective master and pretending that its rival was not there.

Seranis was already waiting for them as the car floated into Airlee. It was impossible, Alvin thought, to surprise these people. Their interlinked minds kept them in touch with everything that was happening in their land. He wondered how they had reacted to his adventures in Shalmirane, which presumably everyone in Lys now knew about.

Seranis seemed to be worried and more uncertain than he had ever seen her before, and Alvin remembered the choice that now lay before him. In the excitement of the last few days he had almost forgotten it; he did not like to spend energy worrying about problems that still lay in the future. But the future was now upon him; he must decide in which of these two worlds he wished to live.

The voice of Seranis was troubled when she began to speak, and Alvin had the sudden impression that something had gone awry with the plans that Lys had been making for him. What had been happening during his absence? Had emissaries gone into Diaspar to tamper with Khedron's mind—and had they failed in their duty?

"Alvin," began Seranis, "there are many things I did not tell you before, but which you must now learn if you are to understand our actions.

"You know one of the reasons for the isolation of our two races. The fear of the Invaders, that dark shadow in the depths of every human mind, turned your people against the world and made them lose themselves in their own dreams. Here in Lys that fear has never been so great, though we bore the burden of the final attack. We had a better reason for our actions, and what we did, we did with open eyes.

"Long ago, Alvin, men sought immortality and at last achieved it. They forgot that a world which had banished death must also banish life. The power to extend his life indefinitely might bring contentment to the individual, but brought stagnation to the race. Ages ago we sacrificed our immortality, but Diaspar still follows the false dream. That is why our ways parted—*and why they must never meet again.*"

Although the words had been more than half expected, the blow seemed none the less for its anticipation. Yet Alvin refused to admit the failure of all his plans—half-formed though they were—and only part of his brain was listening to Seranis now. He understood and noted all her words, but the conscious portion of his mind was retracing the road to Diaspar, trying to imagine every obstacle that could be placed in his way.

Seranis was clearly unhappy. Her voice was almost pleading as it spoke, and Alvin knew that she was talking not only to him but to her son. She must be aware of the understanding and affection that had grown up between them during the days they had spent together. Hilvar was watching his mother intently as she spoke, and it seemed to Alvin that his gaze held not merely concern but also more than a trace of censure.

"We do not wish to make you do anything against your will, but you must surely realize what it would mean if our people met again. Between our culture and yours is a gulf as great as any that ever separated Earth from its ancient colonies. Think of this one fact, Alvin. You and Hilvar are now of nearly the same age—*but both he and I will have been dead for centuries while you are still a youth.* And this is only your first in an infinite series of lives."

The room was very quiet, so quiet that Alvin could hear the strange, plaintive cries of unknown beasts in the fields beyond the village. Presently, he said, almost in a whisper: "What do you want me to do?"

"We hoped that we could give you the choice of staying here or returning to Diaspar, but now that is impossible. Too much has happened for us to leave the decision in your hands. Even in the short time you have been here, your influence has been highly disturbing. No, I am not reproving you; I am sure you intended no harm. But it would have been best to leave the creatures you met in Shalmirane to their own destiny.

"And as for Diaspar—" Seranis gave a gesture of annoyance. "Too many people know where you have gone; we did not act in time. What is most serious, the man who helped you discover Lys has vanished; neither your Council nor our agents can discover him, so he remains a potential danger to our security. Perhaps you are surprised that I am telling you all this, but it is quite safe for me to do so. I am afraid we have only one choice before us; we must send you back to Diaspar with a false set of memories. Those memories have been constructed with great care, and when you return home you will know nothing of us. You will believe that you have had rather dull and dangerous adventures in gloomy underground caverns, where the roofs continually collapsed behind you and you kept alive only through eating unappetizing weeds and drinking from occasional springs. For the rest of your life you will believe this to be the truth, and everyone in Diaspar will accept your story. There will be no mystery, then, to lure any future explorers; they will think they know all there is to be known about Lys."

Seranis paused and looked at Alvin with anxious eyes. "We are very sorry that this is necessary and ask your forgiveness while you still remember us. You may not accept our verdict, but we know many facts that are hidden from you. At least you will have no regrets, for you will believe that you have discovered all that there is to be found."

Alvin wondered if that was true. He was not sure that he would ever settle down to the routine of life in Diaspar, even when he had convinced himself that nothing worthwhile existed beyond its walls. What was more, he had no intention of putting the matter to the test.

"When do you wish me to undergo this—treatment?" Alvin asked.

"Immediately. We are ready now. Open your mind to me, as you did before, and you will know nothing until you find yourself back in Diaspar."

Alvin was silent for a while. Then he said quietly: "I would like to say good-bye to Hilvar."

Seranis nodded.

"I understand. I will leave you here for a while and return when you are ready." She walked over to the stairs that led down to the interior of the house, and left them alone on the roof.

It was some time before Alvin spoke to his friend; he felt a great sadness, yet also an unbroken determination not to permit the wreck of all his hopes. He looked once more down upon the village where he had found a measure of happiness and which he might never see again if those who were ranged behind Seranis had their way. The ground-car was still standing beneath one of the wide-branching trees, with the patient robot hanging in the air above it. A few children had gathered around to examine this strange newcomer, but none of the adults seemed in the least interested.

"Hilvar," said Alvin abruptly, "I'm very sorry about this."

"So am I," Hilvar answered, his voice unstable with emotion. "I had hoped that you could have remained here."

"Do you think that what Seranis wants to do is right?"

"Do not blame my mother. She is only doing as she is asked," replied Hilvar. Though he had not answered his question, Alvin had not the heart to ask it again. It was unfair to put such a strain on his friend's loyalty.

"Then tell me this," asked Alvin, "how could your people stop me if I tried to leave with my memories untouched?"

"It would be easy. If you tried to escape, we would take control of your mind and force you to come back."

Alvin had expected as much and was not discouraged. He wished that he could confide in Hilvar, who was obviously upset by their impending separation, but he dared not risk the failure of his plans. Very carefully, checking every detail, he traced out the only road that could lead him back to Diaspar on the terms he wished.

There was one risk which he had to face, and against which he could do nothing to protect himself. If Seranis broke her promise and dipped into his mind, all his careful preparations might be in vain.

He held out his hand to Hilvar, who grasped it firmly but seemed unable to speak.

"Let's go downstairs to meet Seranis," said Alvin. "I'd like to see some of the people in the village before I go."

Hilvar followed him silently into the peaceful coolness of the house and then out through the hallway and onto the ring of colored glass that surrounded the building. Seranis was waiting for them there, looking calm and resolute. She knew that Alvin was trying to hide something from her, and thought again of the precautions she had taken. As a man may flex his muscles before some great effort, she ran through the compulsion patterns she might have to use.

"Are you ready, Alvin?" she asked.

"Quite ready," replied Alvin, and there was a tone in his voice that made her look at him sharply.

"Then it will be best if you make your mind a blank, as you did before. You will feel and know nothing after that, until you find yourself back in Diaspar."

Alvin turned to Hilvar and said in a quick whisper that Seranis could not hear: "Good-bye, Hilvar, Don't worry—*I'll be back.*" Then he faced Seranis again.

"I don't resent what you are trying to do," he said. "No doubt you believe it is for the best, but I think you are wrong. Diaspar and Lys should not remain apart forever; one day they may need each other desperately. So I am going home with all that I have learned—*and I do not think that you can stop me.*"

He waited no longer, and it was just as well. Seranis never moved, but instantly he felt his body slipping from his control. The power that had brushed aside his own will was even greater than he had expected, and he realized that many hidden minds must be aiding Seranis. Helplessly he began to walk back into the house, and for an awful moment he thought his plan had failed.

Then there came a flash of steel and crystal, and metal arms closed swiftly around him. His body fought against them, as he had known that it must do, but the struggles were useless. The ground fell away beneath him and he caught a glimpse of Hilvar, frozen by surprise, with a foolish smile upon his face.

The robot was carrying him a dozen feet above the ground, much faster than a man could run. It took Seranis only a moment to understand his ruse, and his struggles died away as she relaxed her control. But she was not defeated yet, and presently there happened that which Alvin had feared and done his best to counteract.

There were now two separate entities fighting inside his mind, and one of them was pleading with the robot, begging it to set him down. The real Alvin waited, breathlessly, resisting only a little against forces he knew he could not hope to fight. He had gambled; there was no way of telling beforehand if his uncertainty would obey orders as complex as those that he had given it. Under no circumstances, he had told the robot, must it obey any further commands of his until he was safely inside Diaspar. Those were the orders. If they were obeyed, Alvin had placed his fate beyond the reach of human interference.

Never hesitating, the machine raced on along the path he had so carefully mapped out for it. A part of him was still pleading angrily to be released, but he knew now that he was safe. And presently Seranis understood that too, for the forces inside his brain ceased to war with one another. Once more he was at peace, as ages ago an earlier wanderer had been when, lashed to the mast of his ship, he had heard the song of the Sirens die away across the wine-dark sea.

Chapter

Alvin did not relax until the chamber of the moving ways was around him once more. There had still been the danger that the people of Lys might be able to stop, or even to reverse, the vehicle in which he was traveling, and bring him back helplessly to his starting point. But his return was an uneventful repetition of the outward trip; forty minutes after he had left Lys he was in the Tomb of Yarlan Zey.

The servants of the Council were waiting for him, dressed in the formal black robes which they had not worn for centuries. Alvin felt no surprise, and little alarm, at the presence of this reception committee. He had now overcome so many obstacles that one more made little difference. He had learned a great deal since leaving Diaspar, and with that knowledge had come a confidence verging upon arrogance. Moreover, he now had a powerful, if erratic, ally. The best minds of Lys had been unable to interfere with his plans; somehow, he believed that Diaspar could do no better.

There were rational grounds for this belief, but it was based partly upon something beyond reason—a faith in his destiny which had slowly been growing in Alvin's mind. The mystery of his origin, his success in doing what no earlier man had ever done, the way in which new vistas had opened up before him, and the manner in which obstacles had failed to halt him—all these things added to his self-confidence. Faith in one's own destiny was among the most valuable of the gifts which the gods could bestow upon a man, but Alvin did not know how many it had led to utter disaster.

"Alvin," said the leader of the city's proctors, "we have orders to accompany you wherever you go, until the Council has heard your case and rendered its verdict."

"With what offense am I charged?" asked Alvin. He was still exhilarated by the excitement and elation of his escape from Lys and could not yet take this new development very seriously. Presumably Khedron had talked; he felt a brief annoyance at the Jester for betraying his secret.

"No charge has been made," came the reply. "If necessary, one will be framed after you have been heard."

"And when will that be?"

"Very soon, I imagine." The proctor was obviously ill at ease and was not sure how to handle his unwelcome assignment. At one moment he would treat Alvin as a fellow citizen, and then he would remember his duties as a custodian and would adopt an attitude of exaggerated aloofness.

"This robot," he said abruptly, pointing to Alvin's companion, "where did it come from? Is it one of ours?"

"No," replied Alvin. "I found it in Lys, the country I have been to. I have brought it here to meet the Central Computer."

This calm statement produced a considerable commotion. The fact that there was something outside Diaspar was hard enough to accept, but that Alvin should have brought back one of its inhabitants and proposed to introduce it to the brain of the city was even worse. The proctors looked at each other with such helpless alarm that Alvin could hardly refrain from laughing at them.

As they walked back through the park, his escort keeping discreetly at the rear and talking among itself in agitated whispers, Alvin considered his next move. The first thing he must do was to discover exactly what had happened during his absence. Khedron, Seranis had told him, had vanished. There were countless places where a man could hide in Diaspar, and since the Jester's knowledge of the city was unsurpassed it was not likely that he would be found until he chose to reappear. Perhaps, thought Alvin, he could leave a message where Khedron would be bound to see it, and arrange a rendezvous. However, the presence of his guard might make that impossible.

He had to admit that the surveillance was very discreet. By the time he had reached his apartment, he had almost forgotten the existence of the proctors. He imagined that they would not interfere with his movements unless he attempted to leave Diaspar, and for the time being he had no intention of doing that. Indeed, he was fairly certain that it would be impossible to return to Lys by his original route. By this time, surely, the underground carrier system would have been put out of action by Seranis and her colleagues.

The proctors did not follow him into his room; they knew that there was only the one exit, and stationed themselves outside that. Having had no instructions regarding the robot, they let it accompany Alvin. It was not a machine which they had any desire to interfere with, since its alien construction was obvious. From its behavior they could not tell whether it was a passive servant of Alvin's or whether it was operating under its own volition. In view of this uncertainty, they were quite content to leave it severely alone.

Once the wall had sealed itself behind him, Alvin materialized his favorite divan and threw himself down upon it. Luxuriating in his familiar surroundings, he called out of the memory units his last efforts in painting and sculpture, and examined them with a critical eye. If they had failed to satisfy him before, they were doubly displeasing now, and he could take no further pride in them. The person who had created them no longer existed; into the few days he had been away from Diaspar, it seemed to Alvin that he had crowded the experience of a lifetime.

He canceled all these products of his adolescence, erasing them forever and not merely returning them to the Memory Banks. The room was empty again, apart from the couch on which he was reclining, and the robot that still watched with wide, unfathomable eyes. What did the robot think of Diaspar? wondered Alvin. Then he remembered that it was no stranger here, for it had known the city in the last days of its contact with the stars.

Not until he felt thoroughly at home once more did Alvin begin to call his friends. He began with Eriston and Etania, though out of a sense of duty rather than any real desire to see and speak to them again. He was not sorry when their communicators informed him that they were unavailable, but he left them both a brief message announcing his return. This was quite unnecessary, since by now the whole city would know that he was back. However, he hoped that they would appreciate his thoughtfulness; he was beginning to learn consideration, though he had not yet realized that, like most virtues, it had little merit unless it was spontaneous and unself-conscious.

Then, acting on a sudden impulse, he called the number that Khedron had given him so long ago in the Tower of Loranne. He did not, of course, expect an answer, but there was always the possibility that Khedron had left a message.

His guess was correct; but the message itself was shatteringly unexpected.

The wall dissolved, and Khedron was standing before him. The Jester looked tired and nervous, no longer the confident, slightly cynical person who had set Alvin on the path that led to Lys. There was a haunted look in his eyes, and he spoke as though he had very little time.

"Alvin," he began, "this is a recording. Only you can receive it, but you can make what use of it you wish. It will not matter to me.

"When I got back to the Tomb of Yarlan Zey, I found that Alystra had been following us. She must have told the Council that you had left Diaspar, and that I had helped you. Very soon the proctors were looking for me, and I decided to go into hiding. I am used to that—I have done it before when some of my jests failed to be appreciated." (There, thought Alvin, was a flash of the old Khedron.) "They could not have found me in a thousand years—but someone else nearly did. There are strangers in Diaspar, Alvin; they could only have come from Lys, and they are looking for me. I do not know what this means, and I do not like it. The fact that they nearly caught me, though they are in a city that must be strange to them, suggests that they possess telepathic powers. I could fight the Council, but this is an unknown peril which I do not care to face.

"I am therefore anticipating a step which I think the Council might well force upon me, since it has been threatened before. I am going where no one can follow, and where I shall escape whatever changes are now about to happen to Diaspar. Perhaps I am foolish to do this; that is something which only time can prove. I shall know the answer one day.

"By now you will have guessed that I have gone back into the Hall of Creation, into the safety of the Memory Banks. Whatever happens, I put my trust in the Central Computer and the forces it controls for the benefit of Diaspar. If anything tampers with the Central Computer, we are all lost. If not, I have nothing to fear.

"To me, only a moment will seem to pass before I walk forth into Diaspar again, fifty or a hundred thousand years from now. I wonder what sort of city I shall find? It will be strange if you are there; some day, I suppose, we will meet again. I cannot say whether I look forward to that meeting or fear it.

"I have never understood you, Alvin, though there was a time when I was vain enough to think I did. Only the Central Computer knows the truth, as it knows the truth about those other Uniques who have appeared from time to time down the ages and then were seen no more. Have you discovered what happened to them?

"One reason, I suppose, why I am escaping into the future is because I am impatient. I want to see the results of what you have started, but I am anxious to miss the intermediate stages—which I suspect may be unpleasant. It will be interesting to see, in that world which will be around me in only a few minutes of apparent time from now, whether you are remembered as a creator or as a destroyer—or whether you are remembered at all.

"Good-bye, Alvin. I had thought of giving you some advice, but I do not suppose you would take it. You will go your own way, as you always have, and your friends will be tools to use or discard as occasion suits.

"That is all. I can think of nothing more to say."

For a moment Khedron—the Khedron who no longer existed save as a pattern of electric charges in the memory cells of the city—looked at Alvin with resignation and, it seemed, with sadness. Then the screen was blank again.

Alvin remained motionless for a long time after the image of Khedron had faded. He was searching his soul as he had seldom done before in all his life, for he could not deny the truth of much that Khedron had said. When had he paused, in all his schemes and adventures, to consider the effect of what he was doing upon any of his friends? He had brought anxiety to them and might soon bring worse—all because of his insatiable curiosity and the urge to discover what should not be known.

He had never been fond of Khedron; the Jester's astringent personality prevented any close relationship, even if Alvin had desired it. Yet now, as he thought of Khedron's parting words, he was shaken with remorse. Because of his actions, the Jester had fled from this age into the unknown future.

But surely, thought Alvin, he had no need to blame himself for that. It proved only what he had already known—that Khedron was a coward. Perhaps he was no more of a coward than anyone else in Diaspar, but he had the additional misfortune of possessing a powerful imagination. Alvin could accept some responsibility for his fate, but by no means all.

Who else in Diaspar had he harmed or distressed? He thought of Jeserac; his tutor, who had been patient with what must have been his most difficult pupil. He remembered all the little kindnesses that his parents had shown him over the years; now that he looked back upon them, there were more than he had imagined.

And he thought of Alystra. She had loved him, and he had taken that love or ignored it as he chose. Yet what else was he to have done? Would she have been any happier had he spurned her completely?

He understood now why he had never loved Alystra, or any of the women he had known in Diaspar. That was another lesson that Lys had taught him. Diaspar had forgotten many things, and among them was the true meaning of love. In Airlee he had watched the mothers dandling their children on their knees, and had himself felt that protective tenderness for all small and helpless creatures that is love's unselfish twin. Yet now there was no woman in Diaspar who knew or cared for what had once been the final aim of love.

There were no real emotions, no deep passions, in the immortal city. Perhaps such things only thrived because of their very transience, because they could not last forever and lay always under the shadow which Diaspar had banished.

That was the moment, if such a moment ever existed, when Alvin realized what his destiny must be. Until now he had been the unconscious agent of his own impulses. If he could have known so archaic an analogy, he might have compared himself to a rider on a runaway horse. It had taken him to many strange places, and might do so again, but in its wild galloping it had shown him its powers and taught him where he really wished to go.

Alvin's reverie was rudely interrupted by the chimes of the wall screen. The timbre of the sound told him at once that this was no incoming call, but that someone had arrived to see him. He gave the admission signal, and a moment later was facing Jeserac.

His tutor looked grave, but not unfriendly.

"I have been asked to take you to the Council, Alvin," he said. "It is waiting to hear you." Then Jeserac saw the robot and examined it curiously. "So this is the companion you have brought back from your travels. I think it had better come with us."

This suited Alvin very well. The robot had already extricated him from one dangerous situation, and he might have to call upon it again. He wondered what the machine had thought about the adventures and vicissitudes in which he had involved it, and wished for the thousandth time that he could understand what was going on inside its closely shuttered mind. Alvin had the impression that for the moment it had decided to watch, analyze, and draw its own conclusion, doing nothing of its own volition until it had judged the time was ripe. Then, perhaps quite suddenly, it might decide to act; and what it chose to do might not suit Alvin's plans. The only ally he possessed was bound to him by the most tenuous ties of self interest and might desert him at any moment.

Alystra was waiting for them on the ramp that led out into the street. Even if Alvin had wished to blame her for whatever part she had played in revealing his secret, he did not have the heart to do so. Her distress was too obvious, and her eyes brimmed with tears as she ran up to greet him.

"Oh, Alvin!" she cried. "What are they going to do with you?"

Alvin took her hands in his with a tenderness that surprised them both.

"Don't worry, Alystra," he said. "Everything is going to be all right. After all, at the very worst the Council can only send me back to the Memory Banks—and somehow I don't think that will happen."

Her beauty and her unhappiness were so appealing that, even now, Alvin felt his body responding to her presence after its old fashion. But it was the lure of the body alone; he did not disdain it, but it was no longer enough. Gently he disengaged his hands and turned to follow Jeserac toward the Council Chamber.

Alystra's heart was lonely, but no longer bitter, as she watched him go. She knew now that she had not lost him, for he had never belonged to her. And with the acceptance of that knowledge, she had begun to put herself beyond the power of vain regrets.

Alvin scarcely noticed the curious or horrified glances of his fellow citizens as he and his retinue made their way through the familiar streets. He was marshaling the arguments he might have to use, and arranging his story in the form most favorable to himself. From time to time he assured himself that he was not in the least alarmed and that he was still master of the situation.

They waited only a few minutes in the anteroom, but it was long enough for Alvin to wonder why, if he was unafraid, his legs felt so curiously weak. He had known this sensation before when he had forced himself up the last slopes of that distant hill in Lys, where Hilvar had shown him the waterfall from whose summit they had seen the explosion of light that had drawn them to Shalmirane. He wondered what Hilvar was doing now, and if they would ever meet again. It was suddenly very important to him that they should.

The great doors dilated, and he followed Jeserac into the Council Chamber. The twenty members were already seated around their crescent-shaped table, and Alvin felt flattered as he noticed that there were no empty places. This must be the first time for many centuries that the entire Council had been gathered together without a single abstention. Its rare meetings were usually a complete formality, all ordinary business being dealt with by a few visophone calls and, if necessary, an interview between the President and the Central Computer.

Alvin knew by sight most of the members of the Council, and felt reassured by the presence of so many familiar faces. Like Jeserac, they did not seem unfriendly—merely anxious and puzzled. They were, after all, reasonable men. They might be annoyed that someone had proved them wrong, but Alvin did not believe that they would bear him any resentment. Once this would have been a very rash assumption, but human nature had improved in some respects.

They would give him a fair hearing, but what they thought was not all-important. His judge now would not be the Council. It would be the Central Computer.

Chapter

There were no formalities. The President declared the meeting open and then turned to Alvin.

"Alvin," he said, kindly enough, "we would like you to tell us what has happened to you since you disappeared ten days ago."

The use of the word "disappeared," thought Alvin, was highly significant. Even now, the Council was reluctant to admit that he had really gone outside Diaspar. He wondered if they knew that there had been strangers in the city, and rather doubted it. In that event they would have shown considerably more alarm.

He told his story clearly and without any dramatics. It was strange and unbelievable enough to their ears, and needed no embellishment. Only at one place did he depart from strict accuracy, for he said nothing about the manner of his escape from Lys. It seemed more than likely that he might want to use the same method again.

It was fascinating to watch the way in which the attitude of the Council members altered during the course of his narrative. At first they were skeptical, refusing to accept the denial of all they had believed, the violation of their deepest prejudices. When Alvin told them of his passionate desire to explore the world beyond the city, and his irrational conviction that such a world did exist, they stared at him as if he was some strange and incomprehensible animal. To their minds, indeed, he was. But finally they were compelled to admit that he had been right, and that they had been mistaken. As Alvin's story unfolded, any doubts they may have had slowly dissolved. They might not like what he had told them, but they could no longer deny its truth. If they felt tempted to do so, they had only to look at Alvin's silent companion.

There was only one aspect of his tale that roused their indignation—and then it was not directed toward him. A buzz of annoyance went around the chamber as Alvin explained the anxiety of Lys to avoid contamination with Diaspar, and the steps that Seranis had taken to prevent such a catastrophe. The city was proud of its culture, and with good reason. That anyone should regard them as inferiors was more than the Council members could tolerate.

Alvin was very careful not to give offense in anything he said; he wanted, as far as possible, to win the Council to his side. Throughout, he tried to give the impression that he had seen nothing wrong in what he had done, and that he expected praise rather than censure for his discoveries. It was the best policy he could have adopted, for it disarmed most of his would-be critics in advance. It also had the effect—though he had not intended this—of transferring any blame to the vanished Khedron. Alvin himself, it was clear to his listeners, was too young to see any danger in what he was doing. The Jester, however, should certainly have known better and had acted in a thoroughly irresponsible fashion. They did not yet know how fully Khedron himself had agreed with them.

Jeserac, as Alvin's tutor, was also deserving of some censure, and from time to time several of the Councilors gave him thoughtful glances. He did not seem to mind, though he was perfectly well aware of what they were thinking. There was a certain honor in having instructed the most original mind that had come into Diaspar since the Dawn Ages, and nothing could rob Jeserac of that.

Not until Alvin had finished the factual account of his adventures did he attempt a little persuasion. Somehow, he would have to convince these men of the truths that he had learned in Lys, but now how could he make them really understand something that they had never seen and could hardly imagine?

"It seems a great tragedy," he said, "that the two surviving branches of the human race should have become separated for such an enormous period of time. One day, perhaps, we may know how it happened, but it is more important now to repair the break—to prevent it happening again. When I was in Lys I protested against their view that they were superior to us; they may have much to teach us, but we also have much to teach them. If we both believe that we have nothing to learn from the other, is it not obvious that we will *both* be wrong?"

He looked expectantly along the line of faces, and was encouraged to go on.

"Our ancestors," he continued, "built an empire that reached to the stars. Men came and went at will among all those worlds—and now their descendants are afraid to stir beyond the walls of their city. *Shall I tell you why?*" He paused; there was no movement at all in the great, bare room.

"It is because we are afraid—afraid of something that happened at the beginning of history. I was told the truth in Lys, though I guessed it long ago. Must we always hide like cowards in Diaspar, pretending that nothing else exists—because a billion years ago the Invaders drove us back to Earth?"

He had put his finger on their secret fear—the fear that he had never shared and whose power he could therefore never fully understand. Now let them do what they pleased; he had spoken the truth as he saw it.

The President looked at him gravely.

"Have you anything more to say," he asked, "before we consider what is to be done?"

"Only one thing. I would like to take this robot to the Central Computer."

"But why? You know that the Computer is already aware of everything that has happened in this room."

"I still wish to go," replied Alvin politely but stubbornly. "I ask permission both of the Council and the Computer."

Before the President could reply, a clear, calm voice sounded through the chamber. Alvin had never heard it before in his life, but he knew what it was that spoke. The information machines, which were no more than outlying fragments of this great intelligence, could speak to men—but they did not possess this unmistakable accent of wisdom and authority.

"Let him come to me," said the Central Computer.

Alvin looked at the President. It was to his credit that he did not attempt to exploit his victory. He merely asked, "Have I your permission to leave?"

The President looked around the Council Chamber, saw no disagreement there, and replied a little helplessly: "Very well. The proctors will accompany you, and will bring you back here when we have finished our discussion."

Alvin gave a slight bow of thanks, the great doors expanded before him, and he walked slowly out of the chamber. Jeserac had accompanied him, and when the doors had closed once more, he turned to face his tutor.

"What do you think the Council will do now?" he asked anxiously. Jeserac smiled.

"Impatient as ever, aren't you?" he said. "I do not know what my guess is worth, but I imagine that they will decide to seal the Tomb of Yarlan Zey so that no one can ever again make your journey. Then Diaspar can continue as before, undisturbed by the outside world."

"That is what I am afraid of," said Alvin bitterly.

"And you still hope to prevent it?"

Alvin did not at once reply; he knew that Jeserac had read his intentions, but at least his tutor could not foresee his plans, for he had none. He had come to the stage when he could only improvise and meet each new situation as it arose.

"Do you blame me?" he said presently, and Jeserac was surprised by the new note in his voice. It was a hint of humility, the barest suggestion that for the first time Alvin sought the approval of his fellow men. Jeserac was touched by it, but he was too wise to take it very seriously. Alvin was under a considerable strain, and it would be unsafe to assume that any improvement in his character was permanent.

"That is a very hard question to answer," said Jeserac slowly. "I am tempted to say that all knowledge is valuable, and it cannot be denied that you have added much to our knowledge. But you have also added to our dangers, and in the long run which will be more important? How often have you stopped to consider that?"

For a moment master and pupil regarded each other pensively, each perhaps seeing the other's point of view more clearly than ever before in his life. Then, with one impulse, they turned together down the long passage from the Council Chamber, with their escort still following patiently in the rear.

This world, Alvin knew, had not been made for man. Under the glare of the fierce blue lights—so dazzling that they pained the eyes—the long, broad corridors seemed to stretch to infinity. Down these great passageways, the robots of Diaspar must come and go throughout their endless lives, yet not once in centuries did they echo to the sound of human feet.

Here was the underground city, the city of machines without which Diaspar could not exist. A few hundred yards ahead, the corridor would open into a circular chamber more than a mile across, its roof supported by great columns that must also bear the unimaginable weight of Power Center. Here, according to the maps, the Central Computer brooded eternally over the fate of Diaspar.

The chamber was there, and it was even vaster than Alvin had dared imagine—but where was the Computer? Somehow he had expected to meet a single huge machine, naïve though he knew that this conception was. The tremendous but meaningless panorama beneath him made him pause in wonder and uncertainty.

The corridor along which they had come ended high in the wall of the chamber—surely the largest cavity ever built by man—and on either side long ramps swept down to the distant floor. Covering the whole of that brilliantly lit expanse were hundreds of great white structures, so unexpected that for a moment Alvin thought he must be looking down upon a subterranean city. The impression was startlingly vivid, and it was one that he never wholly lost. Nowhere at all was the sight he had expected—the familiar gleam of metal which since the beginning of time man had learned to associate with his servants.

Here was the end of an evolution almost as long as Man's. Its beginnings were lost in the mists of the Dawn Ages, when humanity had first learned the use of power and sent its noisy engines clanking about the world. Steam, water, wind—all had been harnessed for a little while and then abandoned. For centuries the energy of matter had run the world until it too had been superseded, and with each change the old machines were forgotten and new ones took their place. Very slowly, over thousands of years, the ideal of the perfect machine was approached—that ideal which had once been a dream, then a distant prospect, and at last reality:

No machine may contain any moving parts.

Here was the ultimate expression of that ideal. Its achievement had taken Man perhaps a hundred million years, and in the moment of his triumph he had turned his back upon the machine forever. It had reached finality, and thenceforth could sustain itself eternally while serving him.

Alvin no longer asked himself which of these silent white presences was the Central Computer. He knew that it comprised them all—and that it extended far beyond this chamber, including within its being all the countless other machines in Diaspar, whether they were mobile or motionless. As his own brain was the sum of many billion separate cells, arrayed throughout a volume of space a few inches across, so the physical elements of the Central Computer were scattered throughout the length and breadth of Diaspar. This chamber might hold no more than the switching system whereby all these dispersed units kept in touch with one another.

Uncertain where to go next, Alvin stared down the great sweeping ramps and across the silent arena. The Central Computer must know that he was here, as it knew everything that was happening in Diaspar. He could only wait for its instructions.

The now-familiar yet still awe-inspiring voice was so quiet and so close to him that he did not believe that his escort could also hear it. "Go down the left-hand ramp," it said. "I will direct you from there."

He walked slowly down the slope, the robot floating above him. Neither Jeserac nor the proctors followed; he wondered if they had received orders to remain here, or whether they had decided that they could supervise him just as well from their vantage point without the bother of making this long descent. Or perhaps they had come as close to the central shrine of Diaspar as they cared to approach.

At the foot of the ramp, the quiet voice redirected Alvin, and he walked between an avenue of sleeping titan shapes. Three times the voice spoke to him again, until presently he knew that he had reached his goal.

The machine before which he was standing was smaller

than most of its companions, but he felt dwarfed as he stood beneath it. The five tiers with their sweeping horizontal lines gave the impression of some crouching beast, and looking from it to his own robot Alvin found it hard to believe that both were products of the same evolution, and both described by the same word.

About three feet from the ground a wide transparent panel ran the whole length of the structure. Alvin pressed his forehead against the smooth, curiously warm material and peered into the machine. At first he saw nothing; then, by shielding his eyes, he could distinguish thousands of faint points of light hanging in nothingness. They were ranged one beyond the other in a three-dimensional lattice, as strange and as meaningless to him as the stars must have been to ancient man. Though he watched for many minutes, forgetful of the passage of time, the colored lights never moved from their places and their brilliance never changed.

If he could look into his own brain, Alvin realized, it would mean as little to him. The machine seemed inert and motionless because he could not see its thoughts.

For the first time, he began to have some dim understanding of the powers and forces that sustained the city. All his life he had accepted without question the miracle of the synthesizers which age after age provided in an unending stream all the needs of Diaspar. Thousands of times he had watched that act of creation, seldom remembering that somewhere must exist the prototype of that which he had seen come into the world.

As a human mind may dwell for a little while upon a single thought, so the infinitely greater brains which were but a portion of the Central Computer could grasp and hold forever the most intricate ideas. The patterns of all created things were frozen in these eternal minds, needing only the touch of a human will to make them reality.

The world had indeed gone far since, hour upon hour, the

first cavemen had patiently chipped their arrowheads and knives from the stubborn stone.

Alvin waited, not caring to speak until he had received some further sign of recognition. He wondered how the Central Computer was aware of his presence, and could see him and hear his voice. Nowhere were there any signs of sense organs—none of the grilles or screens or emotionless crystal eyes through which robots normally had knowledge of the world around them.

"State your problem," said the quiet voice in his ear. It seemed strange that this overwhelming expanse of machinery should sum up its thoughts so softly. Then Alvin realized that he was flattering himself; perhaps not even a millionth part of the Central Computer's brain was dealing with him. He was just one of the innumerable incidents that came to its simultaneous attention as it watched over Diaspar.

It was hard to talk to a presence who filled the whole of the space around you. Alvin's words seemed to die in the empty air as soon as he had uttered them.

"What am I?" he asked.

If he had put the question to one of the information machines in the city, he knew what the reply would have been. Indeed, he had often done so, and they had always answered, "You are a Man." But now he was dealing with an intelligence of an altogether different order, and there was no need for painstaking semantic accuracy. The Central Computer would know what he meant, but that did not mean that it would answer him.

Indeed, the reply was exactly what Alvin had feared.

"I cannot answer that question. To do so would be to reveal the purpose of my builders, and hence to nullify it."

"Then my role was planned when the city was laid down?"

"That can be said of all men."

This reply made Alvin pause. It was true enough; the human inhabitants of Diaspar had been designed as carefully as its machines. The fact that he was a Unique gave Alvin rarity, but there was no necessary virtue in that.

He knew that he could learn nothing further here regarding the mystery of his origin. It was useless to try to trick this vast intelligence, or to hope that it would disclose information it had been ordered to conceal. Alvin was not unduly disappointed; he felt that he had already begun to glimpse the truth, and in any case this was not the main purpose of his visit.

He looked at the robot he had brought from Lys, and wondered how to make his next step. It might react violently if it knew what he was planning, so it was essential that it should not overhear what he intended to say to the Central Computer.

"Can you arrange a zone of silence?" he asked.

Instantly, he sensed the unmistakable "dead" feeling, the total blanketing of all sounds, which descended when one was inside such a zone. The voice of the Computer, now curiously flat and sinister, spoke to him: "No one can hear us now. Say what you wish."

Alvin glanced at the robot; it had not moved from its position. Perhaps it suspected nothing, and he had been quite wrong in ever imaginating that it had plans of its own. It might have followed him into Diaspar like a faithful, trusting servant, in which case what he was planning now seemed a particularly churlish trick.

"You have heard how I met this robot," Alvin began. "It must possess priceless knowledge about the past, going back to the days before the city as we know it existed. It may even be able to tell us about the other worlds than Earth, since it followed the Master on his travels. Unfortunately, its speech circuits are blocked. I do not know how effective that block is, but I am asking you to clear it."

His voice sounded dead and hollow as the zone of silence absorbed every word before it could form an echo. He waited, within that invisible and unreverberant void, for his request to be obeyed or rejected.

"Your order involves two problems," replied the Computer. "One is moral, one technical. This robot was designed to obey the orders of a certain man. What right have I to override them, even if I can?"

It was a question which Alvin had anticipated and for which he had prepared several answers.

"We do not know what exact form the Master's prohibition took," he replied. "If you can talk to the robot, you may be able to persuade it that the circumstances in which the block was imposed have now changed."

It was, of course, the obvious approach. Alvin had attempted it himself, without success, but he hoped that the Central Computer, with its infinitely greater mental resources, might accomplish what he had failed to do.

"That depends entirely upon the nature of the block," came the reply. "It is possible to set up a block which, if tampered with, will cause the contents of the memory cells to be erased. However, I think it unlikely that the Master possessed sufficient skill to do that; it requires somewhat specialized techniques. I will ask your machine if an erasing circuit has been set up in its memory units."

"But suppose," said Alvin in sudden alarm, "it causes erasure of memory merely to *ask* if an erasing circuit exists?"

"There is a standard procedure for such cases, which I shall follow. I shall set up secondary instructions, telling the machine to ignore my question if such a situation exists. It is then simple to insure that it will become involved in a logical paradox, so that whether it answers me or whether it says nothing it will be forced to disobey its instructions. In such an event all robots act in the same manner, for their own protection. They clear their input circuits and act as if no question has been asked."

Alvin felt rather sorry that he had raised the point, and after a moment's mental struggle decided that he too would adopt the same tactics and pretend that he had never been asked the question. At least he was reassured on one point—the Central Computer was fully prepared to deal with any booby traps that might exist in the robot's memory units. Alvin had no wish to see the machine reduced to a pile of junk; rather than that, he would willingly return it to Shalmirane with its secrets still intact.

He waited with what patience he could while the silent, impalpable meeting of two intellects took place. Here was an encounter between two minds, both of them created by human genius in the long-lost golden age of its greatest achievement. And now both were beyond the full understanding of any living man.

Many minutes later, the hollow, anechoic voice of the Central Computer spoke again.

"I have established partial contact," it said. "At least I know the nature of the block, and I think I know why it was imposed. There is only one way in which it can be broken. Not until the Great Ones come to Earth will this robot speak again."

"But that is nonsense!" protested Alvin. "The Master's other disciple believed in them, too, and tried to explain what they were like to us. Most of the time it was talking gibberish. The Great Ones never existed, and never will exist."

It seemed a complete impasse, and Alvin felt a sense of bitter, helpless disappointment. He was barred from the truth by the wishes of a man who had been insane, and who had died a billion years ago.

"You may be correct," said the Central Computer, "in saying that the Great Ones never existed. But that does not mean that they never will exist."

There was another long silence while Alvin considered the meaning of this remark, and while the mind of the two robots made their delicate contact again. And then, without any warning, he was in Shalmirane.

Chapter

It was just as he had last seen it, the great ebony bowl drinking the sunlight and reflecting none back to the eye. He stood among the ruins of the fortress, looking out across the lake, whose motionless waters showed that the giant polyp was now a dispersed cloud of animalcules and no longer an organized, sentient being.

The robot was still beside him, but of Hilvar there was no sign. He had no time to wonder what that meant, or to worry about his friend's absence, for almost at once there occurred something so fantastic that all other thoughts were banished from his mind.

The sky began to crack in two. A thin wedge of darkness reached from horizon to zenith, and slowly widened as if night and chaos were breaking in upon the Universe. Inexorably the wedge expanded until it embraced a quarter of the sky. For all his knowledge of the real facts of astronomy, Alvin could not fight against the overwhelming impression that he and his world lay beneath a great blue dome—and that *something* was now breaking through that dome from outside.

The wedge of night had ceased to grow. The powers that

had made it were peering down into the toy universe they had discovered, perhaps conferring among themselves as to whether it was worth their attention. Underneath that cosmic scrutiny, Alvin felt no alarm, no terror. He knew that he was face to face with power and wisdom, before which a man might feel awe but never fear.

And now they had decided—they would waste some fragments of Eternity upon Earth and its peoples. They were coming through the window they had broken in the sky.

Like sparks from some celestial forge, they drifted down to Earth. Thicker and thicker they came, until a waterfall of fire was streaming down from heaven and splashing in pools of liquid light as it reached the ground. Alvin did not need the words that sounded in his ears like a benediction:

"The Great Ones have come."

Thc fire reached him, and it did not burn. It was everywhere, filling the great bowl of Shalmirane with its golden glow. As he watched in wonder, Alvin saw that it was not a featureless flood of light, but that it had form and structure. It began to resolve itself into distinct shapes, to gather into separate fiery whirlpools. The whirlpools spun more and more swiftly on their axes, their centers rising to form columns within which Alvin could glimpse mysterious evanescent shapes. From these glowing totem poles came a faint musical note, infinitely distant and hauntingly sweet.

"The Great Ones have come."

This time there was a reply. As Alvin heard the words: "The servants of the Master greet you. We have been waiting for your coming," he knew that the barriers were down. And in that moment, Shalmirane and its strange visitors were gone, and he was standing once more before the Central Computer in the depths of Diaspar.

It had all been illusion, no more real than the fantasy world of the sagas in which he had spent so many of the hours of his youth. But how had it been created; whence had come the strange images he had seen?

"It was an unusual problem," said the quiet voice of the Central Computer. "I knew that the robot must have some visual conception of the Great Ones in its mind. If I could convince it that the sense impressions it received coincided with that image, the rest would be simple."

"And how did you do that?"

"Basically, by asking the robot what the Great Ones were like, and then seizing the pattern it formed in its thoughts. The pattern was very incomplete, and I had to improvise a good deal. Once or twice the picture I created began to depart badly from the robot's conception, but when that happened I could sense the machine's growing perplexity and modify the image before it became suspicious. You will appreciate that I could employ hundreds of circuits where it could employ only one, and switch from one image to the other so quickly that the change could not be perceived. It was a kind of conjuring trick; I was able to saturate the robot's sensory circuits and also to overwhelm its critical faculties. What you saw was only the final, corrected image—the one which best fitted the Master's revelation. It was crude, but it sufficed. The robot was convinced of its genuineness long enough for the block to be lifted, and in that moment I was able to make complete contact with its mind. It is no longer insane; it will answer any questions you wish."

Alvin was still in a daze; the afterglow of that spurious apocalypse still burned in his mind, and he did not pretend fully to understand the Central Computer's explanation. No matter; a miracle of therapy had been accomplished, and the doors of knowledge had been flung open for him to enter.

Then he remembered the warning that the Central Computer had given him, and asked anxiously: "What about the moral objections you had to overriding the Master's orders?"

"I have discovered why they were imposed. When you examine his life story in detail, as you can now do, you will see that he claimed to have produced many miracles. His disciples believed him, and their conviction added to his power. But, of course, all those miracles had some simple explanation—when indeed they occurred at all. I find it surprising that otherwise intelligent men should have let themselves be deceived in such a manner."

"So the Master was a fraud?"

"No; it is not as simple as that. If he had been a mere impostor, he would never have achieved such success, and his movement would not have lasted so long. He was a good man, and much of what he taught was true and wise. In the end, he believed in his own miracles, but he knew that there was one witness who could refute them. The robot knew all his secrets; it was his mouthpiece and his colleague, yet if it were ever questioned too closely it could destroy the foundations of his power. So he ordered it never to reveal its memories until the last day of the Universe, when the Great Ones would come. It is hard to believe that such a mixture of deception and sincerity could exist in the same man, but such was the case."

Alvin wondered what the robot felt about this escape from its ancient bondage. It was, surely, a sufficiently complex machine to understand such emotions as resentment. It might be angry with the Master for having enslaved it—and equally angry with Alvin and the Central Computer for having tricked it back into sanity.

The zone of silence had been lifted; there was no further need for secrecy. The moment for which Alvin had been waiting had come at last. He turned to the robot, and asked it the question that had haunted him ever since he had heard the story of the Master's saga.

And the robot replied.

Jeserac and the proctors were still waiting patiently when he rejoined them. At the top of the ramp, before they entered the corridor, Alvin looked back across the cave, and the illusion was stronger than ever. Lying beneath him was a dead city of strange white buildings, a city bleached by a fierce light not meant for human eyes. Dead it might be, for it had never lived, but it pulsed with energies more potent than any that had ever quickened organic matter. While the world endured, these silent machines would still be here, never turning their minds from the thoughts that men of genius had given them long ago.

Though Jeserac tried to question Alvin on the way back to the Council Chamber, he learned nothing of his talk with the Central Computer. This was not merely discretion on Alvin's part; he was still too much lost in the wonder of what he had seen, too intoxicated with success, for any coherent conversation. Jeserac had to muster what patience he could, and hope that presently Alvin would emerge from his trance.

The streets of Diaspar were bathed with a light that seemed pale and wan after the glare of the machine city. But Alvin scarcely saw them; he had no regard for the familiar beauty of the great towers drifting past him, or the curious glances of his fellow citizens. It was strange, he thought, how everything that had happened to him led up to this moment. Since he had met Khedron, events seemed to have moved automatically toward a predetermined goal. The monitors—Lys—Shalmirane—at every stage he might have turned aside with unseeing eyes, but something had led him on. Was he the maker of his own destiny, or was he especially favored by Fate? Perhaps it was merely a matter of probabilities, of the operation of the laws of chance. Any man might have found the path his footsteps had traced, and countless times in the past ages others must have gone almost as far. Those earlier Uniques, for example—what had happened to them? Perhaps he was merely the first to be lucky.

All the way back through the streets, Alvin was establishing closer and closer rapport with the machine he had released from its age-long thralldom. It had always been able to receive his thoughts, but previously he had never known whether it would obey any orders he gave it. Now that uncertainty was gone; he could talk to it as he would to another human being, though since he was not alone he directed it not to use verbal speech but such simple thought images as he could understand. He sometimes resented the fact that robots could talk freely to one another on the telepathic level, whereas Man could not—except in Lys. Here was another power that Diaspar had lost or deliberately set aside.

He continued the silent but somewhat one-sided conversation while they were waiting in the anteroom of the Council Chamber. It was impossible not to compare his present situation with that in Lys, when Seranis and her colleagues had tried to bend him to their wills. He hoped that there would be no need for another conflict, but if one should arise he was now far better prepared for it.

His first glance at the faces of the Council members told Alvin what their decision had been. He was neither surprised nor particularly disappointed, and he showed none of the emotion the Councilors might have expected as he listened to the President's summing-up.

"Alvin," began the President, "we have considered with great care the situation which your discovery has brought about, and we have reached this unanimous decision. Because no one wishes any change in our way of life, and because only once in many millions of years is anyone born who is capable of leaving Diaspar even if the means exists, the tunnel system to Lys is unnecessary and may well be a danger. The entrance to the chamber of the moving ways has therefore been sealed.

"Moreover, since it is possible that there may be other ways of leaving the city, a search will be made of the monitor memory units. That search has already begun.

"We have also considered what action, if any, need be taken with regard to you. In view of your youth, and the peculiar circumstances of your origin, it is felt that you cannot be censured for what you have done. Indeed, by disclosing a potential danger to our way of life, you have done the city a service, and we record our appreciation of that fact."

There was a murmur of applause, and expressions of satisfaction spread across the faces of the Councilors. A difficult situation had been speedily dealt with, they had avoided the necessity of reprimanding Alvin, and now they could go their ways again feeling that they, the chief citizens of Diaspar, had done their duty. With reasonably good fortune, it might be centuries before the need arose again.

The President looked expectantly at Alvin; perhaps he hoped that Alvin would reciprocate and express his appreciation of the Council for letting him off so lightly. He was disappointed.

"May I ask one question?" said Alvin politely.

"Of course."

"The Central Computer, I take it, approved of your action?"

In the ordinary way, this would have been an impertinent question to ask. The Council was not supposed to justify its decisions or explain how it had arrived at them. But Alvin himself had been taken into the confidence of the Central Computer, for some strange reason of its own. He was in a privileged position.

The question clearly caused some embarrassment, and the reply came rather reluctantly.

"Naturally we consulted with the Central Computer. It told us to use our own judgment."

Alvin had expected as much. The Central Computer would have been conferring with the Council at the same moment as it was talking to him—at the same moment, in fact, as it was attending to a million other tasks in Diaspar. It knew, as did Alvin, that any decision the Council now made was of no importance. The future had passed utterly beyond its control at the very moment when, in happy ignorance, it had decided that the crisis had been safely dealt with.

Alvin felt no sense of superiority, none of the sweet anticipation of impending triumph, as he looked at these foolish old men who thought themselves the rulers of Diaspar. He had seen the real ruler of the city, and had spoken to it in the grave silence of its brilliant, buried world. That was an encounter which had burned most of the arrogance out of his soul, but enough was left for a final venture that would surpass all that had gone before.

As he took leave of the Council, he wondered if they were surprised at his quiet acquiescence, his lack of indignation at the closing of the path to Lys. The proctors did not accompany him; he was no longer under observation, at least in so open a manner. Only Jeserac followed him out of the Council Chamber and into the colored, crowded streets.

"Well, Alvin," he said. "You were on your best behavior, but you cannot deceive me. What are you planning?"

Alvin smiled.

"I knew that you would suspect something; if you will come with me, I will show you why the subway to Lys is no longer important. And there is another experiment I want to try; it will not harm you, but you may not like it."

"Very well. I am still supposed to be your tutor, but it seems that the roles are now reversed. Where are you taking me?"

"We are going to the Tower of Loranne, and I am going to show you the world outside Diaspar."

Jeserac paled, but he stood his ground. Then, as if not trusting himself with words, he gave a stiff little nod and followed Alvin out onto the smoothly gliding surface of the moving way.

Jeserac showed no fear as they walked along the tunnel through which that cold wind blew forever into Diaspar. The tunnel had changed now; the stone grille that had blocked access to the outer world was gone. It served no structural purpose, and the Central Computer had removed it without comment at Alvin's request. Later, it might instruct the monitors to remember the grille again and bring it back into existence. But for the moment the tunnel gaped unfenced and unguarded in the sheer outer wall of the city.

Not until Jeserac had almost reached the end of the air shaft did he realize that the outer world was now upon him. He looked at the widening circle of sky, and his steps became more and more uncertain until they finally slowed to a halt. Alvin remembered how Alystra had turned and fled from this same spot, and he wondered if he could induce Jeserac to go any further.

"I am only asking you to *look,*" he begged, "not to leave the city. Surely you can manage to do that!"

In Airlee, during his brief stay, Alvin has seen a mother teaching her child to walk. He was irresistibly reminded of this as he coaxed Jeserac along the corridor, making encouraging remarks as his tutor advanced foot by reluctant foot. Jeserac, unlike Khedron, was no coward. He was prepared to fight against his compulsion, but it was a desperate struggle. Alvin was almost as exhausted as the older man by the time he had succeeded in getting Jeserac to a point where he could see the whole, uninterrupted sweep of the desert.

Once there, the interest and strange beauty of the scene, so alien to all that Jeserac had ever known in this or any previous existence, seemed to overcome his fears. He was clearly fascinated by the immense vista of the rolling sand dunes and the far-off, ancient hills. It was late afternoon, and in a little while all this land would be visited by the night that never came to Diaspar.

"I asked you to come here," said Alvin, speaking quickly as if he could hardly control his impatience, "because I realize that you have earned more right than anyone to see where my travels have led me. I wanted you to see the desert, and I also want you to be a witness, so that the Council will know what I have done.

"As I told the Council, I brought this robot home from Lys in the hope that the Central Computer would be able to break the block that has been imposed on its memories by the man known as the Master. By a trick which I still don't fully understand, the Computer did that. Now I have access to all the memories in this machine, as well as to the special skills that had been designed into it. I'm going to use one of those skills now. Watch."

On a soundless order which Jeserac could only guess, the robot floated out of the tunnel entrance, picked up speed, and within seconds was no more than a distant metallic gleam in the sunlight. It was flying low over the desert, across the sand dunes that lay crisscrossed like frozen waves. Jeserac had the unmistakable impression that it was searching—though for what, he could not imagine.

Then, abruptly, the glittering speck soared away from the desert and came to rest a thousand feet above the ground. At the same moment, Alvin gave an explosive sigh of satisfaction and relief. He glanced quickly at Jeserac, as if to say: "This is it!"

At first, not knowing what to expect, Jeserac could see no change. Then, scarcely believing his eyes, he saw that a cloud of dust was slowly rising from the desert.

Nothing is more terrible than movement where no movement should ever be again, but Jeserac was beyond surprise or fear as the sand dunes began to slide apart. Beneath the desert something was stirring like a giant awakening from its sleep, and presently there came to Jeserac's ears the rumble of falling earth and the shriek of rock split asunder by irresistible force. Then, suddenly, a great geyser of sand erupted hundreds of feet into the air and the ground was hidden from sight.

Slowly the dust began to settle back into a jagged wound torn across the face of the desert. But Jeserac and Alvin still kept their eyes fixed steadfastly upon the open sky, which a little while ago had held only the waiting robot. Now at last Jeserac knew why Alvin had seemed so indifferent to the decision of the Council, why he had shown no emotion when he was told that the subway to Lys had been closed.

The covering of earth and rock could blur but could not conceal the proud lines of the ship still ascending from the riven desert. As Jeserac watched, it slowly turned toward them until it had foreshortened to a circle. Then, very leisurely, the circle started to expand.

Alvin began to speak, rather quickly, as if the time were short.

"This robot was designed to be the Master's companion and servant—and, above all, the pilot of his ship. Before he came to Lys, he landed at the Port of Diaspar, which now lies out there beneath those sands. Even in his day, it must have been largely deserted; I think that the Master's ship was one of the last ever to reach Earth. He lived for a while in Diaspar before he went to Shalmirane; the way must still have been open in those days. But he never needed the ship again, and all these ages it has been waiting out there beneath the sands. Like Diaspar itself, like this robot—like everything that the builders of the past considered really important—it was preserved by its own eternity circuits. As long as it had a source of power, it could never wear out or be destroyed; the image carried in its memory cells would never fade, and that image controlled its physical structure."

The ship was now very close, as the controlling robot guided it toward the tower. Jeserac could see that it was about a hundred feet long and sharply pointed at both ends. There appeared to be no windows or other openings, though the thick layer of earth made it impossible to be certain of this.

Suddenly they were spattered with dirt as a section of the hull opened outward, and Jeserac caught a glimpse of a small, bare room with a second door at its far end. The ship was hanging only a foot away from the mouth of the air vent, which it had approached very cautiously like a sensitive, living thing.

"Good-bye, Jeserac," said Alvin. "I cannot go back into Diaspar to say farewell to my friends: please do that for me. Tell Eriston and Etania that I hope to return soon; if I do not, I am grateful for all that they did. And I am grateful to you, even though you may not approve of the way I have applied your lessons.

"And as for the Council—tell it that a road that has once been opened cannot be closed again merely by passing a resolution."

The ship was now only a dark stain against the sky, and of a sudden Jeserac lost it altogether. He never saw its going, but presently there echoed down from the heavens the most awe-inspiring of all the sounds that Man has ever made—the long-drawn thunder of air falling, mile after mile, into a tunnel of vacuum drilled suddenly across the sky.

Even when the last echoes had died away into the desert, Jeserac never moved. He was thinking of the boy who had gone—for to Jeserac, Alvin would always be a child, the only one to come into Diaspar since the cycle of birth and death had been broken, so long ago. Alvin would never grow up; to him the whole Universe was a plaything, a puzzle to be unraveled for his own amusement. In his play he had now found the ultimate, deadly toy which might wreck what was left of human civilization—but whatever the outcome, to him it would still be a game.

The sun was now low on the horizon, and a chill wind was blowing from the desert. But Jeserac still waited, conquering his fears; and presently for the first time in his life he saw the stars.

Chapter

Even in Diaspar, Alvin had seldom seen such luxury as that which lay before him when the inner door of the air lock slid aside. Whatever else he had been, at least the Master was no ascetic. Not until some time later did it occur to Alvin that all this comfort might be no vain extravagance; this little world must have been the Master's only home on many long journeys among the stars.

There were no visible controls of any kind, but the large oval screen which completely covered the far wall showed that his was no ordinary room. Ranged in a half circle before it were three low couches; the rest of the cabin was occupied by two small tables and a number of padded chairs—some of them obviously not designed for human occupants.

When he had made himself comfortable in front of the screen, Alvin looked around for the robot. To his surprise, it had disappeared; then he located it, neatly stowed away in a recess beneath the curved ceiling. It had brought the Master across space to Earth and then, as his servant, followed him into Lys. Now it was ready, as if the intervening aeons had never been, to carry out its old duties once again.

Alvin threw it an experimental command, and the great

screen shivered into life. Before him was the Tower of Loranne, curiously foreshortened and apparently lying on its side. Further trials gave him views of the sky, of the city, and of great expanses of desert. The definition was brilliantly, almost unnaturally, clear, although there seemed to be no actual magnification. Alvin experimented for a little while until he could obtain any view he wished; then he was ready to start.

"Take me to Lys." The command was a simple one, but how could the ship obey it when he himself had no idea of the direction? Alvin had not considered this, and when it did occur to him the machine was already moving across the desert at a tremendous speed. He shrugged his shoulders, accepting thankfully the fact that he now had servants wiser than himself.

It was difficult to judge the scale of the picture racing up the screen, but many miles must be passing every minute. Not far from the city the color of the ground had changed abruptly to a dull gray, and Alvin knew that he was passing over the bed of one of the lost oceans. Once Diaspar must have been very near the sea, though there had never been any hint of this even in the most ancient records. Old though the city was, the oceans must have passed away long before its founding.

Hundreds of miles later, the ground rose sharply and the desert returned. Once Alvin halted his ship above a curious pattern of intersecting lines, showing faintly through the blanket of sand. For a moment it puzzled him; then he realized that he was looking down upon the ruins of some forgotten city. He did not stay for long; it was heartbreaking to think that billions of men had left no other trace of their existence save these furrows in the sand.

The smooth curve of the horizon was breaking up at last, crinkling into mountains that were beneath him almost as soon as they were glimpsed. The machine was slowing now, slowing and falling to earth in a great arc a hundred miles in length. And then below him was Lys, its forests and endless rivers forming a scene of such incomparable beauty that for a while he could go no further. To the east, the land was shadowed and the great lakes floated upon it like pools of darker night. But toward the sunset, the waters danced and sparkled with light, throwing back toward him such colors as he had never imagined.

It was not difficult to locate Airlee—which was fortunate, for the robot could guide him no further. Alvin had expected this, and felt a little glad to have discovered some limits to its powers. It was unlikely that it would ever have heard of Airlee, so the position of the village would never have been stored in its memory cells.

After a little experimenting, Alvin brought his ship to rest on the hillside that had given him his first glimpse of Lys. It was quite easy to control the machine; he had only to indicate his general desires and the robot attended to the details. It would, he imagined, ignore dangerous or impossible orders, though he had no intention of giving any if he could avoid it. Alvin was fairly certain that no one could have seen his arrival. He thought this rather important, for he had no desire to engage in mental combat with Seranis again. His plans were still somewhat vague, but he was running no risks until he had established friendly relations. The robot could act as his ambassador, while he remained safely in the ship.

He met no one on the road to Airlee. It was strange to sit in the spaceship while his field of vision moved effortlessly along the familiar path, and the whispering of the forest sounded in his ears. As yet he was unable to identify himself fully with the robot, and the strain of controlling it was still considerable.

It was nearly dark when he reached Airlee, and the little houses were floating in pools of light. Alvin kept to the shadows and had almost reached Seranis's home before he was discovered. Suddenly there was an angry, high-pitched buzzing and his view was blocked by a flurry of wings. He recoiled involuntarily before the onslaught; then he realized what had happened. Krif was once again expressing his resentment of anything that flew without wings.

Not wishing to hurt the beautiful but stupid creature, Alvin brought the robot to a halt and endured as best he could the blows that seemed to be raining upon him. Though he was sitting in comfort a mile away, he could not avoid flinching and was glad when Hilvar came out to investigate.

At his master's approach Kris departed, still buzzing balefully. In the silence that followed, Hilvar stood looking at the robot for a while. Then he smiled.

"Hello, Alvin," he said. "I'm glad you've come back. Or are you still in Diaspar?"

Not for the first time, Alvin felt an envious admiration for the speed and precision of Hilvar's mind.

"No," he said, wondering as he did so how clearly the robot echoed his voice. "I'm in Airlee, not very far away. But I'm staying here for the present."

Hilvar laughed.

"I think that's just as well. Seranis has forgiven you, but as for the Assembly—well, that is another matter. There is a conference going on here at the moment—the first we have ever had in Airlee."

"Do you mean," asked Alvin, "that your Councilors have actually come here? With your telepathic powers, I should have thought that meetings weren't necessary."

"They are rare, but there are times when they are felt desirable. I don't know the exact nature of the crisis, but three Senators are already here and the rest are expected soon."

Alvin could not help smiling at the way in which events in Diaspar had been mirrored here. Wherever he went, he now seemed to be leaving a trail of consternation and alarm behind him.

"I think it would be a good idea," he said, "if I could talk to this Assembly of yours—as long as I can do so in safety."

"It would be safe for you to come here yourself," said Hilvar, "if the Assembly promises not to try and take over your mind again. Otherwise, I should stay where you are. I'll lead your robot to the Senators—they'll be rather upset to see it."

Alvin felt that keen but treacherous sense of enjoyment and exhilaration as he followed Hilvar into the house. He was meeting the rulers of Lys on more equal terms now; though he felt no rancor against them, it was very pleasant to know that he was now master of the situation, and in command of powers which even yet he had not fully turned to account.

The door of the conference room was locked, and it was some time before Hilvar could attract attention. The minds of the Senators, it seemed, were so completely engaged that it was difficult to break into their deliberations. Then the walls slid reluctantly aside, and Alvin moved his robot swiftly forward into the chamber.

The three Senators froze in their seats as he floated toward them, but only the slightest flicker of surprise crossed Seranis's face. Perhaps Hilvar had already sent her a warning, or perhaps she had expected that, sooner or later, Alvin would return.

"Good evening," he said politely, as if this vicarious entry were the most natural thing in the world. "I've decided to come back."

Their surprise certainly exceeded his expectations. One of the Senators, a young man with graying hair, was the first to recover.

"How did you get here?" he gasped.

The reason for his astonishment was obvious. Just as Diaspar had done, so Lys must also have put the subway out of action.

"Why, I came here just as I did last time," said Alvin, unable to resist amusing himself at their expense.

Two of the Senators looked fixedly at the third, who spread his hands in a gesture of baffled resignation. Then the young man who had addressed him before spoke again.

"Didn't you have any—difficulty?" he asked.

"None at all," said Alvin, determined to increase their confusion. He saw that he had succeeded.

"I've come back," he continued, "under my own free will, and because I have some important news for you. However, in view of our previous disagreement I'm remaining out of sight for the moment. If I appear personally, will you promise not to try to restrict my movements again?"

No one said anything for a while, and Alvin wondered what thoughts were being silently interchanged. Then Seranis spoke for them all.

"We won't attempt to control you again—though I don't think we were very successful before."

"Very well," replied Alvin. "I will come to Airlee as quickly as I can."

He waited until the robot had returned; then, very carefully, he gave the machine its instructions and made it repeat them back to him. Seranis, he was quite sure, would not break her word; nevertheless he preferred to safeguard his line of retreat.

The air lock closed silently behind him as he left the ship. A moment later there was a whispering "hiss . . ." like a long-drawn gasp of surprise, as the air made way for the rising ship. For an instant a dark shadow blotted out the stars; then the ship was gone.

Not until it had vanished did Alvin realize that he had made a slight but annoying miscalculation of the kind that could bring the best-laid plans to disaster. He had forgotten that the robot's senses were more acute than his own, and the night was far darker than he had expected. More than once he lost the path completely, and several times he barely avoided colliding with trees. It was almost pitch-black in the forest, and once something quite large came toward him through the undergrowth. There was the faintest crackling of twigs, and two emerald eyes were looking steadfastly at him from the level of his waist. He called softly, and an incredibly long tongue rasped across his hand. A moment later a powerful body rubbed affectionately against him and departed without a sound. He had no idea what it could be.

Presently the lights of the village were shining through the trees ahead, but he no longer needed their guidance for the path beneath his feet had now become a river of dim blue fire. The moss upon which he was walking was luminous, and his footprints left dark patches which slowly disappeared behind him. It was a beautiful and entrancing sight, and when Alvin stooped to pluck some of the strange moss it glowed for minutes in his cupped hands before its radiance died.

Hilvar met him for the second time outside the house, and for the second time introduced him to Seranis and the Senators. They greeted him with a kind of wary and reluctant respect; if they wondered where the robot had gone, they made no comment.

"I'm very sorry," Alvin began, "that I had to leave your country in such an undignified fashion. It may interest you to know that it was nearly as difficult to escape from Diaspar." He let that remark sink in, then added quickly, "I have told my people all about Lys, and I did my best to give a favorable impression. But Diaspar will have nothing to do with you. In spite of all I could say, it wishes to avoid contamination with an inferior culture."

It was most satisfying to watch the Senators' reactions, and even the urbane Seranis colored slightly at his words. If he could make Lys and Diaspar sufficiently annoyed with each other, thought Alvin, his problem would be more than half solved. Each would be so anxious to prove the superiority if its own way of life that the barriers between them would soon go down.

"Why have you come back to Lys?" asked Seranis.

"Because I want to convince you, as well as Diaspar, that you have made a mistake." He did not add his other reason—

that in Lys was the only friend of whom he could be certain and whose help he now needed.

The Senators were still silent, waiting for him to continue, and he knew that looking through their eyes and listening through their ears were many other unseen intelligences. He was the representative of Diaspar, and the whole of Lys was judging him by what he might say. It was a great responsibility, and he felt humbled before it. He marshaled his thoughts and then began to speak.

His theme was Diaspar. He painted the city as he had last seen it, dreaming on the breast of the desert, its towers glowing like captive rainbows against the sky. From the treasure house of memory he recalled the songs that the poets of old had written in praise of Diaspar, and he spoke of the countless men who had spent their lives to increase its beauty. No one, he told them, could ever exhaust the city's treasures, however long they lived; always there would be something new. For a while he described some of the wonders which the men of Diaspar had wrought; he tried to make them catch a glimpse at least of the loveliness that the artists of the past had created for men's eternal admiration. And he wondered a little wistfully if it were indeed true that the music of Diaspar was the last sound that Earth had ever broadcast to the stars.

They heard him to the end without interruption or questioning. When he had finished it was very late, and Alvin felt more tired than he could ever before remember. The strain and excitement of the long day had told on him at last, and quite suddenly he was asleep.

When he woke, he was in an unfamiliar room and it was some moments before he remembered that he was no longer in Diaspar. As consciousness returned, so the light grew around him, until presently he was bathed in the soft, cool radiance of the morning sun, streaming through the now transparent walls. He lay in drowsy half-awareness, recalling the events of the previous day and wondering what forces he had now set in motion.

With a soft, musical sound, one of the walls began to pleat itself up in a manner so complicated that it eluded the eye. Hilvar stepped through the opening that had been formed and looked at Alvin with an expression half of amusement, half of serious concern.

"Now that you're awake, Alvin," he said, "perhaps you'll at least tell me what your next move is, and how you managed to return here. The Senators are just leaving to look at the subway; they can't understand how you managed to come back through it. Did you?"

Alvin jumped out of bed and stretched himself mightily.

"Perhaps we'd better overtake them," he said. "I don't want to make them waste their time. As for the question you asked me—in a little while I'll show you the answer to that."

They had almost reached the lake before they overtook the three Senators, and both parties exchanged slightly self-conscious greetings. The Committee of Investigation could see that Alvin knew where it was going, and the unexpected encounter had clearly put it somewhat at a loss.

"I'm afraid I misled you last night," said Alvin cheerfully. "I didn't come to Lys by the old route, so your attempt to close it was quite unnecessary. As a matter of fact, the Council of Diaspar also closed it at their end, with equal lack of success."

The Senators' faces were a study in perplexity as one solution after another chased through their brains.

"Then how *did* you get here?" said the leader. There was a sudden, dawning comprehension in his eyes, and Alvin could tell that he had begun to guess the truth. He wondered if he had intercepted the command his mind had just sent winging across the mountains. But he said nothing, and merely pointed in silence to the northern sky.

Too swiftly for the eye to follow, a needle of silver light arched across the mountains, leaving a mile-long trail of incandescence. Twenty thousand feet above Lys, it stopped. There was no deceleration, no slow braking of its colossal speed. It came to a halt instantly, so that the eye that had been following it moved on across a quarter of the heavens before the brain could arrest its motion. Down from the skies crashed a mighty petal of thunder, the sound of air battered and smashed by the violence of the ship's passage. A little later the ship itself, gleaming splendidly in the sunlight, came to rest upon the hillside a hundred yards away.

It was difficult to say who was the most surprised, but Alvin was the first to recover. As they walked—very nearly running—toward the spaceship, he wondered if it normally traveled in this meteoric fashion. The thought was disconcerting, although there had been no sensation of movement on his voyage. Considerably more puzzling, however, was the fact that a day ago this resplendent creature had been hidden beneath a thick layer of iron-hard rock—the coating it had still retained when it had torn itself loose from the desert. Not until Alvin had reached the ship, and burned his fingers by incautiously resting them on the hull, did he understand what had happened. Near the stern there were still traces of earth, but it had been fused into lava. All the rest had been swept away, leaving uncovered the stubborn shell which neither time nor any natural force could ever touch.

With Hilvar by his side, Alvin stood in the open door and looked back at the silent Senators. He wondered what they were thinking—what, indeed, the whole of Lys was thinking. From their expressions, it almost seemed as if they were beyond thought.

"I am going to Shalmirane," said Alvin, "and I will be back in Airlee within an hour or so. But that is only a beginning, and while I am away, there is a thought I would leave with you.

"This is no ordinary flyer of the kind in which men traveled over the Earth. It is a spaceship, one of the fastest ever built. If you want to know where I found it, you will find the answer in Diaspar. But you will have to go there, for Diaspar will never come to you."

He turned to Hilvar, and gestured to the door. Hilvar hesitated for a moment only, looking back once at the familiar scenes around him. Then he stepped forward into the air lock.

The Senators watched until the ship, now moving quite slowly—for it had only a little way to go—had disappeared into the south. Then the gray-haired young man who led the group shrugged his shoulders philosophically and turned to one of his colleagues.

"You've always opposed us for wanting change," he said, "and so far you have won. But I don't think the future lies with either of our groups now. Lys and Diaspar have both come to the end of an era, and we must make the best of it."

"I am afraid you are right," came the gloomy reply. "This is a crisis, and Alvin knew what he was saying when he told us to go to Diaspar. They know about us now, so there is no further purpose in concealment. I think we had better get in touch with our cousins—we may find them more anxious to cooperate now."

"But the subway is closed at both ends!"

"We can open ours; it will not be long before Diaspar does the same."

The minds of the Senators, those in Airlee and those scattered over the whole width of Lys, considered the proposal and disliked it heartily. But they saw no alternative.

Sooner than he had any right to expect, the seed that Alvin had planted was beginning to flower.

The mountains were still swimming in shadow when they reached Shalmirane. From their height the great bowl of the fortress looked very small; it seemed impossible that the fate of Earth had once depended on that tiny ebony circle.

When Alvin brought the ship to rest among the ruins by the lakeside, the desolation crowded in upon him, chilling his soul. He opened the air lock, and the stillness of the place crept into the ship. Hilvar, who had scarcely spoken during the entire flight, asked quietly: "Why have you come here again?"

Alvin did not answer until they had almost reached the edge of the lake. Then he said: "I wanted to show you what this ship was like. And I also hoped that the polyp might be in existence once more; I feel I owe it a debt, and I want to tell it what I've discovered."

"In that case," replied Hilvar, "you will have to wait. You have come back much too soon."

Alvin had expected that; it had been a remote chance and he was not disappointed that it had failed. The waters of the lake were perfectly still, no longer beating with that steady rhythm that had so puzzled them on their first visit. He knelt down at the water's edge and peered into the cold, dark depths.

Tiny translucent bells, trailing almost invisible tentacles, were drifting to and fro beneath the surface. Alvin plunged in his hand and scooped one up. He dropped it at once, with a slight exclamation of annoyance. It had stung him.

Some day—perhaps years, perhaps centuries in the future—these mindless jellies would reassemble and the great polyp would be reborn as its memories linked together and its consciousness flashed into existence once again. Alvin wondered how it would receive the discoveries he had made; it might not be pleased to learn the truth about the Master. Indeed, it might refuse to admit that all its ages of patient waiting had been in vain.

Yet had they? Deluded though these creatures might have been, their long vigil had at last brought its reward. As if by a miracle, they had saved from the past knowledge that else might have been lost forever. Now they could rest at last, and their creed could go the way of a million other faiths that had once thought themselves eternal.

Chapter

Hilvar and Alvin walked in reflective silence back to the waiting ship, and presently the fortress was once more a dark shadow among the hills. It dwindled swiftly until it became a black and lidless eye, staring up forever into space, and soon they lost it in the great panorama of Lys.

Alvin did nothing to check the machine; still they rose until the whole of Lys lay spread beneath them, a green island in an ocher sea. Never before had Alvin been so high; when finally they came to rest the whole crescent of the Earth was visible below. Lys was very small now, only an emerald stain against the rusty desert—but far around the curve of the globe something was glittering like a man-colored jewel. And so for the first time, Hilvar saw the city of Diaspar.

They sat for a long while watching the Earth turn beneath them. Of all Man's ancient powers, this surely was the one he could least afford to lose. Alvin wished he could show the world as he saw it now to the rulers of Lys and Diaspar.

"Hilvar," he said at last, "do you think that what I'm doing is right?"

The question surprised Hilvar, who did not suspect the sudden doubts that sometimes overwhelmed his friend, and still knew nothing of Alvin's meeting with the Central Computer and the impact which that had had upon his mind. It was not an easy question to answer dispassionately; like Khedron, though with less cause, Hilvar felt that his own character was becoming submerged. He was being sucked helplessly into the vortex which Alvin left behind him on his way through life.

"I believe you are right," Hilvar answered slowly. "Our two peoples have been separated for long enough." That, he thought, was true, though he knew that his own feelings must bias his reply. But Alvin was still worried.

"There's one problem that bothers me," he said in a troubled voice, "and that's the difference in our life spans." He said no more, but each knew what the other was thinking.

"I've been worried about that as well," Hilvar admitted, "but I think the problem will solve itself in time when our people get to know each other again. We can't *both* be right—our lives may be too short, and yours are certainly far too long. Eventually there will be a compromise."

Alvin wondered. That way, it was true, lay the only hope, but the ages of transition would be hard indeed. He remembered again those bitter words of Seranis: *"Both he and I will have been dead for centuries while you are still a young man."* Very well; he would accept the conditions. Even in Diaspar all friendships lay under the same shadow; whether it was a hundred or a million years away made little difference at the end.

Alvin knew, with a certainty that passed all logic, that the welfare of the race demanded the mingling of these two cultures; in such a cause individual happiness was unimportant. For a moment Alvin saw humanity as something more than the living background of his own life, and he accepted without flinching the unhappiness his choice must one day bring.

Beneath them the world continued on its endless turning. Sensing his friend's mood, Hilvar said nothing, until presently Alvin broke the silence.

"When I first left Diaspar," he said, "I did not know what I hoped to find. Lys would have satisfied me once—more than satisfied me—yet now everything on Earth seems so small and unimportant. Each discovery I've made has raised bigger questions, and opened up wider horizons. I wonder where it will end. . . ."

Hilvar had never seen Alvin in so thoughtful a mood, and did not wish to interrupt his soliloquy. He had learned a great deal about his friend in the last few minutes.

"The robot told me," Alvin continued, "that this ship can reach the Seven Suns in less than a day. Do you think I should go?"

"Do you think I could stop you?" Hilvar replied quietly.

Alvin smiled.

"That's no answer," he said. "Who knows what lies out there in space? The Invaders may have left the Universe, but there may be other intelligences unfriendly to Man."

"Why should there be?" Hilvar asked. "That's one of the questions our philosophers have been debating for ages. A truly intelligent race is not likely to be unfriendly."

"But the Invaders—?"

"They are an enigma, I admit. If they were really vicious, they must have destroyed themselves by now. And even if they have not—" Hilvar pointed to the unending deserts below. "Once we had an Empire. What have we now that they would covet?"

Alvin was a little surprised that anyone else shared this point of view, so closely allied to his own.

"Do all your people think this way?" he asked.

"Only a minority. The average person doesn't worry about it, but would probably say that if the Invaders really wanted to destroy Earth, they'd have done it ages ago. I don't suppose anyone is actually afraid of them."

"Things are very different in Diaspar," said Alvin. "My people are great cowards. They are terrified of leaving their city, and I don't know what will happen when they hear that I've located a spaceship. Jeserac will have told the Council by now, and I would like to know what it is doing."

"I can tell you that. It is preparing to receive its first delegation from Lys. Seranis has just told me."

Alvin looked again at the screen. He could span the distance between Lys and Diaspar in a single glance; though one of his aims had been achieved, that seemed a small matter now. Yet he was very glad; now, surely, the long ages of sterile isolation would be ending.

The knowledge that he had succeeded in what had once been his main mission cleared away the last doubts from Alvin's mind. He had fulfilled his purpose here on Earth, more swiftly and more thoroughly than he had dared to hope. The way lay clear ahead for what might be his last, and would certainly be his greatest, adventure.

"Will you come with me, Hilvar?" he said, all too conscious of what he was asking.

Hilvar looked at him steadfastly.

"There was no need to ask that, Alvin," he said. "I told Seranis and all my friends that I was leaving with you—a good hour ago."

They were very high when Alvin gave the robot its final instructions. The ship had come almost to rest and the Earth was perhaps a thousand miles below, nearly filling the sky. It looked very uninviting; Alvin wondered how many ships in the past had hovered here for a little while and then continued on their way.

There was an appreciable pause, as if the robot was checking controls and circuits that had not been used for geological ages. Then came a very faint sound, the first that Alvin had ever heard from a machine. It was a tiny humming, which soared swiftly octave by octave until it was lost at the edge of hearing. There was no sense of change of motion, but suddenly he noticed that the stars were drifting across the screen. The Earth reappeared, and rolled past—then appeared again, in a slightly different position. The ship was "hunting," swinging in space like a compass needle seeking the north. For minutes the skies turned and twisted around them, until at last the ship came to rest, a giant projectile aimed at the stars.

Centered in the screen the great ring of the Seven Suns lay in its rainbow-hued beauty. A little of Earth was still visible as a dark crescent edged with the gold and crimson of the sunset. Something was happening now, Alvin knew, beyond all his experience. He waited, gripping his seat, while the seconds drifted by and the Seven Suns glittered on the screen.

There was no sound, only a sudden wrench that seemed to blur the vision—but Earth had vanished as if a giant hand had whipped it away. They were alone in space, alone with the stars and a strangely shrunken sun. Earth was gone as though it had never been.

Again came that wrench, and with it now the faintest murmur of sound, as if for the first time the generators were exerting some appreciable fraction of their power. Yet for a moment it seemed that nothing had happened; then Alvin realized that the sun itself was gone and that the stars were creeping slowly past the ship. He looked back for an instant and saw—nothing. All the heavens behind had vanished utterly, obliterated by a hemisphere of night. Even as he watched, he could see the stars plunge into it, to disappear like sparks falling upon water. The ship was traveling far faster than light, and Alvin knew that the familiar space of Earth and sun held him no more.

When that sudden, vertiginous wrench came for the third time, his heart almost stopped beating. The strange blurring of vision was unmistakable now: for a moment his surrounding seemed distorted out of recognition. The meaning of that distortion came to him in a flash of insight he could not explain. *It was real, and no delusion of his eyes.* Somehow he was catching, as he passed through the thin film of the Present, a glimpse of the changes that were occurring in the space around him.

At the same instant the murmur of the generators rose to a roar that shook the ship—a sound doubly impressive for it was the first cry of protest that Alvin had ever heard from a machine. Then it was all over, and the sudden silence seemed to ring in his ears. The great generators had done their work; they would not be needed again until the end of the voyage. The stars ahead flared blue-white and vanished into the ultraviolet. Yet by some magic of Science or Nature the Seven Suns were still visible, though now their positions and colors were subtly changed. The ship was hurtling toward them along a tunnel of darkness, beyond the boundaries of space and time, at a velocity too enormous for the mind to contemplate.

It was hard to believe that they had now been flung out of the Solar System at a speed which unless it were checked would soon take them through the heart of the Galaxy and into the greater emptiness beyond. Neither Alvin nor Hilvar could conceive the real immensity of their journey; the great sagas of exploration had completely changed Man's outlook toward the Universe and even now, millions of centuries later, the ancient traditions had not wholly died. There had once been a ship, legend whispered, that had circumnavigated the Cosmos between the rising and the setting of the sun. The billions of miles between the stars meant nothing before such speeds. To Alvin this voyage was very little greater, and perhaps less dangerous, than his first journey to Lys.

It was Hilvar who voiced both their thoughts as the Seven Suns slowly brightened ahead.

"Alvin," he remarked, "that formation can't possibly be natural."

The other nodded.

"I've thought that for years, but it still seems fantastic."

"The system may not have been built by Man," agreed Hilvar, "but intelligence must have created it. Nature could never have formed that perfect circle of stars, all equally brilliant. And there's nothing else in the visible Universe like the Central Sun."

"Why should such a thing have been made, then?"

"Oh, I can think of many reasons. Perhaps it's a signal, so that any strange ship entering our Universe will know where to look for life. Perhaps it marks the center of galactic administration. Or perhaps—and somehow I feel that this is the real explanation—it's simply the greatest of all works of art. But it's foolish to speculate now. In a few hours we shall know the truth."

"We shall know the truth." Perhaps, thought Alvin—but how much of it shall we ever know? It seemed strange that now, while he was leaving Diaspar, and indeed Earth itself, at a speed beyond all comprehension, his mind should turn once more to the mystery of his origin. Yet perhaps it was not so surprising; he had learned many things since he had first arrived in Lys, but until now he had not had a single moment for quiet reflection.

There was nothing he could do now but sit and wait; his immediate future was controlled by the wonderful machine—surely one of the supreme engineering achievements of all time—that was now carrying him into the heart of the Universe. Now was the moment for thought and reflection, whether he wished it or not. But first he would tell Hilvar all that had happened to him since their hasty parting only two days before.

Hilvar absorbed the tale without comment and without asking for any explanations; he seemed to understand at once everything that Alvin described, and showed no signs of surprise even when he heard of the meeting with the Central Computer and the operation it had performed upon the robot's mind. It was not that he was incapable of wonder, but that the history of the past was full of marvels that could match anything in Alvin's story.

"It's obvious," he said, when Alvin had finished talking, "that the Central Computer must have received special instructions regarding you when it was built. By now, you must have guessed why."

"I think so. Khedron gave me part of the answer when he explained how the men who designed Diaspar had taken steps to prevent it becoming decadent."

"Do you think you—and the other Uniques before you—are part of the social mechanism which prevents complete stagnation? So that whereas the Jesters are short-term correcting factors, you and your kind are long-term ones?"

Hilvar had expressed the idea better than Alvin could, yet this was not exactly what he had in mind.

"I believe the truth is more complicated than that. It almost looks as if there was a conflict of opinion when the city was built, between those who wanted to shut it off completely from the outside world, and those who wanted to maintain some contacts. The first faction won, but the others did not admit defeat. I think Yarlan Zey must have been one of their leaders, but he was not powerful enough to act openly. He did his best, by leaving the subway in existence and by insuring that at long intervals someone would come out of the Hall of Creation who did not share the fears of all his fellow men. In fact, I wonder—" Alvin paused, and his eyes veiled with thought so that for a moment he seemed oblivious of his surroundings.

"What are you thinking now?" asked Hilvar.

"It's just occurred to me—perhaps *I* am Yarlan Zey. It's perfectly possible. He may have fed his personality into the Memory Banks, relying on it to break the mold of Diaspar before it was too firmly established. One day I must discover what happened to those earlier Uniques; that may help fill in the gaps in the picture."

"And Yarlan Zey—or whoever it was—also instructed the Central Computer to give special assistance to the Uniques, whenever they were created," mused Hilvar, following this line of logic.

"That's right. The ironic thing is that I could have got all the information I needed direct from the Central Computer, without any assistance from poor Khedron. It would have told me more than it ever told him. But there's no doubt that he saved me a good deal of time, and taught me much that I could never have learned by myself."

"I think your theory covers all the known facts," said Hilvar cautiously. "Unfortunately, it still leaves wide open the biggest problem of all—the original purpose of Diaspar. Why did your people try to pretend that the outer world didn't exist? *That's* a question I'd like to see answered."

"It's a question I intend to answer," replied Alvin. "But I don't know when—or how."

So they argued and dreamed, while hour by hour the Seven Suns drifted apart until they had filled that strange tunnel of night in which the ship was riding. Then, one by one, the six outer stars vanished at the brink of darkness and at last only the Central Sun was left. Though it could no longer be fully in their space, it still shone with the pearly light that marked it out from all other stars. Minute by minute its brilliance increased, until presently it was no longer a point but a tiny disc. And now the disc was beginning to expand before them.

There was the briefest of warnings: for a moment a deep, bell-like note vibrated through the room. Alvin clenched the arms of his chair, though it was a futile enough gesture.

Once again the great generators exploded into life, and with an abruptness that was almost blinding, the stars reappeared. The ship had dropped back into space, back into the Universe of suns and planets, the natural world where nothing could move more swiftly than light.

They were already within the system of the Seven Suns, for the great ring of colored globes now dominated the sky. And what a sky it was! All the stars they had known, all the familiar constellations, had gone. The Milky Way was no longer a faint band of mist far to one side of the heavens; they were now at the center of creation, and its great circle divided the Universe in twain.

The ship was still moving very swiftly toward the Central Sun, and the six remaining stars of the system were colored beacons ranged around the sky. Not far from the nearest of them were the tiny sparks of circling planets, worlds that must have been of enormous size to be visible over such a distance.

The cause of the Central Sun's nacreous light was now clearly visible. The great star was shrouded in an envelope of gas which softened its radiation and gave it its characteristic color. The surrounding nebula could only be seen indirectly, and it was twisted into strange shapes that eluded the eye. But it was there, and the longer one stared the more extensive it seemed to be.

"Well, Alvin," said Hilvar, "we have a good many worlds to take our choice from. Or do you hope to explore them all?"

"It's lucky that won't be necessary," admitted Alvin. "If we can make contact anywhere, we'll get the information we need. The logical thing would be to head for the largest planet of the Central Sun."

"Unless it's too large. Some planets, I've heard, were so big that human life could not exist on them—men would be crushed under their own weight."

"I doubt if that will be true here, since I'm sure this system is entirely artificial. In any case, we'll be able to see from space whether there are any cities and buildings."

Hilvar pointed to the robot.

"Our problem has been solved for us. Don't forget—our guide has been here before. He is taking us home—and I wonder what he thinks about it?"

That was something that Alvin had also wondered. But was it accurate—did it make any sense at all—to imagine that the robot felt anything resembling human emotions now that it was returning to the ancient home of the Master, after so many aeons?

In all his dealings with it, since the Central Computer had released the blocks that made it mute, the robot had never shown any sign of feelings or emotion. It had answered his questions and obeyed his commands, but its real personality had proved utterly inaccessible to him. That it had a personality Alvin was sure; otherwise he would not have felt that obscure sense of guilt which afflicted him when he recalled the trick he had played upon it—and upon its now dormant companion.

It still believed in everything that the Master had taught it; though it had seen him fake his miracles and tell lies to his followers, these inconvenient facts did not affect its loyalty. It was able, as had many humans before it, to reconcile two conflicting sets of data.

Now it was following its immemorial memories back to their origin. Almost lost in the glare of the Central Sun was a pale spark of light, with around it the fainter gleams of yet smaller worlds. Their enormous journey was coming to its end; in a little while they would know if it had been in vain.

CHAPTER

The planet they were approaching was now only a few million miles away, a beautiful sphere of multicolored light. There could be no darkness anywhere upon its surface, for as it turned beneath the Central Sun, the other stars would march one by one across its skies. Alvin now saw very clearly the meaning of the Master's dying words: *"It is lovely to watch the colored shadows on the planets of eternal light."*

Now they were so close that they could see continents and oceans and a faint haze of atmosphere. Yet there was something puzzling about its markings, and presently they realized that the divisions between land and water were curiously regular. This planet's continents were not as Nature had left them—but how small a task the shaping of a world must have been to those who built its suns!

"Those aren't oceans at all!" Hilvar exclaimed suddenly. "Look—you can see markings in them!"

Not until the planet was nearer could Alvin see clearly what his friend meant. Then he noticed faint bands and lines along the continental borders, well inside what he had taken to be the limits of the sea. The sight filled him with a sudden doubt, for he knew too well the meaning of those lines. He had seen them once before in the desert beyond Diaspar, and they told him that his journey had been in vain.

"This planet is as dry as Earth," he said dully. "Its water has all gone—those markings are the salt beds where the seas have evaporated."

"They would never have let that happen," replied Hilvar. "I think that, after all, we are too late."

His disappointment was so bitter that Alvin did not trust himself to speak again but stared silently at the great world ahead. With impressive slowness the planet turned beneath the ship, and its surface rose majestically to meet them. Now they could see buildings—minute white incrustations everywhere save on the ocean beds themselves.

Once this world had been the center of the Universe. Now it was still, the air was empty, and on the ground were none of the scurrying dots that spoke of life. Yet the ship was still sliding purposefully over the frozen sea of stone—a sea which here and there had gathered itself into great waves that challenged the sky.

Presently the ship came to rest, as if the robot had at last traced its memories to their source. Below them was a column of snow-white stone springing from the center of an immense marble amphitheater. Alvin waited for a little while; then, as the machine remained motionless, he directed it to land at the foot of the pillar.

Even until now, Alvin had half hoped to find life on this planet. That hope vanished instantly as the air lock opened. Never before in his life, even in the desolation of Shalmirane, had he been in utter silence. On Earth there was always the murmur of voices, the stir of living creatures, or the sighing of the wind. Here were none of these, nor ever would be again.

"Why did you bring us to this spot?" asked Alvin. He felt little interest in the answer, but the momentum of his quest still carried him on even when he had lost all heart to pursue it further.

"The Master left from here," replied the robot.

"I thought that would be the explanation," said Hilvar. "Don't you see the irony of all this? He fled from this world in disgrace—now look at the memorial they built for him!"

The great column of stone was perhaps a hundred times the height of a man, and was set in a circle of metal slightly raised above the level of the plain. It was featureless and bore no inscription. For how many thousands or millions of years, wondered Alvin, had the Master's disciples gathered here to do him honor? And had they ever known that he died in exile on distant Earth?

It made no difference now. The Master and his disciples alike were buried in oblivion.

"Come outside," urged Hilvar, trying to jolt Alvin out of his mood of depression. "We have traveled halfway across the Universe to see this place. At least you can make the effort to step outdoors."

Despite himself, Alvin smiled and followed Hilvar through the air lock. Once outside, his spirits began to revive a little. Even if this world was dead, it must contain much of interest, much that would help him to solve some of the mysteries of the past.

The air was musty, but breathable. Despite the many suns in the sky, the temperature was low. Only the white disc of the Central Sun provided any real heat, and that seemed to have lost its strength in its passage through the nebulous haze around the star. The other suns gave their quota of color, but no warmth.

It took only a few minutes to make sure that the obelisk could tell them nothing. The stubborn material of which it was made showed definite signs of age; its edges were rounded, and the metal on which it was standing had been worn away by the feet of generations of disciples and visitors. It was strange to think that they might be the last of many billions of human beings ever to stand upon this spot.

Hilvar was about to suggest that they should return to the ship and fly across to the nearest of the surrounding buildings when Alvin noticed a long, narrow crack in the marble floor of the amphitheater. They walked along it for a considerable distance, the crack widening all the time until presently it was too broad for a man's legs to straddle.

A moment later they stood beside its origin. The surface of the arena had been crushed and splintered into an enormous shallow depression, more than a mile long. No intelligence, no imagination was needed to picture its cause. Ages ago—though certainly long after this world had been deserted—an immense cylindrical shape had rested here, then lifted once more into space and left the planet to its memories.

Who had they been? Where had they come from? Alvin could only stare and wonder. He would never know if he had missed these earlier visitors by a thousand or a million years.

They walked in silence back to their own ship (how tiny that would have looked beside the monster which once had rested here!) and flew slowly across the arena until they came to the most impressive of the buildings flanking it. As they landed in front of the ornate entrance, Hilvar pointed out something that Alvin had noticed at the same moment.

"These buildings don't look safe. See all that fallen stone over there—it's a miracle they're still standing. If there were any storms on this planet, they would have been flattened ages ago. I don't think it would be wise to go inside any of them."

"I'm not going to; I'll send the robot—it can travel far faster than we can, and it won't make any disturbance which might bring the roof crashing down on top of it."

Hilvar approved of this precaution, but he also insisted on one which Alvin had overlooked. Before the robot left on its reconnaissance, Alvin made it pass on a set of instructions to the almost equally intelligent brain of the ship, so that whatever happened to their pilot they could at least return safely to Earth.

It took little time to convince both of them that this world had nothing to offer. Together they watched miles of empty, dust-carpeted corridors and passageways drift across the screen as the robot explored these empty labyrinths. All buildings designed by intelligent beings, whatever form their bodies may take, must comply with certain basic laws, and after a while even the most alien forms of architecture or design fail to evoke surprise, and the mind becomes hypnotized by sheer repetition, incapable of absorbing any more impressions. These buildings, it seemed, had been purely residential, and the beings who had lived in them had been approximately human in size. They might well have been men; it was true that there were a surprising number of rooms and enclosures that could be entered only by flying creatures, but that did not mean that the builders of this city were winged. They could have used the personal antigravity devices that had once been in common use but of which there was now no trace in Diaspar.

"Alvin," said Hilvar at last, "we could spend a million years exploring these buildings. It's obvious that they've not merely been abandoned—they were carefully stripped of everything valuable that they possessed. We are wasting our time."

"Then what do you suggest?" asked Alvin.

"We should look at two or three other areas of this planet and see if they are the same—as I expect they are. Then we should make an equally quick survey of the other planets, and only land if they seem fundamentally different or we notice something unusual. That's all we can hope to do unless we are going to stay here for the rest of our lives."

It was true enough; they were trying to contact intelligence, not to carry out archaeological research. The former task could be achieved in a few days, if it could be achieved at all. The latter would take centuries of labor by armies of men and robots.

They left the planet two hours later, and were thankful enough to go. Even when it had been bustling with life, Alvin decided, this world of endless buildings would have been very depressing. There were no signs of any parks, any open spaces where there could have been vegetation. It had been an utterly sterile world, and it was hard to imagine the psychology of the beings who had lived here. If the next planet was identical with this, Alvin decided, he would probably abandon the search there and then.

It was not; indeed, a greater contrast would have been impossible to imagine.

This planet was nearer the sun, and even from space it looked hot. It was partly covered with low clouds, indicating that water was plentiful, but there were no signs of any oceans. Nor was there any sign of intelligence; they circled the planet twice without glimpsing a single artifact of any kind. The entire globe, from poles down to the equator, was clothed with a blanket of virulent green.

"I think we should be very careful here," said Hilvar. "This world is alive—and I don't like the color of that vegetation. It would be best to stay in the ship and not to open the air lock at all."

"Not even to send out the robot?"

"No, not even that. You have forgotten what disease is, and though my people know how to deal with it, we are a long way from home and there may be dangers here which we cannot see. I think this is a world that has run amok. Once it may have been all one great garden or park, but when it was abandoned Nature took over again. It could never have been like this while the system was inhabited."

Alvin did not doubt that Hilvar was right. There was something evil, something hostile to all the order and regularity on which Lys and Diaspar were based, in the biological anarchy below. Here a ceaseless battle had raged for a billion years; it would be well to be wary of the survivors.

They came cautiously down over a great level plain, so uniform that its flatness posed an immediate problem. The plain was bordered by higher ground, completely covered with trees whose height could only be guessed—they were so tightly packed, and so enmeshed with undergrowth, that their trunks were virtually buried. There were many winged creatures flying among their upper branches, though they moved so swiftly that it was impossible to tell whether they were birds or insects—or neither.

Here and there a forest giant had managed to climb a few scores of feet above its battling neighbors, who had formed a brief alliance to tear it down and destroy the advantage it had won. Despite the fact that this was a silent war, fought too slowly for the eye to see, the impression of merciless, implacable conflict was overwhelming.

The plain, by comparison, appeared placid and uneventful. It was flat, to within a few inches, right out to the horizon, and seemed to be covered with a thin, wiry grass. Though they descended to within fifty feet of it, there was no sign of any animal life, which Hilvar found somewhat surprising. Perhaps, he decided, it had been scared underground by their approach.

They hovered just above the plain while Alvin tried to convince Hilvar that it would be safe to open the air lock, and Hilvar patiently explained such conceptions as bacteria, fungi, viruses, and microbes—ideas which Alvin found hard to visualize, and harder still to apply to himself. The argument had been in progress for some minutes before they noticed a peculiar fact. The vision screen, which a moment ago had been showing the forest ahead of them, had now become blank.

"Did you turn that off?" said Hilvar, his mind, as usual, just one jump ahead of Alvin's.

"No," replied Alvin, a cold shiver running down his spine as he thought of the only other explanation. "Did *you* turn it off?" he asked the robot.

"No," came the reply, echoing his own.

With a sigh of relief, Alvin dismissed the idea that the robot might have started to act on its own volition—that he might have a mechanical mutiny on his hands.

"Then why is the screen blank?" he asked.

"The image receptors have been covered."

"I don't understand," said Alvin, forgetting for a moment that the robot would only act on definite orders or questions. He recovered himself quickly and asked: "What's covered the receptors?"

"I do not know."

The literal-mindedness of robots could sometimes be as exasperating as the discursiveness of humans. Before Alvin could continue the interrogation, Hilvar interrupted.

"Tell it to lift the ship—slowly," he said, and there was a note of urgency in his voice.

Alvin repeated the command. There was no sense of motion; there never was. Then, slowly, the image re-formed on the vision screen, though for a moment it was blurred and distorted. But it showed enough to end the argument about landing.

The level plain was level no longer. A great bulge had formed immediately below them—a bulge which was ripped open at the top where the ship had torn free. Huge pseudopods were waving sluggishly across the gap, as if trying to recapture the prey that had just escaped from their clutches. As he stared in horrified fascination, Alvin caught a glimpse of a pulsing scarlet orifice, fringed with whiplike tentacles which were beating in unison, driving anything that came into their reach down into that gaping maw.

Foiled of its intended victim, the creature sank slowly into the ground—and it was then that Alvin realized that the plain below was merely the thin scum on the surface of a stagnant sea.

"What was that—*thing?*" he gasped.

"I'd have to go down and study it before I could tell you that," Hilvar replied matter-of-factly. "It may have been some form of primitive animal—perhaps even a relative of our friend in Shalmirane. Certainly it was not intelligent, or it would have known better than to try to eat a spaceship."

Alvin felt shaken, though he knew that they had been in no possible danger. He wondered what else lived down there beneath that innocent sward, which seemed to positively invite him to come out and run upon its springy surface.

"I could spend a lot of time here," said Hilvar, obviously fascinated by what he had just seen. "Evolution must have produced some very interesting results under these conditions. Not only evolution, but *devolution* as well, as higher forms of life regressed when the planet was deserted. By now equilibrium must have been reached and—you're not leaving already?" His voice sounded quite plaintive as the landscape receded below them.

"I am," said Alvin. "I've seen a world with no life, and a world with too much, and I don't know which I dislike more."

Five thousand feet above the plain, the planet gave them one final surprise. They encountered a flotilla of huge, flabby balloons drifting down the wind. From each semitransparent envelope, clusters of tendrils dangled to form what was virtually an inverted forest. Some plants, it seemed, in the effort to escape from the ferocious conflict on the surface, had learned to conquer the air. By a miracle of adaptation, they had managed to prepare hydrogen and store it in bladders, so that they could lift themselves into the comparative peace of the lower atmosphere.

Yet it was not certain that even here they had found security. Their downward-hanging stems and leaves were infested with an entire fauna of spidery animals, which must spend their lives floating far above the surface of the globe, continuing the universal battle for existence on their lonely aerial islands. Presumably they must from time to time have some contact with the ground; Alvin saw one of the great balloons suddenly collapse and fall out of the sky, its broken envelope acting as a crude parachute. He wondered if this was an accident, or part of the life cycle of these strange entities.

Hilvar slept while they waited for the next planet to approach. For some reason which the robot could not explain to them, the ship traveled slowly—at least by comparison with its Universe-spanning haste—now that it was within a Solar System. It took almost two hours to reach the world that Alvin had chosen for his third stop, and he was a little surprised that any mere interplanetary journey should last so long.

He woke Hilvar as they dropped down into the atmosphere.

"What do you make of *that?*" he asked, pointing to the vision screen.

Below them was a bleak landscape of blacks and grays, showing no sign of vegetation or any other direct evidence of life. But there was indirect evidence; the low hills and shallow valleys were dotted with perfectly formed hemispheres, some of them arranged in complex, symmetrical patterns.

They had learned caution on the last planet, and after carefully considering all the possibilities remained poised high in the atmosphere while they sent the robot down to investigate. Through its eyes, they saw one of the hemispheres approach until the robot was floating only a few feet away from the completely smooth, featureless surface.

There was no sign of any entrance, nor any hint of the purpose which the structure served. It was quite large—over a hundred feet high; some of the other hemispheres were larger still. If it was a building, there appeared to be no way in or out.

After some hesitation, Alvin ordered the robot to move forward and touch the dome. To his utter astonishment, it refused to obey him. This indeed was mutiny—or so at first sight it seemed.

"Why won't you do what I tell you?" asked Alvin, when he had recovered from his astonishment.

"It is forbidden," came the reply.

"Forbidden by whom?"

"I do not know."

"Then how—no, cancel that. Was the order built into you?"

"No."

That seemed to eliminate one possibility. The builders of these domes might well have been the race who made the robot, and might have included this taboo in the machine's original instructions.

"When did you receive the order?" asked Alvin.

"I received it when I landed."

Alvin turned to Hilvar, the light of a new hope burning in his eyes.

"There's intelligence here! Can you sense it?"

"No," Hilvar replied. "This place seems as dead to me as the first world we visited."

"I'm going outside to join the robot. Whatever spoke to it may speak to me."

Hilvar did not argue the point, though he looked none too happy. They brought the ship to earth a hundred feet away from the dome, not far from the waiting robot, and opened the air lock.

Alvin knew that the lock could not be opened unless the ship's brain had already satisfied itself that the atmosphere was breathable. For a moment he thought it had made a mistake—the air was so thin and gave such little sustenance to his lungs. Then, by inhaling deeply, he found that he could grasp enough oxygen to survive, though he felt that a few minutes here would be all that he could endure.

Panting hard, they walked up to the robot and to the curving wall of the enigmatic dome. They took one more step—then stopped in unison as if hit by the same sudden blow. In their minds, like the tolling of a mighty gong, had boomed a single message:

DANGER. COME NO CLOSER.

That was all. It was a message not in words, but in pure thought. Alvin was certain that any creature, whatever its level of intelligence, would receive the same warning, in the same utterly unmistakable fashion—deep within its mind.

It was a warning, not a threat. Somehow they knew that it was not directed *against* them; it was for their own protection. Here, it seemed to say, is something intrinsically dangerous, and we, its makers, are anxious that no one shall be hurt through blundering ignorantly into it.

Alvin and Hilvar stepped back several paces, and looked at each other, each waiting for the other to say what was in his mind. Hilvar was the first to sum up the position.

"I was right, Alvin," he said. "There is no intelligence here. That warning is automatic—triggered by our presence when we get too close."

Alvin nodded in agreement.

"I wonder what they were trying to protect," he said. "There could be buildings—anything—under these domes."

"There's no way we can find out, if all the domes warn us off. It's interesting—the difference between the three planets we've visited. They took everything away from the first—they abandoned the second without bothering about it—but they went to a lot of trouble here. Perhaps they expected to come back some day, and wanted everything to be ready for them when they returned."

"But they never did—and that was a long time ago."

"They may have changed their minds."

It was curious Alvin thought, how both he and Hilvar had unconsciously started using the word "they." Whoever or whatever "they" had been, their presence had been strong on that first planet—and was even stronger here. This was a world that had been carefully wrapped up, and put away until it might be needed again.

"Let's go back to the ship," panted Alvin. "I can't breathe properly here."

As soon as the air lock had closed behind them, and they were at ease once more, they discussed their next move. To make a thorough investigation, they should sample a large number of domes, in the hope that they might find one that had no warning and which could be entered. If that failed—but Alvin would not face that possibility until he had to.

He faced it less than an hour later, and in a far more dramatic form than he would have dreamed. They had sent the robot down to half a dozen domes, always with the same result, when they came across a scene that was badly out of place on this tidy, neatly packaged world.

Below them was a broad valley, sparsely sprinkled with the tantalizing, impenetrable domes. At its center was the unmistakable scar of a great explosion—an explosion that had thrown debris for miles in all directions and burned a shallow crater in the ground.

And beside the crater was the wreckage of a spaceship.

Chapter

They landed close to the scene of this ancient tragedy, and walked slowly, conserving their breath, toward the immense, broken hull towering above them. Only a short section—either the prow or the stern—of the ship remained; presumably the rest had been destroyed in the explosion. As they approached the wreck, a thought slowly dawned in Alvin's mind, becoming stronger and stronger until it attained the status of certainty.

"Hilvar," he said, finding it hard to talk and walk at the same time, "I believe this is the ship that landed on the first planet we visited."

Hilvar nodded, preferring not to waste air. The same idea had already occurred to him. It was a good object lesson, he thought, for incautious visitors. He hoped it would not be lost on Alvin.

They reached the hull and stared up into the exposed interior of the ship. It was like looking into a huge building that had been roughly sliced in two; floors and walls and ceilings, broken at the point of the explosion, gave a distorted chart of the ship's cross section. What strange beings, wondered Alvin, still lay where they had died in the wreckage of their vessel?

"I don't understand this," said Hilvar suddenly. "This portion of the ship is badly damaged, but it's still fairly intact. Where's the rest of it? Did it break in two out in space, and this part crash here?"

Not until they had sent the robot exploring again, and had themselves examined the area around the wreckage, did they learn the answer. There was no shadow of doubt; any reservations they might have had were banished when Alvin found the line of low mounds, each ten feet long, on the little hill beside the ship.

"So they landed here," mused Hilvar, "and ignored the warning. They were inquisitive, just as you are. They tried to open that dome."

He pointed to the other side of the crater, to the smooth, still unmarked shell within which the departed rulers of this world had sealed their treasures. But it was no longer a dome; it was now an almost complete sphere, for the ground in which it had been set had been blasted away.

"They wrecked their ship, and many of them were killed. Yet despite that, they managed to make repairs and leave again, cutting off this section and stripping out everything of value. What a task that must have been!"

Alvin scarcely heard him. He was looking at the curious marker that had first drawn him to this spot—the slim shaft ringed by a horizontal circle a third of the way down from its tip. Alien and unfamiliar thought it was, he could respond to the mute message it had carried down the ages.

Underneath those stones, if he cared to disturb them, was the answer to one question at least. It could remain unanswered; whatever these creatures might have been, they had earned their right to rest.

Hilvar scarcely heard the words Alvin whispered as they walked slowly back to the ship.

"I hope they got home," he said.

*   *   *

"And where now?" asked Hilvar, when they were once more out in space.

Alvin stared thoughtfully at the screen before replying.

"Do you think I should go back?" he said.

"It would be the sensible thing to do. Our luck may not hold out much longer, and who knows what other surprises these planets may have waiting for us?"

It was the voice of sanity and caution, and Alvin was now prepared to give it greater heed than he would have done a few days before. But he had come a long way, and waited all his life, for this moment; he would not turn back while there was still so much to see.

"We'll stay in the ship from now on," he said, "and we won't touch surface anywhere. That should be safe enough, surely."

Hilvar shrugged his shoulders, as if refusing to accept any responsibility for what might happen next. Now that Alvin was showing a certain amount of caution, he thought it unwise to admit that he was equally anxious to continue their exploring, though he had long ago abandoned all hope of meeting intelligent life upon any of these planets.

A double world lay ahead of them, a great planet with a smaller satellite beside it. The primary might have been the twin of the second world they had visited; it was clothed in that same blanket of livid green. There would be no point in landing here; this was a story they already knew.

Alvin brought the ship low over the surface of the satellite; he needed no warning from the complex mechanism which protected him to know that there was no atmosphere here. All shadows had a sharp, clean edge, and there were no gradations between night and day. It was the first world on which he had seen something approaching night, for only one of the more distant suns was above the horizon in the area where they made first contact. The landscape was bathed in a dull red light, as though it had been dipped in blood.

For many miles they flew above mountains that were still as

jagged and sharp as in the distant ages of their birth. This was a world that had never known change or decay, had never been scoured by winds and rains. No eternity circuits were needed here to preserve objects in their pristine freshness.

But if there was no air, then there could have been no life—or could there have been?

"Of course," said Hilvar, when Alvin put the question to him, "there's nothing biologically absurd in the idea. Life can't originate in airless space—but it can evolve forms that will survive in it. It must have happened millions of times, whenever an inhabited planet lost its atmosphere."

"But would you expect *intelligent* life forms to exist in a vacuum? Wouldn't they have protected themselves against the loss of their air?"

"Probably, if it occurred *after* they achieved enough intelligence to stop it happening. But if the atmosphere went while they were still in the primitive state, they would have to adapt or perish. After they had adapted, they might then develop a very high intelligence. In fact, they probably would—the incentive would be so great."

The argument, decided Alvin, was a purely theoretical one, as far as this planet was concerned. Nowhere was there any sign that it had ever borne life, intelligent or otherwise. But in that case, what was the purpose of this world? The entire multiple system of the Seven Suns, he was now certain, was artificial, and this world must be part of its grand design.

It could, conceivably, be intended purely for ornament—to provide a moon in the sky of its giant companion. Even in that case, however, it seemed likely that it would be put to *some* use.

"Look," said Hilvar, pointing to the screen. "Over there, on the right."

Alvin changed the ship's course, and the landscape tilted around them. The red-lit rocks blurred with the speed of their motion; then the image stabilized, and sweeping below was the unmistakable evidence of life.

Unmistakable—yet also baffling. It took the form of a wide-spaced row of slender columns, each a hundred feet from its neighbor and twice as high. They stretched into the distance, dwindling in hypnotic perspective, until the far horizon swallowed them up.

Alvin swung the ship to the right, and began to race along the line of columns, wondering as he did so what purpose they could ever have served. They were absolutely uniform, marching in an unbroken file over hills and down into valleys. There was no sign that they had ever supported anything; they were smooth and featureless, tapering very slightly toward the top.

Quite abruptly, the line changed its course, turning sharply through a right angle. Alvin overshot by several miles before he reacted and was able to swing the ship around in the new direction.

The columns continued with the same unbroken stride across the landscape, their spacing perfectly regular. Then, fifty miles from the last change of course, they turned abruptly through another right angle. At this rate, thought Alvin, we will soon be back where we started.

The endless sequence of columns had so mesmerized them that when it was broken they were miles past the discontinuity before Hilvar cried out and made Alvin, who had noticed nothing, turning the ship back. They descended slowly, and as they circled above what Hilvar had found, a fantastic suspicion began to dawn in their minds—though at first neither dared mention it to the other.

Two of the columns had been broken off near their bases, and lay stretched out upon the rocks where they had fallen. Nor was that all; the two columns adjoining the gap had been bent outward by some irresistible force.

There was no escape from the awesome conclusion. Now Alvin knew what they had been flying over; it was something he had seen often enough in Lys, but until this moment the shocking change of scale had prevented recognition.

"Hilvar," he said, still hardly daring to put his thoughts into words, "do you know what this is?"

"It seems hard to believe, but we've been flying around the edge of a corral. This thing is a fence—a fence that hasn't been strong enough."

"People who keep pets," said Alvin, with the nervous laugh men sometimes use to conceal their awe, "should make sure they know how to keep them under control."

Hilvar did not react to his forced levity; he was staring at the broken barricade, his brow furrowed with thought.

"I don't understand it," he said at last. "Where could it have got food on a planet like this? And why did it break out of its pen? I'd give a lot to know what kind of animal it was."

"Perhaps it was left here, and broke out because it was hungry," Alvin surmised. "Or something may have made it annoyed."

"Let's go lower," said Hilvar. "I want to have a look at the ground."

They descended until the ship was almost touching the barren rock, and it was then that they noticed that the plain was pitted with innumerable small holes, no more than an inch or two wide. Outside the stockade, however, the ground was free from these mysterious pockmarks; they stopped abruptly at the line of the fence.

"You are right," said Hilvar. "It was hungry. But it wasn't an animal: it would be more accurate to call it a plant. It had exhausted the soil inside its pen, and had to find fresh food elsewhere. It probably moved quite slowly; perhaps it took years to break down those posts."

Alvin's imagination swiftly filled in the details he could never know with certainty. He did not doubt that Hilvar's analysis was basically correct, and that some botanical monster, perhaps moving too slowly for the eye to see, had fought a sluggish but relentless battle against the barriers that hemmed it in.

It might still be alive, even after all these ages, roving at will over the face of this planet. To look for it, however, would be a hopeless task, since it would mean quartering the surface of an entire globe. They made a desultory search in the few square miles around the gap, and located one great circular patch of pockmarks, almost five hundred feet across, where the creature had obviously stopped to feed—if one could apply that word to an organism that somehow drew its nourishment from solid rock.

As they lifted once more into space, Alvin felt a strange weariness come over him. He had seen so much, yet learned so little. There were many wonders on all these planets, but what he sought had fled them long ago. It would be useless, he knew, to visit the other worlds of the Seven Suns. Even if there was still intelligence in the Universe, where could he seek it now? He looked at the stars scattered like dust across the vision screen, and knew that what was left of time was not enough to explore them all.

A feeling of loneliness and oppression such as he had never before experienced seemed to overwhelm him. He could understand now the fear of Diaspar for the great spaces of the Universe, the terror that had made his people gather in that little microcosm of their city. It was hard to believe that, after all, they had been right.

He turned to Hilvar for support. But Hilvar was standing, fists tightly clenched and with a glazed look in his eyes. His head was tilted on one side; he seemed to be listening, straining every sense into the emptiness around them.

"What is it?" said Alvin urgently. He had to repeat the question before Hilvar showed any sign of hearing it. He was still staring into nothingness when he finally replied.

"There's something coming," he said slowly. "Something that I don't understand."

It seemed to Alvin that the cabin had suddenly become very cold, and the racial nightmare of the Invaders reared up to confront him in all its terror. With an effort of will that sapped his strength, he forced his mind away from panic.

"Is it friendly?" he asked. "Shall I run for Earth?"

Hilvar did not answer the first question—only the second. His voice was very faint, but showed no sign of alarm or fear. It held rather a vast astonishment and curiosity, as if he had encountered something so surprising that he could not be bothered to deal with Alvin's anxious query.

"You're too late," he said. "It's already here."

The Galaxy had turned many times on its axis since consciousness first came to Vanamonde. He could recall little of those first aeons and the creatures who had tended him then—but he could remember still his desolation when they had gone and left him alone among the stars. Down the ages since, he had wandered from sun to sun, slowly evolving and increasing his powers. Once he had dreamed of finding again those who had attended his birth, and though the dream had faded now, it had never wholly died.

On countless worlds he had found the wreckage that life had left behind, but intelligence he had discovered only once—and from the Black Sun he had fled in terror. Yet the Universe was very large, and the search had scarcely begun.

Far away though it was in space and time, the great burst of power from the heart of the Galaxy beckoned to Vanamonde across the light-years. It was utterly unlike the radiation of the stars, and it had appeared in his field of consciousness as suddenly as a meteor trail across a cloudless sky. He moved through space and time toward it, to the latest moment of its existence, sloughing from him in the way he knew the dead, unchanging pattern of the past.

The long metal shape, with its infinite complexities of structure, he could not understand, for it was as strange to him as almost all the things of the physical world. Around it still clung the aura of power that had drawn him across the Universe, but that was of no interest to him now. Carefully, with the delicate nervousness of a wild beast half poised for flight, he reached out toward the two minds he had discovered.

And then he knew that his long search was ended.

Alvin grasped Hilvar by the shoulders and shook him violently, trying to drag him back to a greater awareness of reality.

"Tell me what's happening!" he begged. "What do you want me to do?"

The remote, abstracted look slowly faded from Hilvar's eyes.

"I still don't understand," he said, "but there's no need to be frightened—I'm sure of that. Whatever it is, it won't harm us. It seems simply—interested."

Alvin was about to reply when he was suddenly overwhelmed by a sensation unlike any he had ever known before. A warm, tingling glow seemed to spread through his body; it lasted only a few seconds, but when it was gone he was no longer merely Alvin. Something was sharing his brain, overlapping it as one circle may partly cover another. He was conscious, also, of Hilvar's mind close at hand, equally entangled in whatever creature had descended upon them. The sensation was strange rather than unpleasant, and it gave Alvin his first glimpse of true telepathy—the power which in his people had so degenerated that it could now be used only to control machines.

Alvin had rebelled at once when Seranis had tried to dominate his mind, but he did not struggle against this intrusion. It would have been useless, and he knew that this creature, whatever it might be, was not unfriendly. He let himself relax, accepting without resistance the fact that an infinitely greater intelligence than his own was exploring his mind. But in that belief, he was not wholly right.

One of these minds, Vanamonde saw at once, was more sympathetic and accessible than the other. He could tell that both were filled with wonder at his presence, and that surprised him greatly. It was hard to believe that they could have forgotten; forgetfulness, like mortality, was beyond the comprehension of Vanamonde.

Communication was very difficult; many of the thought-images in their minds were so strange that he could hardly recognize them. He was puzzled and a little frightened by the recurrent fear pattern of the Invaders; it reminded him of his own emotions when the Black Sun first came into his field of knowledge.

But they knew nothing of the Black Sun, and now their own questions were beginning to form in his mind.

"What are you?"

He gave the only reply he could.

"I am Vanamonde."

There came a pause (how long the pattern of their thoughts took to form!) and then the question was repeated. They had not understood; that was strange, for surely their kind had given him his name for it to be among the memories of his birth. Those memories were very few, and they began strangely at a single point in time, but they were crystal clear.

Again their tiny thoughts struggled up into his consciousness.

"Where are the people who built the Seven Suns? What happened to them?"

He did not know; they could scarcely believe him, and their disappointment came sharp and clear across the abyss separating their minds from his. But they were patient and he was glad to help them, for their quest was the same as his and they gave him the first companionship he had ever known.

As long as he lived, Alvin did not believe he would ever again undergo so strange an experience as this soundless conversation. It was hard to believe that he could be little more than a spectator, for he did not care to admit, even to himself, that Hilvar's mind was in some ways so much more capable than his own. He could only wait and wonder, half dazed by the torrent of thought just beyond the limits of his understanding.

Presently Hilvar, rather pale and strained, broke off the contact and turned to his friend.

"Alvin," he said, his voice very tired. "There's something strange here. I don't understand it at all."

The news did a little to restore Alvin's self-esteem and his face must have shown his feelings for Hilvar gave a sudden, sympathetic smile.

"I can't discover what this—Vanamonde—is," he continued. "It's a creature of tremendous knowledge, but it seems to have very little intelligence. Of course," he added, "its mind may be of such a different order that we can't understand it—yet somehow I don't believe that is the right explanation."

"Well, what *have* you learned?" asked Alvin with some impatience. "Does it know anything about the Seven Suns?"

Hilvar's mind still seemed very far away.

"They were built by many races, including our own," he said absently. "It can give me facts like that, but it doesn't seem to understand their meaning. I believe it's conscious of the past, without being able to interpret it. Everything that's ever happened seems jumbled together in its mind."

He paused thoughtfully for a moment; then his face lightened.

"There's only one thing to do; somehow or other, we must get Vanamonde to Earth so that our philosophers can study him."

"Would that be safe?" asked Alvin.

"Yes," answered Hilvar, thinking how uncharacteristic his friend's remark was. "Vanamonde is friendly. More than that, in fact, he seems almost affectionate."

And quite suddenly the thought that all the while had been hovering at the edge of Alvin's consciousness came clearly into view. He remembered Krif and all the small animals that were constantly escaping, to the annoyance or alarm of Hilvar's friends. And he recalled—how long ago that seemed!—the zoological purpose behind their expedition to Shalmirane.

Hilvar had found a new pet.

CHAPTER

How completely unthinkable, Jeserac mused, this conference would have seemed only a few short days ago. The six visitors from Lys sat facing the Council, along a table placed across the open end of the horseshoe. It was ironic to remember that not long ago Alvin had stood at the same spot and heard the Council rule that Diaspar must be closed again from the world. Now the world had broken in upon it with a vengeance—and not only the world, but the Universe.

The Council itself had already changed. No less than five of its members were missing. They had been unable to face the responsibilities and problems now confronting them, and had followed the path that Khedron had already taken. It was, thought Jeserac, proof that Diaspar had failed if so many of its citizens were unable to face their first real challenge in millions of years. Many thousands of them had already fled into the brief oblivion of the Memory Banks, hoping that when they awoke the crisis would be past and Diaspar would be its familiar self again. They would be disappointed.

Jeserac had been co-opted to fill one of the vacant places on the Council. Though he was under something of a cloud, owing to his position as Alvin's tutor, his presence was so obviously essential that no one had suggested excluding him. He sat at one end of the horseshoe-shaped table—a position which gave him several advantages. Not only could he study the profiles of his visitors, but he could also see the faces of his fellow Councilors—and their expressions were sufficiently instructive.

There was no doubt that Alvin had been right, and the Council was slowly realizing the unpalatable truth. The delegates from Lys could think far more swiftly than the finest minds in Diaspar. Nor was that their only advantage, for they also showed an extraordinary degree of co-ordination which Jeserac guessed must be due to their telepathic powers. He wondered if they were reading the Councilors' thoughts, but decided that they would not have broken the solemn assurance without which this meeting would have been impossible.

Jeserac did not think that much progress had been made; for that matter, he did not see how it could have been made. The Council, which had barely accepted the existence of Lys, still seemed incapable of realizing what had happened. But it was clearly frightened—and so, he guessed, were the visitors, though they managed to conceal the fact better.

Jeserac himself was not as terrified as he had expected; his fears were still there, but he had faced them at last. Something of Alvin's own recklessness—or was it courage?—had begun to change his outlook and give him new horizons. He did not believe he would ever be able to set foot beyond the walls of Diaspar, but now he understood the impulse that had driven Alvin to do so.

The President's question caught him unawares, but he recovered himself quickly.

"I think," he said, "that it was sheer chance that this situation never arose before. We know that there were fourteen earlier Uniques, and there must have been some definite plan behind their creation. That plan, I believe, was to insure that Lys and Diaspar would not remain apart forever. Alvin had seen to that, but he has also done something which I do not imagine was ever in the original scheme. Could the Central Computer confirm that?"

The impersonal voice replied at once.

"The Councilor knows that I cannot comment on the instructions given to me by my designers."

Jeserac accepted the mild reproof.

"Whatever the cause, we cannot dispute the facts. Alvin has gone out into space. When he returns, you may prevent him leaving again—though I doubt if you will succeed, for he may have learned a great deal by then. And if what you fear has happened, there is nothing any of us can do about it. Earth is utterly helpless—as she has been for millions of centuries."

Jeserac paused and glanced along the tables. His words had pleased no one, nor had he expected them to do so.

"Yet I don't see why we should be alarmed. Earth is in no greater danger now than she has always been. Why should two men in a single small ship bring the wrath of the Invaders down upon us again? If we'll be honest with ourselves, we must admit that the Invaders could have destroyed our world ages ago."

There was a disapproving silence. This was heresy—and once Jeserac himself would have condemned it as such.

The President interrupted, frowning heavily.

"Is there not a legend that the Invaders spared Earth itself only on condition that Man never went into space again? And have we not now broken those conditions?"

"A legend, yes," said Jeserac. "We accept many things without question, and this is one of them. However, there is no proof of it. I find it hard to believe that anything of such importance would not be recorded in the memories of the Central Computer, yet it knows nothing of this pact. I have asked it, though only through the information machines. The Council may care to ask the question directly."

Jeserac saw no reason why he should risk a second admonishment by trespassing on forbidden territory, and waited for the President's reply.

It never came, for in that moment the visitors from Lys suddenly started in their seats, while their faces froze in simultaneous expressions of incredulity and alarm. They seemed to be listening while some faraway voice poured its message into their ears.

The Councilors waited, their own apprehension growing minute by minute as the soundless conversation proceeded. Then the leader of the delegation shook himself free from his trance, and turned apologetically to the President.

"We have just had some very strange and disturbing news from Lys," he said.

"Has Alvin returned to Earth?" asked the President.

"No—not Alvin. Something else."

As he brought his faithful ship down in the glade of Airlee, Alvin wondered if ever in human history any ship had brought such a cargo to Earth—if, indeed, Vanamonde was located in the physical space of the machine. There had been no sign of him on the voyage; Hilvar believed, and his knowledge was more direct, that only Vanamode's sphere of attention could be said to have any position in space. Vanamonde himself was not located anywhere—perhaps not even *anywhen.*

Seranis and five Senators were waiting for them as they emerged from the ship. One of the Senators Alvin had already met on his last visit; the other two from that previous meeting were, he gathered, now in Diaspar. He wondered how the delegation was faring, and how the city had reacted to the presence of the first intruders from outside in so many millions of years.

"It seems, Alvin," said Seranis drily, after she had greeted her son, "that you have a genius for discovering remarkable entities. Still, I think it will be some time before you can surpass your present achievement."

For once, it was Alvin's turn to be surprised.

"Then Vanamonde's arrived?"

"Yes, hours ago. Somehow he managed to trace the path your ship made on its outward journey—a staggering feat in itself, and one which raises interesting philosophical problems. There is some evidence that he reached Lys at the moment you discovered him, so that he is capable of infinite speeds. And that is not all. In the last few hours he has taught us more of history than we thought existed."

Alvin looked at her in amazement. Then he understood; it was not hard to imagine what the impact of Vanamonde must have been upon this people, with their keen perceptions and their wonderfully interlocking minds. They had reacted with surprising speed, and he had a sudden incongruous picture of Vanamonde, perhaps a little frightened, surrounded by the eager intellects of Lys.

"Have you discovered what he is?" Alvin asked.

"Yes. That was simple, though we still don't know his origin. He's a pure mentality and his knowledge seems to be unlimited. But he's childish, and I mean that quite literally."

"Of course!" cried Hilvar. "I should have guessed!"

Alvin looked puzzled, and Seranis took pity on him.

"I mean that although Vanamonde has a colossal, perhaps an infinite mind, he's immature and undeveloped. His actual intelligence is less than that of a human being"—she smiled a little wryly—"though his thought processes are much faster and he learns very quickly. He also has some powers we do not yet understand. The whole of the past seems open to his mind, in a way that's difficult to describe. He may have used that ability to follow your path back to Earth."

Alvin stood in silence, for once somewhat overcome. He realized how right Hilvar had been to bring Vanamonde to Lys. And he knew how lucky he had been ever to outwit Seranis; that was not something he would do twice in a lifetime.

"Do you mean," he asked, "that Vanamonde has only just been born?"

"By his standards, yes. His actual age is very great, though apparently less than Man's. The extraordinary thing is that he insists that we created him, and there's no doubt that his origin is bound up with all the great mysteries of the past."

"What's happening to Vanamonde now?" asked Hilvar in a slightly possessive voice.

"The historians of Grevarn are questioning him. They are trying to map out the main outlines of the past, but the work will take years. Vanamonde can describe the past in perfect detail, but as he doesn't understand what he sees it's very difficult to work with him."

Alvin wondered how Seranis knew all this; then he realized that probably every waking mind in Lys was watching the progress of the great research. He felt a sense of pride in the knowledge that he had now made as great a mark on Lys as on Diaspar, yet with that pride was mingled frustration. Here was something that he could never fully share nor understand: the direct contact even between human minds was as great a mystery to him as music must be to a deaf man or color to a blind one. Yet the people of Lys were now exchanging thoughts with this unimaginably alien being, whom he had led to Earth but whom he could never detect with any sense that he possessed.

There was no place for him here; when the inquiry was finished, he would be told the answers. He had opened the gates of infinity, and now felt awe—even fear—for all that he had done. For his own peace of mind, he must return to the tiny, familiar world of Diaspar, seeking its shelter while he came to grips with his dreams and his ambition. There was irony here; the one who had spurned the city to venture out among the stars was coming home as a frightened child runs back to its mother.

CHAPTER

Diaspar was none too pleased to see Alvin again. The city was still in a ferment, like a giant beehive that had been violently stirred with a stick. It was still reluctant to face reality, but those who refused to admit the existence of Lys and the outside world no longer had a place to hide. The Memory Banks had ceased to accept them; those who tried to cling to their dreams, and to seek refuge in the future, now walked in vain into the Hall of Creation. The dissolving, heatless flame refused to greet them; they no longer awoke, their minds washed clean, a hundred thousand years further down the river of time. No appeal to the Central Computer was of any avail, nor would it explain the reason for its actions. The intended refugees had to turn sadly back into city, to face the problems of their age.

Alvin and Hilvar had landed at the periphery of the park, not far from Council Hall. Until the last moment, Alvin was not certain that he could bring the ship into the city, through whatever screens fenced its sky from the outer world. The firmament of Diaspar, like all else about it, was artificial, or at least partly so. Night, with its starry reminder of all that Man had lost, was never allowed to intrude upon the city; it was protected also from the storms that sometimes raged across the desert and filled the sky with moving walls of sand.

The invisible guardians let Alvin pass, and as Diaspar lay spread out beneath him, he knew that he had come home. However much the Universe and its mysteries might call him, this was where he was born and where he belonged. It would never satisfy him, yet always he would return. He had gone halfway across the Galaxy to learn this simple truth.

The crowds had gathered even before the ship landed, and Alvin wondered how his fellow citizens would receive him now that he had returned. He could read their faces easily enough, as he watched them through the viewing screen before he opened the air lock. The dominant emotion seemed to be curiosity—in itself something new in Diaspar. Mingled with that was apprehension, while here and there were unmistakable signs of fear. No one, Alvin thought a little wistfully, seemed glad to see him back.

The Council, on the other hand, positively welcomed him—though not out of pure friendship. Though he had caused this crisis, he alone could give the facts on which future policy must be based. He was listened to with deep attention as he described his flight to the Seven Suns and his meeting with Vanamonde. Then he answered innumerable questions, with a patience which probably surprised his interrogators. Uppermost in their minds, he quickly discovered, was the fear of the Invaders, though they never mentioned the name and were clearly unhappy when he broached the subject directly.

"If the Invaders are still in the Universe," Alvin told the Council, "then surely I should have met them at its very center. But there is no intelligent life among the Seven Suns; we had already guessed that before Vanamonde confirmed it. I believe that the Invaders departed ages ago; certainly Vanamonde, who appears to be at least as old as Diaspar, knows nothing of them."

"I have a suggestion," said one of the Councilors suddenly. "Vanamonde may be a descendant of the Invaders, in some way beyond our present understanding. He has forgotten his origin, but that does not mean that one day he may not be dangerous again."

Hilvar, who was present merely as a spectator, did not wait for permission to speak. It was the first time that Alvin had ever seen him angry.

"Vanamonde has looked into my mind," he said, "and I have glimpsed something of his. My people have already learned much about him, though they have not yet discovered what he is. But one thing is certain—he is friendly, and was glad to find us. We have nothing to fear from him."

There was a brief silence after this outburst, and Hilvar relaxed with a somewhat embarrassed expression. It was noticeable that the tension in the Council Chamber lessened from then on, as if a cloud had lifted from the spirits of those present. Certainly the President made no attempt, as he was supposed to do, to censure Hilvar for his interruption.

It was clear to Alvin, as he listened to the debate, that three schools of thought were represented on the Council. The conservatives, who were in a minority, still hoped that the clock could be turned back and that the old order could somehow be restored. Against all reason, they clung to the hope that Diaspar and Lys could be persuaded to forget each other again.

The progressives were an equally small minority; the fact that there were any on the Council at all pleased and surprised Alvin. They did not exactly welcome this invasion of the outer world, but they were determined to make the best of it. Some of them went so far as to suggest that there might be a way of breaking through the psychological barriers which for so long had sealed Diaspar even more effectively than the physical ones.

Most of the Council, accurately reflecting the mood of the city, had adopted an attitude of watchful caution, while they waited for the pattern of the future to emerge. They realized that they could make no general plans, nor try to carry out any definite policy, until the storm had passed.

Jeserac joined Alvin and Hilvar when the session was over. He seemed to have changed since they had last met—and last parted—in the Tower of Loranne, with the desert spread out beneath them. The change was not one that Alvin had expected, though it was one that he was to encounter more and more often in the days to come.

Jeserac seemed younger, as if the fires of life had found fresh fuel and were burning more brightly in his veins. Despite his age, he was one of those who could accept the challenge that Alvin had thrown to Diaspar.

"I have some news for you, Alvin," he said. "I think you know Senator Gerane."

Alvin was puzzled for a moment; then he remembered.

"Of course—he was one of the first men I met in Lys. Isn't he a member of their delegation?"

"Yes; we have grown to know each other quite well. He is a brilliant man, and understands more about the human mind than I would have believed possible—though he tells me that by the standards of Lys he is only a beginner. While he is here, he is starting a project which will be very close to your heart. He is hoping to analyze the compulsion which keeps us in the city, and he believes that once he has discovered how it was imposed, he will be able to remove it. About twenty of us are already co-operating with him."

"And you are one of them?"

"Yes," replied Jeserac, showing the nearest approach to bashfulness that Alvin had ever seen or ever would see. "It is not easy, and certainly not pleasant—but it is stimulating."

"How does Gerane work?"

"He is operating through the sagas. He has had a whole series of them constructed, and studies our reactions when we are experiencing them. I never thought, at my age, that I should go back to my childhood recreations again!"

"What are the sagas?" asked Hilvar.

"Imaginary dream worlds," exclaimed Alvin. "At least, most of them are imaginary, though some are probably based on historical facts. There are millions of them recorded in the memory cells of the city; you can take your choice of any kind of adventure or experience you wish, and it will seem utterly real to you while the impulses are being fed into your mind." He turned to Jeserac.

"What kind of sagas does Gerane take you into?"

"Most of them are concerned, as you might expect, with leaving Diaspar. Some have taken us back to our very earliest lives, to as near to the founding of the city as we can get. Gerane believes that the closer he can get to the origin of this compulsion, the more easily he will be able to undermine it."

Alvin felt very encouraged by this news. His work would be merely half accomplished if he had opened the gates of Diaspar—only to find that no one would pass through them.

"Do you *really* want to be able to leave Diaspar?" asked Hilvar shrewdly.

"No," replied Jeserac, without hesitation. "I am terrified of the idea. But I realize that we were completely wrong in thinking that Diaspar was all the world that mattered, and logic tells me that something has to be done to rectify the mistake. Emotionally, I am still quite incapable of leaving the city; perhaps I always shall be. Gerane thinks he can get some of us to come to Lys, and I am willing to help him with the experiment—even though half the time I hope that it will fail."

Alvin looked at his old tutor with a new respect. He no longer discounted the power of suggestion, nor underestimated the forces which could compel a man to act in defiance of logic. He could not help comparing Jeserac's calm courage with Khedron's panic flight into the future—though with his new understanding of human nature he no longer cared to condemn the Jester for what he had done.

Gerane, he was certain, would accomplish what he had set out to do. Jeserac might be too old to break the pattern of a lifetime, however willing he might be to start afresh. That did not matter, for others would succeed, with the skilled guidance of the psychologists of Lys. And once a few had escaped from their billion-year-old mold, it would only be a question of time before the remainder could follow.

He wondered what would happen to Diaspar—and to Lys—when the barriers were fully down. Somehow, the best elements of both must be saved, and welded into a new and healthier culture. It was a terrifying task, and would need all the wisdom and all the patience that each could bring to bear.

Some of the difficulties of the forthcoming adjustments had already been encountered. The visitors from Lys had, politely enough, refused to live in the homes provided for them in the city. They had set up their own temporary accommodation in the park, among surroundings which reminded them of Lys. Hilvar was the only exception; though he disliked living in a house with indeterminate walls and ephemeral furniture, he bravely accepted Alvin's hospitality, reassured by the promise that they would not stay here for long.

Hilvar had never felt lonely in his life, but he knew loneliness in Diaspar. The city was stranger to him than Lys had been to Alvin, and he was oppressed and overwhelmed by its infinite complexity and by the myriads of strangers who seemed to crowd every inch of space around him. He knew, if only in a tenuous manner, everyone in Lys, whether he had met them or not. In a thousand lifetimes he could never know everyone in Diaspar, and though he realized that this was an irrational feeling, it left him vaguely depressed. Only his loyalty to Alvin held him here in a world that had nothing in common with his own.

He had often tried to analyze his feelings toward Alvin. His friendship sprang, he knew, from the same source that inspired his sympathy for all small and struggling creatures. This would have astonished those who thought of Alvin as willful, stubborn, and self-centered, needing no affection from anyone and incapable of returning it even if it was offered.

Hilvar knew better than this; he had sensed it instinctively even from the first. Alvin was an explorer, and all explorers are seeking something they have lost. It is seldom that they find it, and more seldom still that the attainment brings them greater happiness than the quest.

What Alvin was seeking, Hilvar did not know. He was driven by forces that had been set in motion ages before, by the men of genius who planned Diaspar with such perverse skill—or by the men of even greater genius who had opposed them. Like every human being, Alvin was in some measure a machine, his actions predetermined by his inheritance. That did not alter his need for understanding and sympathy, nor did it render him immune to loneliness or frustration. To his own people, he was so unaccountable a creature that they sometimes forgot that he still shared their emotions. It needed a stranger from a totally different environment to see him as another human being.

Within a few days of arriving in Diaspar, Hilvar had met more people than in his entire life. Met them—and had grown to know practically none. Because they were so crowded together, the inhabitants of the city maintained a reserve that was hard to penetrate. The only privacy they knew was that of the mind, and they still clung to this even as they made their way through the endless social activities of Diaspar. Hilvar felt sorry for them, though he knew that they felt no need for his sympathy. They did not realize what they were missing—they could not understand the warm sense of community, the feeling of *belonging,* which linked everyone together in the telepathic society of Lys. Indeed, though they were polite enough to try to conceal it, it was obvious that most of the people he spoke to looked upon him pityingly as leading an incredibly dull and drab existence.

Eriston and Etania, Alvin's guardians, Hilvar quickly dismissed as kindly but totally baffled nonentities. He found it very confusing to hear Alvin refer to them as his father and mother—words which in Lys still retained their ancient biological meaning. It required a continual effort of imagination to remember that the laws of life and death had been repealed by the makers of Diaspar, and there were times when it seemed to Hilvar that despite all the activity around him, the city was half empty because it had no children.

He wondered what would happen to Diaspar now that its long isolation was over. The best thing the city could do, he decided, was to destroy the Memory Banks which had held it entranced for so many ages. Miraculous though they were—perhaps the supreme triumph of the science that had produced them—they were the creations of a sick culture, a culture that had been afraid of many things. Some of those fears had been based on reality, but others, it now seemed, lay only in the imagination. Hilvar knew a little of the pattern that was beginning to emerge from the exploration of Vanamonde's mind. In a few days, Diaspar would know it too—and would discover how much of its past had been a myth.

Yet if the Memory Banks were destroyed, within a thousand years the city would be dead, since its people had lost the power to reproduce themselves. That was the dilemma that had to be faced, but already Hilvar had glimpsed one possible solution. There was always an answer to any technical problem, and his people were masters of the biological sciences. What had been done could be undone, if Diaspar so wished.

First, however, the city would have to learn what it had lost. Its education would take many years—perhaps many centuries. But it was beginning; very soon the impact of the first lesson would shake Diaspar as profoundly as had contact with Lys itself.

It would shake Lys too. For all the difference between the two cultures, they had sprung from the same roots—and they had shared the same illusions. They would both be healthier when they looked once more, with a calm and steadfast gaze, into the past which they had lost.

Chapter

The amphitheater had been designed to hold the entire waking population of Diaspar, and scarcely one of its ten million places was empty. As he looked down the great curving sweep from his vantage point high up the slope, Alvin was irresistibly reminded of Shalmirane. The two craters were of the same shape, and almost the same size. If one packed the crater of Shalmirane with humanity, it would look very much like this.

There was, however, one fundamental difference between the two. The great bowl of Shalmirane existed; this amphitheater did not. Nor had it ever done so; it was merely a phantom, a pattern of electronic charges, slumbering in the memory of the Central Computer until the need came to call it forth. Alvin knew that in reality he was still in his room, and that all the myriads of people who appeared to surround him were equally in their own homes. As long as he made no attempt to move from this spot, the illusion was perfect. He could believe that Diaspar had been abolished and that all its citizens had been assembled here in this enormous concavity.

Not once in a thousand years did the life of the city stop so that all its people could meet in Grand Assembly. In Lys also,

Alvin knew, the equivalent of this gathering was taking place. There it would be a meeting of minds, but perhaps associated with it would be an apparent meeting of bodies, as imaginary yet as seemingly real as this.

He could recognize most of the faces around him, out to the limits of unaided vision. More than a mile away, and a thousand feet below, was the little circular stage upon which the attention of the entire world was now fixed. It was hard to believe that he could see anything from such a distance, but Alvin knew that when the address began, he would hear and observe everything that happened as clearly as anyone else in Diaspar.

The stage filled with mist; the mist became Callitrax, leader of the group whose task it had been to reconstruct the past from the information which Vanamonde had brought to Earth. It had been a stupendous, almost an impossible undertaking, and not merely because of the spans of time involved. Only once, with the mental help of Hilvar, had Alvin been given a brief glimpse into the mind of the strange being they had discovered—or who had discovered them. To Alvin, the thoughts of Vanamonde were as meaningless as a thousand voices shouting together in some vast, echoing cave. Yet the men of Lys could disentangle them, could record them to be analyzed at leisure. Already, so it was rumored—though Hilvar would neither deny nor confirm this—what they had discovered was so strange that it bore scarcely any resemblance to the history which all the human race had accepted for a billion years.

Callitrax began to speak. To Alvin, as to everyone else in Diaspar, the clear, precise voice seemed to come from a point only a few inches away. Then, in a manner that was hard to define, just as the geometry of a dream defies logic yet rouses no surprise in the mind of the dreamer, Alvin was standing beside Callitrax while at the same time he retained his position high up on the slope of the amphitheater. The paradox did not puzzle him; he simply accepted it without question, like all the other masteries over time and space which science had given him.

Very briefly, Callitrax ran through the accepted history of the race. He spoke of the unknown peoples of the Dawn Civilizations, who had left behind them nothing but a handful of great names and the fading legends of the Empire. Even at the beginning, so the story went, Man had desired the stars—and had at last attained them. For millions of years he had expanded across the Galaxy, gathering system after system beneath his sway. Then, out of the darkness beyond the rim of the Universe, the Invaders had struck and wrenched from him all that he had won.

The retreat to the Solar System had been bitter and must have lasted many ages. Earth itself was barely saved by the fabulous battles that raged around Shalmirane. When all was over, Man was left with only his memories and the world on which he had been born.

Since then, all else had been long-drawn anticlimax. As an ultimate irony, the race that had hoped to rule the Universe had abandoned most of its own tiny world, and had split into the two isolated cultures of Lys and Diaspar—oases of life in a desert that sundered them as effectively as the gulfs between the stars.

Callitrax paused; to Alvin, as to everyone in the great assembly, it seemed that the historian was looking directly at him with eyes that had witnessed things which even now they could not wholly credit.

"So much," said Callitrax, "for the tales we have believed since our records began. I must tell you now that they are false—false in every detail—*so false that even now we have not fully reconciled them with the truth.*"

He waited for the full meaning of his words to strike home. Then, speaking slowly and carefully, he gave to both Lys and

Diaspar the knowledge that had been won from the mind of Vanamonde.

It was not even true that Man had reached the stars. The whole of his little empire was bounded by the orbits of Pluto and Persephone, for interstellar space proved a barrier beyond his power to cross. His entire civilization was huddled around the sun, and was still very young when—the stars reached him.

The impact must have been shattering. Despite his failures, Man had never doubted that one day he would conquer the depths of space. He believed too that if the Universe held his equals, it did not hold his superiors. Now he knew that both beliefs were wrong, and that out among the stars were minds far greater than his own. For many centuries, first in the ships of other races and later in machines built with borrowed knowledge, Man had explored the Galaxy. Everywhere he found cultures he could understand but could not match, and here and there he encountered minds which would soon have passed altogether beyond his comprehension.

The shock was tremendous, but it proved the making of the race. Sadder and infinitely wiser, Man had returned to the Solar System to brood upon the knowledge he had gained. He would accept the challenge, and slowly he evolved a plan which gave hope for the future.

Once the physical sciences had been Man's greatest interest. Now he turned even more fiercely to genetics and the study of the mind. Whatever the cost, he would drive himself to the limits of his evolution.

The great experiment had consumed the entire energies of the race for millions of years. All that striving, all that sacrifice and toil, became only a handful of words in Callitrax's narrative. It had brought Man his greatest victories. He had banished disease; he could live forever if he wished, and in mastering telepathy he had bent the most subtle of all powers to his will.

He was ready to go out again, relying upon his own resources, into the great spaces of the Galaxy. He would meet as an equal the races of the worlds from which he had once turned aside. And he would play his full part in the story of the Universe.

These things he did. From this age, perhaps the most spacious of all history, came the legends of the Empire. It had been an Empire of many races, but this had been forgotten in the drama, too tremendous for tragedy, in which it had come to its end.

The Empire had lasted for at least a million years. It must have known many crises, perhaps even wars, but all these were lost in the sweep of great races moving together toward maturity.

"We can be proud," continued Callitrax, "of the part our ancestors played in this story. Even when they had reached their cultural plateau, they lost none of their initiative. We deal now with conjecture rather than proved fact, but it seems certain that the experiments which were at once the Empire's downfall and its crowning glory were inspired and directed by Man.

"The philosophy underlying these experiments appears to have been this. Contact with other species had shown Man how profoundly a race's world-picture depended upon its physical body and the sense organs with which it was equipped. It was argued that a true picture of the Universe could be attained, if at all, only by a mind that was free from such physical limitations—a pure mentality, in fact. This was a conception common among many of Earth's ancient religious faiths, and it seems strange that an idea which had no rational origin should finally become one of the greatest goals of science.

"No disembodied intelligence had ever been encountered in the natural Universe; the Empire set out to create one. We have forgotten, with so much else, the skills and knowledge that made this possible. The scientists of the Empire had mastered all the forces of Nature, all the secrets of time and space. As our minds are the by-product of an immensely intricate arrangement of brain cells, linked together by the network of the nervous system, so they strove to create a brain whose components were not material, but patterns embossed upon space itself. Such a brain, if one can call it that, would use electrical or yet higher forces for its operation, and would be completely free from the tyranny of matter. It could function with far greater speed than any organic intelligence; it could endure as long as there was an erg of free energy left in the Universe, and no limit could be seen for its powers. Once created, it would develop potentialities which even its makers could not foresee.

"Largely as a result of the experience gained in his own regeneration, Man suggested that the creation of such beings should be attempted. It was the greatest challenge ever thrown out to intelligence in the Universe, and after centuries of debate it was accepted. All the races of the Galaxy joined together in its fulfillment.

"More than a million years were to separate the dream from the reality. Civilizations were to rise and fall, again and yet again the age-long toil of worlds was to be lost, but the goal was never forgotten. One day we may know the full story of this, the greatest sustained effort in all history. Today we only know that its ending was a disaster that almost wrecked the Galaxy.

"Into this period Vanamonde's mind refuses to go. There is a narrow region of time which is blocked to him; but only, we believe, by his own fears. At its beginning we can see the Empire at the summit of its glory, taut with the expectation of coming success. At its end, only a few thousand years later, the Empire is shattered and the stars themselves are dimmed as though drained of their power. Over the Galaxy hangs a pall of fear, a fear with which is linked the name: 'The Mad Mind.'

"What must have happened in that short period is not hard to guess. The pure mentality had been created, but it was either insane, or as seems more likely from other sources, was implacably hostile to matter. For centuries it ravaged the Universe until brought under control by forces at which we cannot guess. Whatever weapon the Empire used in its extremity squandered the resources of the stars; from the memories of that conflict spring some, though not all, of the legends of the Invaders. But of this I shall presently say more.

"The Mad Mind could not be destroyed, for it was immortal. It was driven to the edge of the Galaxy and there imprisoned in a way we do not understand. Its prison was a strange artificial star known as the Black Sun, and there it remains to this day. When the Black Sun dies, it will be free again. How far in the future that day lies there is no way of telling."

Callitrax became silent, as if lost in his own thoughts, utterly unconscious of the fact that the eyes of all the world were upon him. In the long silence, Alvin glanced over the packed multitude around him, seeking to read their minds as they faced this revelation—and this unknown threat which must now replace the myth of the Invaders. For the most part, the faces of his fellow citizens were frozen in disbelief; they were still struggling to reject their false past, and could not yet accept the yet stranger reality that had superseded it.

Callitrax began to speak again in a quiet, more subdued voice as he described the last days of the Empire. This was the age, Alvin realized as the picture unfolded before him, in which he would have like to have lived. There had been adventure then, and a superb and dauntless courage—the courage that could snatch victory from the teeth of disaster.

"Though the Galaxy had been laid waste by the Mad Mind, the resources of the Empire were still enormous, and its spirit was unbroken. With a courage at which we can only marvel, the great experiment was resumed and a search made for the flaw that had caused the catastrophe. There were now, of course, many who opposed the work and predicted further disasters, but they were overruled. The project went ahead and, with the knowledge so bitterly gained, this time it succeeded.

"The new race that was born had a potential intellect that could not even be measured. But it was completely infantile; we do not know if this was expected by its creators, but it seems likely that they knew it to be inevitable. Millions of years would be needed before it reached maturity, and nothing could be done to hasten the process. Vanamonde was the first of these minds; there must be others elsewhere in the Galaxy, but we believe that only a very few were created, for Vanamonde has never encountered any of his fellows.

"The creation of the pure mentalities was the greatest achievement of Galactic civilization; in it Man played a major and perhaps a dominant part. I have made no reference to Earth itself, for its story is merely a tiny thread in an enormous tapestry. Since it had always been drained of its most adventurous spirits, our planet had inevitably become highly conservative, and in the end it opposed the scientists who created Vanamonde. Certainly it played no part at all in the final act.

"The work of the Empire was now finished; the men of that age looked around at the stars they had ravaged in their desperate peril, and they made their decision. They would leave the Universe to Vanamonde.

"There is a mystery here—a mystery we may never solve, for Vanamonde cannot help us. All we know is that the Empire made contact with—something—very strange and very great, far away around the curve of the Cosmos, at the other extremity of space itself. What it was we can only guess, but its call must have been of immense urgency, and immense promise. Within a very short period of time our ancestors and their fellow races have gone upon a journey which we cannot follow. Vanamonde's thoughts seem to be bounded by the confines of the Galaxy, but through his mind we have watched the beginnings of this great and mysterious adventure. Here is the image that we have reconstructed; now you are going to look more than a billion years into the past—"

A pale wraith of its former glory, the slowly turning wheel of the Galaxy hung in nothingness. Throughout its length were the great empty rents which the Mad Mind had torn—wounds that in ages to come the drifting stars would fill. But they would never replace the splendor that had gone.

Man was about to leave his Universe, as long ago he had left his world. And not only Man, but the thousand other races that had worked with him to make the Empire. They were gathered together, here at the edge of the Galaxy, with its whole thickness between them and the goal they would not reach for ages.

They had assembled a fleet before which imagination quailed. Its flagships were suns, its smallest vessels, planets. An entire globular cluster, with all its solar systems and all their teeming worlds, was about to be launched across infinity.

The long line of fire smashed through the heart of the Universe, leaping from star to star. In a moment of time a thousand suns had died, feeding their energies to the monstrous shape that had torn along the axis of the Galaxy, and was now receding into the abyss. . . .

"So the Empire left our Universe, to meet its destiny elsewhere. When its heirs, the pure mentalities, have reached their full stature, it may return again. But that day must still lie far ahead.

"This, in its briefest and most superficial outlines, is the story of Galactic civilization. Our own history, which to us seems so important, is no more than a belated and trivial epilogue, though one so complex that we have not been able to unravel all its details. It seems that many of the older, less adventurous races refused to leave their homes; our direct ancestors were among them. Most of these races fell into decadence and are now extinct, though some may still survive. Our own world barely escaped the same fate. During the Transition Centuries—which actually lasted for millions of years—the knowledge of the past was lost or else deliberately destroyed. The latter, hard though it is to believe, seems more probable. For ages, Man sank into a superstitious yet still scientific barbarism during which he distorted history to remove his sense of impotence and failure. The legends of the Invaders are completely false, although the desperate struggle against the Mad Mind undoubtedly contributed something to them. Nothing drove our ancestors back to Earth except the sickness in their souls.

"When we made this discovery, one problem in particular puzzled us in Lys. The Battle of Shalmirane never occurred—yet Shalmirane existed, and exists to this day. What is more, it was one of the greatest weapons of destruction ever built.

"It took us some time to resolve this puzzle, but the answer, once it was found, was very simple. Long ago our Earth had a single giant satellite, the Moon. When, in the tug of war between the tides and gravity, the Moon at last began to fall, it became necessary to destroy it. Shalmirane was built for that purpose, and around its use were woven the legends you all know."

Callitrax smiled a little ruefully at his immense audience.

"There are many such legends, partly true and partly false, and other paradoxes in our past which have not yet been resolved. That problem, though, is one for the psychologist rather than the historian. Even the records of the Central Computer cannot be wholly trusted, and bear clear evidence of tampering in the very remote past.

"On Earth, only Diaspar and Lys survived the period of decadence—Diaspar thanks to the perfection of its machines, Lys owing to its partial isolation and the unusual intellectual powers of its people. But both cultures, even when they had struggled back to their former level, were distorted by the fears and myths they had inherited.

"These fears need haunt us no longer. It is not my duty as a historian to predict the future, only to observe and interpret the past. But its lesson is clear enough; we have lived too long out of contact with reality, and now the time has come to rebuild our lives."

CHAPTER

Jeserac walked in silent wonder through the streets of a Diaspar he had never seen. So different was it, indeed, from the city in which he had passed all his lives that he would never have recognized it. Yet he knew that it was Diaspar, though *how* he knew, he did not pause to ask.

The streets were narrow, the buildings lower—and the park was gone. Or, rather, it did not yet exist. This was the Diaspar before the change, the Diaspar that had been open to the world and to the Universe. The sky above the city was pale blue and flecked with raveled wisps of cloud, slowly twisting and turning in the winds that blew across the face of this younger Earth.

Passing through and beyond the clouds were more substantial voyagers of the sky. Miles above the city, lacing the heavens with their silent tracery, the ships that linked Diaspar with the outer world came and went upon their business. Jeserac stared for a long time at the mystery and wonder of the open sky, and for a moment fear brushed against his soul. He felt naked and unprotected, conscious that this peaceful, blue dome above his head was no more than the thinnest of shells—that beyond it lay space, with all its mystery and menace.

The fear was not strong enough to paralyze his will. In part of his mind Jeserac knew that his whole experience was a dream, and a dream could not harm him. He would drift through it, savoring all that it brought to him, until he woke once more in the city that he knew.

He was walking into the heart of Diaspar, toward the point where in his own age stood the Tomb of Yarlan Zey. There was no tomb here, in this ancient city—only a low, circular building with many arched doorways leading into it. By one of those doorways a man was waiting for him.

Jeserac should have been overcome with astonishment, but nothing could surprise him now. Somehow it seemed right and natural that he should now be face to face with the man who had built Diaspar.

"You recognize me, I imagine," said Yarlan Zey.

"Of course; I have seen your statue a thousand times. You are Yarlan Zey, and this is Diaspar as it was a billion years ago. I know I am dreaming, and that neither of us is really here."

"Then you need not be alarmed at anything that happens. So follow me, and remember that nothing can harm you, since whenever you wish you can wake up in Diaspar—in your own age."

Obediently, Jeserac followed Yarlan Zey into the building, his mind a receptive, uncritical sponge. Some memory, or echo of a memory, warned him of what was going to happen next, and he knew that once he would have shrunk from it in horror. Now, however, he felt no fear. Not only did he feel protected by the knowledge that this experience was not real, but the presence of Yarlan Zey seemed a talisman against any dangers that might confront him.

There were few people drifting down the glideways that led into the depths of the building, and they had no other company when presently they stood in silence beside the long, streamlined cylinder which, Jeserac knew, could carry him out of the city on a journey that would once have shattered his mind. When his guide pointed to the open door, he paused for no more than a moment on the threshold, and then was through.

"You see?" said Yarlan Zey with a smile. "Now relax, and remember that you are safe—that nothing can touch you."

Jeserac believed him. He felt only the faintest tremor of apprehension as the tunnel entrance slid silently toward him, and the machine in which he was traveling began to gain speed as it hurtled through the depths of the earth. Whatever fears he might have had were forgotten in his eagerness to talk with this almost mythical figure from the past.

"Does it not seem strange to you," began Yarlan Zey, "that though the skies are open to us, we have tried to bury ourselves in the Earth? It is the beginning of the sickness whose ending you have seen in your age. Humanity is trying to hide; it is frightened of what lies out there in space, and soon it will have closed all the doors that lead into the Universe."

"But I saw spaceships in the sky above Diaspar," said Jeserac.

"You will not see them much longer. We have lost contact with the stars, and soon even the planets will be deserted. It took us millions of years to make the outward journey—but only centuries to come home again. And in a little while we will have abandoned almost all of Earth itself."

"Why did you do it?" asked Jeserac. He knew the answer, yet somehow felt impelled to ask the question.

"We needed a shelter to protect us from two fears—fear of death, and fear of space. We were a sick people, and wanted no further part in the Universe—so we pretended that it did not exist. We had seen chaos raging through the stars, and yearned for peace and stability. Therefore Diaspar had to be closed, so that nothing new could ever enter it.

"We designed the city that you know, and invented a false

past to conceal our cowardice. Oh, we were not the first to do that—but we were the first to do it so thoroughly. And we redesigned the human spirit, robbing it of ambition and the fiercer passions, so that it would be contented with the world it now possessed.

"It took a thousand years to build the city and all its machines. As each of us completed his task, his mind was washed clean of its memories, the carefully planned pattern of false ones was implanted, and his identity was stored in the city's circuits until the time came to call it forth again.

"So at last there came a day when there was not a single man alive in Diaspar; there was only the Central Computer, obeying the orders which we had fed into it, and controlling the Memory Banks in which we were sleeping. There was no one who had any contact with the past—and so at this point, history began.

"Then, one by one, in a predetermined sequence, we were called out of the memory circuits and given flesh again. Like a machine that had just been built and was now set operating for the first time, Diaspar began to carry out the duties for which it had been designed.

"Yet some of us had had doubts even from the beginning. Eternity was a long time; we recognized the risks involved in leaving no outlet, and trying to seal ourselves completely from the Universe. We could not defy the wishes of our culture, so we worked in secret, making the modifications we thought necessary.

"The Uniques were our invention. They would appear at long intervals and would, if circumstances allowed them, discover if there was anything beyond Diaspar that was worth the effort of contacting. We never imagined that it would take so long for one of them to succeed—nor did we imagine that his success would be so great."

Despite that suspension of the critical faculties which is the very essence of a dream, Jeserac wondered fleetingly how

Yarlan Zey could speak with such knowledge of things that had happened a billion years after his time. It was very confusing . . . he did not know where in time or space he was.

The journey was coming to an end; the walls of the tunnel no longer flashed past him at such breakneck speed. Yarlan Zey began to speak with an urgency, and an authority, which he had not shown before.

"The past is over; we did our work, for better or for ill, and that is finished with. When you were created, Jeserac, you were given that fear of the outer world, and that compulsion to stay within the city, that you share with everyone else in Diaspar. You know now that that fear was groundless, that it was artificially imposed on you. I, Yarlan Zey, who gave it to you, now release you from its bondage. Do you understand?"

With those last words, the voice of Yarlan Zey became louder and louder, until it seemed to reverberate through all of space. The subterranean carrier in which he was speeding blurred and trembled around Jeserac as if his dream was coming to an end. Yet as the vision faded, he could still hear that imperious voice thundering into his brain: "You are no longer afraid, Jeserac. *You are no longer afraid.*"

He struggled up toward wakefulness, as a diver climbs from the ocean depths back to the surface of the sea. Yarlan Zey had vanished, but there was a strange interregnum when voices which he knew but could not recognize talked to him encouragingly, and he felt himself supported by friendly hands. Then like a swift dawn reality came flooding back.

He opened his eyes, and saw Alvin and Hilvar and Gerane standing anxiously beside him. But he paid no heed to them; his mind was too filled with the wonder that now lay spread before him—the panorama of forests and rivers, and the blue vault of the open sky.

He was in Lys; and he was not afraid.

No one disturbed him as the timeless moment imprinted itself forever on his mind. At last, when he had satisfied himself that this indeed was real, he turned to his companions.

"Thank you, Gerane," he said. "I never believed you would succeed."

The psychologist, looking very pleased with himself, was making delicate adjustments to a small machine that hung in the air beside him.

"You gave us some anxious moments," he admitted. "Once or twice you started to ask questions that couldn't be answered logically, and I was afraid I would have to break the sequence."

"Suppose Yarlan Zey had not convinced me—what would you have done then?"

"We would have kept you unconscious, and taken you back to Diaspar where you could have waked up naturally, without ever knowing that you'd been to Lys."

"And that image of Yarlan Zey you fed into my mind—how much of what he said was the truth?"

"Most of it, I believe. I was much more anxious that my little saga should be convincing rather than historically accurate, but Callitrax has examined it and can find no errors. It is certainly consistent with all that we know about Yarlan Zey and the origins of Diaspar."

"So now we can really open the city," said Alvin. "It may take a long time, but eventually we'll be able to neutralize this fear so that everyone who wishes can leave Diaspar."

"It *will* take a long time," replied Gerane dryly. "And don't forget that Lys is hardly large enough to hold several hundred million extra people, if all your people decide to come here. I don't think that's likely, but it's possible."

"That problem will solve itself," answered Alvin. "Lys may be tiny, but the world is wide. Why should we let the desert keep it all?"

"So you are still dreaming, Alvin," said Jeserac with a smile. "I was wondering what there was left for you to do."

Alvin did not answer; that was a question which had become more and more insistent in his own mind during the past few weeks. He remained lost in thought, falling behind the others, as they walked down the hill toward Airlee. Would the centuries that lay ahead of him be one long anticlimax?

The answer lay in his own hands. He had discharged his destiny; now, perhaps, he could begin to live.

Chapter

There is a special sadness in achievement, in the knowledge that a long-desired goal has been attained at last, and that life must now be shaped toward new ends. Alvin knew that sadness as he wandered alone through the forests and fields of Lys. Not even Hilvar accompanied him, for there are times when a man must be apart even from his closest friends.

He did not wander aimlessly, though he never knew which village would be his next port of call. He was seeking no particular place, but a mood, an influence—indeed a way of life. Diaspar had no need of him now; the ferments he had introduced into the city were working swiftly, and nothing he could do would accelerate or retard the changes that were happening there.

This peaceful land would also change. Often he wondered if he had done wrong, in the ruthless drive to satisfy his own curiosity, by opening up the ancient way between the two cultures. Yet surely it was better that Lys should know the truth—that it also, like Diaspar, had been partly founded upon fears and falsehoods.

Sometimes he wondered what shape the new society would take. He believed that Diaspar must escape from the prison of the Memory Banks, and restore again the cycle of life and death. Hilvar, he knew, was sure that this could be done, though his proposals were too technical for Alvin to follow. Perhaps the time would come again when love in Diaspar was no longer completely barren.

Was *this,* Alvin wondered, what he had always lacked in Diaspar—what he had really been seeking? He knew now that when power and ambition and curiosity were satisfied, there still were left the longings of the heart. No one had really lived until they had achieved that synthesis of love and desire which he had never dreamed existed until he came to Lys.

He had walked upon the planet of the Seven Suns—the first man to do so in a billion years. Yet that meant little to him now; sometimes he thought he would give all his achievements if he could hear the cry of a newborn child, and know that it was his own.

In Lys, he might one day find what he wanted; there was a warmth and understanding about its people, which, he now realized, was lacking in Diaspar. But before he could rest, before he could find peace, there was one decision yet to be made.

Into his hands had come power; that power he still possessed. It was a responsibility he had once sought and accepted with eagerness, but now he knew that he could have no peace while it was still his. Yet to throw it away would be the betrayal of a trust.

He was in a village of tiny canals, at the edge of a wide lake, when he made his decision. The colored houses, which seemed to float at anchor upon the gentle waves, formed a scene of almost unreal beauty. There was life and warmth and comfort here—everything he had missed among the desolate grandeur of the Seven Suns.

One day humanity would once more be ready for space. What new chapter Man would write among the stars, Alvin did not know. That would be no concern of his; his future lay here on Earth.

But he would make one more flight before he turned his back upon the stars.

When Alvin checked the upward rush of the ascending ship, the city was too distant to be recognized as the work of Man, and the curve of the planet was already visible. Presently they could see the line of twilight, thousands of miles away on its unending march across the desert. Above and around were the stars, still brilliant for all the glory they had lost.

Hilvar and Jeserac were silent, guessing but not knowing with certainty why Alvin was making this flight, and why he had asked them to come with him. Neither felt like speech, as the desolate panorama unfolded below them. Its emptiness oppressed them both, and Jeserac felt a sudden contemptuous anger for the men of the past who had let Earth's beauty die through their own neglect.

He hoped that Alvin was right in dreaming that all this could be changed. The power and the knowledge still existed—it needed only the will to turn back the centuries and make the oceans roll again. The water was still there, deep down in the hidden places of the Earth; or if necessary, transmutation plants could be built to make it.

There was so much to do in the years that lay ahead. Jeserac knew that he stood between two ages; around him he could feel the pulse of mankind beginning to quicken again. There were great problems to be faced—but Diaspar would face them. The recharting of the past would take centuries, but when it was finished Man would have recovered almost all that he had lost.

Yet could he regain it all? Jeserac wondered. It was hard to believe that the Galaxy would be reconquered, and even if that were achieved, what purpose would it serve?

Alvin broke into his reverie, and Jeserac turned from the screen.

"I wanted you to see this," said Alvin quietly. "You may never have another chance."

"You're not leaving Earth?"

"No; I want nothing more of space. Even if any other civilizations still survive in this Galaxy, I doubt if they will be worth the effort of finding. There is so much to do here; I know now that this is my home, and I am not going to leave it again."

He looked down at the great deserts, but his eyes saw instead the waters that would be sweeping over them a thousand years from now. Man had rediscovered his world, and he would make it beautiful while he remained upon it. And after that—

"We aren't ready to go out to the stars, and it will be a long time before we can face their challenge again. I have been wondering what I should do with this ship; if it stays here on earth, I shall always be tempted to use it, and will never have any peace of mind. Yet I cannot waste it; I feel that it has been given into my trust, and I must use it for the benefit of the world.

"So this is what I have decided to do. I'm going to send it out of the Galaxy, with the robot in control, to discover what happened to our ancestors—and, if possible, *what* it was they left our Universe to find. It must have been something wonderful for them to have abandoned so much to go in search of it.

"The robot will never tire, however long the journey takes. One day our cousins will receive my message, and they'll know that we are waiting for them here on Earth. They will return, and I hope that by then we will be worthy of them, however great they have become."

Alvin fell silent, staring into a future he had shaped but which he might never see. While Man was rebuilding his world, this ship would be crossing the darkness between the galaxies, and in thousands of years to come it would return. Perhaps he would still be here to meet it, but if not, he was well content.

"I think you are wise," said Jeserac. Then, for the last time, the echo of an ancient fear rose up to plague him. "But suppose," he added, "the ship makes contact with something we do not wish to meet. . . ." His voice faded away as he recognized the source of his anxiety and he gave a wry, self-deprecatory smile that banished the last ghost of the Invaders.

"You forget," said Alvin, taking him more seriously than he expected, "that we will soon have Vanamonde to help us. We don't know what powers he possesses, but everyone in Lys seems to think they are potentially unlimited. Isn't that so, Hilvar?"

Hilvar did not reply at once. It was true that Vanamonde was the other great enigma, the question mark that would always lie across the future of humanity while it remained on earth. Already, it seemed certain, Vanamonde's evolution toward self-consciousness had been accelerated by his contact with the philosophers of Lys. They had great hopes of future co-operation with the childlike supermind, believing that they could foreshorten the aeons which his natural development would require.

"I am not sure," confessed Hilvar. "Somehow, I don't think that we should expect too much from Vanamonde. We can help him now, but we will be only a brief incident in his total life span. I don't think that his ultimate destiny has anything to do with ours."

Alvin looked at him in surprise.

"Why do you feel that?" he asked.

"I can't explain it," said Hilvar. "It's just an intuition." He could have added more, but he kept his silence. These matters were not capable of communication, and though Alvin would not laugh at his dream, he did not care to discuss it even with his friend.

It was more than a dream, he was sure of that, and it would haunt him forever. Somehow it had leaked into his mind, during that indescribable and unsharable contact he had had with Vanamonde. Did Vanamonde himself know what his lonely destiny must be?

One day the energies of the Black Sun would fail and it would release its prisoner. And then, at the end of the Universe, as time itself was faltering to a stop, Vanamonde and the Mad Mind must meet each other among the corpses of the stars.

That conflict might ring down the curtain on Creation itself. Yet it was a conflict that had nothing to do with Man, and whose outcome he would never know. . . .

"Look!" said Alvin suddenly. "This is what I wanted to show you. Do you understand what it means?"

The ship was now above the Pole, and the planet beneath them was a perfect hemisphere. Looking down upon the belt of twilight, Jeserac and Hilvar could see at one instant both sunrise and sunset on opposite sides of the world. The symbolism was so perfect, and so striking, that they were to remember this moment all their lives.

In this universe the night was falling; the shadows were lengthening toward an east that would not know another dawn. But elsewhere the stars were still young and the light of morning lingered; and along the path he once had followed, Man would one day go again.

THE SANDS OF MARS

Introduction

In 2001—where have I seen that date before?—it will be exactly half a century since this novel was published. Or to put it in perhaps better perspective: It is already more than halfway back in time, dear reader, between you and the Wright Brothers' first flight . . .

Though I have not opened it for decades, I have a special fondness for *Sands,* as it was my first full-length novel. When I wrote it, we knew practically nothing about Mars—and what we did "know" was completely wrong. The mirage of Percival Lowell's canals was beginning to fade, though it would not vanish completely until our space probes began arriving in the late 1970s. It was still generally believed that Mars had a thin but useful atmosphere, and that vegetation flourished—at least in the equatorial regions where the temperature often rose above the freezing point. And where there was vegetation, of course, there might be more interesting forms of life—though nothing remotely human. Edgar Rice Burroughs' Martian princesses had joined the canals in mythology.

When I tapped out "The End" on my Remington Noiseless (ha!) Portable in 1951, I could never have imagined that exactly twenty years later I should be sitting on a panel with Ray Bradbury and Carl Sagan at the Jet Propulsion Laboratory, waiting for the first news of the real Mars to arrive from the

Mariner space probes. (See *Mars and the Mind of Man,* Harper & Row, 1973.) But that was only the first trickle of a flood of information: During the next two decades, the *Viking*s were to give stunning images of the gigantic Mariner Valley and, most awe-inspiring of all, Olympus Mons—an extinct volcano more than twice the height of Everest. (Pause for embarrassed cough. Somewhere herein you'll find "There are no mountains on Mars!" Well, that's what even the best observers, straining their eyes to make sense of the tiny disc dancing in the field of their telescopes, believed in the 1950s.)

Soon after maps of the real Mars became available, I received a generous gift from computer genius John Hinkley—his Vistapro image-processing system. This prompted me to do some desktop terraforming (a word, incidentally, invented by science fiction's Grandest of Grand Masters, Jack Williamson.) I must confess that in *The Snows of Olympus: A Garden on Mars* (Norton, 1995) I frequently allowed artistic considerations to override scientific ones. Thus I couldn't resist putting a lake in the caldera of Mount Olympus, unlikely though it is that the most strenuous efforts of future colonists will produce an atmosphere dense enough to permit liquid water at such an altitude.

My next encounter with Mars involved a most ambitious but, alas, unsuccessful space project—the Russian MARS96 mission. Besides all its scientific equipment, the payload carried a CD/ROM disc full of sounds and images, including the whole of the famous Orson Welles "War of the Worlds" broadcast. (I have a recording of the only encounter between H.G. and Orson, made soon after this historic demonstration of the power of the new medium. Listening to the friendly banter between two of the great magicians of our age is like stepping into a time machine.)

It was intended that all these "Visions of Mars" would, some day in the 21st century, serve as greetings to the pioneers of the next New World. I was privileged to send a video recording, made in the garden of my Colombo home. Here is what I said:

Message to Mars

My name is Arthur Clarke, and I am speaking to you from the island of Sri Lanka, once known as Ceylon, in the Indian Ocean, Planet Earth. It is early spring in the year 1993, but this message is intended for the future.

I am addressing men and women—perhaps some of you already born—who will listen to these words when they are living on Mars.

As we approach the new millennium, there is great interest in the planet that may be the first real home for mankind beyond the mother world. During my lifetime, I have been lucky enough to see our knowledge of Mars advance from almost complete ignorance—worse than that, misleading fantasy—to a real understanding of its geography and climate. Certainly we are still very ignorant in many areas, and lack knowledge that you take for granted. But now we have accurate maps of your wonderful world, and can imagine how it might be modified—terraformed—to make it nearer to the heart's desire. Perhaps you are already engaged upon that centuries-long process.

There is a link between Mars and my present home, which I used in what will probably be my last novel, *The Hammer of God.* At the beginning of this century, an amateur astronomer named Percy Molesworth was living here in Ceylon. He spent much time observing Mars, and now there is a huge crater, 175 kilometers wide, named after him in your southern hemisphere.

In my book I've imagined how a New Martian astronomer might one day look back at his ancestral world, to try and see the little island from which Molesworth—and I—often gazed up at your planet.

There was a time, soon after the first landing on the Moon in 1969, when we were optimistic enough to imagine that we might have reached Mars by the 1990s. In another of my stories, I described a survivor of the first ill-fated expedition, watching the Earth in transit across the face of the Sun on May 11, 1984!

Well, there was no one on Mars then to watch that event—but it will happen again on November 10, 2084. By that time I hope that many eyes will be looking back towards the Earth as it slowly crosses the solar disc, looking like a tiny, perfectly circular sunspot. And I've suggested that we should signal to you then with powerful lasers, so that you will see a star beaming a message to you from the very face of the Sun.

I too salute you across the gulfs of space—as I send my greetings and good wishes from the closing decade of the century in which mankind first became a space-faring species, and set forth on a journey that can never end, so long as the universe endures.

Alas, owing to a failure of the launch vehicle, MARS96 ended up at the bottom of the Pacific. But I hope—and fully expect—that one day our descendants on the red planet will be chuckling over this CD/ROM—which is a delightful combination of science, art, and fantasy. (It is still available from the Planetary Society, 65 N. Catalina Ave., Pasadena, Ca. 91106.)

On July 4, 1997, with a little help from the World Wide Web, Mars was news again. *Pathfinder* had made a bumpy landing in the Ares Vallis region and disgorged the tiny but sophisticated rover, *Sojourner,* whose cautious exploration of the surrounding rockscape was watched by millions on Earth. This was the moment when, for most people, Mars ceased to be a distant place in the sky and became a real world.

Shortly afterwards, Donna Shirley—the engineer who had run the program—sent me her autobiography, *Managing Martians* (Broadway Books, 1998), with a dedication: "To Arthur

Clarke, who inspired my summer vacation on Mars." Reading further, I was delighted to discover how this happened: "At age twelve and searching for my own place in the world, I'd read *The Sands of Mars,* a book that pointed me towards the sky."

Colombo, Sri Lanka
January 2001

Chapter

1

"So this is the first time you've been upstairs?" said the pilot, leaning back idly in his seat so that it rocked to and fro in the gimbals. He clasped his hands behind his neck in a nonchalant manner that did nothing to reassure his passenger.

"Yes," said Martin Gibson, never taking his eyes from the chronometer as it ticked away the seconds.

"I thought so. You never got it quite right in your stories—all that nonsense about fainting under the acceleration. Why must people write such stuff? It's bad for business."

"I'm sorry," Gibson replied. "But I think you must be referring to my earlier stories. Space-travel hadn't got started then, and I had to use my imagination."

"Maybe," said the pilot grudgingly. (He wasn't paying the slightest attention to the instruments, and take-off was only two minutes away.) "It must be funny, I suppose, for this to be happening to you, after writing about it so often."

The adjective, thought Gibson, was hardly the one he would have used himself, but he saw the other's point of view. Dozens of his heroes—and villains—had gazed hypnotized by remorseless second-hands, waiting for the rockets to hurl them into infinity. And now—as it always did if one waited long enough—the reality had caught up with the fiction. The same moment lay only ninety seconds in his own future. Yes, it *was* funny, a beautiful case of poetic justice.

The pilot glanced at him, reading his feelings, and grinned cheerfully.

"Don't let your own stories scare you. Why, I once took off standing up, just for a bet, though it was a damn silly thing to do."

"I'm not scared," Gibson replied with unnecessary emphasis.

"Hmmm," said the pilot, condescending to glance at the clock. The second-hand had one more circuit to go. "Then I shouldn't hold on to the seat like that. It's only beryl-manganese; you might bend it."

Sheepishly, Gibson relaxed. He knew that he was building up synthetic responses to the situation, but they seemed none the less real for all that.

"Of course," said the pilot, still at ease but now, Gibson noticed, keeping his eyes fixed on the instrument panel, "it wouldn't be very comfortable if it lasted more than a few minutes—ah, there go the fuel pumps. Don't worry when the vertical starts doing funny things, but let the seat swing where it likes. Shut your eyes if that helps at all. (Hear the igniter jets start then?) We take about ten seconds to build up to full thrust—there's really nothing to it, apart from the noise. You just have to put up with that. I SAID, YOU JUST HAVE TO PUT UP WITH THAT!"

But Martin Gibson was doing nothing of the sort. He had already slipped gracefully into unconsciousness at an acceleration that had not yet exceeded that of a high-speed elevator.

He revived a few minutes and a thousand kilometers* later, feeling quite ashamed of himself. A beam of sunlight was shin-

*The metric system is used throughout this account of space-travel. This decimal system is based upon the meter equalling 39.37 inches. Thus a kilometer would be slightly over one-half mile (0:62 mi.).

ing full on his face, and he realized that the protective shutter on the outer hull must have slid aside. Although brilliant, the light was not as intolerably fierce as he would have expected; then he saw that only a fraction of the full intensity was filtering through the deeply tinted glass.

He looked at the pilot, hunched over his instrument board and busily writing up the log. Everything was very quiet, but from time to time there would come curiously muffled reports—almost miniature explosions—that Gibson found disconcerting. He coughed gently to announce his return to consciousness, and asked the pilot what they were.

"Thermal contraction in the motors," he replied briefly. "They've been running round five thousand degrees and cool mighty fast. You feeling all right now?"

"I'm fine," Gibson answered, and meant it. "Shall I get up?"

Psychologically, he had hit the bottom and bounced back. It was a very unstable position, though he did not realize it.

"If you like," said the pilot doubtfully. "But be careful—hang on to something solid."

Gibson felt a wonderful sense of exhilaration. The moment he had waited for all his life had come. He was in space! It was too bad that he'd missed the take-off, but he'd gloss that part over when he wrote it up.

From a thousand kilometers away, Earth was still very large—and something of a disappointment. The reason was quickly obvious. He had seen so many hundreds of rocket photographs and films that the surprise had been spoilt; he knew exactly what to expect. There were the inevitable moving bands of cloud on their slow march round the world. At the center of the disc, the divisions between land and sea were sharply defined, and an infinite amount of minute detail was visible, but towards the horizon everything was lost in the thickening haze. Even in the cone of clear vision vertically beneath him, most of the features were unrecognizable and therefore meaningless. No doubt a meteorologist would have gone into transports of delight at the animated weather-map displayed below—but most of the meteorologists were up in the space stations, anyway, where they had an even better view. Gibson soon grew tired of searching for cities and other works of man. It was chastening to think that all the thousands of years of human civilization had produced no appreciable change in the panorama below.

Then Gibson began to look for the stars, and met his second disappointment. They were there, hundreds of them, but pale and wan, mere ghosts of the blinding myriads he had expected to find. The dark glass of the port was to blame; in subduing the sun, it had robbed the stars of all their glory.

Gibson felt a vague annoyance. Only one thing had turned out quite as expected. The sensation of floating in mid-air, of being able to propel oneself from wall to wall at the touch of a finger, was just as delightful as he had hoped—though the quarters were too cramped for any ambitious experiments. Weightlessness was an enchanting, a fairylike state, now that there were drugs to immobilize the balance organs and space-sickness was a thing of the past. He was glad of that. How his heroes had suffered! (His heroines too, presumably, but one never mentioned that.) He remembered Robin Blake's first flight, in the original version of "Martian Dust." When he'd written that, he had been heavily under the influence of D. H. Lawrence. (It would be interesting, one day, to make a list of the authors who *hadn't* influenced him at one time or another.)

There was no doubt that Lawrence was magnificent at describing physical sensations, and quite deliberately Gibson had set out to defeat him on his own ground. He had devoted a whole chapter to space-sickness, describing every symptom from the queasy premonitions that could sometimes be willed aside, the subterranean upheavals that even the most optimistic could no longer ignore, the volcanic cataclysms of the final stages and the ultimate, merciful exhaustion.

The chapter had been a masterpiece of stark realism. It was

too bad that his publishers, with an eye on a squeamish Book-of-the-Month Club, had insisted on removing it. He had put a lot of work into that chapter; while he was writing it, he had really *lived* those sensations. Even now—

"It's very puzzling," said the M.O. thoughtfully as the now quiescent author was propelled through the airlock. "He's passed his medical tests O.K., and of course he'll have had the usual injections before leaving Earth. It must be psychosomatic."

"I don't care what it is," complained the pilot bitterly, as he followed the cortege into the heart of Space Station One. "All I want to know is—who's going to clean up my ship?"

No one seemed inclined to answer this heart-felt question, least of all Martin Gibson, who was only vaguely conscious of white walls drifting by his field of vision. Then, slowly, there was a sensation of increasing weight, and a warm, caressing glow began to steal through his limbs. Presently he became fully aware of his surroundings. He was in a hospital ward, and a battery of infrared lamps was bathing him with a glorious, enervating warmth, that sank through his flesh to the very bones.

"Well?" said the medical officer presently.

Gibson grinned feebly.

"I'm sorry about this. Is it going to happen again?"

"I don't know how it happened the first time. It's very unusual; the drugs we have now are supposed to be infallible."

"I think it was my own fault," said Gibson apologetically. "You see, I've got a rather powerful imagination, and I started thinking about the symptoms of space-sickness—in quite an objective sort of way, of course—but before I knew what had happened—"

"Well, just stop it!" ordered the doctor sharply. "Or we'll have to send you right back to Earth. You can't do this sort of thing if you're going to Mars. There wouldn't be much left of you after three months."

A shudder passed through Gibson's tortured frame. But he was rapidly recovering, and already the nightmare of the last hour was fading into the past.

"I'll be O.K.," he said. "Let me out of this muffle-furnace before I cook."

A little unsteadily, he got to his feet. It seemed strange, here in space, to have normal weight again. Then he remembered that Station One was spinning on its axis, and the living quarters were built around the outer walls so that centrifugal force could give the illusion of gravity.

The great adventure, he thought ruefully, hadn't started at all well. But he was determined not to be sent home in disgrace. It was not merely a question of his own pride: the effect on his public and his reputation would be deplorable. He winced as he visualized the headlines: "GIBSON GROUNDED! SPACE-SICKNESS ROUTS AUTHOR-ASTRONAUT." Even the staid literary weeklies would pull his leg, and as for "Time"—no, it was unthinkable!

"It's lucky," said the M.O., "that we've got twelve hours before the ship leaves. I'll take you into the zero-gravity section and see how you manage there, before I give you a clean bill of health."

Gibson also thought that was a good idea. He had always regarded himself as fairly fit, and until now it had never seriously occurred to him that this journey might be not merely uncomfortable but actually dangerous. You could laugh at space-sickness—when you'd never experienced it yourself. Afterwards, it seemed a very different matter.

The Inner Station—"Space Station One," as it was usually called—was just over two thousand kilometers from Earth, circling the planet every two hours. It had been Man's first stepping-stone to the stars, and though it was no longer technically necessary for spaceflight, its presence had a profound effect on the economics of interplanetary travel. All journeys to the Moon or the planets started from here; the unwieldy atomic ships floated alongside this outpost of Earth while the cargoes from the parent world were loaded into their holds. A ferry service of chemically fuelled rockets linked the station to the planet beneath, for by law no atomic drive unit was allowed to operate within a thousand kilometers of the Earth's surface. Even this safety margin was felt by many to be inadequate, for the radioactive blast of a nuclear propulsion unit could cover that distance in less than a minute.

Space Station One had grown with the passing years, by a process of accretion, until its original designers would never have recognized it. Around the central spherical core had accumulated observatories, communications labs with fantastic aerial systems, and mazes of scientific equipment which only a specialist could identify. But despite all these additions, the main function of the artificial moon was still that of refueling the little ships with which Man was challenging the immense loneliness of the Solar System.

"Quite sure you're feeling O.K. now?" asked the doctor as Gibson experimented with his feet.

"I think so," he replied, unwilling to commit himself.

"Then come along to the reception room and we'll get you a drink—a nice hot drink," he added, to prevent any misunderstanding. "You can sit there and read the paper for half an hour before we decide what to do with you."

It seemed to Gibson that anticlimax was being piled on anticlimax. He was two thousand kilometers from Earth, with the stars all around him; yet here he was forced to sit sipping sweet tea—tea!—in what might have been an ordinary dentist's waiting-room. There were no windows, presumably because the sight of the rapidly revolving heavens might have undone the good work of the medical staff. The only way of passing the time was to skim through piles of magazines which he'd already seen, and which were difficult to handle as they were ultra-lightweight editions apparently printed on cigarette paper. Fortunately he found a very old copy of "Argosy" containing a story he had written so long ago that he had completely forgotten the ending, and this kept him happy until the doctor returned.

"Your pulse seems normal," said the M.O., grudgingly. "We'll take you along to the zero-gravity chamber. Just follow me and don't be surprised at anything that happens."

With this cryptic remark he led Gibson out into a wide, brightly lit corridor that seemed to curve upwards in both directions away from the point at which he was standing. Gibson had no time to examine this phenomenon, for the doctor slid open a side door and started up a flight of metal stairs. Gibson followed automatically for a few paces, then realized just what lay ahead of him and stopped with an involuntary cry of amazement.

Immediately beneath his feet, the slope of the stairway was a reasonable forty-five degrees, but it rapidly became steeper until only a dozen meters ahead the steps were rising vertically. Thereafter—and it was a sight that might have unnerved anyone coming across it for the first time—the increase of gradient continued remorselessly until the steps began to overhang and at last passed out of sight above and *behind* him.

Hearing his exclamation, the doctor looked back and gave a reassuring laugh.

"You mustn't always believe your eyes," he said. "Come along and see how easy it is."

Reluctantly Gibson followed, and as he did so he became aware that two very peculiar things were happening. In the first place he was gradually becoming lighter; in the second, despite the obvious steepening of the stairway, the slope beneath his feet remained at a constant forty-five degrees. The vertical direction itself, in fact, was slowly tilting as he moved forward, so that despite its increasing curvature the gradient of the stairway never altered.

It did not take Gibson long to arrive at the explanation. All the apparent gravity was due to the centrifugal force produced as the station spun slowly on its axis, and as he approached the center the force was diminishing to zero. The stairway itself was winding in towards the axis along some sort of spiral—once he'd have known its mathematical name—so that despite the radial gravity field the slope underfoot remained constant. It was the sort of thing that people who lived in space stations must get accustomed to quickly enough; presumably when they returned to Earth the sight of a normal stairway would be equally unsettling.

At the end of the stairs there was no longer any real sense of "up" or "down." They were in a long cylindrical room, criss-crossed with ropes but otherwise empty, and at its far end a shaft of sunlight came blasting through an observation port. As Gibson watched, the beam moved steadily across the metal walls like a questing searchlight, was momentarily eclipsed, then blazed out again from another window. It was the first indication Gibson's senses had given him of the fact that the station was really spinning on its axis, and he timed the rotation roughly by noting how long the sunlight took to return to its original position. The "day" of this little artificial world was less than ten seconds; that was sufficient to give a sensation of normal gravity at its outer walls.

Gibson felt rather like a spider in its web as he followed the doctor hand-over-hand along the guide ropes, towing himself effortlessly through the air until they came to the observation post. They were, he saw, at the end of a sort of chimney jutting out along the axis of the station, so that they were well clear of its equipment and apparatus and had an almost unrestricted view of the stars.

"I'll leave you here for a while," said the doctor. "There's plenty to look at, and you should be quite happy. If not—well, remember there's normal gravity at the bottom of those stairs!"

Yes, thought Gibson; *and* a return trip to Earth by the next rocket as well. But he was determined to pass the test and to get a clean bill of health.

It was quite impossible to realize that the space station itself was rotating, and not the framework of sun and stars: to believe otherwise required an act of faith, a conscious effort of will. The stars were moving so quickly that only the brighter ones were clearly visible and the sun, when Gibson allowed himself to glance at it out of the corner of his eye, was a golden comet that crossed the sky every five seconds. With this fantastic speeding up of the natural order of events, it was easy to see how ancient man had refused to believe that his own solid earth was rotating, and had attributed all movement to the turning celestial sphere.

Partly occulted by the bulk of the station, the Earth was a great crescent spanning half the sky. It was slowly waxing as the station raced along on its globe-encircling orbit; in some forty minutes it would be full, and an hour after that would be totally invisible, a black shield eclipsing the sun while the station passed through its cone of shadow. The Earth would go through all its phases—from new to full and back again—in just two hours. The sense of time became distorted as one thought of these things; the familiar divisions of day and night, of months and seasons, had no meaning here.

About a kilometer from the station, moving with it in its orbit but not at the moment connected to it in any way, were the three spaceships that happened to be "in dock" at the moment. One was the tiny arrowhead of the rocket that had brought him, at such expense and such discomfort, up from Earth an hour ago. The second was a lunar-bound freighter of, he guessed, about a thousand tons gross. And the third, of course, was the *Ares,* almost dazzling in the splendor of her new aluminum paint.

Gibson had never become reconciled to the loss of the sleek, streamlined spaceships which had been the dream of the early twentieth century. The glittering dumb-bell hanging against the stars was not *his* idea of a space-liner; though the world had accepted it, he had not. Of course, he knew the familiar arguments—there was no need for streamlining in a ship that never entered an atmosphere, and therefore the design was dictated purely by structural and power-plant considerations. Since the violently radioactive drive-unit had to be as far away from the crew quarters as possible, the double-sphere and long connecting tube was the simplest solution.

It was also, Gibson thought, the ugliest; but that hardly mattered since the *Ares* would spend practically all her life in deep space where the only spectators were the stars. Presumably she was already fueled and merely waiting for the precisely calculated moment when her motors would burst into life, and she would pull away out of the orbit in which she was circling and had hitherto spent all her existence, to swing into the long hyperbola that led to Mars.

When that happened, he would be aboard, launched at last upon the adventure he had never really believed would come to him.

CHAPTER

The captain's office aboard the *Ares* was not designed to hold more than three men when gravity was acting, but there was plenty of room for six while the ship was in a free orbit and one could stand on walls or ceiling according to taste. All except one of the group clustered at surrealist angles around Captain Norden had been in space before and knew what was expected of them, but this was no ordinary briefing. The maiden flight of a new spaceship is always an occasion, and the *Ares* was the first of her line—the first, indeed, of all spaceships ever to be built primarily for passengers and not for freight. When she was fully commissioned, she would carry a crew of thirty and a hundred and fifty passengers in somewhat spartan comfort. On her first voyage, however, the proportions were almost reversed and at the moment her crew of six was waiting for the single passenger to come aboard.

"I'm still not quite clear," said Owen Bradley, the electronics officer, "what we are supposed to do with the fellow when we've got him. Whose bright idea was this, anyway?"

"I was coming to that," said Captain Norden, running his hands over where his magnificent blond hair had been only a few days before. (Spaceships seldom carry professional barbers, and though there are always plenty of eager amateurs one prefers to put off the evil day as long as possible.) "You all know of Mr. Gibson, of course."

This remark produced a chorus of replies, not all of them respectful.

"I think his stories stink," said Dr. Scott. "The later ones, anyway. 'Martian Dust' wasn't bad, but of course it's completely dated now."

"Nonsense!" snorted astrogator Mackay. "The last stories are much the best, now that Gibson's got interested in fundamentals and has cut out the blood and thunder."

This outburst from the mild little Scott was most uncharacteristic. Before anyone else could join in, Captain Norden interrupted.

"We're not here to discuss literary criticism, if you don't mind. There'll be plenty of time for that later. But there are one or two points the Corporation wants me to make clear before we begin. Mr. Gibson is a very important man—a distinguished guest—and he's been invited to come on this trip so that he can write a book about it later. It's not just a publicity stunt." ("Of course not!" interjected Bradley, with heavy sarcasm.) "But naturally the Corporation hopes that future clients won't be—er—discouraged by what they read. Apart from that, we *are* making history; our maiden voyage ought to be recorded properly. So try and behave like gentlemen for a while; Gibson's book will probably sell half a million copies, and your future reputations may depend on your behavior these next three months!"

"That sounds dangerously like blackmail to me," said Bradley.

"Take it that way if you please," continued Norden cheerfully. "Of course, I'll explain to Gibson that he can't expect the service that will be provided later when we've got stewards and cooks and Lord knows what. He'll understand that, and won't expect breakfast in bed every morning."

"Will he help with the washing-up?" asked someone with a practical turn of mind.

Before Norden could deal with this problem in social etiquette a sudden buzzing came from the communications panel, and a voice began to call from the speaker grille.

"Station One calling *Ares*—your passenger's coming over."

Norden flipped a switch and replied, "O.K.—we're ready." Then he turned to the crew.

"With all these hair-cuts around, the poor chap will think it's graduation day at Alcatraz. Go and meet him, Jimmy, and help him through the airlock when the tender couples up."

Martin Gibson was still feeling somewhat exhilarated at having surmounted his first major obstacle—the M.O. at Space Station One. The loss of gravity on leaving the station and crossing to the *Ares* in the tiny, compressed-air driven tender had scarcely bothered him at all, but the sight that met his eyes when he entered Captain Norden's cabin caused him a momentary relapse. Even when there was no gravity, one liked to pretend that *some* direction was "down," and it seemed natural to assume that the surface on which chairs and table were bolted was the floor. Unfortunately the majority decision seemed otherwise, for two members of the crew were hanging like stalactites from the "ceiling," while two more were relaxed at quite arbitrary angles in mid-air. Only the Captain was, according to Gibson's ideas, the right way up. To make matters worse, their shaven heads gave these normally quite presentable men a faintly sinister appearance, so that the whole tableau looked like a family reunion at Castle Dracula.

There was a brief pause while the crew analyzed Gibson. They all recognized the novelist at once; his face had been familiar to the public ever since his first best-seller, "Thunder in the Dawn," had appeared nearly twenty years ago. He was a chubby yet sharp-featured little man, still on the right side of forty-five, and when he spoke his voice was surprisingly deep and resonant.

"This," said Captain Norden, working round the cabin from left to right, "is my engineer, Lieutenant Hilton. This is Dr. Mackay, our navigator—only a Ph.D., not a *real* doctor, like Dr. Scott here. Lieutenant Bradley is Electronics Officer, and Jimmy Spencer, who met you at the airlock, is our supernumerary and hopes to be Captain when he grows up."

Gibson looked round the little group with some surprise. There were so few of them—five men and a boy! His face must have revealed his thoughts, for Captain Norden laughed and continued.

"Not many of us, are there? But you must remember that this ship is almost automatic—and besides, nothing ever happens in space. When we start the regular passenger run, there'll be a crew of thirty. On this trip, we're making up the weight in cargo, so we're really traveling as a fast freighter."

Gibson looked carefully at the men who would be his only companions for the next three months. His first reaction (he always distrusted first reactions, but was at pains to note them) was one of astonishment that they seemed so ordinary—when one made allowance for such superficial matters as their odd attitudes and temporary baldness. There was no way of guessing that they belonged to a profession more romantic than any that the world had known since the last cowboys traded in their broncos for helicopters.

At a signal which Gibson did not intercept, the others took their leave by launching themselves with fascinatingly effortless precision through the open doorway. Captain Norden settled down in his seat again and offered Gibson a cigarette. The author accepted it doubtfully.

"You don't mind smoking?" he asked. "Doesn't it waste oxygen?"

"There'd be a mutiny," laughed Norden, "if I had to ban smoking for three months. In any case, the oxygen consumption's negligible."

Captain Norden, thought Gibson a little ruefully, was not

fitting at all well into the expected pattern. The skipper of a space-liner, according to the best—or at least the most popular—literary tradition, should be a grizzled, keen-eyed veteran who had spent half his life in the ether and could navigate across the Solar System by the seat of his pants, thanks to his uncanny knowledge of the spaceways. He must also be a martinet; when he gave orders, his officers must jump to attention (not an easy thing under zero gravity), salute smartly, and depart at the double.

Instead, the captain of the *Ares* was certainly less than forty, and might have been taken for a successful business executive. As for being a martinet—so far Gibson had detected no signs of discipline whatsoever. This impression, he realized later, was not strictly accurate. The only discipline aboard the *Ares* was entirely self-imposed; that was the only form possible among the type of men who composed her crew.

"So you've never been in space before," said Norden, looking thoughtfully at his passenger.

"I'm afraid not. I made several attempts to get on the lunar run, but it's absolutely impossible unless you're on official business. It's a pity that space-travel's still so infernally expensive."

Norden smiled.

"We hope the *Ares* will do something to change that. I must say," he added, "that you seem to have managed to write quite a lot about the subject with—ah—the minimum of practical experience."

"Oh, that!" said Gibson airily, with what he hoped was a light laugh. "It's a common delusion that authors must have experienced everything they describe in their books. I read all I could about space-travel when I was younger and did my best to get the local color right. Don't forget that all my interplanetary novels were written in the early days—I've hardly touched the subject in the last few years. It's rather surprising that people still associate my name with it."

Norden wondered how much of this modesty was assumed.

Gibson must know perfectly well that it was his space-travel novels that had made him famous—and had prompted the Corporation to invite him on this trip. The whole situation, Norden realized, had some highly entertaining possibilities. But they would have to wait; in the meantime he must explain to this landlubber the routine of life aboard the private world of the *Ares*.

"We keep normal Earth-time—Greenwich Meridian—aboard the ship and everything shuts down at 'night.' There are no watches, as there used to be in the old days; the instruments can take over when we're sleeping, so we aren't on continuous duty. That's one reason why we can manage with such a small crew. On this trip, as there's plenty of space, we've all got separate cabins. Yours is a regular passenger stateroom; the only one that's fitted up, as it happens. I think you'll find it comfortable. Is all your cargo aboard? How much did they let you take?"

"A hundred kilos. It's in the airlock."

"A hundred kilos?" Norden managed to repress his amazement. The fellow must be emigrating—taking all his family heirlooms with him. Norden had the true astronaut's horror of surplus mass, and did not doubt that Gibson was carrying a lot of unnecessary rubbish. However, if the Corporation had O.K.'d it, and the authorized load wasn't exceeded, he had nothing to complain about.

"I'll get Jimmy to take you to your room. He's our odd-job man for this trip, working his passage and learning something about spaceflight. Most of us start that way, signing up for the lunar run during college vacations. Jimmy's quite a bright lad—he's already got his Bachelor's degree."

By now Gibson was beginning to take it quite for granted that the cabin-boy would be a college graduate. He followed Jimmy—who seemed somewhat overawed by his presence—to the passengers' quarters.

The stateroom was small, but beautifully planned and designed in excellent taste. Ingenious lighting and mirror-faced walls made it seem much larger than it really was, and the pivoted bed could be reversed during the "day" to act as a table. There were very few reminders of the absence of gravity; everything had been done to make the traveler feel at home.

For the next hour Gibson sorted out his belongings and experimented with the room's gadgets and controls. The device that pleased him most was a shaving mirror which, when a button was pressed, transformed itself into a porthole looking out on the stars. He wondered just how it was done.

At last everything was stowed away where he could find it; there was absolutely nothing else for him to do. He lay down on the bed and buckled the elastic belts around his chest and thighs. The illusion of weight was not very convincing, but it was better than nothing and did give some sense of a vertical direction.

Lying at peace in the bright little room that would be his world for the next hundred days, he could forget the disappointments and petty annoyances that had marred his departure from Earth. There was nothing to worry about now; for the first time in almost as long as he could remember, he had given his future entirely into the keeping of others. Engagements, lecture appointments, deadlines—all these things he had left behind on Earth. The sense of blissful relaxation was too good to last, but he would let his mind savor it while he could.

A series of apologetic knocks on the cabin door roused Gibson from sleep an indeterminate time later. For a moment he did not realize where he was; then full consciousness came back; he unclipped the retaining straps and thrust himself off the bed. As his movements were still poorly coordinated he had to make a carom off the nominal ceiling before reaching the door.

Jimmy Spencer stood there, slightly out of breath.

"Captain's compliments, sir, and would you like to come and see the take-off?"

"I certainly would," said Gibson. "Wait until I get my camera."

He reappeared a moment later carrying a brand-new Leica XXA, at which Jimmy stared with undisguised envy, and festooned with auxiliary lenses and exposure meters. Despite these handicaps, they quickly reached the observation gallery, which ran like a circular belt around the body of the *Ares.*

For the first time Gibson saw the stars in their full glory, no longer dimmed either by atmosphere or by darkened glass, for he was on the night side of the ship and the sun-filters had been drawn aside. The *Ares,* unlike the space-station, was not turning on her axis but was held in the rigid reference system of her gyroscopes so that the stars were fixed and motionless in her skies.

As he gazed on the glory he had so often, and so vainly, tried to describe in his books, Gibson found it very hard to analyze his emotions—and he hated to waste an emotion that might profitably be employed in print. Oddly enough neither the brightness nor the sheer numbers of the stars made the greatest impression on his mind. He had seen skies little inferior to this from the tops of mountains on Earth, or from the observation decks of stratoliners; but never before had he felt so vividly the sense that the stars were all around him, down to the horizon he no longer possessed, and even below, under his very feet.

Space Station One was a complicated, brightly polished toy floating in nothingness a few meters beyond the port. There was no way in which its distance or size could be judged, for there was nothing familiar about its shape, and the sense of perspective seemed to have failed. Earth and Sun were both invisible, hidden behind the body of the ship.

Startlingly close, a disembodied voice came suddenly from a hidden speaker.

"One hundred seconds to firing. Please take your positions."

Gibson automatically tensed himself and turned to Jimmy for advice. Before he could frame any questions, his guide said hastily, "I must get back on duty," and disappeared in a graceful power-dive, leaving Gibson alone with his thoughts.

The next minute and a half passed with remarkable slowness, punctuated though it was with frequent time-checks from the speakers. Gibson wondered who the announcer was; it did not sound like Norden's voice, and probably it was merely a recording, operated by the automatic circuit which must now have taken over control of the ship.

"Twenty seconds to go. Thrust will take about ten seconds to build up."

"Ten seconds to go."

"Five seconds, four, three, two, one——"

Very gently, something took hold of Gibson and slid him down the curving side of the porthole-studded wall on to what had suddenly become the floor. It was hard to realize that up and down had returned once more, harder still to connect their reappearance with that distant, attenuated thunder that had broken in upon the silence of the ship. Far away in the second sphere that was the other half of the *Ares,* in that mysterious, forbidden world of dying atoms and automatic machines which no man could ever enter and live, the forces that powered the stars themselves were being unleashed. Yet there was none of that sense of mounting, pitiless acceleration that always accompanies the take-off of a chemically propelled rocket. The *Ares* had unlimited space in which to maneuver; she could take as long as she pleased to break free from her present orbit and crawl slowly out into the transfer hyperbola that would lead her to Mars. In any case, the utmost power of the atomic drive could move her two-thousand-ton mass with an acceleration of only a tenth of a gravity, at the moment it was throttled back to less than half of this small value.

It did not take Gibson long to re-orientate himself. The ship's acceleration was so low—it gave him, he calculated, an effective weight of less than four kilograms—that his movements were still practically unrestricted. Space Station One had not moved from its apparent position, and he had to wait almost a minute before he could detect that the *Ares* was, in fact, slowly drawing away from it. Then he belatedly remembered his camera, and began to record the departure. When he had finally settled (he hoped) the tricky problem of the right exposure to give a small, brilliantly lit object against a jet-black background, the station was already appreciably more distant. In less than ten minutes, it had dwindled to a distant point of light that was hard to distinguish from the stars.

When Space Station One had vanished completely, Gibson went round to the day side of the ship to take some photographs of the receding Earth. It was a huge, thin crescent when he first saw it, far too large for the eye to take in at a single glance. As he watched, he could see that it was slowly waxing, for the *Ares* must make at least one more circuit before she could break away and spiral out towards Mars. It would be a good hour before the Earth was appreciably smaller and in that time it would pass again from new to full.

Well, this is it, thought Gibson. Down there is all my past life, and the lives of all my ancestors back to the first blob of jelly in the first primeval sea. No colonist or explorer setting sail from his native land ever left so much behind as I am leaving now. Down beneath those clouds lies the whole of human history; soon I shall be able to eclipse with my little finger what was, until a lifetime ago, all of Man's dominion and everything that his art had saved from time.

This inexorable drawing away from the known into the unknown had almost the finality of death. Thus must the naked soul, leaving all its treasures behind it, go out at last into the darkness and the night.

Gibson was still watching at the observation post when,

more than an hour later, the *Ares* finally reached escape velocity and was free from Earth. There was no way of telling that this moment had come and passed, for Earth still dominated the sky and the motors still maintained their muffled, distant thunder. Another ten hours of continuous operation would be needed before they had completed their task and could be closed down for the rest of the voyage.

Gibson was sleeping when that moment came. The sudden silence, the complete loss of even the slight gravity the ship had enjoyed these last few hours, brought him back to a twilight sense of awareness. He looked dreamily around the darkened room until his eye found the little pattern of stars framed in the porthole. They were, of course, utterly motionless. It was impossible to believe that the *Ares* was now racing out from the Earth's orbit at a speed so great that even the Sun could never hold her back.

Sleepily, he tightened the fastenings of his bedclothes to prevent himself drifting out into the room. It would be nearly a hundred days before he had any sense of weight again.

Chapter

3

The same pattern of stars filled the porthole when a series of bell-like notes tolling from the ship's public address system woke Gibson from a comparatively dreamless sleep. He dressed in some haste and hurried out to the observation deck, wondering what had happened to Earth overnight.

It is very disconcerting, at least to an inhabitant of Earth, to see two moons in the sky at once. But there they were, side by side, both in their first quarter, and one about twice as large as the other. It was several seconds before Gibson realized that he was looking at Moon and Earth together—and several seconds more before he finally grasped the fact that the smaller and more distant crescent was his own world.

The *Ares* was not, unfortunately, passing very close to the Moon, but even so it was more than ten times as large as Gibson had ever seen it from the Earth. The interlocking chains of crater-rings were clearly visible along the ragged line separating day from night, and the still unilluminated disc could be faintly seen by the reflected earthlight falling upon it. And surely—Gibson bent suddenly forward, wondering if his eyes had tricked him. Yet there was no doubt of it: down in the midst of that cold and faintly gleaming land, waiting for the dawn that was still many days away, minute sparks of light were burning like fireflies in the dusk. They had not been there fifty years ago; they were the lights of the first lunar cities, telling the stars that life had come at last to the Moon after a billion years of waiting.

A discreet cough from nowhere in particular interrupted Gibson's reverie. Then a slightly overamplified voice remarked in a conversational tone:

"If Mr. Gibson will kindly come to the mess-room, he will find some tepid coffee and a few flakes of cereal still left on the table."

He glanced hurriedly at his watch. He had completely forgotten about breakfast—an unprecedented phenomenon. No doubt someone had gone to look for him in his cabin and, failing to find him there, was paging him through the ship's public address system.

When he burst apologetically into the mess-room he found the crew engaged in technical controversy concerning the merits of various types of spaceships.

While he ate, Gibson watched the little group of arguing men, fixing them in his mind and noting their behavior and characteristics. Norden's introduction had merely served to give them labels; as yet they were not definite personalities to him. It was curious to think that before the voyage had ended, he would probably know every one of them better than most of his acquaintances back on Earth. There could be no secrets and no masks aboard the tiny world of the *Ares.*

At the moment, Dr. Scott was talking. (Later, Gibson would realize that there was nothing very unusual about this.) He seemed a somewhat excitable character, inclined to lay down the law at a moment's provocation on subjects about which he could not possibly be qualified to speak. His most successful interrupter was Bradley, the electronics and communications expert—a dryly cynical person who seemed to take a sardonic pleasure in verbal sabotage. From time to time he would throw a small bombshell into the conversation which would halt Scott for a moment, though never for long. Mackay, the little Scots mathematician, also entered the battle from time to time, speaking rather quickly in a precise, almost pedantic fashion. He would, Gibson thought, have been more at home in a university common-room than on a spaceship.

Captain Norden appeared to be acting as a not entirely disinterested umpire, supporting first one side and then the other in an effort to prevent any conclusive victory. Young Spencer was already at work, and Hilton, the only remaining member of the crew, had taken no part in the discussion. The engineer was sitting quietly watching the others with a detached amusement, and his face was hauntingly familiar to Gibson. Where had they met before? Why, of course—what a fool he was not to have realized it!—this was *the* Hilton. Gibson swung round in his chair so that he could see the other more clearly. His half-finished meal was forgotten as he looked with awe and envy at the man who had brought the *Arcturus* back to Mars after the greatest adventure in the history of spaceflight. Only six men had ever reached Saturn; and only three of them were still alive. Hilton had stood, with his lost companions, on those far-off moons whose very names were magic—Titan, Encladus, Tethys, Rhea, Dione . . . He had seen the incomparable splendor of the great rings spanning the sky in symmetry that seemed too perfect for nature's contriving. He had been into that Ultima Thule in which circled the cold outer giants of the Sun's scattered family, and he had returned again to the light and warmth of the inner worlds. Yes, thought Gibson, there are a good many things I want to talk to you about before this trip's over.

The discussion group was breaking up as the various officers drifted—literally—away to their posts, but Gibson's thoughts were still circling Saturn as Captain Norden came across to him and broke into his reverie.

"I don't know what sort of schedule you've planned," he

said, "but I suppose you'd like to look over our ship. After all, that's what usually happens around this stage in one of your stories."

Gibson smiled, somewhat mechanically. He feared it was going to be some time before he lived down his past.

"I'm afraid you're quite right there. It's the easiest way, of course, of letting the reader know how things work, and sketching in the *locale* of the plot. Luckily it's not so important now that everyone knows exactly what a spaceship is like inside. One can take the technical details for granted, and get on with the story. But when I started writing about astronautics, back in the '60s, one had to hold up the plot for thousands of words to explain how the spacesuits worked, how the atomic drive operated, and clear up anything else that might come into the story."

"Then I can take it," said Norden, with the most disarming of smiles, "that there's not a great deal we can teach you about the *Ares*."

Gibson managed to summon up a blush.

"I'd appreciate it very much if you'd show me round—whether you do it according to the standard literary pattern or not."

"Very well," grinned Norden. "We'll start at the control room. Come along."

For the next two hours they floated along the labyrinth of corridors that crossed and criss-crossed like arteries in the spherical body of the *Ares*. Soon, Gibson knew, the interior of the ship would be so familiar to him that he could find his way blindfolded from one end to the other; but he had already lost his way once and would do so again before he had learned his way around.

As the ship was spherical, it had been divided into zones of latitude like the Earth. The resulting nomenclature was very useful, since it at once gave a mental picture of the liner's geography. To go "North" meant that one was heading for the control cabin and the crew's quarters. A trip to the Equator suggested that one was visiting either the great dining-hall occupying most of the central plane of the ship, or the observation gallery which completely encircled the liner. The Southern hemisphere was almost entirely fuel tank, with a few storage holds and miscellaneous machinery. Now that the *Ares* was no longer using her motors, she had been swung round in space so that the Northern Hemisphere was in perpetual sunlight and the "uninhabited" Southern one in darkness. At the South Pole itself was a small metal door bearing a set of impressive official seals and the notice: "To be Opened only under the Express Orders of the Captain or his Deputy." Behind it lay the long, narrow tube connecting the main body of the ship with the smaller sphere, a hundred meters away, which held the power plant and drive units. Gibson wondered what was the point of having a door at all if no one could ever go through it; then he remembered that there must be some provision to enable the servicing robots of the Atomic Energy Commission to reach their work.

Strangely enough, Gibson received one of his strongest impressions not from the scientific and technical wonders of the ship, which he had expected to see in any case, but from the empty passenger quarters—a honeycomb of closely packed cells that occupied most of the North Temperate Zone. The impression was rather a disagreeable one. A house so new that no one has ever lived in it can be more lonely than an old, deserted ruin that has once known life and may still be peopled by ghosts. The sense of desolate emptiness was very strong here in the echoing, brightly lit corridors which would one day be crowded with life, but which now lay bleak and lonely in the sunlight piped through the walls—a sunlight much bluer than on earth and therefore hard and cold.

Gibson was quite exhausted, mentally and physically, when he got back to his room. Norden had been an altogether too conscientious guide, and Gibson suspected that he had been getting some of his own back, and thoroughly enjoying it. He wondered exactly what his companions thought of his literary activities; probably he would not be left in ignorance for long.

He was lying in his bunk, sorting out his impressions, when there came a modest knock on the door.

"Damn," said Gibson, quietly. "Who's that?" he continued, a little louder.

"It's Jim—Spencer, Mr. Gibson. I've got a radiogram for you."

Young Jimmy floated into the room, bearing an envelope with the Signals Officer's stamp. It was sealed, but Gibson surmised that he was the only person on the ship who didn't know its contents. He had a shrewd idea of what they would be, and groaned inwardly. There was really no way of escape from Earth; it could catch you wherever you went.

The message was brief and contained only one redundant word:

> NEW YORKER, REVUE DES QUATRE MONDES, LIFE INTERPLANETARY WANT FIVE THOUSAND WORDS EACH. PLEASE RADIO BY NEXT SUNDAY. LOVE. RUTH.

Gibson sighed. He had left Earth in such a rush that there had been no time for a final consultation with his agent, Ruth Goldstein, apart from a hurried phone-call halfway around the world. But he'd told her quite clearly that he wanted to be left alone for a fortnight. It never made any difference, of course. Ruth always went happily ahead, confident that he would deliver the goods on time. Well, for once he wouldn't be bullied and she could darned well wait; he'd earned this holiday.

He grabbed his scribbling pad and, while Jimmy gazed ostentatiously elsewhere, wrote quickly:

SORRY. EXCLUSIVE RIGHTS ALREADY PROMISED TO SOUTH ALABAMA PIG KEEPER AND POULTRY FANCIER. WILL SEND DETAILS ANY MONTH NOW. WHEN ARE YOU GOING TO POISON HARRY? LOVE, MART.

Harry was the literary, as opposed to the business, half of Goldstein and Co. He had been happily married to Ruth for over twenty years, during the last fifteen of which Gibson had never ceased to remind them both that they were getting in a rut and needed a change and that the whole thing couldn't possibly last much longer.

Goggling slightly, Jimmy Spencer disappeared with this unusual message, leaving Gibson alone with his thoughts. Of course, he would have to start work some time, but meanwhile his typewriter was buried down in the hold where he couldn't see it. He had even felt like attaching one of those "NOT WANTED IN SPACE—MAY BE STOWED IN VACUUM" labels, but had manfully resisted the temptation. Like most writers who had never had to rely solely on their literary earnings, Gibson hated *starting* to write. Once he had begun, it was different . . . sometimes.

His holiday lasted a full week. At the end of that time, Earth was merely the most brilliant of the stars and would soon be lost in the glare of the Sun. It was hard to believe that he had ever known any life but that of the little, self-contained universe that was the *Ares.* And its crew no longer consisted of Norden, Hilton, Mackay, Bradley, and Scott—but of John, Fred, Angus, Owen, and Bob.

He had grown to know them all, though Hilton and Bradley had a curious reserve that he had been unable to penetrate. Each man was a definite and sharply contrasted character; almost the only thing they had in common was intelligence. Gibson doubted if any of them had an I.Q. of less than 120, and he sometimes wriggled with embarrassment as he remembered the crews he had imagined for some of his fictional spaceships. He recalled Master Pilot Graham, from "Five Moons Too Many"—still one of his favorite characters. Graham had been tough (had he not once survived half a minute in vacuum before being able to get to his spacesuit?) and he regularly disposed of a bottle of whiskey a day. He was a distinct contrast to Dr. Angus Mackay, Ph.D. (Astron.), F.R.A.S., who was now sitting quietly in a corner reading a much annotated copy of "The Canterbury Tales" and taking an occasional squirt from a bulbful of milk.

The mistake that Gibson had made, along with so many other writers back in the '50's and '60's, was the assumption that there would be no fundamental difference between ships of space and ships of the sea—or between the men who manned them. There were parallels, it was true, but they were far outnumbered by the contrasts. The reason was purely technical, and should have been foreseen, but the popular writers of the mid-century had taken the lazy course and had tried to use the traditions of Herman Melville and Frank Dana in a medium for which they were grotesquely unfitted.

A ship of space was much more like a stratosphere liner than anything that had ever moved on the face of the ocean, and the technical training of its crew was at a much higher level even than that required in aviation. A man like Norden had spent five years at college, three years in space, and another two back at college on advanced astronautical theory before qualifying for his present position.

Gibson was having a quiet game of darts with Dr. Scott when the first excitement of the voyage burst unexpectedly upon them. There are not many games of skill that can be played in space; for a long time cards and chess had been the classical stand-bys, until some ingenious Englishman had decided that a flight of darts would perform very well in the absence of gravity. The distance between thrower and board had been increased to ten meters, but otherwise the game still obeyed the rules that had been formulated over the centuries amid an atmosphere of beer and tobacco smoke in English pubs.

Gibson had been delighted to find that he was quite good at the game. He almost always managed to beat Scott, despite—or because of—the other's elaborate technique. This consisted of placing the "arrow" carefully in mid-air, and then going back a couple of meters to squint along it before smacking it smartly on its way.

Scott was optimistically aiming for a treble twenty when Bradley drifted into the room bearing a signals form in his hand.

"Don't look now," he said in his soft, carefully modulated voice, "but we're being followed."

Everyone gaped at him as he relaxed in the doorway. Mackay was the first to recover.

"Please elucidate," he said primly.

"There's a Mark III carrier missile coming after us hell for leather. It's just been launched from the Outer Station and should pass us in four days. They want me to catch it with our radio control as it goes by, but with the dispersion it will have at this range that's asking a lot. I doubt if it will go within a hundred thousand kilometers of us."

"What's it in aid of? Someone left their toothbrush behind?"

"It seems to be carrying urgent medical supplies. Here, Doc, you have a look."

Dr. Scott examined the message carefully.

"This *is* interesting. They think they've got an antidote for Martian fever. It's a serum of some kind; the Pasteur Institute's made it. They must be pretty sure of the stuff if they've gone to all this trouble to catch us."

"What, for heaven's sake, is a Mark III missile—not to mention Martian fever?" exploded Gibson at last.

Dr. Scott answered before anyone else could get a word in.

"Martian fever isn't really a Martian disease. It seems to be caused by a terrestrial organism that we carried there and which liked the new climate more than the old one. It has the same sort of effect as malaria: people aren't often killed by it, but its economic effects are very serious. In any one year the percentage of man-hours lost——"

"Thank you very much. I remember all about it now. And the missile?"

Hilton slid smoothly into the conversation.

"That's simply a little automatic rocket with radio control and a very high terminal speed. It's used to carry cargoes between the space-stations, or to chase after spaceships when they've left anything behind. When it gets into radio range it will pick up our transmitter and home on to us. Hey, Bob," he said suddenly, turning to Scott, "why haven't they sent it direct to Mars? It could get there long before we do."

"Because its little passengers wouldn't like it. I'll have to fix up some cultures for them to live in, and look after them like a nursemaid. Not my usual line of business, but I think I can remember some of the stuff I did at St. Thomas's."

"Wouldn't it be appropriate," said Mackay with one of his rare attempts at humor, "if someone went and painted the Red Cross outside?"

Gibson was thinking deeply.

"I was under the impression," he said after a pause, "that life on Mars was very healthy, both physically and psychologically."

"You mustn't believe all you read in books," drawled Bradley. "Why anyone should ever want to go to Mars I can't imagine. It's flat, it's cold, and it's full of miserable half-starved plants looking like something out of Edgar Allan Poe. We've sunk millions into the place and haven't got a penny back. Anyone who goes there of his own free will should have his head examined. Meaning no offense, of course."

Gibson only smiled amicably. He had learned to discount

Bradley's cynicism by about ninety per cent; but he was never quite sure how far the other was only *pretending* to be insulting. For once, however, Captain Norden asserted his authority; not merely to stop Bradley from getting away with it, but to prevent such alarm and despondency from spreading into print. He gave his electronics officer an angry glare.

"I ought to tell you, Martin," he said, "that although Mr. Bradley doesn't like Mars, he takes an equally poor view of Earth and Venus. So don't let his opinions depress you."

"I won't," laughed Gibson. "But there's one thing I'd like to ask."

"What's that?" said Norden anxiously.

"Does Mr. Bradley take as 'poor a view,' as you put it, of Mr. Bradley as he does of everything else?"

"Oddly enough, he does," admitted Norden. "That shows that one at least of his judgments is accurate."

"Touché," murmured Bradley, for once at a loss. "I will retire in high dudgeon and compose a suitable reply. Meanwhile, Mac, will you get the missile's co-ordinates and let me know when it should come into range?"

"All right," said Mackay absently. He was deep in Chaucer again.

Chapter

During the next few days Gibson was too busy with his own affairs to take much part in the somewhat limited social life of the *Ares.* His conscience had smitten him, as it always did when he rested for more than a week, and he was hard at work again.

The typewriter had been disentangled from his belongings and now occupied the place of honor in the little cabin. Sheets of manuscript lay everywhere—Gibson was an untidy worker—and had to be prevented from escaping by elastic bands. There had been a lot of trouble with the flimsy carbon paper, which had a habit of getting into the airflow and gluing itself against the ventilator, but Gibson had now mastered the minor techniques of life under zero gravity. It was amazing how quickly one learned them, and how soon they became a part of everyday life.

Gibson had found it very hard to get his impressions of space down on paper; one could not very well say "space is awfully big" and leave it at that. The take-off from Earth had taxed his skill to the utmost. He had not actually lied, but anyone who read his dramatic description of the Earth falling away beneath the blast of the rocket would certainly never get the impression that the writer had then been in a state of blissful unconsciousness, swiftly followed by a state of far from blissful consciousness.

As soon as he had produced a couple of articles which would keep Ruth happy for a while (she had meanwhile sent three further radiograms of increasing asperity) he went Northwards to the Signals Office. Bradley received the sheets of MSS. with marked lack of enthusiasm.

"I suppose this is going to happen every day from now on," he said glumly.

"I hope so—but I'm afraid not. It depends on my inspiration."

"There's a split infinitive right here on the top of page 2."

"Excellent; nothing like 'em."

"You've put 'centrifugal' on page 3 where you mean 'centripetal.'"

"Since I get paid by the word, don't you think it's generous of me to use such long ones?"

"There are two successive sentences on page 4 beginning with 'And.'"

"Look here, are you going to send the damned stuff, or do I have to do it myself?"

Bradley grinned.

"I'd like to see you try. Seriously, though, I should have warned you to use a black ribbon. Contrast isn't so good with blue, and though the facsimile sender will be able to handle it all right at this range, when we get farther away from Earth it's important to have a nice, clean signal."

As he spoke, Bradley was slipping the quarto sheets into the tray of the automatic transmitter. Gibson watched, fascinated, as they disappeared one by one into the maw of the machine and emerged five seconds later into the wire collecting-basket. It was strange to think that his words were now racing out through space in a continuous stream, getting a million kilometers farther away every three seconds.

He was just collecting his MSS. sheets again when a buzzer sounded somewhere in the jungle of dials, switches, and meter panels that covered practically the entire wall of the little office. Bradley shot across to one of his receivers and proceeded to do incomprehensible things with great rapidity. A piercing whistle started to come from a loudspeaker.

"The carrier's in range at last," said Bradley, "but it's a long way off—at a guess I'd say it will miss us by a hundred thousand kilometers."

"What can we do about that?"

"Very little. I've got our own beacon switched on, and if it picks up our signals it will home on to us automatically and navigate itself to within a few kilometers of us."

"And if it *doesn't* pick us up?"

"Then it will just go shooting on out of the Solar System. It's traveling fast enough to escape from the Sun; so are we, for that matter."

"That's a cheerful thought. How long would it take us?"

"To do what?"

"To leave the system."

"A couple of years, perhaps. Better ask Mackay. I don't know *all* the answers—I'm not like one of the characters in your books!"

"You may be one yet," said Gibson darkly, and withdrew.

The approach of the missile had added an unexpected—and welcome—element of excitement to life aboard the *Ares*. Once the first fine careless rapture had worn off, space-travel could become exceedingly monotonous. It would be different in future days, when the liner was crowded with life, but there were times when her present loneliness could be very depressing.

The missile sweepstake had been organized by Dr. Scott, but the prizes were held firmly by Captain Norden. Some calculations of Mackay's indicated that the projectile would miss the *Ares* by a hundred and twenty-five thousand kilometers, with an uncertainty of plus or minus thirty thousand. Most of the bets had been placed near the most probable value, but some pessimists, mistrusting Mackay completely, had gone out to a quarter of a million kilometers. The bets weren't in cash, but in far more useful commodities such as cigarettes, candies, and other luxuries. Since the crew's personal weight allowance was strictly limited, these were far more valuable than pieces of paper with marks on them. Mackay had even thrown a half-bottle of whiskey into the pool, and had thereby staked a claim to a volume of space about twenty thousand kilometers across. He never drank the stuff himself, he explained, but was taking some to a compatriot on Mars, who couldn't get the genuine article and was unable to afford the passage back to Scotland. No one believed him, which, as the story was more or less true, was a little unfair.

"Jimmy!"

"Yes, Captain Norden."

"Have you finished checking the oxygen gauges?"

"Yes, sir. All O.K."

"What about that automatic recording gear those physicists have put in the hold? Does it look as if it's still working?"

"Well, it's making the same sort of noises as it did when we started."

"Good. You've cleaned up that mess in the kitchen where Mr. Hilton let the milk boil over?"

"Yes, Captain."

"Then you've really finished everything?"

"I suppose so, but I was hoping——"

"That's fine. I've got a rather interesting job for you—something quite out of the usual run of things. Mr. Gibson wants to start polishing up his astronautics. Of course, any of us could tell him all he wants to know, but—er—you're the last one to come from college and maybe you could put things across better. You've not forgotten the beginner's difficulties—

we'd tend to take too much for granted. It won't take much of your time—just go along when he asks and deal with his questions. I'm sure you can manage."

Exit Jimmy, glumly.

"Come in," said Gibson, without bothering to look up from his typewriter. The door opened behind him and Jimmy Spencer came floating into the room.

"Here's the book, Mr. Gibson. I think it will give you everything you want. It's Richardson's 'Elements of Astronautics,' special lightweight edition."

He laid the volume in front of Gibson, who turned over the thin sheets with an interest that rapidly evaporated as he saw how quickly the proportion of words per page diminished. He finally gave up halfway through the book after coming across a page where the only sentence was "Substituting for the value of perihelion distance from Equation 15.3, we obtain . . ." All else was mathematics.

"Are you *quite* sure this is the most elementary book in the ship?" he asked doubtfully, not wishing to disappoint Jimmy. He had been a little surprised when Spencer had been appointed as his unofficial tutor, but had been shrewd enough to guess the reason. Whenever there was a job that no one else wanted to do, it had a curious tendency to devolve upon Jimmy.

"Oh yes, it really *is* elementary. It manages without vector notation and doesn't touch perturbation theory. You should see some of the books Mackay has in his room. Each equation takes a couple of pages of print."

"Well, thanks anyway. I'll give you a shout when I get stuck. It's about twenty years since I did any maths, though I used to be quite hot at it once. Let me know when you want the book back."

"There's no hurry, Mr. Gibson. I don't very often use it now I've got on to the advanced stuff."

"Oh, before you go, maybe you can answer a point that's just cropped up. A lot of people are still worried about meteors, it seems, and I've been asked to give the latest information on the subject. Just how dangerous are they?"

Jimmy pondered for a moment.

"I could tell you, roughly," he said, "but if I were you I'd see Mr. Mackay. He's got tables giving the exact figures."

"Right, I'll do that."

Gibson could quite easily have rung Mackay but any excuse to leave his work was too good to be missed. He found the little astrogator playing tunes on the big electronic calculating machine.

"Meteors?" said Mackay. "Ah, yes, a very interesting subject. I'm afraid, though, that a great deal of highly misleading information has been published about them. It wasn't so long ago that people believed a spaceship would be riddled as soon as it left atmosphere."

"Some of them still do," replied Gibson. "At least, they think that large-scale passenger travel won't be safe."

Mackay gave a snort of disgust.

"Meteors are considerably less dangerous than lightning and the biggest normal one is a lot smaller than a pea."

"But, after all, one ship has been damaged by them!"

"You mean the *Star Queen*? One serious accident in the last five years is quite a satisfactory record. No ship has ever actually been *lost* through meteors."

"What about the *Palls*?"

"No one knows what happened to her. That's only the popular theory. It's not at all popular among the experts."

"So I can tell the public to forget all about the matter?"

"Yes. Of course, there *is* the question of dust. . . ."

"Dust?"

"Well, if by meteors you mean fairly large particles, from a couple of millimeters upwards, you needn't worry. But dust is a nuisance, particularly on space-stations. Every few years someone has to go over the skin to locate the punctures. They're usually far too small to be visible to the eye, but a bit of dust moving at fifty kilometers a second can get through a surprising thickness of metal."

This sounded faintly alarming to Gibson, and Mackay hastened to reassure him.

"There really isn't the slightest need to worry," he repeated. "There's always a certain hull leakage taking place; the air supply simply takes it in its stride."

However busy Gibson might be, or pretend to be, he always found time to wander restlessly around the echoing labyrinths of the ship, or to sit looking at the stars from the equatorial observation galley. He had formed a habit of going there during the daily concert. At 15.00 hours precisely the ship's public address system would burst into life and for an hour the music of Earth would whisper or roar through the empty passageways of the *Ares.* Every day a different person would choose the programs, so one never knew what was coming—though after a while it was easy to guess the identity of the arranger. Norden played light classics and opera; Hilton practically nothing but Beethoven and Tchaikovsky. They were regarded as hopeless lowbrows by Mackay and Bradley, who indulged in astringent chamber music and atonal cacophonies of which no one else could make head or tail, or indeed particularly desired to. The ship's micro-library of books and music was so extensive that it would outlast a lifetime in space. It held, in fact, the equivalent of a quarter of a million books and some thousands of orchestral works, all recorded in electronic patterns, awaiting the orders that would bring them into life.

Gibson was sitting in the observation gallery, trying to see how many of the Pleiades he could resolve with the naked eye, when a small projectile whispered past his ear and attached itself with a "thwack!" to the glass of the port, where it hung vibrating like an arrow. At first sight, indeed, this seemed exactly what it was and for a moment Gibson wondered if the Cherokee were on the warpath again. Then he saw that a large rubber sucker had replaced the head, while from the base, just behind the feathers, a long, thin thread trailed away into the distance. At the end of the thread was Dr. Robert Scott, M.D., hauling himself briskly along like an energetic spider.

Gibson was still composing some suitably pungent remark when, as usual, the doctor got there first.

"Don't you think it's cute?" he said. "It's got a range of twenty meters—only weighs half a kilo, and I'm going to patent it as soon as I get back to Earth."

"Why?" said Gibson, in tones of resignation.

"Good gracious, can't you see? Suppose you want to get from one place to another inside a space-station where there's no rotational gravity. All you've got to do is to fire at any flat surface near your destination, and reel in the cord. It gives you a perfect anchor until you release the sucker."

"And just what's wrong with the usual way of getting around?"

"When you've been in space as long as *I* have," said Scott smugly, "you'll know what's wrong. There are plenty of handholds for you to grab in a ship like this. But suppose you want to go over to a blank wall at the other side of a room, and you launch yourself through the air from wherever you're standing. What happens? Well, you've got to break your fall somehow, usually with your hands, unless you can twist round on the way. Incidentally, do you know the commonest complaint a spaceship M.O. has to deal with? It's sprained wrists, and *that's* why. Anyway, even when you get to your target you'll bounce back unless you can grab hold of something. You might even get stranded in mid-air. I did that once in Space Station Three, in one of the big hangars. The nearest wall was fifteen meters away and I couldn't reach it."

"Couldn't you spit your way towards it?" said Gibson

solemnly. "I thought that was the approved way out of the difficulty."

"You try it someday and see how far it gets you. Anyway, it's not hygienic. Do you know what I had to do? It was most embarrassing. I was only wearing shorts and vest, as usual, and I calculated that they had about a hundredth of my mass. If I could throw them away at thirty meters a second, I could reach the wall in about a minute."

"And did you?"

"Yes. But the Director was showing his wife round the Station that afternoon, so now you know why I'm reduced to earning my living on an old hulk like this, working my way from port to port when I'm not running a shady surgery down by the docks."

"I think you've missed your vocation," said Gibson admiringly. "You should be in my line of business."

"I don't think you believe me," complained Scott bitterly.

"That's putting it mildly. Let's look at your toy."

Scott handed it over. It was a modified air pistol, with a spring-loaded reel of nylon thread attached to the butt.

"It looks like——"

"If you say it's like a ray-gun I'll certify you as infectious. Three people have made that crack already."

"Then it's a good job you interrupted me," said Gibson, handing the weapon back to the proud inventor. "By the way, how's Owen getting on? Has he contacted that missile yet?"

"No, and it doesn't look as if he's going to. Mac says it will pass about a hundred and forty-five thousand kilometers away—certainly out of range. It's a damn shame; there's not another ship going to Mars for months, which is why they were so anxious to catch us."

"Owen's a queer bird, isn't he?" said Gibson with some inconsequence.

"Oh, he's not so bad when you get to know him. It's quite

untrue what they say about him poisoning his wife. She drank herself to death of her own free will," replied Scott with relish.

Owen Bradley, Ph.D., M.I.E.E., M.I.R.E., was very annoyed with life. Like every man aboard the *Ares,* he took his job with a passionate seriousness, however much he might pretend to joke about it. For the last twelve hours he had scarcely left the communications cabin, hoping that the continuous carrier wave from the missile would break into the modulation that would tell him it was receiving his signals and would begin to steer itself towards the *Ares.* But it was completely indifferent, and he had no right to expect otherwise. The little auxiliary beacon which was intended to call such projectiles had a reliable range of only twenty thousand kilometers; though that was ample for all normal purposes, it was quite inadequate now.

Bradley dialed the astrogation office on the ship's intercom, and Mackay answered almost at once.

"What's the latest, Mac?"

"It won't come much closer. I've just reduced the last bearing and smoothed out the errors. It's now a hundred and fifty thousand kilometers away, traveling on an almost parallel course. Nearest point will be a hundred and forty-four thousand, in about three hours. So I've lost the sweep—and I suppose we lose the missile."

"Looks like it, I'm afraid," grunted Bradley, "but we'll see. I'm going down to the workshop."

"Whatever for?"

"To make a one-man rocket and go after the blasted thing, of course. That wouldn't take more than half an hour in one of Martin's stories. Come down and help me."

Mackay was nearer the ship's equator than Bradley; consequently he had reached the workshop at the South Pole first and was waiting in mild perplexity when Bradley arrived, festooned with lengths of coaxial cable he had collected from stores. He outlined his plan briefly.

"I should have done this before, but it will make rather a mess and I'm one of those people who always go on hoping till the last moment. The trouble with our beacon is that it radiates in all directions—it has to, of course, since we never know where a carrier's coming from. I'm going to build a beam array and squirt *all* the power I've got after our runaway."

He produced a rough sketch of a simple Yagi aerial and explained it swiftly to Mackay.

"This dipole's the actual radiator—the others are directors and reflectors. Antique, but it's easy to make and it should do the job. Call Hilton if you want any help. How long will it take?"

Mackay, who for a man of his tastes and interests had a positively atavistic skill with his hands, glanced at the drawings and the little pile of materials Bradley had gathered.

"About an hour," he said, already at work. "Where are you going now?"

"I've got to go out on the hull and disconnect the plumbing from the beacon transmitter. Bring the array round to the airlock when you're ready, will you?"

Mackay knew little about radio, but he understood clearly enough what Bradley was trying to do. At the moment the tiny beacon on the *Ares* was broadcasting its power over the entire sphere of space. Bradley was about to disconnect it from its present aerial system and aim its whole output accurately towards the fleeing projectile, thus increasing its range manyfold.

It was about an hour later that Gibson met Mackay hurrying through the ship behind a flimsy structure of parallel wires, spaced apart by plastic rods. He gaped at it in amazement as he followed Mackay to the lock, where Bradley was already waiting impatiently in his cumbersome spacesuit, the helmet open beside him.

"What's the nearest star to the missile?" Bradley asked.

Mackay thought rapidly.

"It's nowhere near the ecliptic now," he mused. "The last figures I got were—let's see—declination fifteen something north, right ascension about fourteen hours. I suppose that will be—I never can remember these things!—somewhere in Böotes. Oh yes—it won't be far from Arcturus: not more than ten degrees anyway, I'd say at a guess. I'll work out the exact figures in a minute."

"That's good enough to start with. I'll swing the beam around, anyway. Who's in the Signals Cabin now?"

"The Skipper and Fred. I've rung them up and they're listening to the monitor. I'll keep in touch with you through the hull transmitter."

Bradley snapped the helmet shut and disappeared through the airlock. Gibson watched him go with some envy. He had always wanted to wear a spacesuit, but though he had raised the matter on several occasions Norden had told him it was strictly against the rules. Spacesuits were very complex mechanisms and he might make a mistake in one—and then there would be hell to pay and perhaps a funeral to be arranged under rather novel circumstances.

Bradley wasted no time admiring the stars once he had launched himself through the outer door. He jetted slowly over the gleaming expanse of hull with his reaction units until he came to the section of plating he had already removed. Underneath it a network of cables and wires lay nakedly exposed to the blinding sunlight, and one of the cables had already been cut. He made a quick temporary connection, shaking his head sadly at the horrible mismatch that would certainly reflect half the power right back to the transmitter. Then he found Arcturus and aimed the beam towards it. After waving it around hopefully for a while, he switched on his suit radio.

"Any luck?" he asked anxiously.

Mackay's despondent voice came through the loudspeaker.

"Nothing at all. I'll switch you through to communications."

Norden confirmed the news.

"The signal's still coming in, but it hasn't acknowledged us yet."

Bradley was taken aback. He had been quite sure that this would do the trick; at the very least, he must have increased the beacon's range by a factor of ten in this one direction. He waved the beam around for a few more minutes, then gave it up. Already he could visualize the little missile with its strange but precious cargo slipping silently out of his grasp, out towards the unknown limits of the Solar System—and beyond.

He called Mackay again.

"Listen, Mac," he said urgently, "I want you to check those co-ordinates again and then come out here and have a shot yourself. I'm going in to doctor the transmitter."

When Mackay had relieved him, Bradley hurried back to his cabin. He found Gibson and the rest of the crew gathered glumly round the monitor receiver from which the unbroken whistle from the distant, and now receding, missile was coming with a maddening indifference.

There were very few traces of his normally languid, almost feline movements as Bradley pulled out circuit diagrams by the dozen and tore into the communications rack. It took him only a moment to run a pair of wires into the heart of the beacon transmitter. As he worked, he fired a series of questions at Hilton.

"You know something about these carrier missiles. How long must it receive our signal to give it time to home accurately on to us?"

"That depends, of course, on its relative speed and several other factors. In this case, since it's a low-acceleration job, a good ten minutes, I should say."

"And then it doesn't matter even if our beacon fails?"

"No. As soon as the carrier's vectored itself towards you, you can go off the air again. Of course, you'll have to send it another signal when it passes right by you, but that should be easy."

"How long will it take to get here if I *do* catch it?"

"A couple of days, maybe less. What are you trying out now?"

"The power amplifiers of this transmitter run at seven hundred and fifty volts. I'm taking a thousand-volt line from another supply, that's all. It will be a short life and a merry one, but we'll double or treble the output while the tubes last."

He switched on the intercom and called Mackay, who, not knowing the transmitter had been switched off for some time, was still carefully holding the array lined up on Arcturus, like an armor-plated William Tell aiming a crossbow.

"Hello, Mac, you all set?"

"I am practically ossified," said Mackay with dignity. "How much longer——"

"We're just starting now. Here goes."

Bradley threw the switch. Gibson, who had been expecting sparks to start flying, was disappointed. Everything seemed exactly as before; but Bradley, who knew better, looked at his meters and bit his lips savagely.

It would take radio waves only half a second to bridge the gap to that tiny, far-off rocket with its wonderful automatic mechanisms that must remain forever lifeless unless this signal could reach them. The half-second passed, and the next. There had been time for the reply, but still that maddening heterodyne whistle came unbroken from the speaker. Then, suddenly, it stopped. For an age there was absolute silence. A hundred and fifty thousand kilometers away, the robot was investigating this new phenomenon. It took perhaps five seconds to make up its mind—and the carrier wave broke through again, but now modulated into an endless string of "beep-beep-beeps."

Bradley checked the enthusiasm in the cabin.

"We're not out of the wood yet," he said. "Remember it's got to hold our signal for ten minutes before it can complete its course alterations." He looked anxiously at his meters and wondered how long it would be before the output tubes gave up the unequal battle.

They lasted seven minutes, but Bradley had spares ready and was on the air again in twenty seconds. The replacements were still operating when the missile carrier wave changed its modulation once more, and with a sigh of relief Bradley shut down the maltreated beacon.

"You can come indoors now, Mac," he called into the microphone. "We made it."

"Thank heavens for that. I've nearly got sunstroke, as well as calcification of the joints, doing this Cupid's bow act out here."

"When you're finished celebrating," complained Gibson, who had been an interested but baffled spectator, "perhaps you'll tell me in a few short, well-chosen phrases just how you managed to pull this particular rabbit out of the hat."

"By beaming our beacon signal and then overloading the transmitter, of course."

"Yes, I know that. What I don't understand is why you've switched it off again."

"The controlling gear in the missile has done its job," explained Bradley, with the air of a professor of philosophy talking to a mentally retarded child. "That first signal indicated that it had detected our wave; we knew then that it was automatically vectoring on to us. That took it several minutes, and when it had finished it shut off its motors and sent us the second signal. It's still at almost the same distance, of course, but it's heading towards us now and should be passing in a couple of days. I'll have the beacon running again then. That will bring it to within a kilometer or less."

There was a gentle cough at the back of the room.

"I hate to remind you, sir . . ." began Jimmy.

Norden laughed.

"O.K.—I'll pay up. Here are the keys—locker 26. What are you going to do with that bottle of whiskey?"

"I was thinking of selling it back to Dr. Mackay."

"Surely," said Scott, looking severely at Jimmy, "this moment demands a general celebration, at which a toast . . ."

But Jimmy didn't stop to hear the rest. He had fled to collect his loot.

CHAPTER

"An hour ago we had only one passenger," said Dr. Scott, nursing the long metal case delicately through the airlock. "Now we've got several billion."

"How do you think they've stood the journey?" asked Gibson.

"The thermostats seemed to be working well, so they should be all right. I'll transfer them to the cultures I've got ready, and then they should be quite happy until we get to Mars, gorging themselves to their little hearts' content."

Gibson moved over to the nearest observation post. He could see the stubby, white-painted shape of the missile lying alongside the airlock, with the slack mooring cables drifting away from it like the tentacles of some deep-sea creature. When the rocket had been brought almost to rest a few kilometers away by its automatic radio equipment, its final capture had been achieved by much less sophisticated techniques. Hilton and Bradley had gone out with cables and lassoed the missile as it slowly drifted by. Then the electric winches on the *Ares* had hauled it in.

"What's going to happen to the carrier now?" Gibson asked Captain Norden, who was also watching the proceedings.

"We'll salvage the drive and control assembly and leave the carcass in space. It wouldn't be worth the fuel to carry it all back to Mars. So until we start accelerating again, we'll have a little moon of our own."

"Like the dog in Jules Verne's story."

"What, 'From the Earth to the Moon'? I've never read it. At least, I tried once, but couldn't be bothered. That's the trouble with all those old stories. Nothing is deader than yesterday's science-fiction—and Verne belongs to the day before yesterday."

Gibson felt it necessary to defend his profession.

"So you don't consider that science-fiction can ever have any permanent literary value?"

"I don't think so. It may sometimes have a *social* value when it's written, but to the next generation it must always seem quaint and archaic. Just look what happened, for example, to the space-travel story."

"Go on. Don't mind my feelings—as if you would."

Norden was clearly warming to the subject, a fact which did not surprise Gibson in the least. If one of his companions had suddenly been revealed as an expert on reafforestation, Sanskrit, or bimetallism, Gibson would now have taken it in his stride. In any case, he knew that science-fiction was widely—sometimes hilariously—popular among professional astronauts.

"Very well," said Norden. "Let's see what happened there. Up to 1960—maybe 1970—people were still writing stories about the first journey to the Moon. They're all quite unreadable now. When the Moon was reached, it was safe to write about Mars and Venus for another few years. Now *those* stories are dead too; no one would read them except to get a laugh. I suppose the outer planets will be a good investment for another generation; but the interplanetary romances our grandfathers knew really came to an end in the late 1970's."

"But the theme of space-travel is still as popular as ever."

"Yes, but it's no longer science-fiction. It's either purely factual—the sort of thing you are beaming back to Earth now—or else it's pure fantasy. The stories have to go right outside the Solar System and so they might just as well be fairy tales. Which is all that most of them are."

Norden had been speaking with great seriousness, but there was a mischievous twinkle in his eye.

"I contest your argument on two points," said Gibson. "First of all people—lots of people—still read Wells' yarns, though they're a century old. And, to come from the sublime to the ridiculous, they still read *my* early books, like 'Martian Dust,' although facts have caught up with them and left them a long way in the rear."

"Wells wrote literature," answered Norden, "but even so, I think I can prove my point. Which of his stories are most popular? Why, the straight novels like 'Kipps' and 'Mr. Polly.' When the fantasies are read at all, it's in spite of their hopelessly dated prophecies, not because of them. Only 'The Time Machine' is still at all popular, simply because it's set so far in the future that it's not outmoded—and because it contains Wells' best writing."

There was a slight pause. Gibson wondered if Norden was going to take up his second point. Finally he said:

"When did you write 'Martian Dust'?"

Gibson did some rapid mental arithmetic.

"In '73 or '74."

"I didn't know it was as early as that. But that's part of the explanation. Space-travel was just about to begin then, and everybody knew it. You had already begun to make a name with conventional fiction, and 'Martian Dust' caught the rising tide very nicely."

"That only explains why it sold *then*. It doesn't answer my other point. It's still quite popular, and I believe the Martian colony has taken several copies, despite the fact that it describes a Mars that never existed outside my imagination."

"I attribute that to the unscrupulous advertising of your publisher, the careful way you've managed to keep in the public eye, and—just possibly—to the fact that it was the best thing you ever wrote. Moreover, as Mac would say, it managed to capture the *Zeitgeist* of the '70's, and that gives it a curiosity value now."

"Hmm," said Gibson, thinking matters over.

He remained silent for a moment; then his face creased into a smile and he began to laugh.

"Well, share the joke. What's so funny?"

"Our earlier conversation. I was just wondering what H. G. Wells would have thought if he'd known that one day a couple of men would be discussing his stories, halfway between Earth and Mars."

"Don't exaggerate," grinned Norden. "We're only a third of the way so far."

It was long after midnight when Gibson suddenly awoke from a dreamless sleep. Something had disturbed him—some noise like a distance explosion, far away in the bowels of the ship. He sat up in the darkness, tensing against the broad elastic bands that held him to his bed. Only a glimmer of starlight came from the porthole-mirror, for his cabin was on the night side of the liner. He listened, mouth half opened, checking his breath to catch the faintest murmur of sound.

There were many voices in the *Ares* at night, and Gibson knew them all. The ship was alive, and silence would have meant the death of all aboard her. Infinitely reassuring was the unresting, unhurried suspiration of the air-pumps, driving the man-made trade winds of this tiny planet. Against that faint but continuous background were other intermittent noises: the occasional "whirr" of hidden motors carrying out some mysterious and automatic task, the "tick," every thirty seconds precisely, of the electric clock, and sometimes the sound of water racing through the pressurized plumbing system. Certainly none of these could have roused him, for they were as familiar as the beating of his own heart.

Still only half awake, Gibson went to the cabin door and listened for a while in the corridor. Everything was perfectly normal; he knew that he must be the only man awake. For a moment he wondered if he should call Norden, then thought better of it. He might only have been dreaming, or the noise might have been produced by some equipment that had not gone into action before.

He was already back in bed when a thought suddenly occurred to him. Had the noise, after all, been so far away? That was merely his first impression; it might have been quite near. Anyway, he was tired, and it didn't matter. Gibson had a complete and touching faith in the ship's instrumentation. If anything had really gone wrong, the automatic alarms would have alerted everyone. They had been tested several times on the voyage, and were enough to awaken the dead. He could go to sleep, confident that they were watching over him with unresting vigilance.

He was perfectly correct, though he was never to know it; and by the morning he had forgotten the whole affair.

The camera swept out of the stricken council chamber, following the funeral cortege up the endlessly twining stairs, and on to the windy battlements above the sea. The music sobbed into silence; for a moment, the lonely figures with their tragic burden were silhouetted against the setting sun, motionless upon the ramparts of Elsinore. "Good night, sweet prince . . ." The play was ended.

The lights in the tiny theater came on abruptly, and the State of Denmark was four centuries and fifty million kilometers away. Reluctantly, Gibson brought his mind back to the present, tearing himself free from the magic that had held him captive. What, he wondered, would Shakespeare have made of this interpretation, already a lifetime old, yet as untouched by time as the still older splendors of the immortal poetry? And what, above all, would he have made of this fantastic theater, with its latticework of seats floating precariously in mid-air with the flimsiest of supports?

"It's rather a pity," said Dr. Scott, as the audience of six drifted out into the corridor, "that we'll never have as fine a collection of films with us on our later runs. This batch is for the Central Martian Library, and we won't be able to hang on to it."

"What's the next program going to be?" asked Gibson.

"We haven't decided. It may be a current musical, or we may carry on with the classics and screen 'Gone With the Wind.' "

"My grandfather used to rave about that; I'd like to see it now we have the chance," said Jimmy Spencer eagerly.

"Very well," replied Scott. "I'll put the matter to the Entertainments Committee and see if it can be arranged." Since this Committee consisted of Scott and no one else, these negotiations would presumably be successful.

Norden, who had remained sunk in thought since the end of the film, came up behind Gibson and gave a nervous little cough.

"By the way, Martin," he said. "You remember you were badgering me to let you go out in a spacesuit?"

"Yes. You said it was strictly against the rules."

Norden seemed embarrassed, which was somewhat unlike him.

"Well, it *is* in a way, but this isn't a normal trip and you aren't technically a passenger. I think we can manage it after all."

Gibson was delighted. He had always wondered what it was like to wear a spacesuit, and to stand in nothingness with the stars all around one. It never even occurred to him to ask Norden why he had changed his mind, and for this Norden was very thankful.

The plot had been brewing for about a week. Every morning a little ritual took place in Norden's room when Hilton arrived with the daily maintenance schedules, summarizing the ship's performance and the behavior of all its multidinous machines during the past twenty-four hours. Usually there was nothing of any importance, and Norden signed the reports and filed them away with the log book. Variety was the last thing he wanted here, but sometimes he got it.

"Listen, Johnnie," said Hilton (he was the only one who called Norden by his first name; to the rest of the crew he was always "Skipper"). "It's quite definite now about our air-pressure. The drop's practically constant; in about ten days we'll be outside tolerance limits."

"Confound it! That means we'll have to do something. I was hoping it wouldn't matter till we dock."

"I'm afraid we can't wait until then; the records have to be turned over to the Space Safety Commission when we get home, and some nervous old woman is sure to start yelling if pressure drops below limits."

"Where do you think the trouble is?"

"In the hull, almost certainly."

"That pet leak of yours up round the North Pole?"

"I doubt it; this is too sudden. I think we've been holed again."

Norden looked mildly annoyed. Punctures due to meteoric dust happened two or three times a year on a ship of this size. One usually let them accumulate until they were worth bothering about, but this one seemed a little too big to be ignored.

"How long will it take to find the leak?"

"That's the trouble," said Hilton in tones of some disgust. "We've only one leak detector, and fifty thousand square meters of hull. It may take a couple of days to go over it. Now if it had only been a nice big hole, the automatic bulkheads would have gone into operation and located it for us."

"I'm mighty glad they didn't!" grinned Norden. "That would have taken some explaining away!"

Jimmy Spencer, who as usual got the job that no one else wanted to do, found the puncture three days later, after only a dozen circuits of the ship. The blurred little crater was scarcely visible to the eye, but the supersensitive leak detector had registered the fact that the vacuum near this part of the hull was not as perfect as it should have been. Jimmy had marked the place with chalk and gone thankfully back into the airlock.

Norden dug out the ship's plans and located the approximate position from Jimmy's report. Then he whistled softly and his eyebrows climbed towards the ceiling.

"Jimmy," he said, "does Mr. Gibson know what you've been up to?"

"No," said Jimmy. "I've not missed giving him his astronautics classes, though it's been quite a job to manage it as well as——"

"All right, all right! You don't think anyone else would have told him about the leak?"

"I don't know, but I think he'd have mentioned it if they had."

"Well, listen carefully. This blasted puncture is smack in the middle of his cabin wall, and if you breathe a word about it to him, I'll skin you. Understand?"

"Yes," gulped Jimmy, and fled precipitately.

"Now what?" said Hilton, in tones of resignation.

"We've got to get Martin out of the way on some pretext and plug the hole as quickly as we can."

"It's funny he never noticed the impact. It would have made quite a din."

"He was probably out at the time. *I'm* surprised he never noticed the air current; it must be fairly considerable."

"Probably masked by the normal circulation. But anyway, why all the fuss? Why not come clean about it and explain what's happened to Martin? There's no need for all this melodrama."

"Oh, isn't there? Suppose Martin tells his public that a 12th magnitude meteor has holed the ship—and then goes on to say that this sort of thing happens every other voyage? How many of his readers will understand not only that it's no real danger, but that we don't usually bother to do anything even when it does happen? I'll tell you what the popular reaction would be: 'If it was a little one, it might just as well be a big 'un.' The public's never trusted statistics. And can't you see the headlines: '*Ares* Holed by Meteor!' That *would* be bad for trade!"

"Then why not simply tell Martin and ask him to keep quiet?"

"It wouldn't be fair on the poor chap. He's had no news to hang his articles on to for weeks. It would be kinder to say nothing."

"O.K.," sighed Hilton. "It's your idea. Don't blame me if it backfires."

"It won't. I think I've got a watertight plan."

"I don't give a damn if it's watertight. Is it airtight?"

All his life Gibson had been fascinated by gadgets, and the spacesuit was yet another to add to the collection of mechanisms he had investigated and mastered. Bradley had been detailed to make sure that he understood the drill correctly, to take him out into space, and to see that he didn't get lost.

Gibson had forgotten that the suits on the *Ares* had no legs, and that one simply sat inside them. That was sensible enough, since they were built for use under zero gravity, and not for walking on airless planets. The absence of flexible leg-joints greatly simplified the designs of the suits, which were nothing more than perspex-topped cylinders sprouting articulated arms at their upper ends. Along the sides were mysterious flutings and bulges concerned with the air conditioning, radio, heat regulators, and the low-powered propulsion system. There was considerable freedom of movement inside them: one could withdraw one's arms to get at the internal controls, and even take a meal without too many acrobatics.

Bradley had spent almost an hour in the airlock, making certain that Gibson understood all the main controls and catechizing him on their operation. Gibson appreciated his thoroughness, but began to get a little impatient when the lesson showed no sign of ending. He eventually mutinied when Bradley started to explain the suit's primitive sanitary arrangements.

"Hang it all!" he protested, "we aren't going to be outside *that* long!"

Bradley grinned.

"You'd be surprised," he said darkly, "just how many people make that mistake."

He opened a compartment in the airlock wall and took out two spools of line, for all the world like fishermen's reels. They locked firmly into the mountings on the suits so that they could not be accidentally dislodged.

"Number One safety precaution," he said. "Always have a lifeline anchoring you to the ship. Rules are made to be broken—but not this one. To make doubly sure, I'll tie your suit to mine with another ten meters of cord. Now we're ready to ascend the Matterhorn."

The outer door slid aside. Gibson felt the last trace of air tugging at him as it escaped. The feeble impulse set him moving towards the exit, and he drifted slowly out into the stars.

The slowness of motion and the utter silence combined to make the moment deeply impressive. The *Ares* was receding behind him with a terribly inevitability. He was plunging into space—at last—his only link with safety that tenuous thread unreeling at his side. Yet the experience, though so novel, awoke faint echoes of familiarity in his mind.

His brain must have been working with unusual swiftness, for he recalled the parallel almost immediately. This was like the moment in his childhood—a moment, he could have sworn until now, forgotten beyond recall—when he had been taught to swim by being dropped into ten meters of water.

Once again he was plunging headlong into a new and unknown element.

The friction of the reel had checked his momentum when the cord attaching him to Bradley gave a jerk. He had almost forgotten his companion, who was now blasting away from the ship with the little gas jets at the base of his suit, towing Gibson behind him.

Gibson was quite startled when the other's voice, echoing metallically from the speaker in his suit, shattered the silence.

"Don't use your jets unless I tell you. We don't want to build up too much speed, and we must be careful not to get our lines tangled."

"All right," said Gibson, vaguely annoyed at the intrusion into his privacy. He looked back at the ship. It was already several hundred meters away, and shrinking rapidly.

"How much line have we got?" he asked anxiously. There was no reply, and he had a moment of mild panic before remembering to press the "TRANSMIT" switch.

"About a kilometer," Bradley answered when he repeated the question. "That's enough to make one feel nice and lonely."

"Suppose it broke?" asked Gibson, only half joking.

"It won't. It could support your full weight, back on Earth. Even if it did, we could get back perfectly easily with our jets."

"And if they ran out?"

"This is a very cheerful conversation. I can't imagine that happening except through gross carelessness or about three simultaneous mechanical failures. Remember, there's a spare propulsion unit for just such emergencies—and you've got warning indicators in the suit which let you know well before the main tank's empty."

"But just *supposing,*" insisted Gibson.

"In that case the only thing to do would be to switch on the suit's S.O.S. beacon, and wait until someone came out to haul you back. I doubt if they'd hurry, in such circumstances. Anyone who got himself in a mess like that wouldn't receive much sympathy."

There was a sudden jerk; they had come to the end of the line. Bradley killed the rebound with his jets.

"We're a long way from home now," he said quietly.

It took Gibson several seconds to locate the *Ares.* They were on the night side of the ship so that it was almost wholly in shadow; the two spheres were thin, distant crescents that might easily have been taken for Earth and Moon, seen from perhaps a million kilometers away. There was no real sense of contact: the ship was too small and frail a thing to be regarded as a sanctuary any more. Gibson was alone with the stars at last.

He was always grateful that Bradley left him in silence and did not intrude upon his thoughts. Perhaps the other was equally overwhelmed by the splendid solemnity of the moment. The stars were so brilliant and so numerous that at first Gibson could not locate even the most familiar constellations. Then he found Mars, the brightest object in the sky next to the Sun itself, and so determined the plane of the ecliptic. Very gently, with cautious bursts from his gas jets, he swung the suit round so that his head pointed roughly towards the Pole Star. He was "the right way up" again, and the star patterns were recognizable once more.

Slowly he made his way along the Zodiac, wondering how many other men in history had so far shared this experience. (Soon, of course, it would be common enough, and the magic would be dimmed by familiarity.) Presently he found Jupiter, and later Saturn—or so he imagined. The planets could no longer be distinguished from the stars by the steady, unwinking light that was such a useful, though sometimes treacherous, guide to amateur astronomers. Gibson did not search for Earth or Venus, for the glare of the sun would have dazzled him in a moment if he had turned his eyes in that direction.

A pale band of light welding the two hemispheres of the sky together, the whole ring of the Milky Way was visible. Gibson could see quite clearly the vents and tears along its edge, where entire continents of stars seemed trying to break away and go voyaging alone into the abyss. In the Southern Hemisphere, the black chasm of the Coal Sack gaped like a tunnel drilled through the stars into another universe.

The thought made Gibson turn towards Andromeda. There lay the great Nebula—a ghostly lens of light. He could cover it with his thumbnail, yet it was a whole galaxy as vast as the sky-spanning ring of stars in whose heart he was floating now. That misty specter was a million times farther away than the stars—and *they* were a million times more distant than the planets. How pitiful were all men's voyagings and adventures when seen against this background!

Gibson was looking for Alpha Centauri, among the unknown constellations of the Southern Hemisphere, when he caught sight of something which, for a moment, his mind failed to identify. At an immense distance, a white rectangular object was floating against the stars. That, at least, was Gibson's first impression; then he realized that his sense of perspective was at fault and that, in fact, he was really seeing something quite small, only a few meters away. Even then it was some time before he recognized this interplanetary wanderer for what it was—a perfectly ordinary sheet of quarto manuscript paper, very slowly revolving in space. Nothing could have been more commonplace—or more unexpected here.

Gibson stared at the apparition for some time before he convinced himself that it was no illusion. Then he switched on his transmitter and spoke to Bradley.

The other was not in the least surprised.

"There's nothing very remarkable about that," he replied, rather impatiently. "We've been throwing out waste every day for weeks, and as we haven't any acceleration some of it may still be hanging round. As soon as we start braking, of course, we'll drop back from it and all our junk will go shooting out of the Solar System."

How perfectly obvious, thought Gibson, feeling a little foolish, for nothing is more disconcerting than a mystery which suddenly evaporates. It was probably a rough draft of one of his own articles. If it had been a little closer, it would be amusing to retrieve it as a souvenir, and to see what effects its stay in space had produced. Unfortunately it was just out of reach, and there was no way of capturing it without slipping the cord that linked him with the *Ares.*

When he had been dead for ages, that piece of paper would still be carrying its message out among the stars; and what it was, he would never know.

Norden met them when they returned to the airlock. He seemed rather pleased with himself, though Gibson was in no condition to notice such details. He was still lost among the stars and it would be some time before he returned to normal—before his typewriter began to patter softly as he tried to recapture his emotions.

"You managed the job in time?" asked Bradley, when Gibson was out of hearing.

"Yes, with fifteen minutes to spare. We shut off the ventilators and found the leak right away with the good old smoky-candle technique. A blind rivet and a spot of quick-drying paint did the rest; we can plug the outer hull when we're in dock, if it's worth it. Mac did a pretty neat job—he's wasting his talents as a navigator."

CHAPTER

For Martin Gibson, the voyage was running smoothly and pleasantly enough. As he always did, he had now managed to organize his surroundings (by which he meant not only his material environment but also the human beings who shared it with him) to his maximum comfort. He had done a satisfactory amount of writing, some of it quite good and most of it passable, though he would not get properly into his stride until he had reached Mars.

The flight was now entering upon its closing weeks, and there was an inevitable sense of anticlimax and slackening interest, which would last until they entered the orbit of Mars. Nothing would happen until then; for the time being all of the excitements of the voyage were over.

The last high-light, for Gibson, had been the morning when he finally lost the Earth. Day by day it had come closer to the vast pearly wings of the corona, as though about to immolate all its millions in the funeral pyre of the Sun. One evening it had still been visible through the telescope—a tiny spark glittering bravely against the splendor that was soon to overwhelm it. Gibson had thought it might still be visible in the morning, but overnight some colossal explosion had thrown the corona half a million kilometers farther into space, and Earth was lost against that incandescent curtain. It would be a week before it reappeared, and by then Gibson's world would have changed more than he would have believed possible in so short a time.

If anyone had asked Jimmy Spencer just what he thought of Gibson, that young man would have given rather different replies at various stages of the voyage. At first he had been quite overawed by his distinguished shipmate, but that stage had worn off very quickly. To do Gibson credit, he was completely free from snobbery, and he never made unreasonable use of his privileged position on board the *Ares.* Thus from Jimmy's point of view he was more approachable than the rest of the liner's inhabitants—all of whom were in some degree his superior officers.

When Gibson had started taking a serious interest in astronautics, Jimmy had seen him at close quarters once or twice a week and had made several efforts to weigh him up. This had not been at all easy, for Gibson never seemed to be the same person for very long. There were times when he was considerate and thoughtful and generally good company. Yet there were other occasions when he was so grumpy and morose that he easily qualified as the person on the *Ares* most to be avoided.

What Gibson thought of *him* Jimmy wasn't at all sure. He sometimes had an uncomfortable feeling that the author regarded him purely as raw material that might or might not be of value some day. Most people who knew Gibson slightly had that impression, and most of them were right. Yet as he had tried to pump Jimmy directly there seemed no real grounds for these suspicions.

Another puzzling thing about Gibson was his technical background. When Jimmy had started his evening classes, as everyone called them, he had assumed that Gibson was merely anxious to avoid glaring errors in the material he radioed back to Earth, and had no very deep interest in astronautics for its own sake. It soon became clear that this was far from being the case. Gibson had an almost pathetic anxiety to master quite abstruse branches of the science, and to demand mathematical proofs, some of which Jimmy was hard put to provide. The older man must once have had a good deal of technical knowledge, fragments of which still remained with him. How he had acquired it he never explained; nor did he give any reason for his almost obsessive attempts, doomed though they were to repeated failures, to come to grips with scientific ideas far too advanced for him. Gibson's disappointment after these failures was so obvious that Jimmy found himself very sorry for him—except on those occasions when his pupil became bad-tempered and showed a tendency to blame his instructor. Then there would be a brief exchange of discourtesies, Jimmy would pack up his books and the lesson would not be resumed until Gibson had apologized.

Sometimes, on the other hand, Gibson took these setbacks with humorous resignation and simply changed the subject. He would then talk about his experiences in the strange literary jungle in which he lived—a world of weird and often carnivorous beasts whose behavior Jimmy found quite fascinating. Gibson was a good raconteur, with a fine flair for purveying scandal and undermining reputations. He seemed to do this without any malice, and some of the stories he told Jimmy about the distinguished figures of the day quite shocked that somewhat strait-laced youth. The curious fact was that the people whom Gibson so readily dissected often seemed to be his closest friends. This was something that Jimmy found very hard to understand.

Yet despite all these warnings Jimmy talked readily enough when the time came. One of their lessons had grounded on a reef of integro-differential equations and there was nothing to do but abandon ship. Gibson was in one of his amiable moods, and as he closed his books with a sigh he turned to Jimmy and remarked casually:

"You've never told me anything about yourself, Jimmy. What part of England do you come from, anyway?"

"Cambridge—at least, that's where I was born."

"I used to know it quite well, twenty years ago. But you don't live there now?"

"No; when I was about six, my people moved to Leeds. I've been there ever since."

"What made you take up astronautics?"

"It's rather hard to say. I was always interested in science, and of course spaceflight was the coming thing when I was growing up. So I suppose it was just natural. If I'd been born fifty years before, I guess I'd have gone into aeronautics."

"So you're interested in spaceflight purely as a technical problem, and not as—shall we say—something that might revolutionize human thought, open up new planets, and all that sort of thing?"

Jimmy grinned.

"I suppose that's true enough. Of course, I *am* interested in these ideas; but it's the technical side that really fascinates me. Even if there was nothing on the planets, I'd still want to know how to reach them."

Gibson shook his head in mock distress.

"You're going to grow up into one of those cold-blooded scientists who know everything about nothing. Another good man wasted!"

"I'm glad you think it *will* be a waste," said Jimmy with some spirit. "Anyway, why are you so interested in science?"

Gibson laughed, but there was a trace of annoyance in his voice as he replied:

"I'm only interested in science as a means, not as an end in itself."

That, Jimmy was sure, was quite untrue. But something

warned him not to pursue the matter any further, and before he could reply Gibson was questioning him again.

It was all done in such a friendly spirit of apparently genuine interest that Jimmy couldn't avoid feeling flattered, couldn't help talking freely and easily. Somehow it didn't matter if Gibson was indeed studying him as disinterestedly and as clinically as a biologist watching the reactions of one of his laboratory animals. Jimmy felt like talking, and he preferred to give Gibson's motives the benefit of the doubt.

He talked of his childhood and early life, and presently Gibson understood the occasional clouds that sometimes seemed to overlie the lad's normally cheerful disposition. It was an old story—one of the oldest. Jimmy's mother had died when he was a little more than a baby, and his father had left him in the charge of a married sister. Jimmy's aunt had been kind to him, but he had never felt at home among his cousins, had always been an outsider. Nor had his father been a great deal of help, for he was seldom in England, and had died when Jimmy was about ten years old. He appeared to have left very little impression on his son, who, strangely enough, seemed to have clearer memories of the mother whom he could scarcely have known.

Once the barriers were down, Jimmy talked without reticence, as if glad to unburden his mind. Sometimes Gibson asked questions to prompt him, but the questions grew further and further apart and presently came no more.

"I don't think my parents were really very much in love," said Jimmy. "From what Aunt Ellen told me, it was all rather a mistake. There was another man first, but that fell through. My father was the next best thing. Oh, I know this sounds rather heartless, but please remember it all happened such a long time ago, and doesn't mean much to me now."

"I understand," said Gibson quietly; and it seemed as if he really did. "Tell me more about your mother."

"Her father—my granddad, that is—was one of the professors at the university. I think Mother spent all her life in Cambridge. When she was old enough she went to college for her degree—she was studying history. Oh, all this can't possibly interest you!"

"It really does," said Gibson earnestly. "Go on."

So Jimmy talked. Everything he told must have been learned from hearsay, but the picture he gave Gibson was surprisingly clear and detailed. His listener guessed that Aunt Ellen must have been very talkative, and Jimmy a very attentive small boy.

It was one of those innumerable college romances that briefly flower and wither during that handful of years which seems a microcosm of life itself. But this one had been more serious than most. During her last term Jimmy's mother—he still hadn't told Gibson her name—had fallen in love with a young engineering student who was halfway through his college career. It had been a whirlwind romance, and the match was an ideal one despite the fact that the girl was several years older than the boy. Indeed, it had almost reached the stage of an engagement when—Jimmy wasn't quite sure what had happened. The young man had been taken seriously ill, or had had a nervous breakdown, and had never come back to Cambridge.

"My mother never really got over it," said Jimmy, with a grave assumption of wisdom which somehow did not seem completely incongruous. "But another student was very much in love with her, and so she married him. I sometimes feel rather sorry for my father, for he must have known all about the other affair. I never say much of him because—why, Mr. Gibson, don't you feel well?"

Gibson forced a smile.

"It's nothing—just a touch of space-sickness. I get it now and then—it will pass in a minute."

He only wished that the words were true. All these weeks, in total ignorance and believing himself secure against all the shocks of time and chance, he had been steering a collision course with Fate. And now the moment of impact had come; the twenty years that lay behind had vanished like a dream, and he was face to face once more with the ghosts of his own forgotten past.

"There's something wrong with Martin," said Bradley, signing the signals log with a flourish. "It can't be any news he's had from Earth—I've read it all. Do you suppose he's getting homesick?"

"He's left it a little late in the day, if that's the explanation," replied Norden. "After all, we'll be on Mars in a fortnight. But you do rather fancy yourself as an amateur psychologist, don't you?"

"Well, who doesn't?"

"*I* don't for one," began Norden pontifically. "Prying into other people's affairs isn't one of my——"

An anticipatory gleam in Bradley's eyes warned him just in time, and to the other's evident disappointment he checked himself in mid-sentence. Martin Gibson, complete with notebook and looking like a cub reporter attending his first press conference, had hurried into the office.

"Well, Owen, what was it you wanted to show me?" he asked eagerly.

Bradley moved to the main communication rack.

"It isn't really very impressive," he said, "but it means that we've passed another milestone and always gives me a bit of a kick. Listen to this."

He pressed the speaker switch and slowly brought up the volume control. The room was flooded with the hiss and crackle of radio noise, like the sound of a thousand frying pans at the point of imminent ignition. It was a sound that Gibson had heard often enough in the signals cabin and, for all its unvarying monotony, it never failed to fill him with a sense of wonder. He was listening, he knew, to the voices of the stars and nebulae, to radiations that had set out upon their journey before the birth of Man. And buried far down in the depths of that crackling, whispering chaos there might be—there *must* be—the sounds of alien civilizations talking to one another in the deeps of space. But, alas, their voices were lost beyond recall in the welter of cosmic interference which Nature herself had made.

This, however, was certainly not what Bradley had called him to hear. Very delicately, the signals officer made some vernier adjustments, frowning a little as he did so.

"I had it on the nose a minute ago—hope it hasn't drifted off—ah, here it is!"

At first Gibson could detect no alteration in the barrage of noise. Then he noticed that Bradley was silently marking time with his hand—rather quickly, at the rate of some two beats every second. With this to guide him, Gibson presently detected the infinitely faint undulating whistle that was breaking through the cosmic storm.

"What is it?" he asked, already half guessing the answer.

"It's the radio beacon on Deimos. There's one on Phobos as well, but it's not so powerful and we can't pick it up yet. When we get nearer Mars, we'll be able to fix ourselves within a few hundred kilometers by using them. We're at ten times the usable range now, but it's nice to know."

Yes, thought Gibson, it is nice to know. Of course, these radio aids weren't essential when one could see one's destination all the time, but they simplified some of the navigational problems. As he listened with half-closed eyes to that faint pulsing, sometimes almost drowned by the cosmic barrage, he knew how the mariners of old must have felt when they caught the first glimpse of the harbor lights from far out at sea.

"I think that's enough," said Bradley, switching off the speaker and restoring silence. "Anyway, it should give you something new to write about—things have been pretty quiet lately, haven't they?"

He was watching Gibson intently as he said this, but the author never responded. He merely jotted a few words in his notebook, thanked Bradley with absent-minded and unaccustomed politeness, and departed to his cabin.

"You're quite right," said Norden when he had gone. "Something's certainly happened to Martin. I'd better have a word with Doc."

"I shouldn't bother," replied Bradley. "Whatever it is, I don't think it's anything you can handle with pills. Better leave Martin to work it out his own way."

"Maybe you're right," said Norden grudgingly. "But I hope he doesn't take too long over it!"

He had now taken almost a week. The initial shock of discovering that Jimmy Spencer was Kathleen Morgan's son had already worn off, but the secondary effects were beginning to make themselves felt. Among these was a feeling of resentment that anything like this should have happened to *him.* It was such an outrageous violation of the laws of probability—the sort of thing that would never have happened in one of Gibson's own novels. But life was so inartistic and there was really nothing one could do about it.

This mood of childish petulance was now passing, to be replaced by a deeper sense of discomfort. All the emotions he had thought safely buried beneath twenty years of feverish activity were now rising to the surface again, like deep-sea creatures slain in some submarine eruption. On Earth, he could have escaped by losing himself once more in the crowd, but here he was trapped, with nowhere to flee.

It was useless to pretend that nothing had really changed, to say: "Of course I knew that Kathleen and Gerald had a son: what difference does that make now?" It made a great deal of difference. Every time he saw Jimmy he would be reminded of the past and—what was worse—of the future that might have been. The most urgent problem now was to face the facts squarely, and to come to grips with the new situation. Gibson knew well enough that there was only one way in which this could be done, and the opportunity would arise soon enough.

Jimmy had been down to the Southern Hemisphere and was making his way along the equatorial observation deck when he saw Gibson sitting at one of the windows, staring out into space. For a moment he thought the other had not seen him and had decided not to intrude upon his thoughts when Gibson called out: "Hello, Jimmy. Have you got a moment to spare?"

As it happened, Jimmy was rather busy. But he knew that there had been something wrong with Gibson, and realized that the older man needed his presence. So he came and sat on the bench recessed into the observation port, and presently he knew as much of the truth as Gibson thought good for either of them.

"I'm going to tell you something, Jimmy," Gibson began, "which is known to only a handful of people. Don't interrupt me and don't ask any questions—not until I've finished, at any rate.

"When I was rather younger than you, I wanted to be an engineer. I was quite a bright kid in those days and had no difficulty in getting into college through the usual examinations. As I wasn't sure what I intended to do, I took the five-year course in general engineering physics, which was quite a new thing in those days. In my first year I did fairly well—well enough to encourage me to work harder next time. In my second year I did—not brilliantly, but a lot better than average. And in the third year I fell in love. It wasn't exactly for the first time, but I knew it was the real thing at last.

"Now falling in love while you're at college may or may not be a good thing for you; it all depends on circumstances. If it's only a mild flirtation, it probably doesn't matter one way or the other. But if it's really serious, there are two possibilities.

"It may act as a stimulus—it may make you determined to do your best, to show that you're better than the other fellows.

On the other hand, you may get so emotionally involved in the affair that nothing else seems to matter, and your studies go to pieces. That is what happened in my case."

Gibson fell into a brooding silence, and Jimmy stole a glance at him as he sat in the darkness a few feet away. They were on the night side of the ship, and the corridor lights had been dimmed so that the stars could be seen in their unchallenged glory. The constellation of Leo was directly ahead, and there in its heart was the brilliant ruby gem that was their goal. Next to the Sun itself, Mars was by far the brightest of all celestial bodies, and already its disc was just visible to the naked eye. The brilliant crimson light playing full on his face gave Gibson a healthy, even a cheerful appearance quite out of keeping with his feelings.

Was it true, Gibson wondered, that one never really forgot anything? It seemed now as it if might be. He could still see, as clearly as he had twenty years ago, that message pinned on the faculty noticeboard: "The Dean of Engineering wishes to see M. Gibson in his office at 3.00." He had had to wait, of course, until 3.15, and that hadn't helped. Nor would it have been so bad if the Dean had been sarcastic, or icily aloof, or even if he had lost his temper. Gibson could still picture that inhumanly tidy room, with its neat files and careful rows of books, could remember the Dean's secretary padding away on her typewriter in the corner, pretending not to listen.

(Perhaps, now he came to think of it, she wasn't pretending after all. The experience wouldn't have been so novel to her as it was to him.)

Gibson had liked and respected the Dean, for all the old man's finicky ways and meticulous pedantry, and now he had let him down, which made his failure doubly hard to bear. The Dean had rubbed it in with his "more in sorrow than in anger" technique, which had been more effective than he knew or intended. He had given Gibson another chance, but he was never to take it.

What made matters worse, though he was ashamed to admit the fact, was that Kathleen had done fairly well in her own exams. When his results had been published, Gibson had avoided her for several days, and when they met again he had already identified her with the cause of his failure. He could see this so clearly now that it no longer hurt. Had he really been in love if he was prepared to sacrifice Kathleen for the sake of his own self-respect? For that is what it came to; he had tried to shift the blame on to her.

The rest was inevitable. That quarrel on their last long cycle ride together into the country, and their returns by separate routes. The letters that hadn't been opened—above all, the letters that hadn't been written. Their unsuccessful attempt to meet, if only to say good-bye, on his last day in Cambridge. But even this had fallen through; the message hadn't reached Kathleen in time, and though he had waited until the last minute she had never come. The crowded train, packed with cheering students, had drawn noisily out of the station, leaving Cambridge and Kathleen behind. He had never seen either again.

There was no need to tell Jimmy about the dark months that had followed. He need never know what was meant by the simple words: "I had a breakdown and was advised not to return to college." Dr. Evans had made a pretty good job of patching him up, and he'd always be grateful for that. It was Evans who'd persuaded him to take up writing during his convalescence, with results that had surprised them both. (How many people knew that his first novel had been dedicated to his psychoanalyst? Well, if Rachmaninoff could do the same thing with the C Minor Concerto, why shouldn't he?)

Evans had given him a new personality and a vocation through which he could win back his self-confidence. But he couldn't restore the future that had been lost. All his life Gibson would envy the men who had finished what he had only begun—the men who could put after their names the degrees and qualifications he would never possess, and who would find their life's work in fields of which he could be only a spectator.

If the trouble had lain no deeper than this, it might not have mattered greatly. But in salvaging his pride by throwing the blame on to Kathleen he had warped his whole life. She, and through her all women, had become identified with failure and disgrace. Apart from few attachments which had not been taken very seriously by either partner, Gibson had never fallen in love again, and now he realized that he never would. Knowing the cause of his complaint had helped him not in the least to find a cure.

None of these things, of course, need be mentioned to Jimmy. It was sufficient to give the bare facts, and to leave Jimmy to guess what he could. One day, perhaps, he might tell him more, but that depended on many things.

When Gibson had finished, he was surprised to find how nervously he was waiting for Jimmy's reactions. He felt himself wondering if the boy had read between the lines and apportioned blame where it was due, whether he would be sympathetic, angry—or merely embarrassed. It had suddenly become of the utmost importance to win Jimmy's respect and friendship, more important than anything that had happened to Gibson for a very long time. Only thus could he satisfy his conscience and quieten those accusing voices from the past.

He could not see Jimmy's face, for the other was in shadow, and it seemed an age before he broke the silence.

"Why have you told me this?" he asked quietly. His voice was completely neutral—free both from sympathy or reproach.

Gibson hesitated before answering. The pause was natural enough, for, even to himself, he could hardly have explained all his motives.

"I just *had* to tell you," he said earnestly. "I couldn't have been happy until I'd done so. And besides—I felt I might be able to help, somehow."

Again that nerve-racking silence. Then Jimmy rose slowly to his feet.

"I'll have to think about what you've told me," he said, his voice still almost emotionless. "I don't know what to say now."

Then he was gone. He left Gibson in a state of extreme uncertainty and confusion, wondering whether he had made a fool of himself or not. Jimmy's self-control, his failure to react, had thrown him off balance and left him completely at a loss. Only of one thing was he certain: in telling the facts, he had already done a great deal to relieve his mind.

But there was still much that he had not told Jimmy; indeed there was still much that he did not know himself.

CHAPTER

This is completely crazy!" stormed Norden, looking like a berserk Viking chief. "There must be *some* explanation! Good heavens, there aren't any proper docking facilities on Deimos—how do they expect us to unload? I'm going to call the Chief Executive and raise hell!"

"I shouldn't if I were you," drawled Bradley. "Did you notice the signature? This isn't an instruction from Earth, routed through Mars. It originated in the C.E.'s office. The old man may be a Tartar, but he doesn't do things unless he's got a good reason."

"Name just one!"

Bradley shrugged his shoulders.

"*I* don't have to run Mars, so how would I know? We'll find out soon enough." He gave a malicious little chuckle. "I wonder how Mac is going to take it? He'll have to recompute our approach orbit."

Norden leaned across the control panel and threw a switch.

"Hello, Mac—Skipper here. You receiving me?"

There was a short pause; then Hilton's voice came from the speaker.

"Mac's not here at the moment. Any message?"

"All right—you can break it to him. We've had orders from Mars to re-route the ship. They've diverted us from Phobos—no reason given at all. Tell Mac to calculate an orbit to Deimos, and to let me have it as soon as he can."

"I don't understand it. Why, Deimos is just a lot of mountains with no——"

"Yes—we've been through all that! Maybe we'll know the answer when we get there. Tell Mac to contact me as soon as he can, will you?"

Dr. Scott broke the news to Gibson while the author was putting the final touches to one of his weekly articles.

"Heard the latest?" he exclaimed breathlessly. "We've been diverted to Deimos. Skipper's mad as hell—it may make us a day late."

"Does anyone know why?"

"No; it's a complete mystery. We've asked, but Mars won't tell."

Gibson scratched his head, examining and rejecting half a dozen ideas. He knew that Phobos, the inner moon, had been used as a base ever since the first expedition had reached Mars. Only 6,000 kilometers from the surface of the planet, and with a gravity less than a thousandth of Earth's, it was ideal for this purpose.

The *Ares* was due to dock in less than a week, and already Mars was a small disc showing numerous surface markings even to the naked eye. Gibson had borrowed a large Mercator projection of the planet and had begun to learn the names of its chief features—names that had been given, most of them, more than a century ago by astronomers who had certainly never dreamed that men would one day use them as part of their normal lives. How poetical those old mapmakers had been when they had ransacked mythology! Even to look at those words on the map was to set the blood pounding in the veins—Deucalion, Elysium, Eumenides, Arcadia, Atlantis, Utopia, Eos. . . . Gibson could sit for hours, fondling those wonderful names with his tongue, feeling as if in truth Keats' charm'd magic casements were opening before him. But there were no seas, perilous or otherwise, on Mars—though many of its lands were sufficiently forlorn.

The path of the *Ares* was now cutting steeply across the planet's orbit, and in a few days the motors would be checking the ship's outward speed. The change of velocity needed to deflect the voyage orbit from Phobos to Deimos was trivial, though it had involved Mackay in several hours of computing.

Every meal was devoted to discussing one thing—the crew's plans when Mars was reached. Gibson's could be summed up in one phrase—to see as much as possible. It was, perhaps, a little optimistic to imagine that one could get to know a whole planet in two months, despite Bradley's repeated assurances that two days was quite long enough for Mars.

The excitement of the voyage's approaching end had, to some extent, taken Gibson's mind away from his personal problems. He met Jimmy perhaps half a dozen times a day at meals and during accidental encounters, but they had not reopened their earlier conversation. For a while Gibson suspected that Jimmy was deliberately avoiding him, but he soon realized that this was not altogether the case. Like the rest of the crew, Jimmy was very busy preparing for the end of the voyage. Norden was determined to have the ship in perfect condition when she docked, and a vast amount of checking and servicing was in progress.

Yet despite this activity, Jimmy had given a good deal of thought to what Gibson had told him. At first he had felt bitter and angry towards the man who had been responsible, however unintentionally, for his mother's unhappiness. But after a while, he began to see Gibson's point of view and understood a little of the other's feelings. Jimmy was shrewd enough to guess that Gibson had not only left a good deal untold, but had put his own case as favorably as possible. Even allowing for this, however, it was obvious that Gibson genuinely regretted the past, and was anxious to undo whatever damage he could, even though he was a generation late.

It was strange to feel the sensation of returning weight and to hear the distant roar of the motors once again as the *Ares* reduced her speed to match the far smaller velocity of Mars. The maneuvering and the final delicate course-corrections took more than twenty-four hours. When it was over, Mars was a dozen times as large as the full moon from Earth, with Phobos and Deimos visible as tiny stars whose movements could be clearly seen after a few minutes of observation.

Gibson had never really realized how red the great deserts were. But the simple word "red" conveyed no idea of the variety of color on that slowly expanding disc. Some regions were almost scarlet, others yellow-brown, while perhaps the commonest hue was what could best be described as powdered brick.

It was late spring in the southern hemisphere, and the polar cap had dwindled to a few glittering specks of whiteness where the snow still lingered stubbornly on higher ground. The broad belt of vegetation between pole and desert was for the greater part a pale bluish-green, but every imaginable shade of color could be found somewhere on that mottled disc.

The *Ares* was swimming into the orbit of Deimos at a relative speed of less than a thousand kilometers an hour. Ahead of the ship, the tiny moon was already showing a visible disc, and as the hours passed it grew until, from a few hundred kilometers away, it looked as large as Mars. But what a contrast it presented! Here were no rich reds and greens, only a dark chaos of jumbled rocks, of mountains which jutted up towards the stars at all angels in this world of practically zero gravity.

Slowly the cruel rocks slid closer and swept past them, as the *Ares* cautiously felt her way down towards the radio beacon which Gibson had heard calling days before. Presently he saw, on an almost level area a few kilometers below, the first signs that man had ever visited this barren world. Two rows of vertical pillars jutted up from the ground, and between them was slung a network of cables. Almost imperceptibly the *Ares* sank toward Deimos; the main rockets had long since been silenced, for the small auxiliary jets had no difficulty in handling the ship's effective weight of a few hundred kilograms.

It was impossible to tell the moment of contact; only the sudden silence when the jets were cut off told Gibson that the journey was over, and the *Ares* was now resting in the cradle that had been prepared for her. He was still, of course, twenty thousand kilometers from Mars and would not actually reach the planet itself for another day, in one of the little rockets that was already climbing up to meet them. But as far as the *Ares* was concerned, the voyage was ended.

The tiny cabin that had been his home for so many weeks would soon know him no more.

He left the observation deck and hurried up to the control room, which he had deliberately avoided during the last busy hours. It was no longer so easy to move around inside the *Ares*, for the minute gravitational field of Deimos was just sufficient to upset his instinctive movements and he had to make a conscious allowance for it. He wondered just what it would be like to experience a *real* gravitational field again. It was hard to believe that only three months ago the idea of having no gravity at all had seemed very strange and unsettling, yet now he had come to regard it as normal. How adaptable the human body was!

The entire crew was sitting round the chart table, looking very smug and self-satisfied.

"You're just in time, Martin," said Norden cheerfully. "We're going to have a little celebration. Go and get your camera and take our pictures while we toast the old crate's health."

"Don't drink it all before I come back!" warned Gibson, and departed in search of his Leica. When he reentered, Dr. Scott was attempting an interesting experiment.

"I'm fed up with squirting my beer out of a bulb," he explained. "I want to pour it properly into a glass now we've got the chance again. Let's see how long it takes."

"It'll be flat before it gets there," warned Mackay. "Let's see—g's about half a centimeter a second squared, you're pouring from a height of . . ." He retired into a brown study.

But the experiment was already in progress. Scott was holding the punctured beer-tin about a foot above his glass—and, for the first time in three months, the word "above" had some meaning, even if very little. For, with incredible slowness, the amber liquid oozed out of the tin—so slowly that one might have taken it for syrup. A thin column extended downwards, moving almost imperceptibly at first, but then slowly accelerating. It seemed an age before the glass was reached; then a great cheer went up as contact was made and the level of the liquid began to creep upwards.

". . . I calculate it should take a hundred and twenty seconds to get there," Mackay's voice was heard to announce above the din.

"Then you'd better calculate again," retorted Scott. "That's two minutes, and it's already there!"

"Eh?" said Mackay, startled, and obviously realizing for the first time that the experiment was over. He rapidly rechecked his calculations and suddenly brightened as discovering a misplaced decimal point.

"Silly of me! I never was any good at mental arithmetic. I meant twelve seconds, of course."

"And that's the man who got us to Mars!" said someone in shocked amazement. "I'm going to walk back!"

Nobody seemed inclined to repeat Scott's experiment, which though interesting, was felt to have little practical value. Very soon large amounts of liquid were being squirted out of bulbs in the "normal" manner, and the party began to get steadily more cheerful. Dr. Scott recited the whole of that saga of the spaceways—and a prodigious feat of memory it was—which paying passengers seldom encounter and which begins:

"It was the spaceship *Venus* . . ."

Gibson followed for some time the adventures of this all too appropriately named craft and its ingenious though single-minded crew. Then the atmosphere began to get too close for him and he left to clear his head. Almost automatically, he made his way back to his favorite viewpoint on the observation deck.

He had to anchor himself in it, lest the tiny but persistent pull of Deimos dislodge him. Mars, more than half full and slowly waxing, lay dead ahead. Down there the preparations to greet them would already be under way, and even at this moment the little rockets would be climbing invisibly towards Deimos to ferry them down. Fourteen thousand kilometers below, but still six thousand kilometers above Mars, Phobos was transiting the unlighted face of the planet, shining brilliantly against its star-eclipsing crescent. Just what *was* happening on that little moon, Gibson wondered half-heartedly. Oh, well, he'd find out soon enough. Meanwhile he'd polish up his aerography. Let's see—there was the double fork of the Sinus Meridiani (very convenient, that, smack on the equator and in zero longitude) and over to the east was the Syrtis Major. Working from these two obvious landmarks he could fill in the finer detail. Margaritifer Sinus was showing up nicely today, but there was a lot of cloud over Xanthe, and——

"Mr. Gibson!"

He looked round, startled.

"Why, Jimmy—you had enough too?"

Jimmy was looking rather hot and flushed—obviously another seeker after fresh air. He wavered, a little unsteadily, into the observation seat and for a moment stared silently at Mars as if he'd never seen it before. Then he shook his head disapprovingly.

"It's awfully big," he announced to no one in particular.

"It isn't as big as Earth," Gibson protested. "And in any case your criticism's completely meaningless, unless you state what standards you're applying. Just what size do you think Mars should be, anyway?"

This obviously hadn't occurred to Jimmy and he pondered it deeply for some time.

"I don't know," he said sadly. "But it's still too big. *Everything's* too big."

This conversation was going to get nowhere, Gibson decided. He would have to change the subject.

"What are you going to do when you get down to Mars? You've got a couple of months to play with before the *Ares* goes home."

"Well, I suppose I'll wander round Port Lowell and go out and look at the deserts. I'd like to do a bit of exploring if I can manage it."

Gibson thought this quite an interesting idea, but he knew that to explore Mars on any useful scale was not an easy undertaking and required a good deal of equipment, as well as experienced guides. It was hardly likely that Jimmy could attach himself to one of the scientific parties which left the settlements from time to time.

"I've an idea," he said. "They're supposed to show me everything I want to see. Maybe I can organize some trips out into Hellas or Hesperia, where no one's been yet. Would you like to come? We might meet some Martians!"

That, of course, had been the stock joke about Mars ever since the first ships had returned with the disappointing news that there weren't any Martians after all. Quite a number of people still hoped, against all evidence, that there might be intelligent life somewhere in the many unexplored regions of the planet.

"Yes," said Jimmy, "that would be a great idea. No one can stop me, anyway—my time's my own as soon as we get to Mars. It says so in the contract."

He spoke this rather belligerently, as if for the information of any superior officers who might be listening, and Gibson thought it wisest to remain silent.

The silence lasted for some minutes. Then Jimmy began, very slowly, to drift out of the observation port and to slide down the sloping walls of the ship. Gibson caught him before he had traveled very far and fastened two of the elastic handholds to his clothing—on the principle that Jimmy could sleep here just as comfortably as anywhere else. He was certainly much too tired to carry him to his bunk.

Is it true that we only look our true selves when we are asleep? wondered Gibson. Jimmy seemed very peaceful and contented now that he was completely relaxed—although perhaps the ruby light from the great planet above gave him his appearance of well-being. Gibson hoped it was not an illusion. The fact that Jimmy had at last deliberately sought him out was significant. True, Jimmy was not altogether himself, and he might have forgotten the whole incident by morning. But Gibson did not think so. Jimmy had decided, perhaps not yet consciously, to give him another chance.

He was on probation.

Gibson awoke the next day with a most infernal din ringing in his ears. It sounded as if the *Ares* was falling to pieces around him, and he hastily dressed and hurried out into the corridor. The first person he met was Mackay, who didn't stop to explain but shouted after him as he went by. "The rockets are here! The first one's going down in two hours. Better hurry—you're supposed to be on it!"

Gibson scratched his head a little sheepishly.

"Someone ought to have told me," he grumbled. Then he remembered that someone had, so he'd only himself to blame. He hurried back to his cabin and began to throw his property into suitcases. From time to time the *Ares* gave a distinct shudder around him, and he wondered just what was going on.

Norden, looking rather harassed, met him at the airlock.

Dr. Scott, also dressed for departure, was with him. He was carrying, with extreme care, a bulky metal case.

"Hope you two have a nice trip down," said Norden. "We'll be seeing you in a couple of days, when we've got the cargo out. So until then—oh, I almost forgot! I'm supposed to get you to sign this."

"What is it?" asked Gibson suspiciously. "I never sign anything until my agent's vetted it."

"Read it and see," grinned Norden. "It's quite an historic document."

The parchment which Norden had handed him bore these words:

> THIS IS TO CERTIFY THAT MARTIN M. GIBSON, AUTHOR, WAS THE FIRST PASSENGER TO TRAVEL IN THE LINER ARES, OF EARTH, ON HER MAIDEN VOYAGE FROM EARTH TO MARS.

Then followed the date, and space for the signatures of Gibson and the rest of the crew. Gibson wrote his autograph with a flourish.

"I suppose this will end up in the museum of Astronautics, when they decide where they're going to build it," he remarked.

"So will the *Ares,* I expect," said Scott.

"That's a fine thing to say at the end of her first trip!" protested Norden. "But I guess you're right. Well, I must be off. The others are outside in their suits—shout to them as you go across. See you on Mars!"

For the second time, Gibson climbed into a spacesuit, now feeling quite a veteran at this sort of thing.

"Of course, you'll understand," explained Scott, "that when the service is properly organized the passengers will go across to the ferry through a connecting tube. That will cut out all this business."

"They'll miss a lot of fun," Gibson replied as he quickly checked the gauges on the little panel beneath his chin.

The outer door opened before them, and they jetted themselves slowly out across the surface of Deimos. The *Ares,* supported in the cradle of ropes (which must have been hastily prepared within the last week) looked as if a wrecking party had been at work on her. Gibson understood now the cause of the bangings and thumpings that had awakened him. Most of the plating from the Southern Hemisphere had been removed to get at the hold, and the spacesuited members of the crew were bringing out the cargo, which was now being piled on the rocks around the ship. It looked, Gibson thought, a very haphazard sort of operation. He hoped that no one would accidentally give his luggage a push which would send it off irretrievably into space, to become a third and still tinier satellite of Mars.

Lying fifty meters from the *Ares,* and quite dwarfed by her bulk, were the two winged rockets that had come up from Mars during the night. One was already having cargo ferried into it; the other, a much smaller vessel, was obviously intended for passengers only. As Gibson slowly and cautiously followed Scott towards it, he switched over to the general wavelength of his suit and called good-bye to his crewmates. Their envious replies came back promptly, interspersed with much puffing and blowing—for the loads they were shifting, though practically weightless, possessed their normal inertia and so were just as hard to set moving as on Earth.

"That's right!" came Bradley's voice. "Leave us to do all the work!"

"You've one compensation," laughed Gibson. "You must be the highest-paid stevedores in the Solar System!" He could sympathize with Bradley's point of view; this was not the sort of work for which the highly trained technicians of the *Ares* had signed on. But the mysterious diversion of the ship from the tiny though well-equipped port on Phobos had made such improvisations unavoidable.

One couldn't very well make individual good-byes on open circuit with half a dozen people listening, and in any case Gibson would be seeing everyone again in a few days. He would like to have had an extra word with Jimmy, but that would have to wait.

It was quite an experience seeing a new human face again. The rocket pilot came into the airlock to help them with their suits, which were gently deposited back on Deimos for future use simply by opening the outer door again and letting the air current do the rest. Then he led them into the tiny cabin and told them to relax in the padded seats.

"Since you've had no gravity for a couple of months," he said, "I'm taking you down as gently as I can. I won't use more than a normal Earth gravity—but even that may make you feel as if you weigh a ton. Ready?"

"Yes," said Gibson, trying valiantly to forget his last experience of this nature.

There was a gentle, far-away roar and something thrust him firmly down into the depths of his seat. The crags and mountains of Deimos sank swiftly behind; he caught a last glimpse of the *Ares*—a bright silver dumb-bell against that nightmare jumble of rocks.

Only a second's burst of power had liberated them from the tiny moon; they were now floating round Mars in a free orbit. For several minutes the pilot studied his instruments, receiving radio checks from the planet beneath, and swinging the ship round its gyros. Then he punched the firing key again, and the rockets thundered for a few seconds more. The ship had broken free from the orbit of Deimos, and was falling towards Mars. The whole operation was an exact replica, in miniature, of a true interplanetary voyage. Only the times and durations were changed; it would take them three hours, not months, to reach their goal, and they had only thousands instead of millions of kilometers to travel.

"Well," said the pilot, locking his controls and swinging round in his seat. "Had a good trip?"

"Quite pleasant, thanks," said Gibson. "Not much excitement, of course. Everything went very smoothly."

"How's Mars these days?" asked Scott.

"Oh, just the same as usual. All work and not much play. The big thing at the moment is the new dome we're building at Lowell. Three hundred meters clear span—you'll be able to think you're back on earth. We're wondering if we can arrange clouds and rain inside it."

"What's all this Phobos business?" said Gibson, with a nose for news. "It caused us a lot of trouble."

"Oh, I don't think it's anything important. No one seems to know exactly, but there are quite a lot of people up there building a big lab. My guess is that Phobos is going to be a pure research station, and they don't want liners coming and going—and messing up their instruments with just about every form of radiation known to science."

Gibson felt disappointed at the collapse of several interesting theories. Perhaps if he had not been so intent on the approaching planet he might have considered this explanation a little more critically, but for the moment it satisfied him and he gave the matter no further thought.

When Mars seemed in no great hurry to come closer, Gibson decided to learn all he could about the practical details of life on the planet, now that he had a genuine colonist to question. He had a morbid fear of making a fool of himself, either by ignorance or tactlessness, and for the next couple of hours the pilot was kept busy alternating between Gibson and his instruments.

Mars was less than a thousand kilometers away when Gibson released his victim and devoted his whole attention to the expanding landscape beneath. They were passing swiftly over the equator, coming down into the outer fringes of the planet's extremely deep yet very tenuous atmosphere. Presently—and it was impossible to tell when the moment arrived—Mars ceased to be a planet floating in space, and became instead a landscape far below. Deserts and oases fled beneath; the Syrtis Major came and passed before Gibson had time to recognize it. They were fifty kilometers up when there came the first hint that the air was thickening around them. A faint and distant sighing, seeming to come from nowhere, began to fill the cabin. The thin air was tugging at their hurtling projectile with feeble fingers, but its strength would grow swiftly—too swiftly, if their navigation had been at fault. Gibson could feel the deceleration mounting as the ship slackened its speed; the whistle of air was now so loud, even through the insulation of the walls, that normal speech would have been difficult.

This seemed to last for a very long time, though it could only have been a few minutes. At last the wail of the wind died slowly away. The rocket had shed all its surplus speed against air resistance; the refractory material of its nose and knife-edged wings would be swiftly cooling from cherry-red. No longer a spaceship now, but simply a high-speed glider, the little ship was racing across the desert at less than a thousand kilometers an hour, riding down the radio beam into Port Lowell.

Gibson first glimpsed the settlement as a tiny white patch on the horizon, against the dark background of the Aurorae Sinus. The pilot swung the ship round in a great whistling arc to the south, losing altitude and shedding his surplus speed. As the rocket banked, Gibson had a momentary picture of half a dozen large, circular domes, clustered closely together. Then the ground was rushing up to meet him, there was a series of gentle bumps, and the machine rolled slowly to a standstill.

He was on Mars. He had reached what to ancient man had been a moving red light among the stars, what to the men of only a century ago had been a mysterious and utterly unattainable world—and what was now the frontier of the human race.

"There's quite a reception committee," remarked the pilot. "All the transport fleet's come out to see us. I didn't know they had so many vehicles serviceable!"

Two small, squat machines with very wide balloon tires had come racing up to meet them. Each had a pressurized driving cab, large enough to hold two people, but a dozen passengers had managed to crowd on to the little vehicles by grabbing convenient hand-holds. Behind them came two large half-tracked buses, also full of spectators. Gibson had not expected quite such a crowd, and began to compose a short speech.

"I don't suppose you know how to use these things yet," said the pilot, producing two breathing masks. "But you've only got to wear them for a minute while you get over to the Fleas." (The *what?* thought Gibson. Oh, of course, those little vehicles would be the famous Martian "Sand Fleas," the planet's universal transports.) "I'll fix them on for you. Oxygen, O.K.? Right—here we go. It may feel a bit queer at first."

The air slowly hissed from the cabin until the pressure inside and out had been equalized. Gibson felt his exposed skin tingling uncomfortably; the atmosphere around him was now thinner than above the peak of Everest. It had taken three months of slow acclimatization on the *Ares*, and all the resources of modern medical science, to enable him to step out on to the surface of Mars with no more protection than a simple oxygen mask.

It was flattering that so many people had come to meet him. Of course, it wasn't often that Mars could expect so distinguished a visitor, but he knew that the busy little colony had no time for ceremonial.

Dr. Scott emerged beside him, still carrying the large metal case he had nursed so carefully through the whole of the trip. At his appearance a group of the colonists came rushing forward, completely ignored Gibson, and crowded round Scott.

Gibson could hear their voices, so distorted in this thin air as to be almost incomprehensible.

"Glad to see you again, Doc! Here—let us carry it!"

"We've got everything ready, and there are ten cases waiting in hospital now. We should know how good it is in a week."

"Come on—get into the bus and talk later!"

Before Gibson had realized what was happening, Scott and his impediments had been swept away. There was a shrill whine of a powerful motor and the bus tore off towards Port Lowell, leaving Gibson feeling as foolish as he had ever been in his life.

He had completely forgotten the serum. To Mars, its arrival was of infinitely greater importance than a visit by any novelist, however distinguished he might be on his own planet. It was a lesson he would not forget in a hurry.

Luckily, he had not been completely deserted—the Sand Fleas were still left. One of the passengers disembarked and hurried up to him.

"Mr. Gibson? I'm Westerman of the 'Times'—the 'Martian Times,' that is. Very pleased to meet you. This is——"

"Henderson, in charge of port facilities," interrupted a tall, hatchet-faced man, obviously annoyed that the other had got in first. "I've seen that your luggage will be collected. Jump aboard."

It was quite obvious that Westerman would have much preferred Gibson as his own passenger, but he was forced to submit with as good grace as he could manage. Gibson climbed into Henderson's Flea through the flexible plastic bag that was the vehicle's simple but effective airlock, and the other joined him a minute later in the driving cab. It was a relief to discard the breathing mask; the few minutes he had spent in the open had been quite a strain. He also felt very heavy and sluggish—the exact reverse of the sensation one would have expected on reaching Mars. But for three months he had known no gravity at all, and it would take him some time to grow accustomed to even a third of his terrestrial weight.

The vehicle began to race across the landing strip towards the domes of the Port, a couple of kilometers away. For the first time, Gibson noticed that all around him was the brilliant mottled green of the hardy plants that were the commonest life-form on Mars. Overhead the sky was no longer jet black, but a deep and glorious blue. The sun was not far from the zenith, and its rays struck with surprising warmth through the plastic dome of the cabin.

Gibson peered at the dark vault of the sky, trying to locate the tiny moon on which his companions were still at work. Henderson noticed his gaze, took one hand off the steering wheel, and pointed close to the Sun.

"There she is," he said.

Gibson shielded his eyes and stared into the sky. Then he saw, hanging like a distant electric arc against the blue, a brilliant star a little westwards of the Sun. It was far too small even for Deimos, but it was a moment before Gibson realized that his companion had mistaken the object of his search.

That steady, unwinking light, burning so unexpectedly in the daylight sky, was now, and would remain for many weeks, the morning star of Mars. But it was better known as Earth.

CHAPTER

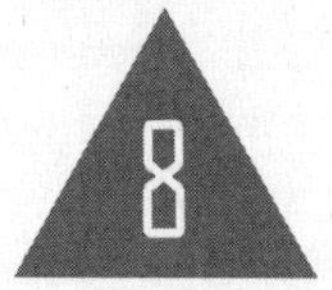

Sorry to have kept you waiting," said Mayor Whittaker, "but you know the way it is—the Chief's been in conference for the last hour. I've only just been able to get hold of him myself to tell him you're here. This way—we'll take the short cut through Records."

It might have been an ordinary office on Earth. The door said, simply enough: "Chief Executive." There was no name; it wasn't necessary. Everyone in the Solar System knew who ran Mars—indeed, it was difficult to think of the planet without thinking of Warren Hadfield at the same time.

Gibson was surprised, when he rose from his desk, to see that the Chief Executive was a good deal shorter than he had imagined. He must have judged the man by his works, and had never guessed that he could give him a couple of inches in height. But the thin, wiry frame and sensitive, rather birdlike head were exactly as he had expected.

The interview began with Gibson somewhat on the defensive, for so much depended on his making a good impression. His way would be infinitely easier if he had the Chief on his side. In fact, if he made an enemy of Hadfield he might just as well go home right away.

"I hope Whittaker's been looking after you," said the Chief when the initial courtesies had been exchanged. "You'll realize that I couldn't see you before—I've only just got back from an inspection. How are you settling down here?"

"Quite well," smiled Gibson. "I'm afraid I've broken a few things by leaving them in mid-air, but I'm getting used to living with gravity again."

"And what do you think of our little city?"

"It's a remarkable achievement. I don't know how you managed to do so much in the time."

Hadfield was eying him narrowly.

"Be perfectly frank. It's smaller than you expected, isn't it?"

Gibson hesitated.

"Well, I suppose it is—but then I'm used to the standards of London and New York. After all, two thousand people would only make a large village back on Earth. Such a lot of Port Lowell's underground, too, and that makes a difference."

The Chief Executive seemed neither annoyed nor surprised.

"Everyone has a disappointment when they see Mars' largest city," he said. "Still, it's going to be a lot bigger in another week, when the new dome goes up. Tell me—just what are your plans now you've got here? I suppose you know I wasn't very much in favor of this visit in the first place."

"I gathered that on Earth," said Gibson, a little taken aback. He had yet to discover that frankness was one of the Chief Executive's major virtues; it was not one that endeared him to many people. "I suppose you were afraid I'd get in the way."

"Yes. But now you're here, we'll do the best for you. I hope you'll do the same for us."

"In what way?" asked Gibson, stiffening defensively.

Hadfield leaned across the table and clasped his hands together with an almost feverish intensity.

"We're at war, Mr. Gibson. We're at war with Mars and all the forces it can bring against us—cold, lack of water, lack of air. And we're at war with Earth. It's a paper war, true, but it's got its victories and defeats. I'm fighting a campaign at the end of a supply line that's never less than fifty million kilometers long. The most urgent goods take at least five months to reach me—and I only get them if Earth decides I can't manage any other way.

"I suppose you realize what I'm fighting for—my primary objective, that is? It's self-sufficiency. Remember that the first expeditions had to bring *everything* with them. Well, we can provide all the basic necessities of life now, from our own resources. Our workshops can make almost anything that isn't too complicated—but it's all a question of manpower. There are some very specialized goods that simply have to be made on Earth, and until our population's at least ten times as big we can't do much about it. Everyone on Mars is an expert at something—but there are more skilled trades back on Earth than there are people on this planet, and it's no use arguing with arithmetic.

"You see those graphs over there? I started keeping them five years ago. They show our production index for various key materials. We've reached the self-sufficiency level—that horizontal red line—for about half of them. I hope that in another five years there will be very few things we'll have to import from Earth. Even now our greatest need is manpower, and that's where you may be able to help us."

Gibson looked a little uncomfortable.

"I can't make any promises. Please remember that I'm here purely as a reporter. Emotionally, I'm on your side, but I've got to describe the facts as I see them."

"I appreciate that. But facts aren't everything. What I hope you'll explain to Earth is the things we hope to do, just as much as the things we've done. They're even more important—but we can achieve them only if Earth gives us its support. Not all your predecessors have realized that."

That was perfectly true, thought Gibson. He remembered a critical series of articles in the "Daily Telegraph" about a year before. The facts had been quite accurate, but a similar account of the first settlers' achievements after five years' colonization of North America would probably have been just as discouraging.

"I think I can see both sides of the question," said Gibson. "You've got to realize that from the point of view of Earth, Mars is a long way away, costs a lot of money, and doesn't offer anything in return. The first glamour of interplanetary exploration has worn off. Now people are asking, 'What do we get out of it?' So far the answer's been, 'Very little.' I'm convinced that your work is important, but in my case it's an act of faith rather than a matter of logic. The average man back on Earth probably thinks the millions you're spending here could be better used improving his own planet—when he thinks of it at all, that is."

"I understand your difficulty; it's a common one. And it isn't easy to answer. Let me put it this way. I suppose most intelligent people would admit the value of a scientific base on Mars, devoted to pure research and investigation?"

"Undoubtedly."

"But they can't see the purpose of building up a self-contained culture, which may eventually become an independent civilization?"

"That's the trouble, precisely. They don't believe it's possible—or, granted the possibility, don't think it's worth while. You'll often see articles pointing out that Mars will always be a drag on the home planet, because of the tremendous natural difficulties under which you're laboring."

"What about the analogy between Mars and the American colonies?"

"It can't be pressed too far. After all, men could breathe the air and find food to eat when they got to America!"

"That's true, but though the problem of colonizing Mars is so much more difficult, we've got enormously greater powers at our control. Given time and material, we can make this a world as good to live on as Earth. Even now, you won't find many of our people who want to go back. They know the importance of what they're doing. Earth may not need Mars yet, but one day it will."

"I wish I could believe that," said Gibson, a little unhappily. He pointed to the rich green tide of vegetation that lapped, like a hungry sea, against the almost invisible dome of the city, at the great plain that hurried so swiftly over the edge of the curiously close horizon, and at the scarlet hills within whose arms the city lay. "Mars is an interesting world, even a beautiful one. But it can never be like Earth."

"Why should it be? And what do you mean by 'Earth,' anyway? Do you mean the South American pampas, the vineyards of France, the coral islands of the Pacific, the Siberian steppes? 'Earth' is every one of those! Wherever men can live, that will be home to someone, some day. And sooner or later men will be able to live on Mars without all this." He waved towards the dome which floated above the city and gave it life.

"Do you really think," protested Gibson, "that men can ever adapt themselves to the atmosphere outside? They won't be men any longer if they do!"

For a moment the Chief Executive did not reply. Then he remarked quietly: "I said nothing about men adapting themselves to Mars. Have you ever considered the possibility of Mars meeting us halfway?"

He left Gibson just sufficient time to absorb the words; then, before his visitor could frame the questions that were leaping to his mind, Hadfield rose to his feet.

"Well, I hope Whittaker looks after you and shows you everything you want to see. You'll understand that the transport situation's rather tight, but we'll get you to all the outposts if you give us time to make the arrangements. Let me know if there's any difficulty."

The dismissal was polite, and, at least for the time being, final. The busiest man on Mars had given Gibson a generous portion of his time, and his questions would have to wait until the next opportunity.

"What do you think of the Chief, now you've met him?" said Mayor Whittaker when Gibson had returned to the outer office.

"He was very pleasant and helpful," replied Gibson cautiously. "Quite an enthusiast about Mars, isn't he?"

Whittaker pursed his lips.

"I'm not sure that's the right word. I think he regards Mars as an enemy to be beaten. So do we all, of course, but the Chief's got better reasons than most. You'd heard about his wife, hadn't you?"

"No."

"She was one of the first people to die of Martian fever, two years after they came here."

"Oh," said Gibson slowly. "I see. I suppose that's one reason why there's been such an effort to find a cure."

"Yes; the Chief's very much set on it. Besides, it's such a drain on our resources. We can't afford to be sick here!"

That last remark, thought Gibson as he crossed Broadway (so called because it was all of fifteen meters wide), almost summed up the position of the colony. He had still not quite recovered from his initial disappointment at finding how small Port Lowell was, and how deficient in all the luxuries to which he was accustomed on Earth. With its rows of uniform metal houses and few public buildings it was more of a military camp than a city, though the inhabitants had done their best to brighten it up with terrestrial flowers. Some of these had grown to impressive sizes under the low gravity, and Oxford Circus was now ablaze with sunflowers thrice the height of a man. Though they were getting rather a nuisance no one had the heart to suggest their removal; if they continued at their present rate of growth it would soon take a skilled lumberjack to fell them without endangering the port hospital.

Gibson continued thoughtfully up Broadway until he came to Marble Arch, at the meeting point of Domes One and Two. It was also, as he had quickly found, a meeting point in many other ways. Here, strategically placed near the multiple airlocks, was "George's," the only bar on Mars.

"Morning, Mr. Gibson," said George. "Hope the Chief was in a good temper."

As he had left the administration building less than ten minutes ago, Gibson thought this was pretty quick work. He was soon to find that news traveled very rapidly in Port Lowell, and most of it seemed to be routed through George.

George was an interesting character. Since tavern keepers were regarded as only relatively, and not absolutely, essential for the well-being of the Port, he had two official professions. On Earth he had been a well-known stage entertainer, but the unreasonable demands of the three or four wives he had acquired in a rush of youthful enthusiasm had made him decide to emigrate. He was now in charge of the Port's little theater and seemed to be perfectly contented with life. Being in the middle forties, he was one of the oldest men on Mars.

"We've got a show on next week," he remarked, when he had served Gibson. "One or two quite good turns. Hope you'll be coming along."

"Certainly," said Gibson. "I'll look forward to it. How often do you have this sort of thing?"

"About once a month. We have film shows three times a week, so we don't really do too badly."

"I'm glad Port Lowell has some night-life."

"You'd be surprised. Still, I'd better not tell you about that or you'll be writing it all up in the papers."

"I don't write for *that* sort of newspaper," retorted Gibson, sipping thoughtfully at the local brew. It wasn't at all bad when you got used to it, though of course it was completely synthetic—the joint offspring of hydroponic farm and chemical laboratory.

The bar was quite deserted, for at this time of day everyone in Port Lowell would be hard at work. Gibson pulled out his notebook and began to make careful entries, whistling a little tune as he did so. It was an annoying habit, of which he was quite unconscious, and George counterattacked by turning up the bar radio.

For once it was a live program, beamed to Mars from somewhere on the night side of Earth, punched across space by heaven-knows-how-many megawatts, then picked up and rebroadcast by the station on the low hills to the south of the city. Reception was good, apart from a trace of solar noise—static from that infinitely greater transmitter against whose background Earth was broadcasting. Gibson wondered if it was really worth all this trouble to send the voice of a somewhat mediocre soprano and a light orchestra from world to world. But half Mars was probably listening with varying degrees of sentimentality and homesickness—both of which would be indignantly denied.

Gibson finished the list of several score questions he had to ask someone. He still felt rather like a new boy at his first school; everything was so strange, nothing could be taken for granted. It was hard to believe that twenty meters on the other side of that transparent bubble lay a sudden death by suffocation. Somehow this feeling had never worried him on the *Ares;* after all, space was like that. But it seemed all wrong here, where one could look out across that brilliant green plain, now a battlefield on which the hardy Martian plants fought their annual struggle for existence—a struggle which would end in death for victors and vanquished alike with the coming of winter.

Suddenly Gibson felt an almost overwhelming desire to leave the narrow streets and go out beneath the open sky. For almost the first time, he found himself really missing Earth, the planet he had thought had so little more to offer him. Like Falstaff, he felt like babbling of green fields—with the added irony that green fields were all around him, tantalizingly visible yet barred from him by the laws of nature.

"George," said Gibson abruptly, "I've been here awhile and I haven't been outside yet. I'm not supposed to without someone to look after me. You won't have any customers for an hour or so. Be a sport and take me out through the airlock—just for ten minutes."

No doubt, thought Gibson a little sheepishly, George considered this a pretty crazy request. He was quite wrong; it had happened so often before that George took it very much for granted. After all, his job was attending to the whims of his customers, and most of the new boys seemed to feel this way after their first few days under the dome. George shrugged his shoulders philosophically, wondering if he should apply for additional credits as Port psychotherapist, and disappeared into his inner sanctum. He came back a moment later, carrying a couple of breathing masks and their auxiliary equipment.

"We won't want the whole works on a nice day like this," he said, while Gibson clumsily adjusted his gear. "Make sure that sponge rubber fits snugly around your neck. All right—let's go. But only ten minutes, mind!"

Gibson followed eagerly, like a sheepdog behind its master, until they came to the dome exit. There were two locks here, a large one, wide open, leading into Dome Two, and a smaller one which led out on to the open landscape. It was simply a metal tube, about three meters in diameter, leading through the glass-brick wall which anchored the flexible plastic envelope of the dome to the ground.

There were four separate doors, none of which could be opened unless the remaining three were closed. Gibson fully approved of these precautions, but it seemed a long time before the last of the doors swung inwards from its seals and that vivid green plain lay open before him. His exposed skin was tingling under the reduced pressure, but the thin air was reasonably warm and he soon felt quite comfortable. Completely ignoring George, he plowed his way briskly through the low, closely packed vegetation, wondering as he did why it clustered so thickly round the dome. Perhaps it was attracted by the warmth of the slow seepage of oxygen from the city.

He stopped after a few hundred meters, feeling at last clear of that oppressive canopy and once more under the open sky of heaven. The fact that his head, at least, was still totally enclosed somehow didn't seem to matter. He bent down and examined the plants among which he was standing knee-deep.

He had, of course, seen photographs of Martian plants many times before. They were not really very exciting, and he was not enough of a botanist to appreciate their peculiarities. Indeed if he had met such plants in some out-of-the-way part of Earth he would hardly have looked at them twice. None were higher than his waist, and those around him now seemed to be made of sheets of brilliant green parchment, very thin but very tough, designed to catch as much sunlight as possible without losing precious water. These ragged sheets were spread like little sails in the sun, whose progress across the sky they would follow until they dipped westwards at dusk. Gibson wished there were some flowers to add a touch of contrasting color to the vivid emerald, but there were no flowers on Mars. Perhaps there had been, once, when the air was thick enough to support insects, but now most of the Martian plant-life was self-fertilized.

George caught up with him and stood regarding the natives with a morose indifference. Gibson wondered if he was annoyed at being so summarily dragged out of doors, but his qualms of conscience were unjustified. George was simply brooding over his next production, wondering whether to risk a Noel Coward play after the disaster that had resulted the last time his company had tried its hand with period pieces. Suddenly he snapped out of his reverie and said to Gibson, his voice thin but clearly audible over this short distance: "This is rather amusing. Just stand still for a minute and watch that plant in your shadow."

Gibson obeyed this peculiar instruction. For a moment nothing happened. Then he saw that, very slowly, the parchment sheets were folding in on one another. The whole process was over in about three minutes; at the end of that time the plant had become a little ball of green paper, tightly crumpled together and only a fraction of its previous size.

George chuckled.

"It thinks night's fallen," he said, "and doesn't want to be caught napping when the sun's gone. If you move away, it will think things over for half an hour before it risks opening shop again. You could probably give it a nervous breakdown if you kept this up all day."

"Are these plants any use?" said Gibson. "I mean, can they be eaten, or do they contain any valuable chemicals?"

"They certainly can't be eaten—they're not poisonous but they'd make you feel mighty unhappy. You see they're not really like plants on Earth at all. That green is just a coincidence. It isn't—what do you call the stuff——"

"Chlorophyll?"

"Yes. They don't depend on the air as our plants do; everything they need they get from the ground. In fact they can grow in a complete vacuum, like the plants on the Moon, if they've got suitable soil and enough sunlight."

Quite a triumph of evolution, thought Gibson. But to what purpose? he wondered. Why had life clung so tenaciously to this little world, despite the worst that nature could do? Perhaps the Chief Executive had obtained some of his own optimism from these tough and resolute plants.

"Hey!" said George. "It's time to go back."

Gibson followed meekly enough. He no longer felt weighed down by that claustrophobic oppression which was, he knew, partly due to the inevitable reaction at finding Mars something of an anticlimax. Those who had come here for a definite job, and hadn't been given time to brood, would probably by-pass this stage altogether. But he had been turned loose to collect his impressions, and so far his chief one was a feeling of helplessness as he compared what man had so far achieved on Mars with the problems still to be faced. Why, even now three-quarters of the planet was still unexplored! That was some measure of what remained to be done.

The first days at Port Lowell had been busy and exciting enough. It had been a Sunday when he had arrived and Mayor Whittaker had been sufficiently free from the cares of office to show him round the city personally, once he had been installed in one of the four suites of the Grand Martian Hotel. (The other three had not yet been finished.) They had started at Dome One, the first to be built, and the Mayor had proudly traced the growth of his city from a group of pressurized huts only ten years ago. It was amusing—and rather touching—to see how the colonists had used wherever possible the names of familiar streets and squares from their own far-away cities. There was also a scientific system of numbering the streets in Port Lowell, but nobody ever used it.

Most of the living houses were uniform metal structures, two stories high, with rounded corners and rather small windows. They held two families and were none too large, since the birth-rate of Port Lowell was the highest in the known universe. This, of course, was hardly surprising since almost the entire population lay between the ages of twenty and thirty, with a few of the senior administrative staff creeping up into the forties. Every house had a curious porch which puzzled Gibson until he realized that it was designed to act as an air-lock in an emergency.

Whittaker had taken him first to the administrative center, the tallest building in the city. If one stood on its roof, one could almost reach up and touch the dome floating above. There was nothing very exciting about Admin. It might have been any office building on Earth, with its rows of desks and typewriters and filing cabinets.

Main Air was much more interesting. This, truly, was the heart of Port Lowell; if it ever ceased to function, the city and all those it held would soon be dead. Gibson had been somewhat vague about the manner in which the settlement obtained its oxygen. At one time he had been under the impression that it was extracted from the surrounding air, having forgotten that even such scanty atmosphere as Mars possessed contained less than one per cent of the gas.

Mayor Whittaker had pointed to the great heap of red sand that had been bulldozed in from outside the dome. Everyone called it "sand," but it had little resemblance to the familiar sand of Earth. A complex mixture of metallic oxides, it was nothing less than the debris of a world that had rusted to death.

"All the oxygen we need's in these ores," said Whittaker, kicking at the caked powder. "And just about every metal you can think of. We've had one or two strokes of luck on Mars: this is the biggest."

He bent down and picked up a lump more solid than the rest.

"I'm not much of a geologist," he said, "but look at this. Pretty, isn't it? Mostly iron oxide, they tell me. Iron isn't much use, of course, but the other metals are. About the only one we can't get easily direct from the sand is magnesium. The best source of that's the old sea bed; there are some salt flats a hundred meters thick out in Xanthe and we just go and collect when we need it."

They walked into the low, brightly lit building, towards which a continual flow of sand was moving on a conveyor belt. There was not really a great deal to see, and though the engineer in charge was only too anxious to explain just what was happening, Gibson was content merely to learn that the ores were cracked in electric furnaces, the oxygen drawn off, purified and compressed, and the various metallic messes sent on for more complicated operations. A good deal of water was also produced here—almost enough for the settlement's needs, though other sources were available as well.

"Of course," said Mayor Whittaker, "in addition to storing the oxygen we've got to keep the air pressure at the correct value and to get rid of the CO_2. You realize, don't you, that the dome's kept up purely by the internal pressure and hasn't any other support at all?"

"Yes," said Gibson. "I suppose if that fell off the whole thing would collapse like a deflated balloon."

"Exactly. We keep 150 millimeters pressure in summer, a little more in winter. That gives almost the same oxygen pressure as in Earth's atmosphere. And we remove the CO_2 simply by letting plants do the trick. We imported enough for this job, since the Martian plants don't go in for photosynthesis."

"Hence the hypertrophied sunflowers in Oxford Circus, I suppose."

"Well, those are intended to be more ornamental than functional. I'm afraid they're getting a bit of a nuisance; I'll have to stop them from spraying seeds all over the city, or whatever it is that sunflowers do. Now let's walk over and look at the farm."

The name was a singularly misleading one for the big food-production plant filling Dome Three. The air was quite humid here, and the sunlight was augmented by batteries of fluorescent tubes so that growth could continue day and night. Gibson knew very little about hydroponic farming and so was not really impressed by the figures which Mayor Whittaker proudly poured into his ear. He could, however, appreciate that one of the greatest problems was meat production, and admired the ingenuity which had partly overcome this by extensive tissue-culture in great vats of nutrient fluid.

"It's better than nothing," said the Mayor a little wistfully. "But what I wouldn't give for a genuine lamb-chop! The trouble with natural meat production is that it takes up so much space and we simply can't afford it. However, when the new dome's up we're going to start a little farm with a few sheep and cows. The kids will love it—they've never seen any animals, of course."

This was not quite true, as Gibson was soon to discover: Mayor Whittaker had momentarily overlooked two of Port Lowell's best-known residents.

By the end of the tour Gibson began to suffer from slight mental indigestion. The mechanics of life in the city were so complicated, and Mayor Whittaker tried to show him *everything.* He was quite thankful when the trip was over and they returned to the Mayor's home for dinner.

"I think that's enough for one day," said Whittaker, "but I wanted to show you round because we'll all be busy tomorrow and I won't be able to spare much time. The Chief's away, you know, and won't be back until Thursday, so I've got to look after everything."

"Where's he gone?" asked Gibson, out of politeness rather than real interest.

"Oh, up to Phobos," Whittaker replied, with the briefest possible hesitation. "As soon as he gets back he'll be glad to see you."

The conversation had then been interrupted by the arrival of Mrs. Whittaker and family, and for the rest of the evening Gibson was compelled to talk about Earth. It was his first, but not by any means his last, experience of the insatiable interest which the colonists had in the home planet. They seldom admitted it openly, pretending to a stubborn indifference about the "old world" and its affairs. But their questions, and above all their rapid reactions to terrestrial criticisms and comments, belied this completely.

It was strange to talk to children who had never known Earth, who had been born and had spent all their short lives under the shelter of the great domes. What, Gibson wondered, did Earth mean to them? Was it any more real than the fabulous lands of fairy tales? All they knew of the world from which their parents had emigrated was at second hand, derived from books and pictures. As far as their own senses were concerned, Earth was just another star.

They had never known the coming of the seasons. Outside the dome, it was true, they could watch the long winter spread death over the land as the Sun descended in the northern sky, could see the strange plants wither and perish, to make way for the next generation when spring returned. But no hint of this came through the protecting barriers of the city. The engineers at the power plant simply threw in more heater circuits and laughed at the worst that Mars could do.

Yet these children, despite their completely artificial environment, seemed happy and well, and quite unconscious of all the things which they had missed. Gibson wondered just what their reactions would be if they ever came to Earth. It would be a very interesting experiment, but so far none of the children born on Mars were old enough to leave their parents.

The lights of the city were going down when Gibson left the Mayor's home after his first day on Mars. He said very little as Whittaker walked back with him to the hotel, for his mind was too full of jumbled impressions. In the morning he would start to sort them out, but at the moment his chief feeling was that the greatest city on Mars was nothing more than an over-mechanized village.

Gibson had not yet mastered the intricacies of the Martian calendar, but he knew that the week-days were the same as on Earth and that Monday followed Sunday in the usual way. (The months also had the same names, but were fifty to sixty days in length.) When he left the hotel at what he thought was a reasonable hour, the city appeared quite deserted. There were none of the gossiping groups of people who had watched his progress with such interest on the previous day. Everyone was at work in office, factory, or lab, and Gibson felt rather like a drone who had strayed into a particularly busy hive.

He found Mayor Whittaker beleaguered by secretaries and talking into two telephones at once. Not having the heart to intrude, Gibson tiptoed away and started a tour of exploration himself. There was not, after all, any great danger of becoming lost. The maximum distance he would travel in a straight line was less than half a kilometer. It was not the kind of exploration of Mars he had ever imagined in any of his books. . . .

So he had passed his first few days in Port Lowell wandering round and asking questions during working hours, spending the evenings with the families of Mayor Whittaker or other members of the senior staff. Already he felt as if he had lived here for years. There was nothing new to be seen; he had met everyone of importance, up to and including the Chief Executive himself.

But he knew he was still a stranger; he had really seen less than a thousand millionth of the whole surface of Mars. Beyond the shelter of the dome, beyond the crimson hills, over the edge of the emerald plain—all the rest of this world was mystery.

CHAPTER

Well, it's certainly nice to see you all again," said Gibson, carrying the drinks carefully across from the bar. "Now I suppose you're going to paint Port Lowell red. I presume the first move will be to contact the local girl friends?"

"That's never very easy," said Norden. "They *will* get married between trips and you've got to be tactful. By the way, George, what's happened to Miss Margaret Mackinnon?"

"You mean Mrs. Henry Lewis," said George. "Such a fine baby boy, too."

"Has she called it John?" asked Bradley, not particularly *sotto voce.*

"Oh, well," sighed Norden, "I hope she's saved me some of the wedding cake. Here's to you, Martin."

"And to the *Ares,*" said Gibson, clinking glasses. "I hope you've put her together again. She looked in a pretty bad way the last time I saw her."

Norden chuckled.

"Oh, that! No, we'll leave all the plating off until we reload. The rain isn't likely to get in!"

"What do you think of Mars, Jimmy?" asked Gibson. "You're the only other new boy here besides myself."

"I haven't seen much of it yet," Jimmy replied cautiously. "Everything seems rather small, though."

Gibson spluttered violently and had to be patted on the back.

"I remember your saying just the opposite when we were on Deimos. But I guess you've forgotten it. You were slightly drunk at the time."

"I've never been drunk," said Jimmy indignantly.

"Then I compliment you on a first-rate imitation: it deceived me completely. But I'm interested in what you say, because that's exactly how I felt after the first couple of days, as soon as I'd seen all there was to look at inside the dome. There's only one cure—you have to go outside and stretch your legs. I've had a couple of short walks around, but now I've managed to grab a Sand Flea from Transport. I'm going to gallop up into the hills tomorrow. Like to come?"

Jimmy's eyes glistened.

"Thanks very much—I'd love to."

"Hey, what about us?" protested Norden.

"You've done it before," said Gibson. "But there'll be one spare seat, so you can toss for it. We've got to take an official driver; they won't let us go out by ourselves with one of their precious vehicles, and I suppose you can hardly blame them."

Mackay won the toss, whereupon the others immediately explained that they didn't really want to go anyway.

"Well, that settles that," said Gibson. "Meet me at Transport Section, Dome Four, at 10 tomorrow. Now I must be off. I've got three articles to write—or at any rate one article with three different titles."

The explorers met promptly on time, carrying the full protective equipment which they had been issued on arrival but so far had found no occasion to use. This comprised the headpiece, oxygen cylinders, and air purifier—all that was necessary out of doors on Mars on a warm day—and the heat-insulating suit with its compact power cells. This could keep one warm and comfortable even when the temperature outside was more than a hundred below. It would not be needed on this trip, unless an accident to the Flea left them stranded a long way away from home.

The driver was a tough young geologist who claimed to have spent as much time outside Port Lowell as in it. He looked extremely competent and resourceful, and Gibson felt no qualms at handing his valuable person into his keeping.

"Do these machines ever break down outside?" he asked as they climbed into the Flea.

"Not very often. They've got a terrific safety factor and there's really very little to go wrong. Of course, sometimes a careless driver gets stuck, but you can usually haul yourself out of anything with the winch. There have only been a couple of cases of people having to walk home in the last month."

"I trust we won't make a third," said Mackay, as the vehicle rolled into the lock.

"I shouldn't worry about that," laughed the driver, waiting for the outer door to open. "We won't be going far from base, so we can always get back even if the worst comes to the worst."

With a surge of power they shot through the lock and out of the city. A narrow road had been cut through the low, vivid vegetation—a road which circled the port and from which other highways radiated to the nearby mines, to the radio station and observatory on the hills, and to the landing ground on which even now the *Ares'* freight was being unloaded as the rockets ferried it down from Deimos.

"Well," said the driver, halting at the first junction. "It's all yours. Which way do we go?"

Gibson was struggling with a map three sizes too big for the cabin. Their guide looked at it with scorn.

"I don't know where you got hold of *that,*" he said. "I suppose Admin gave it to you. It's completely out of date, anyway. If you'll tell me where you want to go I can take you there without bothering about that thing."

"Very well," Gibson replied meekly. "I suggest we climb up into the hills and get a good look round. Let's go to the Observatory."

The Flea leapt forward along the narrow road and the brilliant green around them merged into a featureless blur.

"How fast can these things go?" asked Gibson, when he had climbed out of Mackay's lap.

"Oh, at least a hundred on a good road. But as there aren't any good roads on Mars, we have to take it easy. I'm doing sixty now. On rough ground you'll be lucky to average half that."

"And what about range?" said Gibson, obviously still a little nervous.

"A good thousand kilometers on one charge, even allowing pretty generously for heating, cooking, and the rest. For really long trips we tow a trailer with spare power cells. The record's about five thousand kilometers; I've done three before now, prospecting out in Argyre. When you're doing that sort of thing, you arrange to get supplies dropped from the air."

Though they had now been traveling for no more than a couple of minutes, Port Lowell was already falling below the horizon. The steep curvature of Mars made it very difficult to judge distances, and the fact that the domes were now half concealed by the curve of the planet made one imagine that they were much larger objects at a far greater distance than they really were.

Soon afterwards, they began to reappear as the Flea started climbing towards higher ground. The hills above Port Lowell were less than a kilometer high, but they formed a useful break for the cold winter winds from the south, and gave vantage points for radio station and observatory.

They reached the radio station half an hour after leaving the city. Feeling it was time to do some walking, they adjusted their masks and dismounted from the Flea, taking turns to go through the tiny collapsible airlock.

The view was not really very impressive. To the north, the domes of Port Lowell floated like bubbles on an emerald sea. Over to the west Gibson could just catch a glimpse of crimson from the desert which encircled the entire planet. As the crest of the hills still lay a little above him, he could not see southwards, but he knew that the green band of vegetation stretched for several hundred kilometers until it petered out into the Mare Erythraeum. There were hardly any plants here on the hilltop, and he presumed that this was due to the absence of moisture.

He walked over to the radio station. It was quite automatic, so there was no one he could buttonhole in the usual way, but he knew enough about the subject to guess what was going on. The giant parabolic reflector lay almost on its back, pointing a little east of the zenith—pointing to Earth, sixty million kilometers Sunwards. Along its invisible beam were coming and going the messages that linked these two worlds together. Perhaps at this very moment one of his own articles was flying Earthwards—or one of Ruth Goldstein's directives was winging its way towards him.

Mackay's voice, distorted and feeble in this thin air, made him turn round.

"Someone's coming in to land down there—over on the right."

With some difficulty, Gibson spotted the tiny arrowhead of the rocket moving swiftly across the sky, racing in on a free glide just as he had done a week before. It banked over the city and was lost behind the domes as it touched down on the landing strip. Gibson hoped it was bringing in the remainder of his luggage, which seemed to have taken a long time to catch up with him.

The Observatory was about five kilometers farther south, just over the brow of the hills, where the lights of Port Lowell would not interfere with its work. Gibson had half expected to see the gleaming domes which on Earth were the trademarks of the astronomers, but instead the only dome was the small plastic bubble of the living quarters. The instruments themselves were in the open, though there was provision for covering them up in the very rare event of bad weather.

Everything appeared to be completely deserted as the Flea approached. They halted beside the largest instrument—a reflector with a mirror which, Gibson guessed, was less than a meter across. It was an astonishingly small instrument for the chief observatory on Mars. There were two small refractors, and a complicated horizontal affair which Mackay said was a mirror-transit—whatever that might be. And this, apart from the pressurized dome, seemed to be about all.

There was obviously someone at home, for a small Sand Flea was parked outside the building.

"They're quite a sociable crowd," said the driver as he brought the vehicle to a halt. "It's a pretty dull life up here and they're always glad to see people. And there'll be room inside the dome for us to stretch our legs and have dinner in comfort."

"Surely we can't expect them to provide a meal for us," protested Gibson, who had a dislike of incurring obligations he couldn't readily discharge. The driver looked genuinely surprised; then he laughed heartily.

"This isn't Earth, you know. On Mars, everyone helps everyone else—we have to, or we'd never get anywhere. But I've brought our provisions along—all I want to use is their stove. If you'd ever tried to cook a meal inside a Sand Flea with four aboard you'd know why."

As predicted, the two astronomers on duty greeted them warmly, and the little plastic bubble's air-conditioning plant was soon dealing with the odors of cookery. While this was going on, Mackay had grabbed the senior member of the staff and started a technical discussion about the Observatory's work. Most of it was quite over Gibson's head, but he tried to gather what he could from the conversation.

Most of the work done here was, it seemed, positional astronomy—the dull but essential business of finding longitudes and latitudes, providing time signals and linking radio fixes with the main Martian grid. Very little observational work was done at all; the huge instruments on Earth's moon had taken *that* over long ago, and these small telescopes, with the additional handicap of an atmosphere above them, could not hope to compete. The parallaxes of a few nearer stars had been measured, but the very slight increase of accuracy provided by the wider orbit of Mars made it hardly worth while.

As he ate his dinner—finding to his surprise that his appetite was better than at any time since reaching Mars—Gibson felt a glow of satisfaction at having done a little to brighten the dull lives of these devoted men. Because he had never met enough of them to shatter the illusion, Gibson had an altogether disproportionate respect for astronomers, whom he regarded as leading lives of monkish dedication on their remote mountain eyries. Even his first encounter with the excellent cocktail bar on Mount Palomar had not destroyed this simple faith.

After the meal, at which everyone helped so conscientiously with the washing-up that it took twice as long as necessary, the visitors were invited to have a look through the large reflector. Since it was early afternoon, Gibson did not imagine that there would be a great deal to see; but this was an oversight on his part.

For a moment the picture was blurred, and he adjusted the focusing screw with clumsy fingers. It was not easy to observe with the special eyepiece needed when one was wearing a breathing mask, but after a while Gibson got the knack of it.

Hanging in the field of view, against the almost black sky near the zenith, was a beautiful pearly crescent like a three-day-old moon. Some markings were just visible on the illuminated portion, but though Gibson strained his eyes to the utmost he could not identify them. Too much of the planet was in darkness for him to see any of the major continents.

Not far away floated an identically shaped but much smaller and fainter crescent, and Gibson could distinctly see some of the familiar craters along its edge. They formed a beautiful couple, the twin planets Earth and Moon, but somehow they seemed too remote and ethereal to give him any feeling of homesickness or regret for all that he had left behind.

One of the astronomers was speaking, his helmet held close to Gibson's.

"When it's dark you can see the lights of the cities down there on the night side. New York and London are easy. The prettiest sight, though, is the reflections of the Sun off the sea. You get it near the edge of the disc when there's no cloud about—a sort of brilliant, shimmering star. It isn't visible now because it's mostly land on the crescent portion."

Before leaving the Observatory, they had a look at Deimos, which was rising in its leisurely fashion in the east. Under the highest power of the telescope the rugged little moon seemed only a few kilometers away, and to his surprise Gibson could see the *Ares* quite clearly as two gleaming dots close together. He also wanted to look at Phobos, but the inner moon had not yet risen.

When there was nothing more to be seen, they bade farewell to the two astronomers, who waved back rather glumly as the Flea drove off along the brow of the hill. The driver explained that he wanted to make a private detour to pick up some rock specimens, and as to Gibson one part of Mars was very much like another he raised no objection.

There was no real road over the hills, but ages ago all irregularities had been worn away so that the ground was perfectly smooth. Here and there a few stubborn boulders still jutted above the surface, displaying a fantastic riot of color and shape, but these obstacles were easily avoided. Once or twice they passed small trees—if one could call them that—of a type which Gibson had never seen before. They looked rather like pieces of coral, completely stiff and petrified. According to their driver they were immensely old, for though they were certainly alive no one had yet been able to measure their rate of growth. The smallest value which could be derived for their age was fifty thousand years, and their method of reproduction was a complete mystery.

Towards mid-afternoon they came to a low but beautifully colored cliff—"Rainbow Ridge," the geologist called it—which reminded Gibson irresistibly of the more flamboyant Arizona canyons, though on a much smaller scale. They got out of the Sand Flea and, while the driver chipped off his samples, Gibson happily shot off half a reel of the new Multichrome film he had brought with him for just such occasions. If it could bring out all those colors perfectly it must be as good as the makers claimed, but unfortunately he'd have to wait until he got back to Earth before it could be developed. No one on Mars knew anything about it.

"Well," said the driver, "I suppose it's time we started for home if we want to get back for tea. We can drive back the way we came, and keep to the high ground, or we can go round behind the hills. Any preferences?"

"Why not drive down into the plain? That would be the most direct route," said Mackay, who was now getting a little bored.

"And the slowest—you can't drive at any speed through those overgrown cabbages."

"I always hate retracing my steps," said Gibson. "Let's go round the hills and see what we can find there."

The driver grinned.

"Don't raise any false hopes. It's much the same on both sides. Here we go!"

The Flea bounced forward and Rainbow Ridge soon disappeared behind them. They were now winding their way through completely barren country, and even the petrified trees had vanished. Sometimes Gibson saw a patch of green which he thought was vegetation, but as they approached it invariably turned into another mineral outcrop. This region was fantastically beautiful, a geologist's paradise, and Gibson hoped that it would never be ravaged by mining operations. It was certainly one of the show places of Mars.

They had been driving for half an hour when the hills sloped down into a long, winding valley which was unmistakably an ancient watercourse. Perhaps fifty million years ago, the driver told them, a great river had flowed this way to lose its waters in the Mare Erythraeum—one of the few Martian "seas" to be correctly, if somewhat belatedly, named. They stopped the Flea and gazed down the empty river bed with mingled feelings. Gibson tried to picture this scene as it must have appeared in those remote days, when the great reptiles ruled the Earth and Man was still a dream of the distant future. The red cliffs would scarcely have changed in all that time, but between them the river would have made its unhurried way to the sea, flowing slowly under the weak gravity. It was a scene that might almost have belonged to Earth; and had it ever been witnessed by intelligent eyes? No one knew. Perhaps there had indeed been Martians in those days, but time had buried them completely.

The ancient river had left a legacy, for there was still moisture along the lower reaches of the valley. A narrow band of vegetation had come thrusting up from Erythraeum, its brilliant green contrasting vividly with the crimson of the cliffs. The plants were those which Gibson had already met on the other side of the hills, but here and there were strangers. They were tall enough to be called trees, but they had no leaves—only thin, whiplike branches which continually trembled despite the stillness of the air. Gibson thought they were some of the most sinister things he had ever seen—just the sort of ominous plant that would suddenly flick out its tentacles at an unsuspecting passer-by. In fact, as he was perfectly well aware, they were as harmless as everything else on Mars.

They had zigzagged down into the valley and were climbing the other slope when the driver suddenly brought the Flea to a halt.

"Hello!" he said. "This is odd. I didn't know there was any traffic in these parts."

For a moment Gibson, who was not really as observant as he liked to think, was at a loss. Then he noticed a faint track running along the valley at right angles to their present path.

"There have been some heavy vehicles here," said the driver. "I'm sure this track didn't exist the last time I came this way—let's see, about a year ago. And there haven't been any expeditions into Erythraeum in that time."

"Where does it lead?" asked Gibson.

"Well, if you go up the valley and over the top you'll be back in Port Lowell; that was what I intended to do. The other direction only leads out into the Mare."

"We've got time—let's go along it a little way."

Willingly enough, the driver swung the Flea around and headed down the valley. From time to time the track vanished as they went over smooth, open rock, but it always reappeared again. At last, however, they lost it completely.

The driver stopped the Flea.

"I know what's happened," he said. "There's only one way it could have gone. Did you notice that pass about a kilometer back? Ten to one it leads up there."

"And where would that take anyone?"

"That's the funny thing—it's a complete cul-de-sac. There's a nice little amphitheater about two kilometers across, but you can't get out of it anywhere except the way you came in. I spent a couple of hours there once when we did the first survey of this region. It's quite a pretty little place, sheltered and with some water in the spring."

"A good hide-out for smugglers," laughed Gibson.

The driver grinned.

"That's an idea. Maybe there's a gang bringing in contraband beefsteaks from Earth. I'd settle for one a week to keep my mouth shut."

The narrow pass had obviously once contained a tributary of the main river, and the going was a good deal rougher than in the main valley. They had not driven very far before it became quite clear that they were on the right track.

"There's been some blasting here," said the driver. "This bit of road didn't exist when I came this way. I had to make a detour up that slope, and nearly had to abandon the Flea."

"What do you think's going on?" asked Gibson, now getting quite excited.

"Oh, there are several research projects that are so specialized that one doesn't hear a lot about them. Some things can't be done near the city, you know. They may be building a magnetic observatory here—there's been some talk of that. The generators at Port Lowell would be pretty well shielded by the hills. But I don't think that's the explanation, for I'd have heard—Good Lord!"

They had suddenly emerged from the pass, and before them lay an almost perfect oval of green, flanked by the low, ocher hills. Once this might have been a lovely mountain lake; it was still a solace to the eye weary of lifeless, multicolored rock. But for the moment Gibson scarcely noticed the brilliant carpet of vegetation; he was too astonished by the cluster of domes, like a miniature of Port Lowell itself, grouped at the edge of the little plain.

They drove in silence along the road that had been cut through the living green carpet. No one was moving outside the domes, but a large transporter vehicle, several times the size of the Sand Flea, showed that someone was certainly at home.

"This is quite a set-up," remarked the driver as he adjusted his mask. "There must be a pretty good reason for spending all this money. Just wait here while I go over and talk to them."

They watched him disappear into the airlock of the larger dome. It seemed to his impatient passengers that he was gone rather a long time. Then they saw the outer door open again and he walked slowly back towards them.

"Well?" asked Gibson eagerly as the driver climbed back into the cab. "What did they have to say?"

There was a slight pause; then the driver started the engine and the Sand Flea began to move off.

"I say—what about this famous Martian hospitality? Aren't we invited in?" cried Mackay.

The driver seemed embarrassed. He looked, Gibson thought, exactly like a man who had just discovered he's made a fool of himself. He cleared his throat nervously.

"It's a plant research station," he said, choosing his words with obvious care. "It's not been going for very long, which is why I hadn't heard of it before. We can't go inside because the whole place is sterile and they don't want spores brought in—we'd have to change all our clothes and have a bath of disinfectant."

"I see," said Gibson. Something told him it was no use asking any further questions. He knew, beyond all possibility of error, that his guide had told him only part of the truth—and the least important part at that. For the first time the little discrepancies and doubts that Gibson had hitherto ignored or forgotten began to crystallize in his mind. It had started even before he reached Mars, with the diversion of the *Ares* from Phobos. And now he had stumbled upon this hidden research station. It had been as big a surprise to their experienced guide as to them, but he was attempting to cover up his accidental indiscretion.

There was something going on. What it was, Gibson could not imagine. It must be big, for it concerned not only Mars but Phobos. It was something unknown to most of the colonists, yet something they would co-operate in keeping secret when they encountered it.

Mars was hiding something; and it could only be hiding it from Earth.

CHAPTER

The Grand Martian Hotel now had no less than two residents, a state of affairs which imposed a severe strain on its temporary staff. The rest of his shipmates had made private arrangements for their accommodation in Port Lowell, but as he knew no one in the city Jimmy had decided to accept official hospitality. Gibson wondered if this was going to be a success; he did not wish to throw too great a strain on their still somewhat provisional friendship, and if Jimmy saw too much of him the results might be disastrous. He remembered an epigram which his best enemy had once concocted: "Martin's one of the nicest fellows you could meet, as long as you don't do it too often." There was enough truth in this to make it sting, and he had no wish to put it to the test again.

His life in the Port had now settled down to a fairly steady routine. In the morning he would work, putting on paper his impressions of Mars—rather a presumptuous thing to do when he considered just how much of the planet he had so far seen. The afternoon was reserved for tours of inspection and interviews with the city's inhabitants. Sometimes Jimmy went with him on these trips, and once the whole of the *Ares* crew came along to the hospital to see how Dr. Scott and his colleagues were progressing with their battle against Martian fever. It was still too early to draw any conclusions, but Scott seemed fairly optimistic. "What we'd like to have," he said rubbing his hands ghoulishly, "is a really good epidemic so that we could test the stuff properly. We haven't enough cases at the moment."

Jimmy had two reasons for accompanying Gibson on his tours of the city. In the first place, the older man could go almost anywhere he pleased and so could get into all the interesting places which might otherwise be out of bounds. The second reason was a purely personal one—his increasing interest in the curious character of Martin Gibson.

Though they had now been thrown so closely together, they had never reopened their earlier conversation. Jimmy knew that Gibson was anxious to be friends and to make some recompense for whatever had happened in the past. He was quite capable of accepting this offer on a purely impersonal basis, for he realized well enough that Gibson could be extremely useful to him in his career. Like most ambitious young men, Jimmy had a streak of coldly calculating self-interest in his make-up, and Gibson would have been slightly dismayed at some of the appraisals which Jimmy had made of the advantages to be obtained from his patronage.

It would, however, be quite unfair to Jimmy to suggest that these material considerations were uppermost in his mind. There were times when he sensed Gibson's inner loneliness—the loneliness of the bachelor facing the approach of middle age. Perhaps Jimmy also realized—though not consciously as yet—that to Gibson he was beginning to represent the son he had never had. It was not a role that Jimmy was by any means sure he wanted, yet there were often times when he felt sorry for Gibson and would have been glad to please him. It is, after all, very difficult not to feel a certain affection towards someone who likes you.

The accident that introduced a new and quite unexpected

element into Jimmy's life was really very trivial. He had been out alone one afternoon and, feeling thirsty, had dropped into the small café opposite the Administration building. Unfortunately he had not chosen his time well, for while he was quietly sipping a cup of tea which had never been within millions of kilometers of Ceylon, the place was suddenly invaded. It was the twenty-minute afternoon break when all work stopped on Mars—a rule which the Chief Executive had enforced in the interests of efficiency, though everyone would have much preferred to do without it and leave work twenty minutes earlier instead.

Jimmy was rapidly surrounded by an army of young women, who eyed him with alarming candor and a complete lack of diffidence. Although half a dozen men had been swept in on the flood, they crowded round one table for mutual protection, and judging by their intense expressions, continued to battle mentally with the files they had left on their desks. Jimmy decided to finish his drink as quickly as he could and get out.

A rather tough-looking woman in her late thirties—probably a senior secretary—was sitting opposite him, talking to a much younger girl on his side of the table. It was quite a squeeze to get past, and as Jimmy pushed into the crowd swirling through the narrow gangway, he tripped over an outstretched foot. He grabbed the table as he fell and managed to avoid complete disaster, but only at the cost of catching his elbow a sickening crack on the glass top. Forgetting in his agony that he was no longer back in the *Ares,* he relieved his feelings with a few well-chosen words. Then, blushing furiously, he recovered and bolted to freedom. He caught a glimpse of the elder woman trying hard not to laugh, and the younger one not even attempting such self-control.

And then, though it seemed inconceivable in retrospect, he forgot all about them both.

It was Gibson who quite accidentally provided the second

stimulus. They were talking about the swift growth of the city during the last few years, and wondering if it would continue in the future. Gibson had remarked on the abnormal age distribution caused by the fact that no one under twenty-one had been allowed to emigrate to Mars, so that there was a complete gap between the ages of ten and twenty-one—a gap which, of course, the high birth-rate of the colony would soon fill. Jimmy had been listening half-heartedly when one of Gibson's remarks made him suddenly look up.

"That's funny," he said. "Yesterday I saw a girl who couldn't have been more than eighteen."

And then he stopped. For, like a delayed-action bomb, the memory of that girl's laughing face as he had stumbled from the café suddenly exploded in his mind.

He never heard Gibson tell him that he must have been mistaken. He only knew that, whoever she was and wherever she had come from, he had to see her again.

In a place the size of Port Lowell, it was only a matter of time before one met everybody: the laws of chance would see to that. Jimmy, however, had no intention of waiting until these doubtful allies arranged a second encounter. The following day, just before the afternoon break, he was drinking tea at the same table in the little café.

This not very subtle move had caused him some mental anguish. In the first case, it might seem altogether too obvious. Yet why shouldn't he have tea here when most of Admin did the same? A second and weightier objection was the memory of the previous day's debacle. But Jimmy remembered an apt quotation about faint hearts and fair ladies.

His qualms were unnecessary. Though he waited until the café had emptied again, there was no sign of the girl or her companion. They must have gone somewhere else.

It was an annoying but only temporary setback to so resourceful a young man as Jimmy. Almost certainly she worked in the Admin building, and there were innumerable excuses for visiting that. He could think up enquiries about his pay, though these would hardly get him into the depths of the filing system or the stenographer's office, where she probably worked.

It would be best simply to keep an eye on the building when the staff arrived and left, though how this could be done unobtrusively was a considerable problem. Before he had made any attempt to solve it, Fate stepped in again, heavily disguised as Martin Gibson, slightly short of breath.

"I've been looking everywhere for you, Jimmy. Better hurry up and get dressed. You know there's a show tonight? Well, we've all been invited to have dinner with the Chief before going. That's in two hours."

"What does one wear for formal dinners on Mars?" asked Jimmy.

"Black shorts and white tie, I think," said Gibson, a little doubtfully. "Or is it the other way round? Anyway, they'll tell us at the hotel. I hope they can find something that fits me."

They did, but only just. Evening dress on Mars, where in the heat and air-conditioned cities all clothes were kept to a minimum, consisted simply of a white silk shirt with two rows of pearl buttons, a black bow tie, and black satin shorts with a belt of wide aluminum links on an elastic backing. It was smarter than might have been expected, but when fitted out Gibson felt something midway between a Boy Scout and Little Lord Fauntleroy. Norden and Hilton, on the other hand, carried it off quite well, Mackay and Scott were less successful, and Bradley obviously didn't give a damn.

The Chief's residence was the largest private house on Mars, though on Earth it would have been a very modest affair. They assembled in the lounge for a chat and sherry—real sherry—before the meal. Mayor Whittaker, being Hadfield's second-in-command, had also been invited, and as he listened to them talking to Norden, Gibson understood for the first time with what respect and admiration the colonists regarded the men who provided their sole link with Earth. Hadfield was holding forth at some length about the *Ares,* waxing quite lyrical over her speed and payload, and the effects these would have on the economy of Mars.

"Before we go in," said the Chief, when they had finished the sherry, "I'd like you to meet my daughter. She's just seeing to the arrangements—excuse me a moment while I fetch her."

He was gone only a few seconds.

"This is Irene," he said, in a voice that tried not to be proud but failed completely. One by one he introduced her to his guests, coming to Jimmy last.

Irene looked at him and smiled sweetly.

"I think we've met before," she said.

Jimmy's colour heightened, but he held his ground and smiled back.

"So we have," he replied.

It was really very foolish of him not to have guessed. If he had even started to think properly he would have known who she must have been. On Mars, the only man who could break the rules was the one who enforced them. Jimmy remembered hearing that the Chief had a daughter, but he had never connected the facts together. It all fell into place now: when Hadfield and his wife came to Mars they had brought their only child with them as part of the contract. No one else had ever been allowed to do so.

The meal was an excellent one, but it was largely wasted on Jimmy. He had not exactly lost his appetite—that would have been unthinkable—but he ate with a distracted air. As he was seated near the end of the table, he could see Irene only by dint of craning his neck in a most ungentlemanly fashion. He was very glad when the meal was over and they adjourned for coffee.

The other two members of the Chief Executive's household were waiting for the guests. Already occupying the best seats, a pair of beautiful Siamese cats regarded the visitors with fathomless eyes. They were introduced as Topaz and Turquoise, and Gibson, who loved cats, immediately started to try and make friends with them.

"Are you fond of cats?" Irene asked Jimmy.

"Rather," said Jimmy, who loathed them. "How long have they been here?"

"Oh, about a year. Just fancy—they're the only animals on Mars! I wonder if they appreciate it?"

"I'm sure Mars does. Don't they get spoiled?"

"They're too independent. I don't think they really care for anyone—not even Daddy, though he likes to pretend they do."

With great subtlety—though to any spectator it would have been fairly obvious that Irene was always one jump ahead of him—Jimmy brought the conversation round to more personal matters. He discovered that she worked in the accounting section, but knew a good deal of everything that went on in Administration, where she one day hoped to hold a responsible executive post. Jimmy guessed that her father's position had been, if anything, a slight handicap to her. Though it must have made life easier in some ways, in others it would be a definite disadvantage, as Port Lowell was fiercely democratic.

It was very hard to keep Irene on the subject of Mars. She was much more anxious to hear about Earth, the planet which she had left when a child and so must have, in her mind, a dreamlike unreality. Jimmy did his best to answer her questions, quite content to talk about anything which held her interest. He spoke of Earth's great cities, its mountains and seas, its blue skies and scudding clouds, its rivers and rainbows—all the things which Mars had lost. And as he talked, he fell deeper and deeper beneath the spell of Irene's laughing eyes. That was the only word to describe them: she always seemed to be on the point of sharing some secret joke.

Was she still laughing at him? Jimmy wasn't sure—and he didn't mind. What rubbish it was, he thought, to imagine that one became tongue-tied on these occasions! He had never been more fluent in his life. . . .

He was suddenly aware that a great silence had fallen. Everyone was looking at him and Irene.

"Humph!" said the Chief Executive. "If you two have quite finished, we'd better get a move on. The show starts in ten minutes."

Most of Port Lowell seemed to have squeezed into the little theater by the time they arrived. Mayor Whittaker, who had hurried ahead to check the arrangements, met them at the door and shepherded them into their seats, a reserved block occupying most of the front row. Gibson, Hadfield, and Irene were in the center, flanked by Norden and Hilton—much to Jimmy's chagrin. He had no alternative but to look at the show.

Like all such amateur performances, it was good in parts. The musical items were excellent and there was one mezzo-soprano who was up to the best professional standards of Earth. Gibson was not surprised when he saw against her name on the program: "Late of the Royal Covent Garden Opera."

A dramatic interlude then followed, the distressed heroine and oldtime villain hamming it for all they were worth. The audience loved it, cheering and booing the appropriate characters and shouting gratuitous advice.

Next came one of the most astonishing ventriloquist acts that Gibson had ever seen. It was nearly over before he realized—only a minute before the performer revealed it deliberately—that there was a radio receiver inside the doll and an accomplice off-stage.

The next item appeared to be a skit on life in the city, and was so full of local allusions that Gibson understood only part of it. However, the antics of the main character—a harassed official obviously modelled on Mayor Whittaker—drew roars of laughter. These increased still further when he began to be pestered by a fantastic person who was continually asking ridiculous questions, noting the answers in a little book (which he was always losing), and photographing everything in sight.

It was several minutes before Gibson realized just what was going on. For a moment he turned a deep red; then he realized that there was only one thing he could do. He would have to laugh louder than anyone else.

The proceedings ended with community singing, a form of entertainment which Gibson did not normally go out of his way to seek—rather the reverse, in fact. But he found it more enjoyable than he had expected, and as he joined in the last choruses a sudden wave of emotion swept over him, causing his voice to peter out into nothingness. For a moment he sat, the only silent man in all that crowd, wondering what had happened to him.

The faces around provided the answer. Here were men and women united in a single task, driving towards a common goal, each knowing that their work was vital to the community. They had a sense of fulfillment which very few could know on Earth, where all the frontiers had long ago been reached. It was a sense heightened and made more personal by the fact that Port Lowell was still so small that everyone knew everybody else.

Of course, it was too good to last. As the colony grew, the spirit of these pioneering days would fade. Everything would become too big and too well organized; the development of the planet would be just another job of work. But for the present it was a wonderful sensation, which a man would be lucky indeed to experience even once in his lifetime. Gibson knew it was felt by all those around him, yet he could not share it. He was an outsider: that was the role he had always preferred to play—and now he had played it long enough. If it was not too late, he wanted to join in the game.

That was the moment, if indeed there was such a single point in time, when Martin Gibson changed his allegiance from Earth to Mars. No one ever knew. Even those beside him, if they noticed anything at all, were aware only that for a few seconds he had stopped singing, but had now joined in the chorus again with redoubled vigor.

In twos and threes, laughing, talking and singing, the audience slowly dissolved into the night, Gibson and his friends started back towards the hotel, having said good-bye to the Chief and Mayor Whittaker. The two men who virtually ran Mars watched them disappear down the narrow streets; then Hadfield turned to his daughter and remarked quietly: "Run along home now, dear—Mr. Whittaker and I are going for a little walk. I'll be back in half an hour."

They waited, answering good-nights from time to time, until the tiny square was deserted. Mayor Whittaker, who guessed what was coming, fidgeted slightly.

"Remind me to congratulate George on tonight's show," said Hadfield.

"Yes," Whittaker replied. "I loved the skit on our mutual headache, Gibson. I suppose you want to conduct a post-mortem on his latest exploit?"

The Chief was slightly taken aback by this direct approach.

"It's rather too late now—and there's no real evidence that any real harm was done. I'm just wondering how to prevent future accidents."

"It was hardly the driver's fault. He didn't know about the Project and it was pure bad luck that he stumbled on it."

"Do you think Gibson suspects anything?"

"Frankly, I don't know. He's pretty shrewd."

"Of all the times to send a reporter here! I did everything I could to keep him away, heaven knows!"

"He's bound to find out that something's happening before he's here much longer. I think there's only one solution."

"What's that?"

"We'll just have to tell him. Perhaps not everything, but enough."

They walked in silence for a few yards. Then Hadfield remarked:

"That's pretty drastic. You're assuming he can be trusted completely."

"I've seen a good deal of him these last weeks. Fundamentally, he's on our side. You see, we're doing the sort of things he's been writing about all his life, though he can't quite believe it yet. What would be fatal would be to let him go back to Earth, suspecting something but not knowing what."

There was another long silence. They reached the limit of the dome and stared across the glimmering Martian landscape, dimly lit by the radiance spilling out from the city.

"I'll have to think it over," said Hadfield, turning to retrace his footsteps. "Of course, a lot depends on how quickly things move."

"Any hints yet?"

"No, confound them. You never can pin scientists down to a date."

A young couple, arms twined together, strolled past them obliviously. Whittaker chuckled.

"That reminds me. Irene seems to have taken quite a fancy to that youngster—what's his name—Spencer."

"Oh, I don't know. It's a change to see a fresh face around. And space travel is so much more romantic than the work we do here."

"All the nice girls love a sailor, eh? Well, don't say I didn't warn you!"

That something had happened to Jimmy was soon perfectly obvious to Gibson, and it took him no more than two guesses to arrive at the correct answer. He quite approved of the lad's choice: Irene seemed a very nice child, from what little he had seen of her. She was rather unsophisticated, but this was not necessarily a handicap. Much more important was the fact that she had a gay and cheerful disposition, though once or twice

Gibson had caught her in a mood of wistfulness that was very attractive. She was also extremely pretty; Gibson was now old enough to realize that this was not all-important, though Jimmy might have different views on the subject.

At first, he decided to say nothing about the matter until Jimmy raised it himself. In all probability, the boy was still under the impression that no one had noticed anything in the least unusual. Gibson's self-control gave way, however, when Jimmy announced his intention of taking a temporary job in Port Lowell. There was nothing odd about this; indeed, it was a common practice among visiting space-crews, who soon got bored if they had nothing to do between trips. The work they chose was invariably technical and related in some way to their professional activities; Mackay, for example, was running evening classes in mathematics, while poor Dr. Scott had had no holiday at all, but had gone straight to the hospital immediately on reaching Port Lowell.

But Jimmy, it seemed, wanted a change. They were short of staff in the accounting section, and he thought his knowledge of mathematics might help. He put up an astonishingly convincing argument, to which Gibson listened with genuine pleasure.

"My dear Jimmy," he said, when it was finished. "Why tell *me* all this? There's nothing to stop your going right ahead if you want to."

"I know," said Jimmy, "but you see a lot of Mayor Whittaker and it might save trouble if you had a word with him."

"I'll speak to the Chief if you like."

"Oh no, I shouldn't——" Jimmy began. Then he tried to retrieve his blunder. "It isn't worth bothering him about such details."

"Look here, Jimmy," said Gibson with great firmness. "Why not come clean? Is this your idea, or did Irene put you up to it?"

It was worth traveling all the way to Mars to see Jimmy's expression. He looked rather like a fish that had been breathing air for some time and had only just realized it.

"Oh," he said at last, "I didn't know you knew. You won't tell anyone, will you?"

Gibson was just about to remark that this would be quite unnecessary, but there was something in Jimmy's eyes that made him abandon all attempts at humor. The wheel had come full circle; he was back again in that twenty-year-old-buried spring. He knew exactly what Jimmy was feeling now, and knew also that nothing which the future could bring to him would ever match the emotions he was discovering, still as new and fresh as on the first morning of the world. He might fall in love again in later days, but the memory of Irene would shape and color all his life—just as Irene herself must be the memory of some ideal he had brought with him into this universe.

"I'll do what I can," said Gibson gently, and meant it with all his heart. Though history might repeat itself, it never did so exactly, and one generation could learn from the errors of the last. Some things were beyond planning or foresight, but he would do all he could to help; and this time, perhaps, the outcome might be different.

Chapter

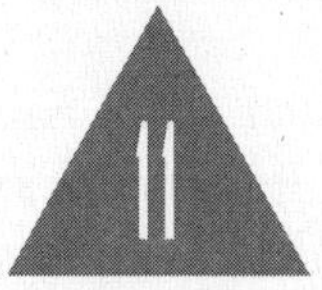

The amber light was on. Gibson took a last sip of water, cleared his throat gently, and checked that the papers of his script were in the right order. No matter how many times he broadcast, his throat always felt this initial tightness. In the control room, the program engineer held up her thumb; the amber changed abruptly to red.

"Hello, Earth. This is Martin Gibson speaking to you from Port Lowell, Mars. It's a great day for us here. This morning the new dome was inflated and now the city's increased its size by almost a half. I don't know if I can convey any impression of what a triumph this means, what a feeling of victory it gives to us here in the battle against Mars. But I'll try.

"You all know that it's impossible to breathe the Martian atmosphere—it's far too thin and contains practically no oxygen. Port Lowell, our biggest city, is built under six domes of transparent plastic held up by the pressure of the air inside—air which we can breathe comfortably though it's still much less dense than yours.

"For the last year a seventh dome has been under construction, a dome twice as big as any of the others. I'll describe it as it was yesterday, when I went inside before the inflation started.

"Imagine a great circular space half a kilometer across, surrounded by a thick wall of glass bricks twice as high as a man. Through this wall lead the passages to the other domes, and the exits direct on to the brilliant green Martian landscape all around us. These passages are simply metal tubes with great doors which close automatically if air escapes from any of the domes. On Mars, we don't believe in putting all our eggs in one basket!

"When I entered Dome Seven yesterday, all this great circular space was covered with a thin transparent sheet fastened to the surrounding wall, and lying limp on the ground in huge folds beneath which we had to force our way. If you can imagine being inside a deflated balloon you'll know exactly how I felt. The envelope of the dome is a very strong plastic, almost perfectly transparent and quite flexible—a kind of thick cellophane.

"Of course, I had to wear my breathing mask, for though we were sealed off from the outside there was still practically no air in the dome. It was being pumped in as rapidly as possible, and you could see the great sheets of plastic straining sluggishly as the pressure mounted.

"This went on all through the night. The first thing this morning I went into the dome again, and found that the envelope had now blown itself into a big bubble at the center, though round the edges it was still lying flat. That huge bubble—it was about a hundred meters across—kept trying to move around like a living creature, and all the time it grew.

"About the middle of the morning it had grown so much that we could see the complete dome taking shape; the envelope had lifted away from the ground everywhere. Pumping was stopped for a while to test for leaks, then resumed again around midday. By now the sun was helping too, warming up the air and making it expand.

"Three hours ago the first stage of the inflation was finished. We took off our masks and let out a great cheer. The air still wasn't really thick enough for comfort, but it was breathable and the engineers could work inside without bothering about masks any more. They'll spend the next few days checking the great envelope for stresses, and looking for leaks. There are bound to be some, of course, but as long as the air loss doesn't exceed a certain value it won't matter.

"So now we feel we've pushed our frontier on Mars back a little further. Soon the new buildings will be going up under Dome Seven, and we're making plans for a small park and even a lake—the only one on Mars, that will be, for free water can't exist here in the open for any length of time.

"Of course, this is only a beginning, and one day it will seem a very small achievement; but it's a great step forward in our battle—it represents the conquest of another slice of Mars. And it means living space for another thousand people. Are you listening, Earth? Good night."

The red light faded. For a moment Gibson sat staring at the microphone, musing on the fact that his first words, though traveling at the speed of light, would only now be reaching Earth. Then he gathered up his papers and walked through the padded doors into the control room.

The engineer held up a telephone for him. "A call's just come through for you, Mr. Gibson," she said. "Someone's been pretty quick off the mark!"

"They certainly have," he replied with a grin. "Hello, Gibson here."

"This is Hadfield. Congratulations. I've just been listening—it went out over our local station, you know."

"I'm glad you liked it."

Hadfield chuckled.

"You've probably guessed that I've read most of your earlier scripts. It's been quite interesting to watch the change of attitude."

"What change?"

"When you started, we were 'they.' Now we're 'we.' Not very well put, perhaps, but I think my point's clear."

He gave Gibson no time to answer this, but continued without a break.

"I really rang up about this. I've been able to fix your trip to Skia at last. We've got a passenger jet going over there on Wednesday, with room for three aboard. Whittaker will give you the details. Good-bye."

The phone clicked into silence. Very thoughtfully, but not a little pleased, Gibson replaced it on the stand. What the Chief had said was true enough. He had been here for almost a month, and in that time his outlook towards Mars had changed completely. The first schoolboy excitement had lasted no more than a few days; the subsequent disillusionment only a little longer. Now he knew enough to regard the colony with a tempered enthusiasm not wholly based on logic. He was afraid to analyze it, lest it disappear completely. Some part of it, he knew, came from his growing respect for the people around him—his admiration for the keen-eyed competence, the readiness to take well-calculated risks, which had enabled them not merely to survive on this heartbreakingly hostile world, but to lay the foundations of the first extra-terrestrial culture. More than ever before, he felt a longing to identify himself with their work, wherever it might lead.

Meanwhile, his first real chance of seeing Mars on the large scale had arrived. On Wednesday he would be taking off for Port Schiaparelli, the planet's second city, ten thousand kilometers to the east of Trivium Charontis. The trip had been planned a fortnight ago, but every time something had turned up to postpone it. He would have to tell Jimmy and Hilton to get ready—they had been the lucky ones in the draw. Perhaps Jimmy might not be quite so eager to go now as he had been once. No doubt he was now anxiously counting the days left to him on Mars, and would resent anything that took him away from Irene. But if he turned down *this* chance, Gibson would have no sympathy for him at all.

"Neat job, isn't she?" said the pilot proudly. "There are only six like her on Mars. It's quite a trick designing a jet that can fly in this atmosphere, even with the low gravity to help you."

Gibson did not know enough about aerodynamics to appreciate the finer points of the aircraft, though he could see that the wing area was abnormally large. The four jet units were neatly buried just outboard of the fuselage, only the slightest of bulges betraying their position. If he had met such a machine on a terrestrial airfield Gibson would not have given it a second though, though the sturdy tractor undercarriage might have surprised him. This machine was built to fly fast and far—and to land on any surface which was approximately flat.

He climbed in after Jimmy and Hilton and settled himself as comfortably as he could in the rather restricted space. Most of the cabin was taken up by large packing cases securely strapped in position—urgent freight for Skia, he supposed. It hadn't left a great deal of space for the passengers.

The motors accelerated swiftly until their thin whines hovered at the edge of hearing. There was the familiar pause while the pilot checked his instruments and controls; then the jets opened full out and the runway began to slide beneath them. A few seconds later there came the sudden reassuring surge of power as the take-off rockets fired and lifted them effortlessly up into the sky. The aircraft climbed steadily into the south, then swung round to starboard in a great curve that took it over the city.

The aircraft leveled out on an easterly course and the great island of Aurorae Sinus sank over the edge of the planet. Apart from a few oases, the open desert now lay ahead for thousands of kilometers.

The pilot switched his controls to automatic and came amidships to talk to his passengers.

"We'll be at Charontis in about four hours," he said. "I'm afraid there isn't much to look at on the way, though you'll see some fine color effects when we go over Euphrates. After that it's more or less uniform desert until we hit the Syrtis Major."

Gibson did some rapid mental arithmetic.

"Let's see—we're flying east and we started rather late—it'll be dark when we get there."

"Don't worry about that—we'll pick up the Charontis beacon when we're a couple of hundred kilometers away. Mars is so small that you don't often do a long-distance trip in daylight all the way."

"How long have you been on Mars?" asked Gibson, who had now ceased taking photos through the observation ports.

"Oh, five years."

"Flying all the time?"

"Most of it."

"Wouldn't you prefer being in spaceships?"

"Not likely. No excitement in it—just floating around in nothing for months." He grinned at Hilton, who smiled amiably but showed no inclination to argue.

"Just what do you mean by 'excitement'?" said Gibson anxiously.

"Well, you've got some scenery to look at, you're not away from home for very long, and there's always the chance you may find something new. I've done half a dozen trips over the poles, you know—most of them in summer, but I went across the Mare Boreum last winter. A hundred and fifty degrees below outside! That's the record so far for Mars."

"I can beat that pretty easily," said Hilton. "At night it reaches two hundred below on Titan." It was the first time Gibson had ever heard him refer to the Saturnia expedition.

"By the way, Fred," he asked, "is this rumor true?"

"What rumor?"

"*You* know—that you're going to have another shot at Saturn."

Hilton shrugged his shoulders.

"It isn't decided—there are a lot of difficulties. But I think it will come off; it would be a pity to miss the chance. You see, if we can leave next year we can go past Jupiter on the way, and have our first really good look at him. Mac's worked out a very interesting orbit for us. We go rather close to Jupiter—right inside *all* the satellites—and let his gravitational field swing us round so that we head out in the right direction for Saturn. It'll need rather accurate navigation to give us just the orbit we want, but it can be done."

"Then what's holding it up?"

"Money, as usual. The trip will last two and a half years and will cost about fifty million. Mars can't afford it—it would mean doubling the usual deficit! At the moment we're trying to get Earth to foot the bill."

"It would come to that anyway in the long run," said Gibson. "But give me all the facts when we get home and I'll write a blistering exposé about cheeseparing terrestrial politicians. You mustn't underestimate the power of the press."

The talk then drifted from planet to planet, until Gibson suddenly remembered that he was wasting a magnificent chance of seeing Mars at first hand. Obtaining permission to occupy the pilot's seat—after promising not to touch anything—he went forward and settled himself comfortably behind the controls.

Five kilometers below, the colored desert was streaking past him to the west. They were flying at what, on Earth, would have been a very low altitude, for the thinness of the Martian air made it essential to keep as near the surface as safety allowed. Gibson had never before received such an impression of sheer speed, for though he had flown in much faster machines on Earth, that had always been at heights where the ground was invisible. The nearness of the horizon added to the effect, for an object which appeared over the edge of the planet would be passing beneath a few minutes later.

From time to time the pilot came forward to check the course, though it was a pure formality, as there was nothing he need do until the voyage was nearly over. At mid-point some coffee and light refreshments were produced, and Gibson rejoined his companions in the cabin. Hilton and the pilot were now arguing briskly about Venus—quite a sore point with the Martian colonists, who regarded that peculiar planet as a complete waste of time.

The sun was now very low in the west and even the stunted Martian hills threw long shadows across the desert. Down there the temperature was already below freezing point, and falling fast. The few hardy plants that had survived in this almost barren waste would have folded their leaves tightly together, conserving warmth and energy against the rigors of the night.

Gibson yawned and stretched himself. The swiftly unfolding landscape had an almost hypnotic effect and it was difficult to keep awake. He decided to catch some sleep in the ninety or so minutes that were left of the voyage.

Some change in the failing light must have woken him. For a moment it was impossible to believe that he was not still dreaming; he could only sit and stare, paralyzed with sheer astonishment. No longer was he looking out across a flat, almost featureless landscape meeting the deep blue of the sky at the far horizon. Desert and horizon had both vanished; in their place towered a range of crimson mountains, reaching north and south as far as the eye could follow. The last rays of the setting sun caught their peaks and bequeathed to them its dying glory; already the foothills were lost in the night that was sweeping onwards to the west.

For long seconds the splendor of the scene robbed it of all reality and hence all menace. Then Gibson awoke from his trance, realizing in one dreadful instant that they were flying far too low to clear those Himalayan peaks.

The sense of utter panic lasted only a moment—to be followed at once by a far deeper terror. Gibson had remembered now what the first shock had banished from his mind—the simple fact he should have thought of from the beginning.

There were no mountains on Mars.

Hadfield was dictating an urgent memorandum to the Interplanetary Development Board when the news came through. Port Schiaparelli had waited the regulation fifteen minutes after the aircraft's expected time of arrival, and Port Lowell Control had stood by for another ten before sending out the "Overdue" signal. One precious aircraft from the tiny Martian fleet was already standing by to search the line of flight as soon as dawn came. The high speed and low altitude essential for flight would make such a search very difficult, but when Phobos rose the telescopes up there could join in with far greater prospects of success.

The news reached Earth an hour later, at a time when there was nothing much else to occupy press or radio. Gibson would have been well satisfied by the resultant publicity: everywhere people began reading his last articles with a morbid interest. Ruth Goldstein knew nothing about it until an editor she was dealing with arrived waving the evening paper. She immediately sold the second reprint rights of Gibson's latest series for half as much again as her victim had intended to pay, then retired to her private room and wept copiously for a full minute. Both these events would have pleased Gibson enormously.

In a score of newspaper offices, the copy culled from the morgue began to be set up in type so that no time would be wasted. And in London a publisher who had paid Gibson a rather large advance began to feel very unhappy indeed.

* * *

Gibson's shout was still echoing through the cabin when the pilot reached the controls. Then he was flung to the floor as the machine turned over in an almost vertical bank in a desperate attempt to swing round to the north. When Gibson could climb to his feet again, he caught a glimpse of a strangely blurred orange cliff sweeping down upon them from only kilometers away. Even in that moment of panic, he could see that there was something very curious about that swiftly approaching barrier, and suddenly the truth dawned upon him at last. This was no mountain range, but something that might be no less deadly. They were running into a wind-borne wall of sand reaching from the desert almost to the edge of the stratosphere.

The hurricane hit them a second later. Something slapped the machine violently from side to side, and through the insulation of the hull came an angry whistling roar that was the most terrifying sound Gibson had ever heard in his life. Night had come instantly upon them and they were flying helplessly through a howling darkness.

It was all over in five minutes, but it seemed a lifetime. Their sheer speed had saved them, for the ship had cut through the heart of the hurricane like a projectile. There was a sudden burst of deep ruby twilight, the ship ceased to be pounded by a million sledge-hammers, and a ringing silence seemed to fill the little cabin. Through the rear observation port Gibson caught a last glimpse of the storm as it moved westwards, tearing up the desert in its wake.

His legs feeling like jellies, Gibson tottered thankfully into his seat and breathed an enormous sigh of relief. For a moment he wondered if they had been thrown badly off course, then realized that this scarcely mattered considering the navigational aids they carried.

It was only then, when his ears had ceased to be deafened by the storm, that Gibson had his second shock. The motors had stopped.

The little cabin was very tense and still. Then the pilot

called out over his shoulder: "Get your masks on! The hull may crack when we come down." His fingers feeling very clumsy, Gibson dragged his breathing equipment from under the seat and adjusted it over his head. When he had finished, the ground already seemed very close, though it was hard to judge distances in the failing twilight.

A low hill swept by and was gone into the darkness. The ship banked violently to avoid another, then gave a sudden spasmodic jerk as it touched ground and bounced. A moment later it made contact again and Gibson tensed himself for the inevitable crash.

It was an age before he dared relax, still unable to believe that they were safely down. Then Hilton stretched himself in his seat, removed his mask, and called out to the pilot: "That was a very nice landing, Skipper. Now how far have we got to walk?"

For a moment there was no reply. Then the pilot called, in a rather strained voice: "Can anyone light me a cigarette? I've got the twitch."

"Here you are," said Hilton, going forward. "Let's have the cabin lights on now, shall we?"

The warm, comfortable glow did much to raise their spirits by banishing the Martian night, which now lay all around. Everyone began to feel ridiculously cheerful and there was much laughing at quite feeble jokes. The reaction had set in: they were so delighted at still being alive that the thousand kilometers separating them from the nearest base scarcely seemed to matter.

"That was quite a storm," said Gibson. "Does this sort of thing happen very often on Mars? And why didn't we get any warnings?"

The pilot, now that he had got over his initial shock, was doing some quick thinking, the inevitable court of enquiry obviously looming large in his mind. Even on autopilot, he *should* have gone forward more often. . . .

"I've never seen one like it before," he said, "though I've done at least fifty trips between Lowell and Skia. The trouble is that we don't know anything about Martian meteorology, even now. And there are only half a dozen met stations on the planet—not enough to give us an accurate picture."

"What about Phobos? Couldn't they have seen what was happening and warned us?"

The pilot grabbed his almanac and ruffled rapidly through the pages.

"Phobos hasn't risen yet," he said after a brief calculation. "I guess the storm blew up suddenly out of Hades—appropriate name, isn't it?— and has probably collapsed again now. I don't suppose it went anywhere near Charontis, so *they* couldn't have warned us either. It was just one of those accidents that's nobody's fault."

This thought seemed to cheer him considerably, but Gibson found it hard to be so philosophical.

"Meanwhile," he retorted, "we're stuck in the middle of nowhere. How long will it take them to find us? Or is there any chance of repairing the ship?"

"Not a hope of that; the jets are ruined. They were made to work on air, not sand, you know!"

"Well, can we radio Skia?"

"Not now we're on the ground. But when Phobos rises in—let's see—an hour's time, we'll be able to call the observatory and they can relay us on. That's the way we've got to do all our long-distance stuff here, you know. The ionosphere's too feeble to bounce signals round the way you do on Earth. Anyway, I'll go and check that the radio is O.K."

He went forward and started tinkering with the ship's transmitter, while Hilton busied himself checking the heaters and cabin air pressure, leaving the two remaining passengers looking at each other a little thoughtfully.

"This is a fine kettle of fish!" exploded Gibson, half in anger and half in amusement. "I've come safely from Earth to

Mars—more than fifty million kilometers—and as soon as I set foot inside a miserable aeroplane *this* is what happens! I'll stick to spaceships in future."

Jimmy grinned. "It'll give us something to tell the others when we get back, won't it? Maybe we'll be able to do some real exploring at last." He peered through the windows, cupping his hands over his eyes to keep out the cabin light. The surrounding landscape was now in complete darkness, apart from the illumination from the ship.

"There seem to be hills all round us; we were lucky to get down in one piece. Good Lord—there's a cliff here on this side—another few meters and we'd have gone smack into it!"

"Any idea where we are?" Gibson called to the pilot. This tactless remark earned him a very stony stare.

"About 120 east, 20 north. The storm can't have thrown us very far off course."

"Then we're somewhere in the Aetheria," said Gibson, bending over the maps. "Yes—there's a hilly region marked here. Not much information about it."

"It's the first time anyone's ever landed here—that's why. This part of Mars is almost unexplored; it's been thoroughly mapped from the air, but that's all."

Gibson was amused to see how Jimmy brightened at this news. There was certainly something exciting about being in a region where no human foot had ever trodden before.

"I hate to cast a gloom over the proceedings," remarked Hilton, in a tone of voice hinting that this was exactly what he was going to do, "but I'm not at all sure you'll be able to radio Phobos even when it does rise."

"What!" yelped the pilot. "The set's O.K.—I've just tested it."

"Yes—but have you noticed where we are? We can't even *see* Phobos. That cliff's due south of us and blocks the view completely. That means that they won't be able to pick up our microwave signals. What's even worse, they won't be able to locate us in their telescopes."

There was a shocked silence.

"*Now* what do we do?" asked Gibson. He had a horrible vision of a thousand-kilometer trek across the desert to Charontis, but dismissed it from his mind at once. They couldn't possibly carry the oxygen for the trip, still less the food and equipment necessary. And no one could spend the night unprotected on the surface of Mars, even here near the Equator.

"We'll just have to signal in some other way," said Hilton calmly. "In the morning we'll climb those hills and have a look round. Meanwhile I suggest we take it easy." He yawned and stretched himself, filling the cabin from ceiling to floor. "We've got no immediate worries; there's air for several days, and power in the batteries to keep us warm almost indefinitely. We may get a bit hungry if we're here more than a week, but I don't think that's at all likely to happen."

By a kind of unspoken mutual consent, Hilton had taken control. Perhaps he was not even consciously aware of the fact, but he was now the leader of the little party. The pilot had delegated his own authority without a second thought.

"Phobos rises in an hour, you said?" asked Hilton.

"Yes."

"When does it transit? I can never remember what this crazy little moon of yours gets up to."

"Well, it rises in the west and sets in the east about four hours later."

"So it'll be due south around midnight?"

"That's right. Oh Lord—that means we won't be able to see it anyway. It'll be eclipsed for at least an hour!"

"*What* a moon!" snorted Gibson. "When you want it most badly, you can't even see the blasted thing!"

"That doesn't matter," said Hilton calmly. "We'll know just where it is, and it won't do any harm to try the radio then. That's all we can do tonight. Has anyone got a pack of cards?

No? Then what about entertaining us, Martin, with some of your stories?"

It was a rash remark, and Gibson seized his chance immediately.

"I wouldn't dream of doing that," he said. "*You're* the one who has the stories to tell."

Hilton stiffened, and for a moment Gibson wondered if he had offended him. He knew that Hilton seldom talked about the Saturnian expedition, but this was too good an opportunity to miss. The chance would never come again, and, as is true of all great adventures, its telling would do their morale good. Perhaps Hilton realized this too, for presently he relaxed and smiled.

"You've got me nicely cornered, haven't you, Martin? Well, I'll talk—but on one condition."

"What's that?"

"No direct quotes, please!"

"As if I would!"

"And when you *do* write it up, let me see the manuscript first."

"Of course."

This was better than Gibson had dared to hope. He had no immediate intention of writing about Hilton's adventures, but it was nice to know that he could do so if he wished. The possibility that he might never have the chance simply did not cross his mind.

Outside the walls of the ship, the fierce Martian night reigned supreme—a night studded with needle-sharp, unwinking stars. The pale light of Deimos made the surrounding landscape dimly visible, as if lit with a cold phosphorescence. Out of the east Jupiter, the brightest object in the sky, was rising in his glory. But the thoughts of the four men in the crashed aircraft were six hundred million kilometers still farther from the sun.

It still puzzled many people—the curious fact that man had

visited Saturn but not Jupiter, so much closer at hand. But in space-travel, sheer distance is of no importance, and Saturn had been reached because of a single astonishing stroke of luck that still seemed too good to be true. Orbiting Saturn was Titan, the largest satellite in the Solar System—about twice the size of Earth's moon. As far back as 1944 it had been discovered that Titan possessed an atmosphere. It was not an atmosphere one could breathe: it was immensely more valuable than that. For it was an atmosphere of methane, one of the ideal propellants for atomic rockets.

This had given rise to a situation unique in the history of spaceflight. For the first time, an expedition could be sent to a strange world with the virtual certainty that refueling would be possible on arrival.

The *Arcturus* and her crew of six had been launched in space from the orbit of Mars. She had reached the Saturnian systems only nine months later, with just enough fuel to land safely on Titan. Then the pumps had been started, and the great tanks replenished from the countless trillions of tons of methane that were there for the taking. Refueling on Titan whenever necessary, the *Arcturus* had visited every one of Saturn's fifteen known moons, and had even skirted the great ring system itself. In a few months, more was learned about Saturn than in all the previous centuries of telescopic examination.

There had been a price to pay. Two of the crew had died of radiation sickness after emergency repairs to one of the atomic motors. They had been buried on Dione, the fourth moon. And the leader of the expedition, Captain Envers, had been killed by an avalanche of frozen air on Titan; his body had never been found. Hilton had assumed command, and had brought the *Arcturus* safely back to Mars a year later, with only two men to help him.

All these bare facts Gibson knew well enough. He could still remember listening to those radio messages that had come trickling back through space, relayed from world to world. But it was a different thing altogether to hear Hilton telling the story in his quiet, curiously impersonal manner, as if he had been a spectator rather than a participant.

He spoke of Titan and its smaller brethren, the little moons which, circling Saturn, made the planet almost a scale model of the Solar System. He described how at last they had landed on the innermost moon of all, Mimas, only half as far from Saturn as the Moon is from the Earth.

"We came down in a wide valley between a couple of mountains, where we were sure the ground would be pretty solid. We weren't going to make the mistake we did on Rhea! It was a good landing, and we climbed into our suits to go outside. It's funny how impatient you always are to do that, no matter how many times you've set down on a new world.

"Of course, Mimas hasn't much gravity—only a hundredth of Earth's. That was enough to keep us from jumping off into space. I liked it that way; you knew you'd always come down safely again if you waited long enough.

"It was early in the morning when we landed. Mimas has a day a bit shorter than Earth's—it goes round Saturn in twenty-two hours, and as it keeps the same face towards the planet its day and month are the same length—just as they are on the Moon. We'd come down in the northern hemisphere, not far from the Equator, and most of Saturn was above the horizon. It looked quite weird—a huge crescent horn sticking up into the sky, like some impossibly bent mountain thousands of miles high.

"Of course you've all seen the films we made—especially the speeded-up color one showing a complete cycle of Saturn's phases. But I don't think they can give you much idea of what it was like to live with that enormous thing always there in the sky. It was so big, you see, that one couldn't take it in a single view. If you stood facing it and held your arms wide open, you could just imagine your finger tips touching the opposite ends of the rings. We couldn't see the rings themselves very well, because they were almost edge-on, but you could always tell they were there by the wide, dusky band of shadow they cast on the planet.

"None of us ever got tired of watching it. It's spinning so fast, you know—the pattern was always changing. The cloud formations, if that's what they were, used to whip round from one side of the disc to the other in a few hours, changing continually as they moved. And there were the most wonderful colors—greens and browns and yellows chiefly. Now and then there'd be great, slow eruptions, and something as big as Earth would rise up out of the depths and spread itself sluggishly in a huge stain halfway round the planet.

"You could never take your eyes off it for long. Even when it was new and so completely invisible, you could still tell it was there because of the great hole in the stars. And here's a funny thing which I haven't reported because I was never quite sure of it. Once or twice, when we were in the planet's shadow and its disc should have been completely dark, I thought I saw a faint phosphorescent glow coming from the night side. It didn't last long—if it really happened at all. Perhaps it was some kind of chemical reaction going on down there in that spinning cauldron.

"Are you surprised that I want to go to Saturn again? What I'd like to do is to get *really* close this time—and by that I mean within a thousand kilometers. It should be quite safe and wouldn't take much power. All you need do is to go into a parabolic orbit and let yourself fall in like a comet going round the Sun. Of course, you'd only spend a few minutes actually close to Saturn, but you could get a lot of records in that time.

"And I want to land on Mimas again, and see that great shining crescent reaching halfway up the sky. It'll be worth the journey, just to watch Saturn waxing and waning, and to see the storms chasing themselves round his Equator. Yes—it would be worth it, even if *I* didn't get back this time."

There were no mock heroics in this closing remark. It was

merely a simple statement of fact, and Hilton's listeners believed him completely. While the spell lasted, every one of them would be willing to strike the same bargain.

Gibson ended the long silence by going to the cabin window and peering out into the night.

"Can we have the lights off?" he called. Complete darkness fell as the pilot obeyed his request. The others joined him at the window.

"Look," said Gibson. "Up there—you can just see it if you crane your neck."

The cliff against which they were lying was no longer a wall of absolute and unrelieved darkness. On its very topmost peaks a new light was playing, spilling over the broken crags and filtering down into the valley. Phobos had leapt out of the west and was climbing on its meteoric rise towards the south, racing backwards across the sky.

Minute by minute the light grew stronger, and presently the pilot began to send out his signals. He had barely begun when the pale moonlight was snuffed out so suddenly that Gibson gave a cry of astonishment. Phobos had gone hurtling into the shadow of Mars, and though it was still rising it would cease to shine for almost an hour. There was no way of telling whether or not it would peep over the edge of the great cliff and so be in the right position to receive their signals.

They did not give up hope for almost two hours. Suddenly the light reappeared on the peaks, but shining now from the east. Phobos had emerged from its eclipse, and was now dropping down towards the horizon which it would reach in little more than an hour. The pilot switched off his transmitter in disgust.

"It's no good," he said. "We'll have to try something else."

"I know!" Gibson exclaimed excitedly. "Can't we carry the transmitter up the top of the hill?"

"I'd thought of that, but it would be the devil's own job to get it out without proper tools. The whole thing—aerials and all—is built into the hull."

"There's nothing more we can do tonight, anyway," said Hilton. "I suggest we all get some sleep before dawn. Good night, everybody."

It was excellent advice, but not easy to follow. Gibson's mind was still racing ahead, making plans for the morrow. Not until Phobos had at last plunged down into the east, and its light had ceased to play mockingly on the cliff above them, did he finally pass into a fitful slumber.

Even then he dreamed that he was trying to fix a belt-drive from the motors to the tractor undercarriage so that they could taxi the last thousand kilometers to Port Schiaparelli. . . .

Chapter

When Gibson woke it was long after dawn. The sun was invisible behind the cliffs, but its rays reflected from the scarlet crags above them flooded the cabin with an unearthly, even a sinister light. He stretched himself stiffly; these seats had not been designed to sleep in, and he had spent an uncomfortable night.

He looked round for his companions—and realized that Hilton and the pilot had gone. Jimmy was still fast asleep; the others must have awakened first and gone out to explore. Gibson felt a vague annoyance at being left behind, but knew that he would have been still more annoyed if they had interrupted his slumbers.

There was a short message from Hilton pinned prominently on the wall. It said simply: "Went outside at 6.30. Will be gone about an hour. We'll be hungry when we get back. Fred."

The hint could hardly be ignored. Besides, Gibson felt hungry himself. He rummaged through the emergency food pack which the aircraft carried for such accidents, wondering as he did so just how long it would have to last them. His attempts to brew a hot drink in the tiny pressure-boiler aroused

Jimmy, who looked somewhat sheepish when he realized he was the last to wake.

"Had a good sleep?" asked Gibson, as he searched round for the cups.

"Awful," said Jimmy, running his hands through his hair. "I feel I haven't slept for a week. Where are the others?"

His question was promptly answered by the sounds of someone entering the airlock. A moment later Hilton appeared, followed by the pilot. They divested themselves of masks and heating equipment—it was still around freezing point outside—and advanced eagerly on the pieces of chocolate and compressed meat which Gibson had portioned out with impeccable fairness.

"Well," said Gibson anxiously, "what's the verdict?"

"I can tell you one thing right away," said Hilton between mouthfuls. "We're damn lucky to be alive."

"I know that."

"You don't know the half of it—you haven't seen just where we landed. We came down parallel to this cliff for almost a kilometer before we stopped. If we'd swerved a couple of degrees to starboard—bang! When we touched down we did swing inwards a bit, but not enough to do any damage.

"We're in a long valley, running east and west. It looks like a geological fault rather than an old river bed, though that was my first guess. The cliff opposite us is a good hundred meters high, and practically vertical—in fact, it's got a bit of overhang near the top. Maybe it can be climbed farther along, but we didn't try. There's no need to, anyway—if we want Phobos to see us we've only got to walk a little way to the north, until the cliff doesn't block the view. In fact, I think that may be the answer—if we can push this ship out into the open. It'll mean we can use the radio, and will give the telescopes and air search a better chance of spotting us."

"How much does this thing weigh?" said Gibson doubtfully.

"About thirty tons with full load. There's a lot of stuff we can take out, of course."

"No there isn't!" said the pilot. "That would mean letting down our pressure, and we can't afford to waste air."

"Oh Lord, I'd forgotten that. Still, the ground's fairly smooth and the undercart's perfectly O.K."

Gibson made noises indicating extreme doubt. Even under a third of Earth's gravity, moving the aircraft was not going to be an easy proposition.

For the next few minutes his attention was diverted to the coffee, which he had tried to pour out before it had cooled sufficiently.

Releasing the pressure on the boiler immediately filled the room with steam, so that for a moment it looked as if everyone was going to inhale their liquid refreshment. Making hot drinks on Mars was always a nuisance, since water under normal pressure boiled at around sixty degrees Centigrade, and cooks who forgot this elementary fact usually met with disaster.

The dull but nourishing meal was finished in silence, as the castaways pondered their pet plans for rescue. They were not really worried; they knew that an intensive search would now be in progress, and it could only be a matter of time before they were located. But that time could be reduced to a few hours if they could get some kind of signal to Phobos.

After breakfast they tried to move the ship. By dint of much pushing and pulling they managed to shift it a good five meters. Then the caterpillar tracks sank into soft ground, and as far as their combined efforts were concerned the machine might have been completely bogged. They retired, panting, into the cabin to discuss the next move.

"Have we anything white which we could spread out over a large area?" asked Gibson.

This excellent idea came to nothing when an intensive search of the cabin revealed six handkerchiefs and a few pieces of grimy rag. It was agreed that, even under the most favorable conditions, these would not be visible from Phobos.

"There's only one thing for it," said Hilton. "We'll have to rip out the landing lights, run them out on a cable until they're clear of the cliff, and aim them at Phobos. I didn't want to do this if it could be avoided; it might make a mess of the wing and it's a pity to break up a good aeroplane."

By his glum expression, it was obvious that the pilot agreed with these sentiments.

Jimmy was suddenly struck with an idea.

"Why not fix up a heliograph?" he asked. "If we flashed a mirror on Phobos they ought to be able to see that."

"Across six thousand kilometers?" said Gibson doubtfully.

"Why not? They've got telescopes that magnify more than a thousand up there. Couldn't you see a mirror flashing in the sun if it was only six kilometers away?"

"I'm sure there's something wrong with that calculation, though I don't know what," said Gibson. "Things never work out as simply as that. But I agree with the general idea. Now who's got a mirror?"

After a quarter hour's search, Jimmy's scheme had to be abandoned. There simply was no such thing as a mirror on the ship.

"We could cut out a piece of the wing and polish that up," said Hilton thoughtfully. "That would be almost as good."

"This magnesium alloy won't take much of a polish," said the pilot, still determined to defend his machine to the last.

Gibson suddenly shot to his feet.

"Will someone kick me three times round the cabin?" he announced to the assembly.

"With pleasure," grinned Hilton, "but tell us why."

Without answering, Gibson went to the rear of the ship and began rummaging among his luggage, keeping his back to the interested spectators. It took him only a moment to find what he wanted; then he swung quickly round.

"Here's the answer," he said triumphantly.

A flash of intolerable light suddenly filled the cabin, flooding every corner with a harsh brilliance and throwing distorted shadows on the wall. It was as if lightning had struck the ship, and for several minutes everyone was half-blinded, still carrying on their retinas a frozen picture of the cabin as seen in that moment of searing incandescence.

"I'm sorry," said Gibson contritely. "I've never used it at full power indoors before—that was intended for night work in the open."

"Phew!" said Hilton, rubbing his eyes. "I thought you'd let off an atomic bomb. Must you scare everyone to death when you photograph them?"

"It's only like *this* for normal indoor use," said Gibson, demonstrating. Everyone flinched again, but this time the flash seemed scarcely noticeable. "It's a special job I had made for me before I left Earth. I wanted to be quite sure I could do color photography at night if I wanted to. So far I haven't had a real chance of using it."

"Let's have a look at the thing," said Hilton.

Gibson handed over the flash-gun and explained its operation.

"It's built round a super-capacity condenser. There's enough for about a hundred flashes on one charge, and it's practically full."

"A hundred of the high-powered flashes?"

"Yes; it'll do a couple of thousand of the normal ones."

"Then there's enough electrical energy to make a good bomb in that condenser. I hope it doesn't spring a leak."

Hilton was examining the little gas-discharge tube, only the size of a marble, at the center of the small reflector.

"Can wc focus this thing to get a good beam?" he asked.

"There's a catch behind the reflector—that's the idea. It's rather a broad beam, but it'll help."

Hilton looked very pleased.

"They ought to see this thing on Phobos, even in broad daylight, if they're watching this part with a good telescope. We mustn't waste flashes, though."

"Phobos is well up now, isn't it?" asked Gibson. "I'm going out to have a shot right away."

He got to his feet and began to adjust his breathing equipment.

"Don't use more than ten flashes," warned Hilton. "We want to save them for night. And stand in any shadow you can find."

"Can I go out too?" asked Jimmy.

"All right," said Hilton. "But keep together and don't go wandering off to explore. I'm going to stay here and see if there's anything we can do with the landing lights."

The fact that they now had a definite plan of action had raised their spirits considerably. Clutching his camera and the precious flash-gun close to his chest, Gibson bounded across the valley like a young gazelle. It was a curious fact that on Mars one quickly adjusted one's muscular efforts to the lower gravity, and so normally used strides no greater than on Earth. But the reserve of power was available, when necessity or high spirits demanded it.

They soon left the shadow of the cliff, and had a clear view of the open sky. Phobos was already high in the west, a little half-moon which would rapidly narrow to a thin crescent as it raced towards the south. Gibson regarded it thoughtfully, wondering if at this very moment someone might be watching this part of Mars. It seemed highly probable, for the approximate position of their crash would be known. He felt an irrational impulse to dance around and wave his arms—even to shout: "Here we are—can't you see us?"

What would this region look like in the telescopes which were, he hoped, now sweeping Aetheria? They would show the mottled green of the vegetation through which he was trudging, and the great cliff would be clearly visible as a red band casting a broad shadow over the valley when the sun was low. There would be scarcely any shadow now, for it was only a few hours from noon. The best thing to do, Gibson decided, was to get in the middle of the darkest area of vegetation he could find.

About a kilometer from the crashed ship the ground sloped down slightly, and here, in the lowest part of the valley, was a wide brownish belt which seemed to be covered with tall weeds. Gibson headed for this, Jimmy following close behind.

They found themselves among slender, leathery plants of a type they had never seen before. The leaves rose vertically out of the ground in long, thin streamers, and were covered with numberless pods which looked as if they might contain seeds. The flat sides were all turned towards the Sun, and Gibson was interested to note that while the sunlit sides of the leaves were black, the shadowed parts were a grayish white. It was a simple but effective trick to reduce loss of heat.

Without wasting time to botanize, Gibson pushed his way into the center of the little forest. The plants were not crowded too closely together, and it was fairly easy to force a passage through them. When he had gone far enough he raised his flash-gun and squinted along it at Phobos.

The satellite was now a thin crescent not far from the Sun, and Gibson felt extremely foolish aiming his flash into the full glare of the summer sky. But the time was really well chosen, for it would be dark on the side of Phobos towards them and the telescopes there would be observing under favorable conditions.

He let off his ten shots in five pairs, spaced well apart. This seemed the most economical way of doing it while still making sure that the signals would look obviously artificial.

"That'll do for today," said Gibson. "We'll save the rest of our ammunition until after dark. Now let's have a look at these plants. Do you know what they remind me of?"

"Overgrown seaweed," replied Jimmy promptly.

"Right first time. I wonder what's in those pods? Have you got a knife on you—thanks."

Gibson began carving at the nearest frond until he had punctured one of the little black balloons. It apparently held gas, and under considerable pressure, for a faint hiss could be heard as the knife penetrated.

"What queer stuff!" said Gibson. "Let's take some back with us."

Not without difficulty, he hacked off one of the long black fronds near the roots. A dark brown fluid began to ooze out of the severed end, releasing tiny bubbles of gas as it did so. With this souvenir hanging over his shoulder, Gibson began to make his way back to the ship.

He did not know that he was carrying with him the future of a world.

They had gone only a few paces when they encountered a denser patch and had to make a detour. With the sun as a guide there was no danger of becoming lost, especially in such a small region, and they had made no attempt to retrace their footsteps exactly. Gibson was leading the way, and finding it somewhat heavy going. He was just wondering whether to swallow his pride and change places with Jimmy when he was relieved to come across a narrow, winding track leading more or less in the right direction.

To any observer, it would have been an interesting demonstration of the slowness of some mental processes. For both Gibson and Jimmy had walked a good six paces before they remembered the simple but shattering truth that footpaths do not, usually, make themselves.

"It's about time our two explorers came back, isn't it?" said the pilot as he helped Hilton detach the floodlights from the underside of the aircraft's wing. This had proved, after all, to be a fairly straight-forward job, and Hilton hoped to find enough wiring inside the machine to run the lights far enough away from the cliff to be visible from Phobos when it rose again. They would not have the brilliance of Gibson's flash, but their steady beams would give them a better chance of being detected.

"How long have they been gone now?" said Hilton.

"About forty minutes. I hope they've had the sense not to get lost."

"Gibson's too careful to go wandering off. I wouldn't trust young Jimmy by himself, though—he'd want to start looking for Martians!"

"Oh, here they are. They seem to be in a bit of a hurry."

Two tiny figures had emerged from the middle distance and were bounding across the valley. Their haste was so obvious that the watchers downed tools and observed their approach with rising curiosity.

The fact that Gibson and Jimmy had returned so promptly represented a triumph of caution and self-control. For a long moment of incredulous astonishment they had stood staring at that pathway through the thin brown plants. On Earth, nothing could have been more commonplace; it was just the sort of track that cattle make across a hill, or wild animals through a forest. Its very familiarity had at first prevented them from noticing it, and even when they had forced their minds to accept its presence, they still kept trying to explain it away.

Gibson had spoken first, in a very subdued voice—almost as if he was afraid of being overheard.

"It's a path all right, Jimmy. But what could have made it, for heaven's sake? No one's ever been here before."

"It must have been some kind of animal."

"A fairly large one, too."

"Perhaps as big as a horse."

"Or a tiger."

The last remark produced an uneasy silence. Then Jimmy said: "Well, if it comes to a fight, that flash of yours should scare anything."

"Only if it had eyes," said Gibson. "Suppose it had some other sense?"

It was obvious that Jimmy was trying to think of good reasons for pressing ahead.

"I'm sure we could run faster, and jump higher, than anything else on Mars."

Gibson liked to believe that his decision was based on prudence rather than cowardice.

"We're not taking any risks," he said firmly. "We're going straight back to tell the others. *Then* we'll think about having a look round."

Jimmy had sense enough not to grumble, but he kept looking back wistfully as they returned to the ship. Whatever faults he might have, lack of courage was not among them.

It took some time to convince the others that they were not attempting a rather poor practical joke. After all, everyone knew why there couldn't be animal life on Mars. It was a question of metabolism: animals burned fuel so much faster than plants, and therefore could not exist in this thin, practically inert atmosphere. The biologists had been quick to point this out as soon as conditions on the surface of Mars had been accurately determined, and for the last ten years the question of animal life on the planet had been regarded as settled—except by incurable romantics.

"Even if you saw what you think," said Hilton, "there must be some natural explanation."

"Come and see for yourself," retorted Gibson." I tell you it was a well-worn track."

"Oh, I'm coming," said Hilton.

"So am I," said the pilot.

"Wait a minute! We can't all go. At least one of us has got to stay behind."

For a moment Gibson felt like volunteering. Then he realized that he would never forgive himself if he did.

"*I* found the track," he said firmly.

"Looks as if I've got a mutiny on my hands," remarked Hilton. "Anyone got some money? Odd man out of you three stays behind."

"It's a wild goose chase, anyway," said the pilot, when he produced the only head. "I'll expect you home in an hour. If you take any longer I'll want you to bring back a genuine Martian princess, *à la* Edgar Rice Burroughs."

Hilton, despite his skepticism, was taking the matter more seriously.

"There'll be three of us," he said, "so it should be all right even if we do meet anything unfriendly. But just in case *none* of us come back, you're to sit right here and not go looking for us. Understand?"

"Very well. I'll sit tight."

The trio set off across the valley towards the little forest, Gibson leading the way. After reaching the tall thin fronds of "seaweed," they had no difficulty in finding the track again. Hilton stared at it in silence for a good minute, while Gibson and Jimmy regarded him with "I told you so" expressions. Then he remarked: "Let's have your flash-gun, Martin. I'm going first."

It would have been silly to argue. Hilton was taller, stronger, and more alert. Gibson handed over his weapon without a word.

There can be no weirder sensation than that of walking along a narrow track between high leafy walls, knowing that at any moment you may come face to face with a totally unknown and perhaps unfriendly creature. Gibson tried to remind himself that animals which had never before encountered man were seldom hostile—though there were enough exceptions to this rule to make life interesting.

They had gone about halfway through the forest when the track branched into two. Hilton took the turn to the right, but soon discovered that this was a *cul-de-sac.* It led to a clearing about twenty meters across, in which all the plants had been cut—or eaten—to within a short distance of the ground, leaving only the stumps showing. These were already beginning to sprout again, and it was obvious that this patch had been deserted for some time by whatever creatures had come here.

"Herbivores," whispered Gibson.

"And fairly intelligent," said Hilton. "See the way they've left the roots to come up again? Let's go back along the other branch."

They came across the second clearing five minutes later. It was a good deal larger than the first, and it was not empty.

Hilton tightened his grip on the flash-gun, and in a single smooth, well-practiced movement Gibson swung his camera into position and began to take the most famous photographs ever made on Mars. Then they all relaxed, and stood waiting for the Martians to notice them.

In that moment centuries of fantasy and legend were swept away. All Man's dreams of neighbors not unlike himself vanished into limbo. With them, unlamented, went Wells' tentacled monstrosities and the other legions of crawling, nightmare horrors. And there vanished also the myth of coldly inhuman intelligences which might look down dispassionately on Man from their fabulous heights of wisdom—and might brush him aside with no more malice than he himself might destroy a creeping insect.

There were ten of the creatures in the glade, and they were all too busy eating to take any notice of the intruders. In appearance they resembled very plump kangaroos, their almost spherical bodies balanced on two large, slender hindlimbs. They were hairless, and their skin had a curious waxy sheen like polished leather. Two thin forearms, which seemed to be completely flexible, sprouted from the upper part of the body and ended in tiny hands like the claws of a bird—too small and feeble, one would have thought, to have been of much practical use. Their heads were set directly on the trunk with no suspicion of a neck, and bore two large pale eyes with wide pupils. There were no nostrils—only a very odd triangular mouth with three stubby bills which were making short work of the foliage. A pair of large, almost transparent ears hung limply from the head, twitching occasionally and sometimes folding themselves into trumpets which looked as if they might be extremely efficient sound detectors, even in this thin atmosphere.

The largest of the beasts was about as tall as Hilton, but all the others were considerably smaller. One baby, less than a meter high, could only be described by the overworked adjective "cute." It was hopping excitedly about in an effort to reach the more succulent leaves, and from time to time emitted thin, piping cries which were irresistibly pathetic.

"How intelligent would you say they are?" whispered Gibson at last.

"It's hard to say. Notice how they're careful not to destroy the plants they eat? Of course, that may be pure instinct—like bees knowing how to build their hives."

"They move very slowly, don't they? I wonder if they're warm-blooded."

"I don't see why they should have blood at all. Their metabolism must be pretty weird for them to survive in this climate."

"It's about time they took some notice of us."

"The big fellow knows we're here. I've caught him looking at us out of the corner of his eye. Do you notice the way his ears keep pointing towards us?"

"Let's go out into the open."

Hilton thought this over.

"I don't see how they can do us much harm, even if they want to. Those little hands look rather feeble—but I suppose those three-sided beaks could do some damage. We'll go forward, very slowly, for six paces. If they come at us, I'll give them a flash with the gun while you make a bolt for it. I'm sure we can outrun them easily. They certainly don't look built for speed."

Moving with a slowness which they hoped would appear reassuring rather than stealthy, they walked forward into the glade. There was now no doubt that the Martians saw them; half a dozen pairs of great, calm eyes stared at them, then looked away as their owners got on with the more important business of eating.

"They don't even seem to be inquisitive," said Gibson, somewhat disappointed. "Are we as uninteresting as all this?"

"Hello—Junior's spotted us! What's he up to?"

The smallest Martian had stopped eating and was staring at the intruders with an expression that might have meant anything from rank disbelief to hopeful anticipation of another meal. It gave a couple of shrill squeaks which were answered by a noncommittal "honk" from one of the adults. Then it began to hop towards the interested spectators.

It halted a couple of paces away, showing not the slightest signs of fear or caution.

"How do you do?" said Hilton solemnly. "Let me introduce us. On my right, James Spencer; on my left, Martin Gibson. But I'm afraid I didn't quite catch your name."

"Squeak," said the small Martian.

"Well, Squeak, what can we do for you?"

The little creature put out an exploring hand and tugged at Hilton's clothing. Then it hopped towards Gibson, who had been busily photographing this exchange of courtesies. Once again it put forward an enquiring paw, and Gibson moved the camera round out of harm's way. He held out his hand, and the little fingers closed round it with surprising strength.

"Friendly little chap, isn't he?" said Gibson, having disentangled himself with difficulty. "At least he's not as stuck-up as his relatives."

The adults had so far taken not the slightest notice of the

proceedings. They were still munching placidly at the other side of the glade.

"I wish we had something to give him, but I don't suppose he could eat any of our food. Lend me your knife, Jimmy. I'll cut down a bit of seaweed for him, just to prove that we're friends."

This gift was gratefully received and promptly eaten, and the small hands reached out for more.

"You seem to have made a hit, Martin," said Hilton.

"I'm afraid it's cupboard love," sighed Gibson. "Hey, leave my camera alone—you can't eat that!"

"I say," said Hilton suddenly. "There's something odd here. What color would you say this little chap is?"

"Why, brown in the front and—oh, a dirty gray at the back."

"Well, just walk to the other side of him and offer another bit of food."

Gibson obliged, Squeak rotating on his haunches so that he could grab the new morsel. And as he did so, an extraordinary thing happened.

The brown covering on the front of his body slowly faded, and in less than a minute had become a dingy gray. At the same time, exactly the reverse happened on the creature's back, until the interchange was complete.

"Good Lord!" said Gibson. "It's just like a chameleon. What do you think the idea is? Protective coloration?"

"No, it's cleverer than that. Look at those others over there. You see, they're always brown—or nearly black—on the side towards the sun. It's simply a scheme to catch as much heat as possible, and avoid re-radiating it. The plants do just the same—I wonder who thought of it first? It wouldn't be any use on an animal that had to move quickly, but some of those big chaps haven't changed position in the last five minutes."

Gibson promptly set to work photographing this peculiar phenomenon—not a very difficult feat to do, as wherever he moved Squeak always turned hopefully towards him and sat waiting patiently. When he had finished, Hilton remarked:

"I hate to break up this touching scene, but we said we'd be back in an hour."

"We needn't all go. Be a good chap, Jimmy—run back and say that we're all right."

But Jimmy was staring at the sky—the first to realize that for the last five minutes an aircraft had been circling high over the valley.

Their united cheer disturbed even the placidly browsing Martians, who looked round disapprovingly. It scared Squeak so much that he shot backwards in one tremendous hop, but soon got over his fright and came forward again.

"See you later!" called Gibson over his shoulder as they hurried out of the glade. The natives took not the slightest notice.

They were halfway out of the little forest when Gibson suddenly became aware of the fact that he was being followed. He stopped and looked back. Making heavy weather, but still hopping along gamely behind him, was Squeak.

"Shoo!" said Gibson, flapping his arms around like a distraught scarecrow. "Go back to Mother! I haven't got anything for you."

It was not the slightest use, and his pause had merely enabled Squeak to catch up with him. The others were already out of sight, unaware that Gibson had dropped back. They therefore missed a very interesting cameo as Gibson tried, without hurting Squeak's feelings, to disengage himself from his new-found friend.

He gave up the direct approach after five minutes, and tried guile. Fortunately he had failed to return Jimmy's knife, and after much panting and hacking managed to collect a small pile of "seaweed" which he laid in front of Squeak. This, he hoped, would keep him busy for quite a while.

He had just finished this when Hilton and Jimmy came hurrying back to find what had happened to him.

"O.K.—I'm coming along now," he said. "I had to get rid of Squeak somehow. *That'll* stop him following."

The pilot in the crashed aircraft had been getting anxious, for the hour was nearly up and there was still no sign of his companions. By climbing on to the top of the fuselage he could see halfway across the valley, and to the dark area of vegetation into which they had disappeared. He was examining this when the rescue aircraft came driving out of the east and began to circle the valley.

When he was sure it had spotted him he turned his attention to the ground again. He was just in time to see a group of figures emerging into the open plain—and a moment later he rubbed his eyes in rank disbelief.

Three people had gone into the forest; but four were coming out. And the fourth looked a very odd sort of person indeed.

CHAPTER

After what was later to be christened the most successful crash in the history of Martian exploration, the visit to Trivium Charontis and Port Schiaparelli was, inevitably, something of an anticlimax. Indeed Gibson had wished to postpone it altogether and to return to Port Lowell immediately with his prize. He had soon abandoned all attempts to jettison Squeak, and as everyone in the colony would be on tenterhooks to see a real, live Martian it had been decided to fly the little creature back with them.

But Port Lowell would not let them return; indeed, it was ten days before they saw the capital again. Under the great domes, one of the decisive battles for the possession of the planet was now being fought. It was a battle which Gibson knew of only through the radio reports—a silent but deadly battle which he was thankful to have missed.

The epidemic which Dr. Scott had asked for had arrived. At its peak, a tenth of the city's population was sick with Martian fever. But the serum from Earth broke the attack, and the battle was won with only three fatal casualties. It was the last time that the fever ever threatened the colony.

Taking Squeak to Port Schiaparelli involved considerable

difficulties, for it meant flying large quantities of his staple diet ahead of him. At first it was doubted if he could live in the oxygenated atmosphere of the domes, but it was soon discovered that this did not worry him in the least—though it reduced his appetite considerably. The explanation of this fortunate accident was not discovered until a good deal later. What never was discovered at all was the reason for Squeak's attachment to Gibson. Someone suggested, rather unkindly, that it was because they were approximately the same shape.

Before they continued their journey, Gibson and his colleagues, with the pilot of the rescue plane and the repair crew who arrived later, made several visits to the little family of Martians. They discovered only the one group, and Gibson wondered if these were the last specimens left on the planet. This, as it later turned out, was not the case.

The rescue plane had been searching along the track of their flight when it had received a radio message from Phobos reporting brilliant flashes in Aetheria. (Just how those flashes had been made had puzzled everyone considerably until Gibson, with justifiable pride, gave the explanation.) When they discovered it would take only a few hours to replace the jet units on their plane, they had decided to wait while the repairs were carried out and to use the time studying the Martians in their natural haunts. It was then that Gibson first suspected the secret of their existence.

In the remote past they had probably been oxygen breathers, and their life processes still depended on the element. They could not obtain it direct from the soil, where it lay in such countless trillions of tons; but the plants they ate could do so. Gibson quickly found that the numerous "pods" in the seaweedlike fronds contained oxygen under quite high pressure. By slowing down their metabolism, the Martians had managed to evolve a balance—almost a symbiosis—with the plants which provided them, literally, with food and air. It was a precarious balance which, one would have thought, might have been upset at any time by some natural catastrophe. But conditions on Mars had long ago reached stability, and the balance would be maintained for ages yet—unless Man disturbed it.

The repairs took a little longer than expected, and they did not reach Port Schiaparelli until three days after leaving Port Lowell. The second city of Mars held less than a thousand people, living under two domes on a long, narrow plateau. This had been the site of the original landing on Mars, and so the position of the city was really an historical accident. Not until some years later, when the planet's resources began to be better known, was it decided to move the colony's center of gravity to Lowell and not to expand Schiaparelli any further.

The little city was in many respects an exact replica of its larger and more modern rival. Its specialty was light engineering, geological—or rather aerological—research, and the exploration of the surrounding regions. The fact that Gibson and his colleagues had accidentally stumbled on the greatest discovery so far made on Mars, less than an hour's flight from the city, was thus the cause of some heartburning.

The visit must have had a demoralizing effect on all normal activity in Port Schiaparelli, for wherever Gibson went everything stopped while crowds gathered around Squeak. A favorite occupation was to lure him into a field of uniform illumination and to watch him turn black all over, as he blissfully tried to extract the maximum advantage from this state of affairs. It was in Schiaparelli that someone hit on the deplorable scheme of projecting simple pictures onto Squeak, and photographing the result before it faded. One day Gibson was very annoyed to come across a photo of his pet bearing a crude but recognizable caricature of a well-known television star.

On the whole, their stay in Port Schiaparelli was not a very happy one. After the first three days they had seen everything worth seeing, and the few trips they were able to make into the surrounding countryside did not provide much of interest. Jimmy was continually worrying about Irene, and putting through expensive calls to Port Lowell. Gibson was impatient to get back to the big city which, not so long ago, he had called an overgrown village. Only Hilton, who seemed to possess unlimited reserves of patience, took life easily and relaxed while the others fussed around him.

There was one excitement during their stay in the city. Gibson had often wondered, a little apprehensively, what would happen if the pressurizing dome ever failed. He received the answer—or as much of it as he had any desire for—one quiet afternoon when he was interviewing the city's chief engineer in his office. Squeak had been with them, propped up on his large, flexible lower limbs like some improbable nursery doll.

As the interview progressed, Gibson became aware that his victim was showing more than the usual signs of restiveness. His mind was obviously very far away, and he seemed to be waiting for something to happen. Suddenly, without warning, the whole building trembled slightly as if hit by an earthquake. Two more shocks, equally spaced, came in quick succession. From a loudspeaker on the wall a voice called urgently: "Blowout! Practice only! You have ten seconds to reach shelter! Blowout! Practice only!"

Gibson had jumped out of his chair, but immediately realized there was nothing he need do. From far away there came a sound of slamming doors—then silence. The engineer got to his feet and walked over to the window, overlooking the city's only main street.

"Everyone seems to have got to cover," he said. "Of course, it isn't possible to make these tests a complete surprise. There's one a month, and we have to tell people what day it will be because they might think it was the real thing."

"Just what are we all supposed to do?" asked Gibson, who had been told at least twice but had become a little rusty on the subject.

"As soon as you hear the signal—that's the three ground explosions—you've got to get under cover. If you're indoors you have to grab your breathing mask to rescue anyone who can't make it. You see, if pressure goes every house becomes a self-contained unit with enough air for several hours."

"And anyone out in the open?"

"It would take a few seconds for the pressure to go right down, and as every building has its own airlock it should always be possible to reach shelter in time. Even if you collapsed in the open, you'd probably be all right if you were rescued inside two minutes—unless you'd got a bad heart. And no one comes to Mars if he's got a bad heart."

"Well, I hope you never have to put this theory into practice."

"So do we! But on Mars one has to be prepared for anything. Ah, there goes the All Clear."

The speaker had burst into life again.

"Exercise over. Will all those who failed to reach shelter in the regulation time please inform Admin in the usual way? End of message."

"Will they?" asked Gibson. "I should have thought they'd keep quiet."

The engineer laughed.

"That depends. They probably will if it was their own fault. But it's the best way of showing up weak points in our defenses. Someone will come and say: 'Look here—I was cleaning one of the ore furnaces when the alarm went; it took me two minutes to get out of the blinking thing. What am *I* supposed to do if there's a real blow-out?' Then we've got to think of an answer, if we can."

Gibson looked enviously at Squeak, who seemed to be asleep, though an occasional twitch of the great translucent ears showed that he was taking some interest in the conversation.

"It would be nice if we could be like him and didn't have to bother about air-pressure. Then we could really do something with Mars."

"I wonder!" said the engineer thoughtfully. "What have *they* done except survive? It's always fatal to adapt oneself to one's surroundings. The thing to do is to alter your surroundings to suit you."

The words were almost an echo of the remark that Hadfield had made at their first meeting. Gibson was to remember them often in the years to come.

Their return to Port Lowell was almost a victory parade. The capital was in a mood of elation over the defeat of the epidemic, and it was now anxiously waiting to see Gibson and his prize. The scientists had prepared quite a reception for Squeak, the zoologists in particular being busily at work explaining away their early explanations for the absence of animal life on Mars.

Gibson had handed his pet over to the experts only when they had solemnly assured him that no thought of dissection had ever for a moment entered their minds. Then, full of ideas, he had hurried to see the Chief.

Hadfield had greeted him warmly. There was, Gibson was interested to note, a distinct change in the Chief's attitude towards him. At first it had been—well, not unfriendly, but at least somewhat reserved. He had not attempted to conceal the fact that he considered Gibson's presence on Mars something of a nuisance—another burden to add to those he already carried. This attitude had slowly changed until it was now obvious that the Chief Executive no longer regarded him as an unmitigated calamity.

"You've added some interesting citizens to my little empire," Hadfield said with a smile. "I've just had a look at your engaging pet. He's already bitten the Chief Medical Officer."

"I hope they're treating him properly," said Gibson anxiously.

"Who—the C.M.O.?"

"No—Squeak, of course. What I'm wondering is whether there are any other forms of animal life we haven't discovered yet—perhaps more intelligent."

"In other words, are these the only genuine Martians?"

"Yes."

"It'll be years before we know for certain, but I rather expect they are. The conditions which make it possible for them to survive don't occur in many places on the planet."

"That was one thing I wanted to talk to you about." Gibson reached into his pocket and brought out a frond of the brown "seaweed." He punctured one of the fronds, and there was the faint hiss of escaping gas.

"If this stuff is cultivated properly, it may solve the oxygen problem in the cities and do away with all our present complicated machinery. With enough sand for it to feed on, it would give you all the oxygen you need."

"Go on," said Hadfield noncommittally.

"Of course, you'd have to do some selective breeding to get the variety that gave most oxygen," continued Gibson, warming to his subject.

"Naturally," replied Hadfield.

Gibson looked at his listener with a sudden suspicion, aware that there was something odd about his attitude. A faint smile was playing about Hadfield's lips.

"I don't think you're taking me seriously!" Gibson protested bitterly.

Hadfield sat up with a start.

"On the contrary!" he retorted. "I'm taking you much more seriously than you imagine." He toyed with his paperweight, then apparently came to a decision. Abruptly he leaned towards his desk microphone and pressed a switch.

"Get me a Sand Flea and a driver," he said. "I want them at Lock One West in thirty minutes."

He turned to Gibson.

"Can you be ready by then?"

"What—yes, I suppose so. I've only got to get my breathing gear from the hotel."

"Good—see you in half an hour."

Gibson was there ten minutes early, his brain in a whirl. Transport had managed to produce a vehicle in time, and the Chief was punctual as ever. He gave the driver instructions which Gibson was unable to catch, and the Flea jerked out of the dome on to the road circling the city.

"I'm doing something rather rash, Gibson," said Hadfield as the brilliant green landscape flowed past them. "Will you give me your word that you'll say nothing of this until I authorize you?"

"Why, certainly," said Gibson, startled.

"I'm trusting you because I believe you're on our side, and haven't been as big a nuisance as I expected."

"Thank you," said Gibson dryly.

"*And* because of what you've just taught us about our own planet. I think we owe you something in return."

The Flea had swung round to the south, following the track that led up into the hills. And, quite suddenly, Gibson realized where they were going.

"Were you very upset when you heard that we'd crashed?" asked Jimmy anxiously.

"Of course I was," said Irene. "Terribly upset. I couldn't sleep for worrying about you."

"Now it's all over, though, don't you think it was worth it?"

"I suppose so, but somehow it keeps reminding me that in a month you'll be gone again. Oh, Jimmy, what shall we do then?"

Deep despair settled upon the two lovers. All Jimmy's present satisfaction vanished into gloom. There was no escaping from this inevitable fact. The *Ares* would be leaving Deimos in less than four weeks, and it might be years before he could return to Mars. It was a prospect too terrible for words.

"I can't possibly stay on Mars, even if they'd let me," said Jimmy. "I can't earn a living until I'm qualified, and I've still got two years' post-graduate work *and* a trip to Venus to do! There's only one thing for it!"

Irene's eyes brightened; then she relapsed into gloom.

"Oh, we've been through that before. I'm sure Daddy wouldn't agree."

"Well, it won't do any harm to try. I'll get Martin to tackle him."

"Mr. Gibson? Do you think he would?"

"I know he will, if I ask him. And he'll make it sound convincing."

"I don't see why he should bother."

"Oh, he likes me," said Jimmy with easy self-assurance. "I'm sure he'll agree with us. It's not right that you should stick here on Mars and never see anything of Earth. Paris—New York—London—why, you haven't lived until you've visited them. Do you know what I think?"

"What?"

"Your father's being selfish in keeping you here."

Irene pouted a little. She was very fond of her father and her first impulse was to defend him vigorously. But she was now torn between two loyalties, though in the long run there was no doubt which would win.

"Of course," said Jimmy, realizing that he might have gone too far, "I'm sure he really means to do the best for you, but he's got so many things to worry about. He's probably forgotten what Earth is like and doesn't realize what you're losing! No, you must get away before it's too late."

Irene still looked uncertain. Then her sense of humor, so much more acute than Jimmy's, came to the rescue.

"I'm quite sure that if we were on Earth, and you had to go

back to Mars, you'd be able to prove just as easily that I ought to follow you there!"

Jimmy looked a little hurt, then realized that Irene wasn't really laughing at him.

"All right," he said. "That's settled. I'll talk to Martin as soon as I see him—and ask him to tackle your dad. So let's forget all about it until then, shall we?"

They did, very nearly.

The little amphitheater in the hills above Port Lowell was just as Gibson had remembered it, except that the green of its lush vegetation had darkened a little, as if it had already received the first warning of the still far-distant autumn. The Sand Flea drove up to the largest of the four small domes, and they walked over to the airlock.

"When I was here before," said Gibson dryly, "I was told we'd have to be disinfected before we could enter."

"A slight exaggeration to discourage unwanted visitors," said Hadfield, unabashed. The outer door had opened at his signal, and they quickly stripped off their breathing apparatus. "We used to take such precautions, but they're no longer necessary."

The inner door slid aside and they stepped through into the dome. A man wearing the white smock of the scientific worker—the *clean* white smock of the very senior scientific worker—was waiting for them.

"Hello, Baines," said Hadfield. "Gibson—this is Professor Baines. I expect you've heard of each other."

They shook hands. Baines, Gibson knew, was one of the world's greatest experts on plant genetics. He had read a year or two ago that he had gone to Mars to study its flora.

"So you're the chap who's just discovered *Oxyfera,*" said Baines dreamily. He was a large, rugged man with an absent-minded air which contrasted strangely with his massive frame and determined features.

"Is that what you call it?" asked Gibson. "Well, I *thought* I'd discovered it. But I'm beginning to have doubts."

"You certainly discovered something quite as important," Hadfield reassured him. "But Baines isn't interested in animals, so it's no good talking to him about your Martian friends."

They were walking between low temporary walls which, Gibson saw, partitioned the dome into numerous rooms and corridors. The whole place looked as if it had been built in a great hurry; they came across beautiful scientific apparatus supported on rough packing cases, and everywhere there was an atmosphere of hectic improvisation. Yet, curiously enough, very few people were at work. Gibson obtained the impression that whatever task had been going on here was now completed and that only a skeleton staff was left.

Baines led them to an airlock connecting with one of the other domes, and as they waited for the last door to open he remarked quietly: "This may hurt your eyes a bit." With this warning, Gibson put up his hand as a shield.

His first impression was one of light and heat. It was almost as if he had moved from Pole to Tropics in a single step. Overhead, batteries of powerful lamps were blasting the hemispherical chamber with light. There was something heavy and oppressive about the air that was not only due to the heat, and he wondered what sort of atmosphere he was breathing.

This dome was not divided up by partitions; it was simply a large, circular space laid out into neat plots on which grew all the Martian plants which Gibson had ever seen, and many more besides. About a quarter of the area was covered by tall brown fronds which Gibson recognized at once.

"So you've known about them all the time?" he said, neither surprised nor particularly disappointed. (Hadfield was quite right: the Martians were *much* more important.)

"Yes," said Hadfield. "They were discovered about two years ago and aren't very rare along the equatorial belt. They only grow where there's plenty of sunlight, and your little crop was the farthest north they've ever been found."

"It takes a great deal of energy to split the oxygen out of the sand," explained Baines. "We've been helping them here with these lights, and trying some experiments of our own. Come and look at the result."

Gibson walked over to the plot, keeping carefully to the narrow path. These plants weren't, after all, exactly the same as those he had discovered, though they had obviously descended from the same stock. The most surprising difference was the complete absence of gas-pods, their place having been taken by myriads of minute pores.

"This is the important point," said Hadfield. "We've bred a variety which releases its oxygen directly into the air, because it doesn't need to store it any more. As long as it's got plenty of light and heat, it can extract all its needs from the sand and will throw off the surplus. *All the oxygen you're breathing now comes from these plants*—there's no other source in this dome."

"I see," said Gibson slowly. "So you'd already thought of my idea—and gone a good deal further. But I still don't understand the need for all this secrecy."

"What secrecy?" said Hadfield with an air of injured innocence.

"Really!" protested Gibson. "You've just asked me not to say anything about this place."

"Oh, that's because there will be an official announcement in a few days, and we haven't wanted to raise false hopes. But there hasn't been any real secrecy."

Gibson brooded over this remark all the way back to Port Lowell. Hadfield had told him a good deal, but had he told him everything? Where—if at all—did Phobos come into the picture? Gibson wondered if his suspicions about the inner moon were completely unfounded; it could obviously have no connection with this particular project. He felt like trying to force Hadfield's hand by a direct question, but thought better of it. He might only make himself look a fool if he did.

The domes of Port Lowell were climbing up over the steeply convex horizon when Gibson broached the subject that had been worrying him for the past fortnight.

"The *Ares* is going back to Earth in three weeks, isn't she?" he remarked to Hadfield. The other merely nodded; the question was obviously a purely rhetorical one for Gibson knew the answer as well as anybody.

"I've been thinking," said Gibson slowly, "that I'd like to stay on Mars a bit longer. Maybe until next year."

"Oh," said Hadfield. The exclamation revealed neither congratulation nor disapproval, and Gibson felt a little piqued that his shattering announcement had fallen flat. "What about your work?" continued the Chief.

"All that can be done just as easily here as on Earth."

"I suppose you realize," said Hadfield, "that if you stay here you'll have to take up some useful profession." He smiled a little wryly. "That wasn't very tactful, was it? What I mean is that you'll have to do something to help run the colony. Have you any particular ideas in this line?"

This was a little more encouraging; at least it meant that Hadfield had not dismissed the suggestion at once. But it was a point that Gibson had overlooked in his first rush of enthusiasm.

"I wasn't thinking of making a permanent home here," he said a little lamely. "But I want to spend some time studying the Martians, and I'd like to see if I can find any more of them. Besides, I don't want to leave Mars just when things are getting interesting."

"What do you mean?" said Hadfield swiftly.

"Why—these oxygen plants, and getting Dome Seven into operation. I want to see what comes of all this in the next few months."

Hadfield looked thoughtfully at his passenger. He was less

surprised than Gibson might have imagined, for he had seen this sort of thing happen before. He had even wondered if it was going to happen to Gibson, and was by no means displeased at the turn of events.

The explanation was really very simple. Gibson was happier now than he had ever been on Earth; he had done something worth while, and felt that he was becoming part of the Martian community. The identification was now nearly complete, and the fact that Mars had already made one attempt on his life had merely strengthened his determination to stay. If he returned to Earth, he would not be going home—he would be sailing into exile.

"Enthusiasm isn't enough, you know," said Hadfield.

"I quite understand that."

"This little world of ours is founded on two things—skill and hard work. Without both of them, we might just as well go back to Earth."

"I'm not afraid of work, and I'm sure I could learn some of the administrative jobs you've got here—and a lot of the routine technical ones."

This, Hadfield thought, was probably true. Ability to do these things was a function of intelligence, and Gibson had plenty of that. But more than intelligence was needed; there were personal factors as well. It would be best not to raise Gibson's hopes until he had made further enquiries and discussed the matter with Whittaker.

"I'll tell you what to do," said Hadfield. "Put in a provisional application to stay, and I'll have it signaled to Earth. We'll get their answer in about a week. Of course, if they turn you down there's nothing we can do."

Gibson doubted this, for he knew just how much notice Hadfield took of terrestrial regulations when they interfered with his plans. But he merely said: "And if Earth agrees, then I suppose it's up to you?"

"Yes. I'll start thinking about my answer then."

That, thought Gibson, was satisfactory as far as it went. Now that he had taken the plunge, he felt a great sense of relief, as if everything was now outside his control. He had merely to drift with the current, awaiting the progress of events.

The door of the airlock opened before them and the Flea crunched into the city. Even if he had made a mistake, no great harm would be done. He could always go back to Earth by the next ship—or the one after.

But there was no doubt that Mars had changed him. He knew what some of his friends would say when they read the news. "Have you heard about Martin? Looks as if Mars has made a man out of him! Who'd have thought it?"

Gibson wriggled uncomfortably. He had no intention of becoming an elevating object lesson for anyone, if he could help it. Even in his most maudlin moments he had never had the slightest use for those smug Victorian parables about lazy, self-centered men becoming useful members of the community. But he had a horrible fear that something uncommonly like this was beginning to happen to him.

CHAPTER

"Out with it, Jimmy. What's on your mind? You don't seem to have much appetite this morning."

Jimmy toyed fretfully with the synthetic omelette on his plate, which he had already carved into microscopic fragments.

"I was thinking about Irene, and what a shame it is she's never had a chance of seeing Earth."

"Are you sure she wants to? I've never heard anyone here say a single good word for the place."

"Oh, she wants to all right. I've asked her."

"Stop beating about the bush. What are you two planning now? Do you want to elope in the *Ares*?"

Jimmy gave a rather sickly grin.

"That's an idea, but it would take a bit of doing! Honestly though—don't you think Irene ought to go back to Earth to finish her education? If she stays here she'll grow up into a—a——"

"A simple unsophisticated country girl—a raw colonial? Is that what you were thinking?"

"Well, something like that, but I wish you wouldn't put it so crudely."

"Sorry—I didn't mean to. As a matter of fact, I rather agree with you; it's a point that's occurred to me. I think someone ought to mention it to Hadfield."

"That's exactly what——" began Jimmy excitedly.

"—what you and Irene want me to do?"

Jimmy threw up his hands in mock despair.

"It's no good trying to kid you. Yes."

"If you'd said that at the beginning, think of the time we'd have saved. But tell me frankly, Jimmy—just how serious are you about Irene?"

Jimmy looked back at him with a level, steadfast gaze that was in itself a sufficient answer.

"I'm dead serious; you ought to know that. I want to marry her as soon as she's old enough—and I can earn my living."

There was a dead silence, then Gibson replied:

"You could do a lot worse; she's a very nice girl. And I think it would do her a lot of good to have a year or so on Earth. Still, I'd rather not tackle Hadfield at the moment. He's very busy and—well, he's already got one request from me."

"Oh?" said Jimmy, looking up with interest.

Gibson cleared his throat.

"It's got to come out some time, but don't say anything to the others yet. I've applied to stay on Mars."

"Good Lord!" exclaimed Jimmy. "That's—well, quite a thing to do."

Gibson suppressed a smile.

"Do you think it's a good thing?"

"Why, yes. I'd like to do it myself."

"Even if Irene was going back to Earth?" asked Gibson dryly.

"That isn't fair! But how long do you expect to stay?"

"Frankly, I don't know; it depends on too many factors. For one thing, I'll have to learn a job!"

"What sort of job?"

"Something that's congenial—and productive. Any ideas?"

Jimmy sat in silence for a moment, his forehead wrinkled with concentration. Gibson wondered just what he was thinking. Was he sorry that they might soon have to separate? In the last few weeks the strain and animosities which had once both repelled and united them had dissolved away. They had reached a state of emotional equilibrium which was pleasant, yet not as satisfactory as Gibson would have hoped. Perhaps it was his own fault; perhaps he had been afraid to show his deeper feelings and had hidden them behind banter and even occasional sarcasm. If so, he was afraid he might have succeeded only too well. Once he had hoped to earn Jimmy's trust and confidence; now, it seemed, Jimmy only came to him when he wanted something. No—that wasn't fair. Jimmy certainly liked him, perhaps as much as many sons liked their fathers. That was a positive achievement of which he could be proud. He could take some credit, too, for the great improvement in Jimmy's disposition since they had left Earth. He was no longer awkward and shy; though he was still rather serious, he was never sullen. This, thought Gibson, was something in which he could take a good deal of satisfaction. But now there was little more he could do. Jimmy was slipping out of his world—Irene was the only thing that mattered to him now.

"I'm afraid I don't seem to have any ideas," said Jimmy. "Of course, you could have my job here! Oh, that reminds me of something I picked up in Admin the other day." His voice dropped to a conspiratorial whisper and he leaned across the table. "Have you ever heard of 'Project Dawn'?"

"No; what is it?"

"That's what I'm trying to find out. It's something very secret, and I think it must be pretty big."

"Oh!" said Gibson, suddenly alert. "Perhaps I have heard about it after all. Tell me what you know."

"Well, I was working late one evening in the filing section, and was sitting on the floor between some of the cabinets, sorting out papers, when the Chief and Mayor Whittaker came in.

They didn't know I was there, and were talking together. I wasn't trying to eavesdrop, but you know how it is. All of a sudden Mayor Whittaker said something that made me sit up with a bang. I think these were his exact words: 'Whatever happens, there's going to be hell to pay as soon as Earth knows about Project Dawn—even if it's successful.' Then the Chief gave a queer little laugh, and said something about success excusing everything. That's all I could hear; they went out soon afterwards. What do you think about it?"

"Project Dawn!" There was a magic about the name that made Gibson's pulse quicken. Almost certainly it must have some connection with the research going on up in the hills above the city—but that could hardly justify Whittaker's remark. Or could it?

Gibson knew a little about the interplay of political forces between Earth and Mars. He appreciated, from occasional remarks of Hadfield's and comments in the local press, that the colony was now passing through a critical period. On Earth, powerful voices were raised in protest against its enormous expense, which, it seemed, would extend indefinitely into the future with no sign of any ultimate reduction. More than once Hadfield had spoken bitterly of schemes which he had been compelled to abandon on grounds of economy, and of other projects for which permission could not be obtained at all.

"I'll see what I can find out from my—er—various sources of information" said Gibson. "Have you mentioned it to anyone else?"

"No."

"I shouldn't, if I were you. After all, it may not be anything important. I'll let you know what I find out."

"You won't forget to ask about Irene?"

"As soon as I get the chance. But it may take some time—I'll have to catch Hadfield in the right mood!"

As a private detective agency, Gibson was not a success. He made two rather clumsy direct attempts before he decided that the frontal approach was useless. George the barman had been his first target, for he seemed to know everything that was happening on Mars and was one of Gibson's most valuable contacts. This time, however, he proved of no use at all.

"Project Dawn?" he said, with a puzzled expression. "I've never heard of it."

"Are you quite sure?" asked Gibson, watching him narrowly.

George seemed to lose himself in deep thought.

"Quite sure," he said at last. And that was that. George was such an excellent actor that it was quite impossible to guess whether he was lying or speaking the truth.

Gibson did a trifle better with the editor of the "Martian Times." Westerman was a man he normally avoided, as he was always trying to coax articles out of him and Gibson was invariably behind with his terrestrial commitments. The staff of two therefore looked up with some surprise as their visitor entered the tiny office of Mars' only newspaper.

Having handed over some carbon copies as a peace offering, Gibson sprang his trap.

"I'm trying to collect all the information I can on 'Project Dawn,'" he said casually. "I know it's still under cover, but I want to have everything ready when it can be published."

There was dead silence for several seconds. Then Westerman remarked: "I think you'd better see the Chief about that."

"I didn't want to bother him—he's so busy," said Gibson innocently.

"Well, I can't tell you anything."

"You mean you don't know anything about it?"

"If you like. There are only a few dozen people on Mars who could even tell you what it is."

That, at least, was a valuable piece of information.

"Do you happen to be one of them?" asked Gibson.

Westerman shrugged his shoulders.

"I keep my eyes open, and I've done a bit of guessing."

That was all that Gibson could extract from him. He strongly suspected that Westerman knew little more about the matter than he did himself, but was anxious to conceal his ignorance. The interview had, however, confirmed two main facts. "Project Dawn" certainly did exist, and it was extremely well hidden. Gibson could only follow Westerman's example, keeping his eyes open and guessing what he could.

He decided to abandon the quest for the time being and to go round to the Biophysics Lab, where Squeak was the guest of honor. The little Martian was sitting on his haunches taking life easily while the scientists stood conversing in a corner, trying to decide what to do next. As soon as he saw Gibson, he gave a chirp of delight and bounded across the room, bringing down a chair as he did so but luckily missing any valuable apparatus. The bevy of biologists regarded this demonstration with some annoyance; presumably it could not be reconciled with their views on Martian psychology.

"Well," said Gibson to the leader of the team, when he had disentangled himself from Squeak's clutches. "Have you decided how intelligent he is yet?"

The scientist scratched his head.

"He's a queer little beast. Sometimes I get the feeling he's just laughing at us. The odd thing is that he's quiet different from the rest of his tribe. We've got a unit studying them in the field, you know."

"In what way is he different?"

"The others don't show any emotions at all, as far as we can discover. They're completely lacking in curiosity. You can stand beside them and if you wait long enough they'll eat right round you. As long as you don't actively interfere with them they'll take no notice of you."

"And what happens if you do?"

"They'll try and push you out of the way, like some obstacle. If they can't do that, they'll just go somewhere else. Whatever you do, you can't make them annoyed."

"Are they good-natured, or just plain stupid?"

"I'd be inclined to say it's neither one nor the other. They've had no natural enemies for so long that they can't imagine that anyone would try to hurt them. By now they must be largely creatures of habit; life's so tough for them that they can't afford expensive luxuries like curiosity and the other emotions."

"Then how do you explain this little fellow's behavior?" asked Gibson, pointing to Squeak, who was now investigating his pockets. "He's not really hungry—I've just offered him some food—so it must be pure inquisitiveness."

"It's probably a phase they pass through when they're young. Think how a kitten differs from a full-grown cat—or a human baby from an adult, for that matter."

"So when Squeak grows up he'll be like the others?"

"Probably, but it isn't certain. We don't know what capacity he has for learning new habits. For instance, he's very good at finding his way out of mazes—once you can persuade him to make the effort."

"Poor Squeak!" said Gibson. "Sometimes I feel quite guilty about taking you away from home. Still, it was your own idea. Let's go for a walk."

Squeak immediately hopped towards the door.

"Did you see that?" exclaimed Gibson. "He understands what I'm saying."

"Well, so can a dog when it hears a command. It may simply be a question of habit again—you've been taking him out this time every day and he's got used to it. Can you bring him back inside half an hour? We're fixing up the encephalograph to get some EEG records of his brain."

These afternoon walks were a way of reconciling Squeak to his fate and at the same time salving Gibson's conscience. He sometimes felt rather like a baby-snatcher who had abandoned his victim immediately after stealing it. But it was all in the cause of science, and the biologists had sworn they wouldn't hurt Squeak in any way.

The inhabitants of Port Lowell were now used to seeing this strangely assorted pair taking their daily stroll along the streets, and crowds no longer gathered to watch them pass. When it was outside school hours Squeak usually collected a retinue of young admirers who wanted to play with him, but it was now early afternoon and the juvenile population was still in durance vile. There was no one in sight when Gibson and his companion swung into Broadway, but presently a familiar figure appeared in the distance. Hadfield was carrying out his daily tour of inspection, and as usual he was accompanied by his pets.

It was the first time that Topaz and Turquoise had met Squeak, and their aristocratic calm was seriously disturbed, though they did their best to conceal the fact. They tugged on their leads and tried to shelter unobtrusively behind Hadfield, while Squeak took not the slightest notice of them at all.

"Quite a menagerie!" laughed Hadfield. "I don't think Topaz and Turquoise appreciate having a rival—they've had the place to themselves so long that they think they own it."

"Any news from Earth yet?" asked Gibson, anxiously.

"Oh, about your application? Good heavens, I only sent it off two days ago! You know just how quickly things move down there. It will be at least a week before we get an answer."

The Earth was always "down," the outer planets "up," so Gibson had discovered. The terms gave him a curious mental picture of a great slope leading down to the Sun, with the planets lying on it at varying heights.

"I don't really see what it's got to do with Earth," Gibson continued. "After all, it's not as if there's any question of allocating shipping space. I'm here already—in fact it'll save trouble if I *don't* go back!"

"You surely don't imagine that such commonsense arguments carry much weight with the policy-makers back on Earth!" retorted Hadfield. "Oh, dear no! Everything has to go through the Proper Channels."

Gibson was fairly sure that Hadfield did not usually talk about his superiors in this light-hearted fashion, and he felt that peculiar glow of satisfaction that comes when one is permitted to share a deliberate indiscretion. It was another sign that the C.E. trusted him and considered that he was on his side. Dare he mention the two other matters that were occupying his mind—Project Dawn and Irene? As far as Irene was concerned, he had made his promise and would have to keep it sooner or later. But first he really ought to have a talk with Irene herself—yes, that was a perfectly good excuse for putting it off.

He put it off so long that the matter was taken right out of his hands. Irene herself made the plunge, no doubt egged on by Jimmy, from whom Gibson had a full report the next day. It was easy to tell from Jimmy's face what the result had been.

Irene's suggestion must have been a considerable shock to Hadfield, who no doubt believed that he had given his daughter everything she needed, and thus shared a delusion common among parents. Yet he had taken it calmly and there had been no scenes. Hadfield was too intelligent a man to adopt the attitude of the deeply wounded father. He had merely given lucid and compelling reasons why Irene couldn't possibly go to Earth until she was twenty-one, when he planned to return for a long holiday during which they could see the world together. And that was only three years away.

"Three years!" lamented Jimmy. "It might just as well be three lifetimes!"

Gibson deeply sympathized, but tried to look on the bright side of things.

"It's not so long, really. You'll be fully qualified then and earning a lot more money than most young men at that age. And it's surprising how quickly the time goes."

This Job's comforting produced no alleviation of Jimmy's gloom. Gibson felt like adding the comment that it was just as well that ages on Mars were still reckoned by Earth time, and not according to the Martian year of 687 days. However, he thought better of it and remarked instead: "What does Hadfield think about all this, anyway? Has he discussed you with Irene?"

"I don't think he knows anything about it."

"You can bet your life he does! You know, I really think it would be a good idea to go and have it out with him."

"I've thought of that, once or twice," said Jimmy. "But I guess I'm scared."

"You'll have to get over that some time if he's going to be your father-in-law!" retorted Gibson. "Besides, what harm could it do?"

"He might stop Irene seeing me in the time we've still got."

"Hadfield isn't that sort of man, and if he was he'd have done it long ago."

Jimmy thought this over and was unable to refute it. To some extent Gibson could understand his feelings, for he remembered his own nervousness at his first meeting with Hadfield. In this he had had much less excuse than Jimmy, for experience had long ago taught him that few great men remain great when one gets up close to them. But to Jimmy, Hadfield was still the aloof and unapproachable master of Mars.

"If I *do* go and see him," said Jimmy at last, "what do you think I ought to say?"

"What's wrong with the plain, unvarnished truth? It's been known to work wonders on such occasions."

Jimmy shot him a slightly hurt look; he was never quite sure whether Gibson was laughing with him or at him. It was Gibson's own fault, and was the chief obstacle to their complete understanding.

"Look," said Gibson. "Come along with me to the Chief's house tonight, and have it out with him. After all, look at it from his point of view. For all he can tell, it may be just an ordinary flirtation with neither side taking it very seriously. But if you go and tell him you want to get engaged—then it's a different matter."

He was much relieved when Jimmy agreed with no more argument. After all, if the boy had anything in him he should make these decisions himself, without any prompting. Gibson was sensible enough to realize that, in his anxiety to be helpful, he must not run the risk of destroying Jimmy's self-reliance.

It was one of Hadfield's virtues that one always knew where to find him at any given time—though woe betide anyone who bothered him with routine official matters during the few hours when he considered himself off duty. This matter was neither routine nor official; and it was not, as Gibson had guessed, entirely unexpected either, for Hadfield had shown no surprise at all when he saw whom Gibson had brought with him. There was no sign of Irene, she had thoughtfully effaced herself. As soon as possible, Gibson did the same.

He was waiting in the library, running through Hadfield's books and wondering how many of them the Chief had actually had time to read, when Jimmy came in.

"Mr. Hadfield would like to see you," he said.

"How did you get on?"

"I don't know yet, but it wasn't so bad as I'd expected."

"It never is. And don't worry. I'll give you the best reference I can without actual perjury."

When Gibson entered the study, he found Hadfield sunk in one of the armchairs, staring at the carpet as though he had never seen it before in his life. He motioned his visitor to take the other chair.

"How long have you known Spencer?" he asked.

"Only since leaving Earth. I'd never met him before boarding the *Ares.*"

"And do you think that's long enough to form a clear opinion of his character?"

"Is a lifetime long enough to do that?" countered Gibson.

Hadfield smiled, and looked up for the first time.

"Don't evade the issue," he said, though without irritation. "What do you really think about him? Would *you* be willing to accept him as a son-in-law?"

"Yes," said Gibson, without hesitation. "I'd be glad to."

It was just as well that Jimmy could not overhear their conversation in the next ten minutes—though in other ways, perhaps, it was rather a pity, for it would have given him much more insight into Gibson's feelings. In his carefully probing cross-examination, Hadfield was trying to learn all he could about Jimmy, but he was testing Gibson as well. This was something that Gibson should have anticipated; the fact that he had overlooked it in serving Jimmy's interests was no small matter to his credit. When Hadfield's interrogation suddenly switched its point of attack, he was totally unprepared for it.

"Tell me, Gibson," said Hadfield abruptly. "Why are you taking all this trouble for young Spencer? You say you only met him five months ago."

"That's perfectly true. But when we were a few weeks out I discovered that I'd known both his parents very well—we were all at college together."

It had slipped out before he could stop it. Hadfield's eyebrows went up slightly; no doubt he was wondering why Gibson had never taken his degree. But he was far too tactful to pursue this subject, and merely asked a few casual questions about Jimmy's parents, and when he had known them.

At least, they seemed casual questions—just the kind Hadfield might have been expected to ask, and Gibson answered them innocently enough. He had forgotten that he was dealing with one of the keenest minds in the Solar System, one at least as good as his own at analyzing the springs and motives of human conduct. When he realized what had happened, it was already too late.

"I'm sorry," said Hadfield, with deceptive smoothness, "but

this whole story of yours simply lacks conviction. I don't say that what you've told me isn't the truth. It's perfectly possible that you might take such an interest in Spencer because you knew his parents very well twenty years ago. But you've tried to explain away too much, and it's quite obvious that the whole affair touches you at an altogether deeper level." He leaned forward suddenly and stabbed at Gibson with his finger.

"I'm not a fool, Gibson, and men's minds are my business. You've no need to answer this if you don't want to, but I think you owe it to me now. *Jimmy Spencer is your son, isn't he?"*

The bomb had dropped—the explosion was over. And in the silence that followed Gibson's only emotion was one of overwhelming relief.

"Yes," he said. "He is my son. How did you guess?"

Hadfield smiled; he looked somewhat pleased with himself, as if he had just settled a question that had been bothering him for some time.

"It's extraordinary how blind men can be to the effects of their own actions—and how easily they assume that no one else has any powers of observation. There's a slight but distinct likeness between you and Spencer; when I first met you together I wondered if you were related and was quite surprised when I heard you weren't."

"It's very curious," interjected Gibson, "that we were together in the *Ares* for three months, and no one noticed it there."

"Is it so curious? Spencer's crewmates thought they knew his background, and it never occurred to them to associate it with you. That probably blinded them to the resemblance which I—who hadn't any preconceived ideas—spotted at once. But I'd have dismissed it as pure coincidence if you hadn't told me your story. That provided the missing clues. Tell me—does Spencer know this?"

"I'm sure he doesn't even suspect it."

"Why are you so sure? And why haven't you told him?"

The cross-examination was ruthless, but Gibson did not resent it. No one had a better right than Hadfield to ask these questions. And Gibson needed someone in whom to confide—just as Jimmy had needed him, back in the *Ares* when this uncovering of the past had first begun. To think that he had started it all himself. He had certainly never dreamed where it would lead. . . .

"I think I'd better go back to the beginning," said Gibson, shifting uneasily in his chair. "When I left college I had a complete breakdown and was in hospital for over a year. After I came out I'd lost all contact with my Cambridge friends; though a few tried to keep in touch with me, I didn't want to be reminded of the past. Eventually, of course, I ran into some of them again, but it wasn't until several years later that I heard what had happened to Kathleen—to Jimmy's mother. By then, she was already dead."

He paused, still remembering, across all these years, the puzzled wonder he had felt because the news had brought him so little emotion.

"I heard there was a son, and thought little of it. We'd always been—well, careful, or so we believed—and I just assumed that the boy was Gerald's. You see, I didn't know when they were married, or when Jimmy was born. I just wanted to forget the whole business, and pushed it out of my mind. I can't even remember now if it even occurred to me that the boy might be mine. You may find it hard to believe this, but it's the truth.

"And then I met Jimmy, and that brought it all back again. I felt sorry for him at first, and then began to get fond of him. But I never guessed who he was. I even found myself trying to trace his resemblance to Gerald—though I can hardly remember him now."

Poor Gerald! He, of course, had known the truth well enough, but he had loved Kathleen and had been glad to marry her on any terms he could. Perhaps he was to be pitied as much as she, but that was something that now would never be known.

"And when," persisted Hadfield, "did you discover the truth?"

"Only a few weeks ago, when Jimmy asked me to witness some official document he had to fill in—it was his application to start work here, in fact. That was when I first learned his date of birth."

"I see," said Hadfield thoughtfully. "But even that doesn't give absolute proof, does it?"

"I'm perfectly sure," Gibson replied with such obvious pique that Hadfield could not help smiling, "that there was no one else. Even if I'd had any doubts left, you've dispelled them yourself."

"And Spencer?" asked Hadfield, going back to his original question. "You've not told me why you're so confident he knows nothing. Why shouldn't he have checked a few dates? His parents' wedding day, for example? Surely what you've told him must have roused his suspicions?"

"I don't think so," said Gibson slowly, choosing his words with the delicate precision of a cat walking over a wet roadway. "You see, he rather idealizes his mother, and though he may guess I haven't told him everything, I don't believe he's jumped to the right conclusion. He's not the sort who could have kept quiet about it if he had. And besides, he'd still have no proof even if he knows when his parents were married—which is more than most people do. No, I'm sure Jimmy doesn't know, and I'm afraid it will be rather a shock to him when he finds out."

Hadfield was silent; Gibson could not even guess what he was thinking. It was not a very creditable story, but at least he had shown the virtue of frankness.

Then Hadfield shrugged his shoulders in a gesture that seemed to hold a lifetime's study of human nature.

"He likes you," he said. "He'll get over it all right."

Gibson relaxed with a sigh of relief. He knew that the worst was past.

"Gosh, you've been a long time," said Jimmy. "I thought you were never going to finish; what happened?"

Gibson took him by the arm.

"Don't worry," he said. "It's quite all right. Everything's going to be all right now."

He hoped and believed he was telling the truth. Hadfield had been sensible, which was more than some fathers would have been even in this day and age.

"I'm not particularly concerned," he had said, "who Spencer's parents were or were not. This isn't the Victorian era. I'm only interested in the fellow himself, and I must say I'm favorably impressed. I've also had quite a chat about him with Captain Norden, by the way, so I'm not relying merely on tonight's interview. Oh yes, I saw all this coming a long time ago! There was even a certain inevitability about it, since there are very few youngsters of Spencer's age on Mars."

He had spread his hands in front of him—in a habit which Gibson had noticed before—and stared intently at his fingers as if seeing them for the first time in his life.

"The engagement can be announced tomorrow," he'd said softly. "And now—what about *your* side of the affair?" He'd stared keenly at Gibson, who returned his gaze without flinching.

"I want to do whatever is best for Jimmy," he had said. "Just as soon as I can decide what that is."

"And you still want to stay on Mars?" asked Hadfield.

"I'd thought of that aspect of it too," Gibson had said. "But if I went back to Earth, what good would that do? Jimmy'll never be there more than a few months at a time—in fact, from now on I'll see a lot more of him if I stay on Mars!"

"Yes, I suppose that's true enough," Hadfield had said, smiling. "How Irene's going to enjoy having a husband who spends half his life in space remains to be seen—but then, sailors' wives have managed to put up with this sort of thing for quite a long time." He paused abruptly.

"Do you know what I think you ought to do?" he said.

"I'd be very glad of your views," Gibson had replied with feeling.

"Do nothing until the engagement's over and the whole thing's settled. If you revealed your identity now I don't see what good it would do, and it might conceivably cause harm. Later, though, you must tell Jimmy who you are—or who he is, whichever way you like to look at it. But I don't think the right moment will come for quite a while."

It was the first time that Hadfield had referred to Spencer by his Christian name. He was probably not even conscious of it, but to Gibson it was a clear and unmistakable sign that he was already thinking of Jimmy as his son-in-law. The knowledge brought him a sudden sense of kinship and sympathy towards Hadfield. They were united in selfless dedication towards the same purpose—the happiness of the two children in whom they saw their own youth reborn.

Looking back upon it later, Gibson was to identify this moment with the beginning of his friendship with Hadfield—the first man to whom he was ever able to give his unreserved admiration and respect. It was a friendship that was to play a greater part in the future of Mars than either could have guessed.

CHAPTER

It had opened just like any other day in Port Lowell. Jimmy and Gibson had breakfasted quietly together—very quietly, for they were both deeply engrossed with their personal problems. Jimmy was still in what could best be described as an ecstatic condition, though he had occasional fits of depression at the thought of leaving Irene, while Gibson was wondering if Earth had yet made any move regarding his application. Sometimes he was sure the whole thing was a great mistake, and even hoped that the papers had been lost. But he knew he'd have to go through with it, and decided to stir things up at Admin.

He could tell that something was wrong the moment he entered the office. Mrs. Smyth, Hadfield's secretary, met him as she always did when he came to see the Chief. Usually she showed him in at once; sometimes she explained that Hadfield was extremely busy, or putting a call through to Earth, and could he come back later? This time she simply said: "I'm sorry, Mr. Hadfield isn't there. He won't be back until tomorrow."

"Won't be back?" queried Gibson. "Has he gone to Skia?"

"Oh no," said Mrs. Smyth, wavering slightly but obviously

on the defensive. "I'm afraid I can't say. But he'll be back in twenty-four hours."

Gibson decided to puzzle over this later. He presumed that Mrs. Smyth knew all about his affairs, so she could probably answer his questions.

"Do you know if there's been any reply yet to my application?" he asked.

Mrs. Smyth looked even unhappier.

"I think there has," she said. "But it was a personal signal to Mr. Hadfield and I can't discuss it. I expect he'll want to see you about it as soon as he gets back."

This was most exasperating. It was bad enough not to have a reply, but it was even worse to have one you weren't allowed to see. Gibson felt his patience evaporating.

"Surely there's no reason why you shouldn't tell me about it!" he exclaimed. "Especially if I'll know tomorrow, anyway."

"I'm really awfully sorry, Mr. Gibson. But I know Mr. Hadfield will be most annoyed if I say anything now."

"Oh, very well," said Gibson, and went off in a huff.

He decided to relieve his feelings by tackling Mayor Whittaker—always assuming that he was still in the city. He was, and he did not look particularly happy to see Gibson, who settled himself firmly down in the visitor's chair in a way that obviously meant business.

"Look here, Whittaker," he began. "I'm a patient man and I think you'll agree I don't often make unreasonable requests." As the other showed no signs of making the right reply, Gibson continued hastily:

"There's something very peculiar going on round here and I'm anxious to get to the bottom of it."

Whittaker sighed. He had been expecting this to happen sooner or later. A pity Gibson couldn't have waited until tomorrow: it wouldn't have mattered then. . . .

"What's made you suddenly jump to this conclusion?" he asked.

"Oh, lots of things—and it isn't at all sudden. I've just tried to see Hadfield, and Mrs. Smyth told me he's not in the city and then closed up like a clam when I tried to ask a few innocent questions."

"I can just imagine her doing that!" grinned Whittaker cheerfully.

"If you try the same thing I'll start throwing the furniture around. At least if you can't tell me what's going on, for goodness' sake tell me *why* you can't tell me. It's Project Dawn, isn't it?"

That made Whittaker sit up with a start.

"How did you know?" he asked.

"Never mind; I can be stubborn too."

"I'm not trying to be stubborn," said Whittaker plaintively. "Don't think we like secrecy for the sake of it; it's a confounded nuisance. But suppose you start telling me what you know."

"Very well, if it'll soften you up. Project Dawn is something to do with that plant genetics place up in the hills where you've been cultivating—what do you call it?—*Oxyfera.* As there seems no point in keeping that quiet, I can only assume it's part of a much bigger plan. I suspect Phobos is mixed up with it, though I can't imagine how. You've managed to keep it so secret that the few people on Mars who know anything about it just won't talk. But you haven't been trying to conceal it from Mars so much as from Earth. Now what have you got to say?"

Whittaker appeared to be not in the least abashed.

"I must compliment you on your—er—perspicacity," he said. "You may also be interested to know that, a couple of weeks ago, I suggested to the Chief that we ought to take you fully into our confidence. But he couldn't make up his mind, and since then things have happened rather more rapidly than anyone expected."

He doodled absentmindedly on his writing pad, then came to a decision.

"I won't jump the gun," he said, "and I can't tell you what's happening now. But here's a little story that may amuse you. Any resemblance to—ah—real persons and places is quite coincidental."

"I understand," grinned Gibson. "Go on."

"Let's suppose that in the first rush of interplanetary enthusiasm world A has set up a colony on world B. After some years it finds that this is costing a lot more than it expected, and has given no tangible returns for the money spent. Two factions then arise on the mother world. One, the conservative group, wants to close the project down—to cut its losses and get out. The other group, the progressives, wants to continue the experiment because they believe that in the long run Man has got to explore and master the material universe, or else he'll simply stagnate on his own world. But this sort of argument is no use with the taxpayers, and the conservatives are beginning to get the upper hand.

"All this, of course, is rather unsettling to the colonists, who are getting more and more independently minded and don't like the idea of being regarded as poor relations living on charity. Still, they don't see any way out—until one day a revolutionary scientific discovery is made. (I should have explained at the beginning that planet B has been attracting the finest brains of A, which is another reason why A is getting annoyed.) This discovery opens up almost unlimited prospects for the future of B, but to apply it involves certain risks, as well as the diversion of a good deal of B's limited resources. Still, the plan is put forward—and is promptly turned down by A. There is a protracted tug-of-war behind the scenes, but the home planet is adamant.

"The colonists are then faced with two alternatives. They can force the issue out into the open, and appeal to the public on world A. Obviously they'll be at a great disadvantage, as the men on the spot can shout them down. The other choice is to carry on with the plan without informing Earth—I mean, planet A—and this is what they finally decided to do.

"Of course, there were a lot of other factors involved—political and personal, as well as scientific. It so happened that the leader of the colonists was a man of unusual determination who wasn't scared of anything or anyone, on either of the planets. He had a team of first-class scientists behind him, and they backed him up. So the plan went ahead; but no one knows yet if it will be successful. I'm sorry I can't tell you the end of the story; you know how these serials always break off at the most exciting place."

"I think you've told me just about everything," said Gibson. "Everything, that is, except one minor detail. I *still* don't know what Project Dawn is." He rose to go. "Tomorrow I'm coming back to hear the final installment of your gripping serial."

"There won't be any need to do that," Whittaker replied. He glanced unconsciously at the clock. "You'll know long before then."

As he left the Administration Building, Gibson was intercepted by Jimmy.

"I'm supposed to be at work," he said breathlessly, "but I had to catch you. Something important's going on."

"I know," replied Gibson rather impatiently. "Project Dawn's coming to the boil, and Hadfield's left town."

"Oh," replied Jimmy, a little taken aback. "I didn't think you'd have heard. But you won't know this, anyway. Irene's very upset. She told me her father said good-bye last night as if—well, as if he mightn't see her again."

Gibson whistled. That put things in a different light. Project Dawn was not only big, it might be dangerous. This was a possibility he had not considered.

"Whatever's happening," he said, "we'll know all about it tomorrow—Whittaker's just told me that. But I think I can guess where Hadfield is right now."

"Where?"

"He's up on Phobos. For some reason, that's the key to Project Dawn, and that's where you'll find the Chief right now."

Gibson would have made a large bet on the accuracy of this guess. It was just as well that there was no one to take it, for he was quite wrong. Hadfield was now almost as far away from Phobos as he was from Mars. At the moment he was sitting in some discomfort in a small spaceship, which was packed with scientists and their hastily dismantled equipment. He was playing chess, and playing it very badly, against one of the greatest physicists in the Solar System. His opponent was playing equally badly, and it would soon have become quite obvious to any observer that they were simply trying to pass the time. Like everyone on Mars, they were waiting; but they were the only ones who knew exactly what they were waiting for.

The long day—one of the longest that Gibson had ever known—slowly ebbed away. It was a day of wild rumors and speculation: everyone in Port Lowell had some theory which they were anxious to air. But as those who knew the truth said nothing, and those who knew nothing said too much, when night came the city was in a state of extreme confusion. Gibson wondered if it was worth while staying up late, but around midnight he decided to go to bed. He was fast asleep when, invisibly, soundlessly, hidden from him by the thickness of the planet, Project Dawn came to its climax. Only the men in the watching spaceship saw it happen, and changed suddenly from grave scientists to shouting, laughing schoolboys as they turned to race for home.

In the very small hours of the morning Gibson was wakened by a thunderous banging on his door. It was Jimmy, shouting to him to get up and come outside. He dressed hastily, but when he reached the door Jimmy had already gone out into the street. He caught him up at the doorway. From all sides, people were beginning to appear, rubbing their eyes sleepily and wondering what had happened. There was a rising buzz of voices and distant shouts; Port Lowell sounded like a beehive that had been suddenly disturbed.

It was a full minute before Gibson understood what had awakened the city. Dawn was just breaking; the eastern sky was aglow with the first light of the rising Sun. The eastern sky? *My God, that dawn was breaking in the west.*

No one could have been less superstitious than Gibson, but for a moment the upper levels of his mind were submerged by a wave of irrational terror. It lasted only a moment; then reason reasserted itself. Brighter and brighter grew the light spilling over the horizon; now the first rays were touching the hills above the city. They were moving swiftly—far, far too swiftly for the Sun—and suddenly a blazing, golden meteor leapt up out of the desert, climbing almost vertically towards the zenith.

Its very speed betrayed its identity. This was Phobos—or what had been Phobos a few hours before. Now it was a yellow disc of fire, and Gibson could feel the heat of its burning upon his face. The city around him was now utterly silent, watching the miracle and slowly waking to a dim awareness of all that it might mean to Mars.

So this was Project Dawn—it had been well named. The pieces of the jig-saw puzzle were falling into place, but the main pattern was still not clear. To have turned Phobos into a second sun was an incredible feat of—presumably—nuclear engineering, yet Gibson did not see how it could solve the colony's problems. He was still worrying over this when the seldom used public-address system of Port Lowell burst into life and Whittaker's voice came drifting softly down the streets.

"Hello, everybody," he said, "I guess you're all awake by now and have seen what's happened. The Chief Executive's on his way back from space and would like to speak to you. Here he is."

There was a click; then someone said, *sotto voce:* "You're on to Port Lowell, sir." A moment later Hadfield's voice came out of the speakers. He sounded tired but triumphant, like a man who had fought a great battle and won through to victory.

"Hello, Mars," he said. "Hadfield speaking. I'm still in space on the way home—I'll be landing in about an hour.

"I hope you like your new sun. According to our calculations, it will take nearly a thousand years to burn itself out. We triggered Phobos off when it was well below your horizon, just in case the initial radiation peak was too high. The reaction's now stabilized at exactly the level we expected, though it may increase by a few per cent during the next week. It's mainly a meson resonance reaction, very efficient but not very violent, and there's no chance of a fully fledged atomic explosion with the material composing Phobos.

"Your new luminary will give you about a tenth of the Sun's heat, which will bring up the temperature of much of Mars to nearly the same value as Earth's. But that isn't the reason why we blew up Phobos—at least, it isn't the main reason.

"Mars wants oxygen more badly than heat—and all the oxygen needed to give it an atmosphere almost as good as Earth's is lying beneath your feet, locked up in the sand. Two years ago we discovered a plant that can break the sand down and release the oxygen. It's a tropical plant—it can exist only on the equator and doesn't really flourish even there. If there was enough sunlight available, it could spread over Mars—with some assistance from us—and in fifty years there'd be an atmosphere here that men could breathe. *That's* the goal we're aiming at: when we've reached it, we can go where we please on Mars and forget about our domed cities and breathing masks. It's a dream that many of you will live to see realized, and it'll mean that we've given a new world to mankind.

"Even now, there are some benefits we'll derive right away. It will be very much warmer, at least when Phobos and the Sun are shining together, and the winters will be much milder. Even though Phobos isn't visible above latitude seventy degrees, the new convection winds will warm the polar regions too, and will prevent our precious moisture from being locked up in the ice caps for half of every year.

"There'll be some disadvantages—the seasons and nights are going to ge complicated now!—but they'll be far outweighed by the benefits. And every day, as you see the beacon we have now lit climbing across the sky, it will remind you of the new world we're bringing to birth. We're making history, remember, for this is the first time that Man has tried his hand at changing the face of a planet. If we succeed here, others will do the same elsewhere. In the ages to come, whole civilizations on worlds of which we've never heard will owe their existence to what we've done tonight.

"That's all I've got to say now. Perhaps you may regret the sacrifice we've had to make to bring life to this world again. But remember this—though Mars has lost a Moon, it's gained a Sun—and who can doubt which is the more valuable?

"And now—good night to you all."

But no one in Port Lowell went back to sleep. As far as the city was concerned, the night was over and the new day had dawned. It was hard to take one's eyes off that tiny golden disc as it climbed steadily up the sky, its warmth growing greater minute by minute. What would the Martian plants be making of it? Gibson wondered. He walked along the street until he came to the nearest section of the dome, and looked out through the transparent wall. It was, as he had expected: they had all awakened and turned their faces to the new Sun. He wondered just what they would do when both Suns were in the sky together. . . .

The Chief's rocket landed half an hour later, but Hadfield and the scientists of Project Dawn avoided the crowds by coming into the city on foot through Dome Seven, and sending the transport on to the main entrance as a decoy. This ruse worked so well that they were all safely indoors before anyone realized what had happened, or could start celebrations which they were too tired to appreciate. However, this did not prevent numerous private parties forming all over the city—parties at which everyone tried to claim that they had known what Project Dawn was all the time.

Phobos was approaching the zenith, much nearer and therefore much warmer than it had been on rising, when Gibson and Jimmy met their crewmates in the crowd that had good-naturedly but firmly insisted to George that he had better open up the bar. Each party claimed it had only homed on this spot because it was sure it would find the other there.

Hilton, who as Chief Engineer might be expected to know more about nucleonics than anyone else in the assembly, was soon pushed to the fore and asked to explain just what had happened. He modestly denied his competence to do anything of the sort.

"What they've done up on Phobos," he protested, "is years ahead of anything I ever learned at college. Why, even meson reactions hadn't been discovered then—let alone how to harness them. In fact, I don't think anyone on Earth knows how to do that, even now. It must be something that Mars has learned for itself."

"Do you mean to tell me," said Bradley, "that Mars is ahead of Earth in nuclear physics—or anything else for that matter?"

This remark nearly caused a riot and Bradley's colleagues had to rescue him from the indignant colonists—which they did in a somewhat leisurely fashion. When peace had been restored, Hilton nearly put *his* foot in it by remarking: "Of course, you know that a lot of Earth's best scientists have been coming here in the last few years, so it's not as surprising as you might think."

The statement was perfectly true, and Gibson remembered the remark that Whittaker had made to him that very morning. Mars had been a lure to many others besides himself, and now he could understand why. What prodigies of persuasion, what intricate negotiations and downright deceptions Hadfield must have performed in these last few years! It had, perhaps, been not too difficult to attract the really first-rate minds; they could appreciate the challenge and respond to it. The second-raters, the equally essential rank-and-file of science, would have been harder to find. One day, perhaps, he would learn the secrets behind the secret, and discover just how Project Dawn had been launched and guided to success.

What was left of the night seemed to pass very swiftly. Phobos was dropping down into the eastern sky when the Sun rose up to greet its rival. It was a duel that all the city watched in silent fascination—a one-sided conflict that could have only a predetermined outcome. When it shone alone in the night sky, it was easy to pretend that Phobos was almost as brilliant as the Sun, but the first light of the true dawn banished the illusion. Minute by minute Phobos faded, though it was still well above the horizon, as the Sun came up out of the desert. Now one could tell how pale and yellow it was by comparison. There was little danger that the slowly turning plants would be confused in their quest for light; when the Sun was shining, one scarcely noticed Phobos at all.

But it was bright enough to perform its task, and for a thousand years it would be the lord of the Martian night. And thereafter? When its fires were extinguished, by the exhaustion of whatever elements it was burning now, would Phobos become again an ordinary moon, shining only by the Sun's reflected glory?

Gibson knew that it would not matter. Even in a century it would have done its work, and Mars would have an atmosphere which it would not lose again for geological ages. When at last Phobos guttered and died, the science of that distant day would have some other answer—perhaps an answer as inconceivable to this age as the detonation of a world would have been only a century ago.

For a little while, as the first day of the new age grew to maturity, Gibson watched his double shadow lying upon the ground. Both shadows pointed to the west, but though one scarcely moved, the fainter lengthened even as he watched, becoming more and more difficult to see, until at last it was snuffed out as Phobos dropped down below the edge of Mars.

Its sudden disappearance reminded Gibson abruptly of something that he—and most of Port Lowell—had forgotten in the last few hours' excitement. By now the news would have reached Earth; perhaps—though he wasn't sure of this—Mars must now be spectacularly brighter in terrestrial skies.

In a very short time, Earth would be asking some extremely pointed questions.

Chapter

It was one of those little ceremonies so beloved by the TV newsreels. Hadfield and all his staff were gathered in a tight group at the edge of the clearing, with the domes of Port Lowell rising behind them. It was, thought the cameraman, a nicely composed picture, though the constantly changing double illumination made things a little difficult.

He got the cue from the control room and started to pan from left to right to give the viewers a bit of movement before the real business began. Not that there was really much to see: the landscape was so flat and they'd miss all its interest in this monochrome transmission. (One couldn't afford the bandwidth for color on a live transmission all the way to Earth; even on black-and-white it was none too easy.) He had just finished exploring the scene when he got the order to swing back to Hadfield, who was now making a little speech. That was going out on the other sound channel and he couldn't hear it, though in the control room it would be mated to the picture he was sending. Anyway, he knew just what the Chief would be saying—he'd heard it all before.

Mayor Whittaker handed over the shovel on which he had been gracefully leaning for the last five minutes, and Hadfield began to tip in the sand until he had covered the roots of the tall, drab Martian plant standing there, held upright in its wooden frame. The "airweed," as it was now universally called, was not a very impressive object: it scarcely looked strong enough to stand upright, even under this low gravity. It certainly didn't look as if it could control the future of a planet. . . .

Hadfield had finished his token gardening; someone else could complete the job and fill in the hole. (The planting team was already hovering in the background, waiting for the bigwigs to clear out of the way so that they could get on with their work.) There was a lot of hand-shaking and back-slapping; Hadfield was hidden by the crowd that had gathered round him. The only person who wasn't taking the slightest notice of all this was Gibson's pet Martian, who was rocking on his haunches like one of those weighted dolls that always come the same way up however you put them down. The cameraman swung towards him and zoomed to a close-up; it would be the first time anyone on Earth would have seen a real Martian—at least in a live program like this.

Hello—what was he up to? Something had caught his interest—the twitching of those huge, membranous ears gave him away. He was beginning to move in short, cautious hops. The cameraman chased him and widened the field at the same time to see where he was going. No one else had noticed that he'd begun to move; Gibson was still talking to Whittaker and seemed to have completely forgotten his pet.

So *that* was the game! This was going to be good; the folk back on Earth would love it. Would he get there before he was spotted? Yes—he'd made it! With one final bound he hopped down into the little pit, and the small triangular beak began to nibble at the slim Martian plant that had just been placed there with such care. No doubt he thought it so kind of his friends to go to all this trouble for him. . . . Or did he really know he was being naughty? That devious approach had been so skillful that it was hard to believe it was done in complete innocence. Anyway, the cameraman wasn't going to spoil his fun; it would make too good a picture. He cut for a moment back to Hadfield and Company, still congratulating themselves on the work which Squeak was rapidly undoing.

It was too good to last. Gibson spotted what was happening and gave a great yell which made everyone jump. Then he raced towards Squeak, who did a quick look round, decided that there was nowhere to hide, and just sat still with an air of injured innocence. He let himself be led away quietly, not aggravating his offense by resisting the forces of the law when Gibson grabbed one of his ears and tugged him away from the scene of the crime. A group of experts then gathered anxiously around the airweed, and to everyone's relief it was soon decided that the damage was not fatal.

It was a trivial incident, which no one would have imagined to have any consequences beyond the immediate moment. Yet, though he never realized the fact, it was to inspire one of Gibson's most brilliant and fruitful ideas.

Life for Martian Gibson had suddenly become very complicated—and intensely interesting. He had been one of the first to see Hadfield after the inception of Project Dawn. The C.E. had called for him, but had been able to give him only a few minutes of his time. That, however, had been enough to change the pattern of Gibson's future.

"I'm sorry I had to keep you waiting," Hadfield said, "but I got the reply from Earth only just before I left. The answer is that you can stay here if you can be absorbed into our administrative structure—to use the official jargon. As the future of our 'administrative structure' depended somewhat largely on Project Dawn, I thought it best to leave the matter until I got back home."

The weight of uncertainty had lifted from Gibson's mind. It was all settled now; even if he had to make a mistake—and he did not believe he had—there was now no going back. He had thrown in his lot with Mars; he would be part of the colony in its fight to regenerate this world that was now stirring sluggishly in its sleep.

"And what job have you got for me?" Gibson asked a little anxiously.

"I've decided to regularize your unofficial status," said Hadfield, with a smile.

"What do you mean?"

"Do you remember what I said at our very first meeting? I asked you to help us by giving Earth not the mere facts of the situation, but also some idea of our goals and—I suppose you could call it—the spirit we've built up here on Mars. You've done well, despite the fact that you didn't know about the project on which we'd set our greatest hopes. I'm sorry I had to keep Dawn from you, but it would have made your job much harder if you'd known our secret and weren't able to say anything. Don't you agree?"

Gibson had not thought of it in that light, but it certainly made sense.

"I've been very interested," Hadfield continued, "to see what result your broadcasts and articles have had. You may not know that we've got a delicate method of testing this."

"How?" asked Gibson in surprise.

"Can't you guess? Every week about ten thousand people, scattered all over Earth, decide they want to come here, and something like three per cent pass the preliminary tests. Since your articles started appearing regularly, that figure's gone up to fifteen thousand a week, and it's still rising."

"Oh," said Gibson, very thoughtfully. He gave an abrupt little laugh. "I also seem to remember," he added, "that you didn't want me to come here in the first place."

"We all make mistakes, but I've learned to profit by mine," smiled Hadfield. "To sum it all up, what I'd like you to do is to lead a small section which, frankly, will be our propaganda department. Of course, we'll think of a nicer name for it! Your job will be to sell Mars. The opportunities are far greater now that we've really got something to put in our shop window. If we can get enough people clamoring to come here, then Earth will be forced to provide the shipping space. And the quicker that's done, the sooner we can promise Earth we'll be standing on our own feet. What do you say?"

Gibson felt a fleeting disappointment. Looked at from one point of view, this wasn't much of a change. But the C.E. was right: he could be of greater use to Mars in this way than in any other.

"I can do it," he said. "Give me a week to sort out my terrestrial affairs and clear up my outstanding commitments."

A week was somewhat optimistic, he thought, but that should break the back of the job. He wondered what Ruth was going to say. She'd probably think he was mad, and she'd probably be right.

"The news that you're going to stay here," said Hadfield with satisfaction, "will cause a lot of interest and will be quite a boost to our campaign. You've no objection to our announcing it right away?"

"I don't think so."

"Good. Whittaker would like to have a word with you now about the detailed arrangements. You realize, of course, that your salary will be that of a Class II Administrative Officer of your age?"

"Naturally I've looked into that," said Gibson. He did not add, because it was unnecessary, that this was largely of theoretical interest. His salary on Mars, though less than a tenth of his total income, would be quite adequate for a comfortable standard of living on a planet where there were very few luxuries. He was not sure just how he could use his terrestrial credits, but no doubt they could be employed to squeeze something through the shipping bottleneck.

After a long session with Whittaker—who nearly succeeded in destroying his enthusiasm with laments about lack of staff and accommodation—Gibson spent the rest of the day writing dozens of radiograms. The longest was to Ruth, and was chiefly, but by no means wholly, concerned with business affairs. Ruth had often commented on the startling variety of things she did for her ten per cent, and Gibson wondered what she was going to say to this request that she keep an eye on one James Spencer, and generally look after him when he was in New York—which, since he was completing his studies at M.I.T., might be fairly often.

It would have made matters much simpler if he could have told her the facts; she would probably guess them, anyway. But that would be unfair to Jimmy; Gibson had made up his mind that he would be the first to know. There were times when the strain of not telling him was so great that he felt almost glad they would soon be parting. Yet Hadfield, as usual, had been right. He had waited a generation—he must wait a little longer yet. To reveal himself now might leave Jimmy confused and hurt—might even cause the breakdown of his engagement to Irene. The time to tell him would be when they had been married and, Gibson hoped, were still insulated from any shocks which the outside world might administer.

It was ironic that, having found his son so late, he must now lose him again. Perhaps that was part of the punishment for the selfishness and lack of courage—to put it no more strongly—he had shown twenty years ago. But the past must bury itself; he must think of the future now.

Jimmy would return to Mars as soon as he could—there was no doubt of that. And even if he had missed the pride and satisfaction of parenthood, there might be compensations later in watching his grandchildren come into the world he was helping to remake. For the first time in his life, Gibson had a future to which he could look forward with interest and excitement—a future which would not be merely a repetition of the past.

* * *

Earth hurled its thunderbolt four days later. The first Gibson knew about it was when he saw the headline across the front page of the "Martian Times." For a moment the two words staring back at him were so astounding that he forgot to read on.

> HADFIELD RECALLED
>
> We have just received news that the Interplanetary Development Board has requested the Chief Executive to return to Earth on the *Ares,* which leaves Deimos in four days. No reason is given.

That was all, but it would set Mars ablaze. No reason was given—and none was necessary. Everyone knew exactly why Earth wanted to see Warren Hadfield.

"What do you think of this?" Gibson asked Jimmy as he passed the paper across the breakfast table.

"Good Lord!" gasped Jimmy. "There'll be trouble now! What do you think he'll do?"

"What can he do?"

"Well, he can refuse to go. Everyone here would certainly back him up."

"That would only make matters worse. He'll go, all right. Hadfield isn't the sort of man to run away from a fight."

Jimmy's eyes suddenly brightened.

"That means that Irene will be going too."

"Trust you to think of that!" laughed Gibson. "I suppose you hope it will be an ill wind blowing the pair of you some good. But don't count on it—Hadfield *might* leave Irene behind."

He thought this very unlikely. When the Chief returned, he would need all the moral support he could get.

Despite the amount of work he had awaiting him, Gibson paid one brief call to Admin, where he found everyone in a state of mingled indignation and suspense. Indignation because of Earth's cavalier treatment of the Chief: suspense because no one yet knew what action he was going to take. Hadfield had arrived early that morning, and so far had not seen anyone except Whittaker and his private secretary. Those who had caught a glimpse of him stated that for a man who was, technically, about to be recalled in disgrace, he looked remarkably cheerful.

Gibson was thinking over this news as he made a detour towards the Biology Lab. He had missed seeing his little Martian friend for two days, and felt rather guilty about it. As he walked slowly along Regent Street, he wondered what sort of defense Hadfield would be able to put up. Now he understood that remark that Jimmy had overheard. *Would* success excuse everything? Success was still a long way off; as Hadfield had said, to bring Project Dawn to its conclusion would take half a century, even assuming the maximum assistance from Earth. It was essential to secure that support, and Hadfield would do his utmost not to antagonize the home planet. The best that Gibson could do to support him would be to provide long-range covering fire from his propaganda department.

Squeak, as usual, was delighted to see him, though Gibson returned his greeting somewhat absentmindedly. As he invariably did, he proffered Squeak a fragment of airweed from the supply kept in the Lab. That simple action must have triggered something in his subconscious mind, for he suddenly paused, then turned to the chief biologist.

"I've just had a wonderful idea," he said. "You know you were telling me about the tricks you've been able to teach Squeak?"

"Teach him! The problem now is to stop him learning them!"

"You also said you were fairly sure the Martians could communicate with each other, didn't you?"

"Well, our field party's proved that they can pass on simple thoughts, and even some abstract ideas like color. That doesn't prove much, of course. Bees can do the same."

"Then tell me what you think of this. Why shouldn't we teach them to cultivate the airweed for us? You see what a colossal advantage they've got—they can go anywhere on Mars they please, while we'd have to do everything with machines. They needn't *know* what they're doing, of course. We'd simply provide them with the shoots—it does propagate that way, doesn't it?—teach them the necessary routine, and reward them afterwards."

"Just a moment! It's a pretty idea, but haven't you overlooked some practical points? I think we could train them in the way you suggest—we've certainly learned enough about their psychology for that—but may I point out that there are only ten known specimens, including Squeak?"

"I hadn't overlooked that," said Gibson impatiently. "I simply don't believe the group I found is the only one in existence. That would be a quite incredible coincidence. Certainly they're rather rare, but there must be hundreds, if not thousands, of them over the planet. I'm going to suggest a photo-reconnaissance of all the airweed forests—we should have no difficulty in spotting their clearings. But in any case I'm taking the long-term view. Now that they've got far more favorable living conditions, they'll start to multiply rapidly, just as the Martian plant life's already doing. Remember, even if we left it to itself the airweed would cover the equatorial regions in four hundred years—according to your own figures. With the Martians *and* us to help it spread, we might cut years off Project Dawn!"

The biologist shook his head doubtfully, but began to do some calculations on a scribbling pad. When he had finished he pursed his lips.

"Well, I . . ." he said. "I can't actually prove it's impossible; there are too many unknown factors—including the most important one of all—the Martians' reproduction rate. Incidentally, I suppose you know that they're marsupials? That's just been confirmed."

"You mean like kangaroos?"

"Yes. Junior lives under cover until he's a big enough boy to go out into the cold, hard world. We think several of the females are carrying babies, so they may reproduce yearly. And since Squeak was the only infant we found, that means they must have a terrifically high death-rate—which isn't surprising in this climate."

"Just the conditions we want!" exclaimed Gibson. "Now there'll be nothing to stop them multiplying, providing we see they get all the food they need."

"Do you want to breed Martians or cultivate airweed?" challenged the biologist.

"Both," grinned Gibson. "They go together like fish and chips, or ham and eggs."

"Don't!" pleaded the other, with such a depth of feeling that Gibson apologized at once for his lack of tact. He had forgotten that no one on Mars had tasted such things for years.

The more Gibson thought about his new idea, the more it appealed to him. Despite the pressure of his personal affairs, he found time to write a memorandum to Hadfield on the subject, and hoped that the C.E. would be able to discuss it with him before returning to Earth. There was something inspiring in the thought of regenerating not only a world, but also a race which might be older than Man.

Gibson wondered how the changed climatic conditions of a hundred years hence would affect the Martians. If it became too warm for them, they could easily migrate north or south—if necessary into the sub-polar regions where Phobos was never visible. As for the oxygenated atmosphere—they had been used to that in the past and might adapt themselves to it again. There was considerable evidence that Squeak now obtained much of his oxygen from the air in Port Lowell, and seemed to be thriving on it.

There was still no answer to the great question which the discovery of the Martians had raised. Were they the degenerate survivors of a race which had achieved civilization long ago, and let it slip from its grasp when conditions became too severe? This was the romantic view, for which there was no evidence at all. The scientists were unanimous in believing that there had never been any advanced culture on Mars—but they had been proved wrong once and might be so again. In any case, it would be an extremely interesting experiment to see how far up the evolutionary ladder the Martians would climb, now that their world was blossoming again.

For it was their world, not Man's. However he might shape it for his own purposes, it would be his duty always to safeguard the interests of its rightful owners. No one could tell what part they might have to play in the history of the universe. And when, as was one day inevitable, Man himself came to the notice of yet higher races, he might well be judged by his behavior here on Mars.

CHAPTER

I'm sorry you're not coming back with us, Martin," said Norden as they approached Lock One West, "but I'm sure you're doing the right thing, and we all respect you for it."

"Thanks," said Gibson sincerely. "I'd like to have made the return trip with you all—still, there'll be plenty of chances later! Whatever happens, I'm not going to be on Mars *all* my life!" He chuckled. "I guess you never thought you'd be swapping passengers in this way."

"I certainly didn't. It's going to be a bit embarrassing in some respects. I'll feel like the captain of the ship who had to carry Napoleon to Elba. How's the Chief taking it?"

"I've not spoken to him since the recall came through, though I'll be seeing him tomorrow before he goes up to Deimos. But Whittaker says he seems confident enough, and doesn't appear to be worrying in the slightest."

"What do *you* think's going to happen?"

"On the official level, he's bound to be reprimanded for misappropriation of funds, equipment, personnel—oh, enough things to land him in jail for the rest of his life. But as half the executives and all the scientists on Mars are involved, what can Earth do about it? It's really a very amusing situation.

The C.E.'s a public hero on two worlds, and the Interplanetary Development Board will have to handle him with kid gloves. I think the verdict will be: 'You shouldn't have done it, but we're rather glad you did.' "

"And then they'll let him come back to Mars?"

"They're bound to. No one else can do his job."

"Someone will have to, one day."

"True enough, but it would be madness to waste Hadfield when he's still got years of work in him. And heaven help anyone who was sent here to replace him!"

"It certainly *is* a peculiar position. I think a lot's been going on that we don't know about. Why did Earth turn down Project Dawn when it was first suggested?"

"I've been wondering about that, and intend to get to the bottom of it some day. Meanwhile my theory is this—I think a lot of people on Earth don't want Mars to become too powerful, still less completely independent. Not for any sinister reason, mark you, but simply because they don't like the idea. It's too wounding to their pride. They want the Earth to remain the center of the universe."

"You know," said Norden, "it's funny how you talk about 'Earth' as if it were some combination of miser and bully, preventing all progress here. After all, it's hardly fair! What you're actually grumbling at are the administrators in the Interplanetary Development Board and all its allied organizations—and they're really trying to do their best. Don't forget that everything you've got here is due to the enterprise and initiative of Earth. I'm afraid you colonists"—he gave a wry grin as he spoke—"take a very self-centered view of things. I can see both sides of the question. When I'm here I get your point of view and can sympathize with it. But in three months' time I'll be on the other side and will probably think you're a lot of grumbling, ungrateful nuisances here on Mars!"

Gibson laughed, not altogether comfortably. There was a good deal of truth in what Norden had said. The sheer difficulty and expense of interplanetary travel, and the time it took to get from world to world, made inevitable some lack of understanding, even intolerance, between Earth and Mars. He hoped that as the speed of transport increased these psychological barriers would be broken down and the two planets would come closer together in spirit as well as in time.

They had now reached the lock and were waiting for the transport to take Norden out to the airstrip. The rest of the crew had already said good-bye and were now on their way up to Deimos. Only Jimmy had received special dispensation to fly up with Hadfield and Irene when they left tomorrow. Jimmy had certainly changed his status, thought Gibson with some amusement, since the *Ares* had left Earth. He wondered just how much work Norden was going to get out of him on the homeward voyage.

"Well, John, I hope you have a good trip back," said Gibson, holding out his hand as the airlock door opened. "When will I be seeing you again?"

"In about eighteen months—I've got a trip to Venus to put in first. When I get back here, I expect to find quite a difference—airweed and Martians everywhere!"

"I don't promise much in that time," laughed Gibson. "But we'll do our best not to disappoint you!"

They shook hands, and Norden was gone. Gibson found it impossible not to feel a twinge of envy as he thought of all the things to which the other was returning—all the unconsidered beauties of Earth which he had once taken for granted, and now might not see again for many years.

He still had two farewells to make, and they would be the most difficult of all. His last meeting with Hadfield would require considerable delicacy and tact. Norden's analogy, he thought, had been a good one: it would be rather like an interview with a dethroned monarch about to sail into exile.

In actual fact it proved to be like nothing of the sort. Hadfield was still master of the situation, and seemed quite unperturbed by his future. When Gibson entered he had just finished sorting out his papers; the room looked bare and bleak and three wastepaper baskets were piled high with discarded forms and memoranda. Whittaker, as acting Chief Executive, would be moving in tomorrow.

"I've run through your note on the Martians and the airweed," said Hadfield, exploring the deeper recesses of his desk. "It's a very interesting idea, but no one can tell me whether it will work or not. The position's extremely complicated and we haven't enough information. It really comes down to this—would we get a better return for our efforts if we teach Martians to plant airweed, or if we do the job ourselves? Anyway, we'll set up a small research group to look into the idea, though there's not much we can do until we've got some more Martians! I've asked Dr. Petersen to handle the scientific side, and I'd like you to deal with the administrative problems as they arise—leaving any major decisions to Whittaker, of course. Petersen's a very sound fellow, but he lacks imagination. Between the two of you, we should get the right balance."

"I'll be very glad to do all I can," said Gibson, quite pleased with the prospect, though wondering a little nervously how he would cope with his increasing responsibilities. However, the fact that the Chief had given him the job was encouraging: it meant that Hadfield, at any rate, was sure that he could handle it.

As they discussed administrative details, it became clear to Gibson that Hadfield did not expect to be away from Mars for more than a year. He even seemed to be looking forward to his trip to Earth, regarding it almost in the light of an overdue holiday. Gibson hoped that this optimism would be justified by the outcome.

Towards the end of their interview, the conversation turned inevitably to Irene and Jimmy. The long voyage back to Earth would provide Hadfield with all the opportunities he needed to study his prospective son-in-law, and Gibson hoped that Jimmy would be on his best behavior. It was obvious that Hadfield was contemplating this aspect of the trip with quiet amusement. As he remarked to Gibson, if Irene and Jimmy could put up with each other in such close quarters for three months, their marriage was bound to be a success. If they couldn't—then the sooner they found out, the better.

As he left Hadfield's office, Gibson hoped that he had made his own sympathy clear. The C.E. knew that he had all Mars behind him, and Gibson would do his best to gain him the support of Earth as well. He looked back at the unobtrusive lettering on the door. There would be no need to change that, whatever happened, since the words designated the position and not the man. For twelve months or so Whittaker would be working behind that door, the democratic ruler of Mars and the—within reasonable limits—conscientious servant of Earth. Whoever came and went, the lettering on the door would remain. That was another of Hadfield's ideas—the tradition that the post was more important than the man. He had not, Gibson thought, given it a very good start, for anonymity was scarcely one of Hadfield's personal characteristics.

The last rocket to Deimos left three hours later with Hadfield, Irene, and Jimmy aboard. Irene had come round to the Grand Martian Hotel to help Jimmy pack and to say good-bye to Gibson. She was bubbling over with excitement and so radiant with happiness that it was a pleasure simply to sit and watch her. Both her dreams had come true at once: she was going back to Earth, and she was going with Jimmy. Gibson hoped that neither experience would disappoint her; he did not believe it would.

Jimmy's packing was complicated by the number of souvenirs he had gathered on Mars—chiefly plant and mineral specimens collected on various trips outside the Dome. All these had to be carefully weighed, and some heartrending decisions were involved when it was discovered that he had exceeded his personal allowance by two kilograms. But finally the last suitcase was packed and on its way to the airport.

"Now don't forget," said Gibson, "to contact Mrs. Goldstein as soon as you arrive; she'll be expecting to hear from you."

"I won't," Jimmy replied. "It's good of you to take all this trouble. We really do appreciate everything you've done—don't we, Irene?"

"Yes," she answered, "we certainly do. I don't know how we'd have got on without you."

Gibson smiled, a little wistfully.

"Somehow," he said, "I think you'd still have managed in one way or another! But I'm glad everything's turned out so well for you, and I'm sure you're going to be very happy. And—I hope it won't be too long before you're both back on Mars."

As he gripped Jimmy's hand in farewell, Gibson felt once again that almost overwhelming desire to reveal his identity and, whatever the consequences, to greet Jimmy as his son. But if he did so, he knew now, the dominant motive would be pure egotism. It would be an act of possessiveness, of inexcusable self-assertion, and it would undo all the good he had wrought in these past months. Yet as he dropped Jimmy's hand, he glimpsed something in the other's expression that he had never seen before. It could have been the dawn of the first puzzled surmise, the birth of the still half-conscious thought that might grow at last to fully fledged understanding and recognition. Gibson hoped it was so; it would make his task easier when the time came.

He watched them go hand-in-hand down the narrow street, oblivious to all around them, their thoughts even now winging outwards into space. Already they had forgotten him; but, later, they would remember.

* * *

It was just before dawn when Gibson left the main airlock and walked away from the still sleeping city. Phobos had set an hour ago; the only light was that of the stars and Deimos, now high in the west. He looked at his watch—ten minutes to go if there had been no hitch.

"Come on, Squeak," he said. "Let's take a nice brisk walk to keep warm." Though the temperature around them was at least fifty below, Squeak did not seem unduly worried. However, Gibson thought it best to keep his pet on the move. He was, of course, perfectly comfortable himself, as he was wearing his full protective clothing.

How these plants had grown in the past few weeks! They were now taller than a man, and though some of this increase might be normal, Gibson was sure that much of it was due to Phobos. Project Dawn was already leaving its mark on the planet. Even the North Polar Cap, which should now be approaching its midwinter maximum, had halted in its advance over the opposite hemisphere—and the remnants of the southern cap had vanished completely.

They came to a stop about a kilometer from the city, far enough away for its lights not to hinder observation. Gibson glanced again at his watch. Less than a minute left; he knew what his friends were feeling now. He stared at the tiny, barely visible gibbous disc of Deimos, and waited.

Quite suddenly, Deimos became conspicuously brighter. A moment later it seemed to split into two fragments as a tiny, incredibly bright star detached itself from its edge and began to creep slowly westwards. Even across these thousands of kilometers of space, the glare of the atomic rockets was so dazzling that it almost hurt the eye.

He did not doubt that they were watching him. Up there in the *Ares*, they would be at the observation windows, looking down upon the great crescent world which they were leaving now, as a lifetime ago, it seemed, he had bade farewell to Earth.

What was Hadfield thinking now? Was he wondering if he

would ever see Mars again? Gibson no longer had any real doubts on this score. Whatever battles Hadfield might have to face, he would win through as he had done in the past. He was returning to Earth in triumph, not in disgrace.

That dazzling blue-white star was several degrees from Deimos now, falling behind as it lost speed to drop Sunwards—and Earthwards.

The rim of the Sun came up over the eastern horizon; all around him, the tall green plants were stirring in their sleep—a sleep already interrupted once by the meteoric passage of Phobos across the sky. Gibson looked once more at the two stars descending in the west, and raised his hand in a silent farewell.

"Come along, Squeak," he said. "Time to get back—I've got work to do." He tweaked the little Martian's ears with his gloved fingers.

"And that goes for you too," he added. "Though you don't know it yet, we've both got a pretty big job ahead of us."

They walked together towards the great domes, now glistening faintly in the first morning light. It would be strange in Port Lowell, now that Hadfield had gone and another man was sitting behind the door marked "Chief Executive."

Gibson suddenly paused. For a fleeting moment, it seemed he saw into the future, fifteen or twenty years ahead. Who would be Chief then, when Project Dawn was entering its middle phase and its end could already be foreseen?

The question and the answer came almost simultaneously. For the first time, Gibson knew what lay at the end of the road on which he had now set his feet. One day, perhaps, it would be his duty, and his privilege, to take over the work which Hadfield had begun. It might have been sheer self-deception, or it might have been the first consciousness of his own still hidden powers—but whichever it was, he meant to know.

With a new briskness in his step, Martin Gibson, writer, late of Earth, resumed his walk towards the city. His shadow merged with Squeak's as the little Martian hopped beside him; while overhead the last hues of night drained from the sky, and all around, the tall, flowerless plants were unfolding to face the sun.

About the Author

Sir Arthur Charles Clarke was born in Minehead, England, in 1917 and now lives in Colombo, Sri Lanka. He is a graduate and Fellow of King's College, London, and Chancellor of the International Space University and the University of Moratuwa near the Arthur C. Clarke Center for Modern Technologies.

Sir Arthur has twice been Chairman of the British Interplanetary Society. While serving as an RAF radar officer in 1945, he published the theory of communications satellites, most of which operate in what is now called the Clarke Orbit. The impact of this invention upon global politics resulted in his nomination for the 1994 Nobel Peace Prize.

He has written over seventy books, and shared an Oscar nomination with Stanley Kubrick for the movie based on his novel *2001: A Space Odyssey.* The recipient of three Hugo Awards and three Nebula Awards as well as an International Fantasy Award and a John W. Campbell Award, he was named a Grand Master by the Science Fiction Writers of America. His "Mysterious World," "Strange Powers," and "Mysterious Universe" TV series have been shown worldwide. His many honors include several doctorates in science and literature, and a host of prizes and awards including the Vidya Jyothi (Light of Science) Award from the President of Sri Lanka in 1986, and the CBE (Commander of the British Empire) from H.M. Queen Elizabeth in 1989. In a global satellite ceremony in 1995 he received NASA's highest civilian honor, its Distinguished Public Service Medal. And in 1998, he was awarded a Knighthood "for services to literature" in the New Year's Honours List.

His recreations are SCUBA diving on Indian Ocean wrecks with his company, Underwater Safaris; table-tennis (despite Post Polio Syndrome); observing the Moon through his fourteen-inch telescope; and playing with his Chihuahua, "Pepsi", and his six computers.